REBEL
OF A
KINGDOM

Book Three of the Black Hallows Series

By G.N. Wright

This is a work of fiction. The names, characters, places, and incidents are a product of the authors imagination or have been used fictitiously. Any resemblance to actual persons and things living or dead, locales, or events is entirely coincidental.

COVER DESIGN: Outlined with Love Designs
EDITOR: Samantha Bee
PUBLISHER: G.N. Wright via Amazon KDP

DEDICATION

This is dedicated to Marcus and Elle. The first couple in my head to inspire me enough to write their story.

TRIGGER WARNING

This is a full-length romance that is the third book of a dark romance series. It contains brief references to sexual assault and violence and other themes that some readers may find triggering.

Contents

These violent delights have violent ends.

- William Shakespeare

-

Prologue

Zack
Three and a Half Years Ago

I ignore my phone for the third time, letting it ring out. Who the fuck is calling me at this time of night? Hell knows, but I'm not answering. I'm too focused on the training video in front of me. I've been doing some Krav Maga with a few old friends from Prep school. I continue to ignore the phone and study the fighting techniques on the video in front of me, observing, learning, absorbing. It's something that has always come easily to me. Picking up new skills, learning new things, mastering new arts. It's how at just twenty-one years old I have already made millions off security software that I invented. My net worth grows every day, and I am set to make my first billion, by the time I hit my next birthday.

Being raised by two extremely talented parents makes you want to push hard at everything you do. I want to show them how grateful I am for everything they have done for me. I wouldn't be the man I am today without them. My concentration is cut off yet again and I curse before answering the phone ready to tell whoever it is to fuck off.

"What?" I snap down the line. Not many people have my personal number and I know the twins and my parents are already in bed. Who the fuck won't stop calling me?

"Zack, this is Michael Riviera. We met a few months ago." A deep, serious voice hits my ear.

"I remember," I snap in irritation. Who gave him my number? Why the hell would he think he can call me like this? He may be friends with my parents, but I don't give a fuck about that. A year ago, I found out I have a sister. She has the same birth mom; except she didn't get left for someone else to raise. I'm thankful I ended up with my mom and dad, but I do wonder about the half sibling my human incubator actually decided to keep. Why her and not me?

"I still don't know if I'm ready to meet her," I add, before he can say anything else. Why the fuck would I want to meet the girl my biological mom didn't abandon? What did she have that I didn't? Besides, who says being blood makes you a family? I've got four family members all asleep under this roof that prove that's bullshit.

"If that's why you're calling you're wasting your breath."

"She's been taken," he says evenly, hesitating slightly before he adds, "kidnapped."

"Kidnapped?" I splutter, pulling the phone from my ear to make sure he's still on the line. "What the fuck do you mean kidnapped?" I must have heard him wrong. I pause the video, finally giving him my full attention. If she had actually been kidnapped, he should be calling the police, not me. Why the hell is he so calm?

"Black Hallows is an extremely dangerous place, Mr. Royton. A lion's den run by the devil himself. Your sister was offered up as collateral." His tone is eerily void of any emotion, yet even though I barely know him I can still hear the undercurrent of panic lacing his words. While his voice remains steady, his words are rushed and firm, the complete opposite of his usual cheerful, content tone.

"I don't--" I start, but I don't really know what to say. I don't know her, but she is still my sister. What if something were to happen to Lily, or Logan? They're a pair of little shits, but I love them both. It doesn't matter if they aren't my blood, they are my family, and I would die to protect them. Would anyone do the same for her?

The overwhelming anxiety in my gut has me stumbling to the closet and putting on shoes before I can even process that I'm doing it. I may not be ready to meet her, but I don't want it to ever be too late to even try.

"What do you need?" I throw on a light jacket and grab my car keys, hesitating only slightly before I unlock my desk and zone in on the unused handgun that lies there. I've never taken it anywhere but the shooting range, I've never needed to. It was something I bought after the first time I went shooting with my friend Max. We began training after that and he taught me to always be prepared for anything. I don't think any longer before I pull it out and stuff it in the back of my jeans.

"I need you here within the hour, can you do that?" The relief in his voice also highlights his desperation. It must be bad if he is relying this much on a stranger to save her. I might have more money and influence than a

*lot of other people my age, but still, I don't feel like I am
up to whatever I need to do to help him.*
"On my way."

I startle awake from the memories of that awful
fucking night. I'd give anything to erase it from existence,
but then if I did, I wouldn't be here right now. Waking up
on the sofa with my perfect, little niece asleep in my lap. I
stroke a little blonde curl behind her ear as she snores
softly. Elle was right, the little squirt has run me ragged,
but I wouldn't have it any other way.

Blood never meant anything to me growing up. I
had my mom and dad and the twins and that was
enough, but the first time I locked eyes with Elle it
changed everything. I already had all the family I could
ever wish for, but then all of a sudden there she was. She
looked so similar to me, even covered in blood.

Seeing her in that state struck me to my core. Like
a direct fucking hit right to my soul. It changed everything
and I knew she had carved a place in my heart, just as
much as the twins. Except more. Not because she was
my real blood, but because she desperately needed
someone to protect her. Realization hit me back then that
I was the lucky one. I spent so much time thinking that
she was picked over me, but now I know that doesn't
mean shit. All that matters now is that we're family.

Careful not to startle my niece, I quietly reach for
the remote and switch off Frozen. Cass fell asleep
halfway through our second watch, something I knew
would happen when she was yawning as she begged me
to put it on again. I'm not ashamed to admit I know every

song word for word thanks to her. I scoop her up into my arms and start towards the stairs so I can get her settled in bed.

The alarm for the security perimeter blares through the house as I reach the bottom of the stairs. What the fuck?

I'm immediately on guard. It's too early for Elle to be home, but even so, she wouldn't set the alarm off. All of us have our own codes for the gate and security has a list of approved visitors, none of which would be coming here at this hour. That means whoever is here, wasn't invited. Fuck.

Cassie stirs slightly in my arms at the commotion, I rub my hand up and down her back in an attempt to settle her. I don't know how to look after her and save her from whatever threat we might be about to face. Fuck. Ironic that the last time I felt this level of dread is the very night I was just dreaming about. The same fear I felt then courses through my body now. I was too late back then. I couldn't save Elle from the terrible things that happened to her. I won't allow the same thing to happen to my niece.

My phone vibrating in my pocket breaks me out of my thoughts. I maneuver Cass until I can pull it out and see it's one of the guards stationed on the perimeter.

"Sir," he starts, but I cut him off.

"David, what the fuck is going on?" I snap into the phone. I can't contain the anger that pulses through me right now.

"I'm not sure. We've lost contact with the guards on the gate. Peter and I are doing a perimeter check now and --" BANG. The gunshot deafens me and cuts off whatever he was about to say. It doesn't take fucking rocket science to figure out who is breaking through.

They found her.

The blood in my veins turns to fucking ice, how the fuck did they find us? I waste no time storming through the house until I reach Elle's room. I head straight for her closet and push inside, popping the back panel to reveal the panic room I had installed. I punch in the code and enter, ensuring to close the door behind me. I tuck Cassie into the bed and then dial Elle on my phone. No answer. Fuck. I won't let them have her. I can't.

I open the safe and pull out the first gun my hand finds. I check it's loaded and take one last look at my niece sleeping softly. I don't know where my guards are or how long it will be until Elle comes home, but I can't just stay here. The Donovan's have already taken enough.

I feel a crushing sense of worry as I leave the panic room and lock her in. My heart pounding in my chest as I move stealthily towards my office, but as I'm near I hear footsteps coming towards me. Bracing myself, I push up against the wall, gun raised and ready to fire. I almost shoot until I see the familiar face.

"Peter!" I lower my gun, "I almost fucking shot you." I take him in, checking for injuries, he seems fine, but he looks startled and nervous. He's only been with us a few months and so far, there hasn't been any threats, so I guess I understand his unease. This is his first security job.

16

"Sorry, sir. Spitfire?" he asks using Cassie's codename.

"Secured in the nest," I confirm while looking around. "How many?"

"Six, sir." His face is set in a grimace. He knows we're outnumbered, but I can't concentrate on that right now.

I nod my head. "Let's go."

We don't have to move far before I hear them. I look back at Peter. From the employment file, I know we are close in age. Right now, though, his youth is more apparent than my own. His discomfort with the situation is obvious. I can't trust him with my life if he's distracted. I signal for him to stay hidden and gesture that I will go first. I trust my own shooting to catch a couple of them off guard at least and then he can jump in and help. He shifts slightly on his feet before nodding. I don't have the luxury of time to wonder anymore about whether he can handle this. I leave him behind and enter the main living area and come face to face with the last man I ever wanted in my home. Greg Donovan.

I don't hesitate in raising my gun and shooting the guy closest to me, clocking him right between the eyes. The silencer muffles the shot and I swing the gun to the left slightly as soon as he drops, giving me a clear shot to the fucking rapist piece of shit. I squeeze the trigger, but at the same time I am tackled from behind and thrown to the ground. My shot goes low, missing Greg completely and I fight to use my legs and flip the guy off me, giving me the upper hand. My victory is short lived, as I am quickly overpowered by the two men who join the fray. I manage to knock the guns from their hands, but one of them produces a blade and doesn't hesitate in plunging it into my thigh and twisting it.

The pain is unreal, but I can't focus on my injuries when panic takes over as Greg Donovan appears above me. His men have forced me to my knees and rendered me to his mercy. How the fuck did he know to come here? How long has he known about Cassie?

Blood pours from the wound in my thigh, and hopelessness takes over. Even if chicken shit Peter waltzes in with the aim of a trained assassin, he would be overtaken by the crowd in this room. My only comfort is knowing that Cassie is safe, and Elle has the Rebels with her.

"Ah here he is, the man of the house." Greg smiles like he's really enjoying himself. He doesn't even sound sarcastic as he says it. He's sitting in the middle of the sofa with one arm stretched out across the back and the other palming a Glock. There are three men behind me and another two behind Greg. All of them ignoring their dead friend laying a few feet from me.

"What a pleasure to finally meet you, Zack. I'm sure I don't have to introduce myself." He preens at me as his hand curls around his gun. I've never wanted to kill someone more.

I am staring at the man who raped and tortured my little sister and he already has me on my knees and bleeding. This is not how I was trained, not how I imagined ever meeting him. I always thought it would be me overpowering him. If we were one on one, he wouldn't stand a chance. I breathe through the numbness

I'm now feeling in my leg from the blood loss, and stare back at him defiantly.

That feeling is soon squashed when Peter finally enters the room. Except the nervous kid I left in hiding doesn't come in guns blazing. No, the traitorous fuck walks in with a sleeping Cassie in his arms. No. No. No. Please no. What the fuck is he doing?

I scramble to move as Greg clicks the safety off his gun and aims it at me using it to gesture to one his men behind me. They move immediately, one of them kicking me to the floor so I'm on my back. He presses his foot onto the wound in my thigh and I have to grit my teeth hard to keep from screaming out.

"Peter," I grit through my teeth. "Why? We trusted you." I can barely get my words out, the shock of what I am seeing causes them to catch in my throat. My pants are coming quick and fast as the realization of what is happening settles in.

"He's just returning my daughter." Greg smirks at his victory as Cassie is placed in his arms. The worst fucking sight I've ever seen. His lips curl around the words 'my daughter' and my insides twist in disgust.

"I had no choice," Peter starts with a tremble. "They took my sister--" he doesn't get to finish his sentence before Greg puts a bullet in the center of his head. Again, the shot is quieted by a silencer, but Cassie still begins to stir, and I tremble at the thought of her waking to this.

Greg isn't phased in the slightest by the murder he just committed, just like I wasn't when I took down one of his men. The only similarity between us, I'm sure. He curls the arm still holding the gun around Cassie.

"Where were we? Ah yes, the returning of my daughter." He says the words so affectionately, but they still sound like poison coming from him. "It's about time I welcomed her to the fold, I've already missed so much."

"I'm going to fucking kill you," I spit out as the foot on my leg is pressed down further. I relish the pain as it means I'm still alive, still able to fight. The desire I feel to inflict violence on every single one of them outweighs any other emotion I could ever feel.

"Hmm, I can finally see the family resemblance," he muses as he stands. He turns to leave before flicking his wrist at the guard pinning me down. "Dispose of the bodies," he gestures to Peter and his dead man. Then looks at me adding, "Make him bleed slowly. I want Elle to come home to a nice little present before I bring her to join us."

The last thing I see is my niece being carried away from her home before the bullet pierces my chest and blackness descends.

Chapter 1

ELLE

There is chaos in blood. Chaos in my blood. Fear, pain, regret, despair, death.... Blood. There is just so much fucking blood. It pours through my fingers as I desperately try to keep pressure on his wounds. He's been shot. My brother and my savior has been shot. In our home. In our safe place. Right under our fucking noses.

There's so much blood that it's soaked through his once crisp white shirt, forcing it to cling to his skin. I can feel it pumping out against my hand as it spills its way out of his body, attempting to draw the life from him. It doesn't matter how hard I apply pressure; the blood still continues to pour.

Fuck this is bad, so fucking bad. I hear Z's voice in my head. Remember your training Elle. *Panic is what will get you killed.* How can I feel anything other than panic right now? My brother is bleeding out in my arms and my daughter is gone.

The sad truth is, I've prepared for this, trained for it. I know exactly how to stem his bleeding and what drugs he'd need to stop his pain, yet I can't force myself to move and do any of it. Z always taught me to expect the unexpected, that way you can never be surprised. I got cocky, overconfident, and now I'm paying the highest fucking price imaginable.

My heart hammers against my rib cage as my body attempts to shut down in terror. I struggle to just keep breathing, every inhale feeling like glass shards are shredding their way down into my lungs. I watch my fingers as they tremble against the escaping blood seeping from my brother's body. I can't lose him; I need to save him.

If it weren't for him, I wouldn't be here. He changed everything, my family, my blood, my life, all of it would be nothing if it weren't for him. He became my anchor when I thought I lost everything.

I think back to the night we met when I climbed into a car with him and drove away from everything I had ever known. It was just me and him, two strangers with no past, yet he didn't let me slip away. It's just us two again now and I need to save him like he saved me.

The Rebels are going to walk in here any minute and find us... Will a minute be too long? Will the Devils of this town change my life forever again, in just one night?

Zack jolts beneath me and I bring my gaze to his. His eyes are a worse sight than all of his blood. There isn't just pain there, but devastation, panic, pure and utter despair. I would give anything to take it away.

"It's okay Z, just hang on for me okay?" I plead with him.

He tries to reply, but he is struggling to even breathe. When Arthur and Zack walked me through basic first aid and some advanced stuff, I thought it was ridiculous. Now, as my brother's blood soaks into the carpet, I've never been more grateful in my life. His shortness of breath and where the bullet has hit his chest makes me think it's a collapsed lung, not always life threatening, but with the amount of blood he's losing it isn't good.

The stab wound in his leg is another thing entirely. It doesn't seem to have hit any major arteries, or he'd already be dead, but this is so fucking bad. I try to concentrate, think about what I need to do to save his life, but I can't keep my mind from my daughter.

Cassie.

Her name is a whisper in my mind playing on repeat. Piercing my heart over and over, every second. I thought I knew what fear was, thought I had felt it that awful night. I thought waking up drugged, beaten, raped, and tied down would be the worst thing that would ever happen to me. I was wrong. This is worse. They have her. I'd go through every single moment of trauma again just to have her back.

My shining light, the very reason for my existence has been taken and I wasn't here to protect her. I'm drowning, suffocating, spiraling into the depths of a void I won't ever recover from. I let them find her, let them take her, and now I am nothing. With her, I am strong, powerful, have everything I will ever need. Without her?

I'm an abyss of emptiness that can only be filled with the blood of my enemies.

They have my baby girl. My daughter is with her biological father for the first time in her life and I've never felt the terror that I feel now. Is she alive? Have they touched her? Will I ever see her again? Will I survive long enough to avenge her?

The bile clogs my throat as every disgusting crime the Donovan's have ever committed flashes across my mind. Is she going to pay for the crimes I have committed against them?

Please don't hurt her, not my baby.

I struggle to control my own body as I choke down the vomit. The impending panic attack attempts to overpower me entirely. My heart threatens to burst inside my chest and my hands begin to tingle with numbness as I try my hardest to keep firm pressure on Zack's wounds.

I want to shut down. I need to. I want to forget. To not exist in a world where my daughter isn't by my side. But I can't. That won't bring my daughter back. No. The only thing that will do that is blood, death, and murder.

Oh, there is going to be so much fucking murder. They think they hurt me before. That I wanted vengeance before? That was nothing. A fucking blip on the radar compared to what I feel now. I wanted their blood for what they did to me, but that wasn't enough for them. It's never fucking enough. Now they have taken my only reason for survival and I will make it rain fucking crimson to get her back.

I lock eyes with Zack again. Not once since the day I met him have I ever seen pure terror in his stare.

Not even the night we met, and considering I was naked and bleeding it would have been expected. But no, not even then. Now though, now he looks like the world has fucking ended. If we don't get Cassie back, it just might. I'll make it.

I try to center my panic and focus my thoughts on the only thing that is in my control right now, and that's Zack's life. He's pleading at me with his eyes, but I am too focused on trying to stem the blood flow and not spiral into a fucking frenzy. But even amongst all the chaos I don't miss the cocking sound of a gun. It echoes in the deafening silence.

Fuck.

Fuck!!! My panic left my back open to vulnerabilities. I forgot the most important rule of my training; check the threat has been neutralized. My gun lies discarded and useless next to Zack's body, just out of my reach. My knives are still embedded in my dress, but they won't help me now. I freeze and Zack closes his eyes in defeat, he doesn't want to watch what is going to happen next. He knows. This is it, the time for my death, our death. I am going to die right here next to him, failing to save him. Failing to save my daughter.

We won't get to see Cassie again or any of our family, I won't get that future I had started to picture with Marcus and the Rebels will have to deal with the loss of one more person in their life. I try to take a deep breath, but I'm suffocating, and as the cry catches in my throat, I finally register the tears spilling down my face.

How the fuck did we get here? We were so careful, and it was all for nothing. Every possible future I had imagined for me and Cassie is about to die right here with me. I think about everything I am going to miss; her first day of school, graduation, her wedding day, when she has kids of her own. All of it causing me more pain than I'm about to feel in my death. I say a silent prayer that Ash will get our baby girl back, he has to. I close my eyes so I can see the image of Cassie in my head, I want her face to be the last thing I see.

Cassie, I'm so sorry, baby girl. Mommy loves you.

That is the last thought I have before the presence behind me speaks. "The Donovan's send their regards."

The bang of the gun roars into the night. My entire body flinching, awaiting the impact, but it doesn't come. Instead, a body drops next to me with a hard thud.

"Regards." Asher's pained tone hits my ear and I whip my head around, letting out a gasp of breath. I see whoever the shooter was is face down in his own blood with a hole in the back of his head. The cry I was so desperately trying to hold in bursts out of me. Shakes wrack my entire body so hard that they force Zack's body to tremble along with me. I never thought about the true danger that I put myself in. I've been close to death multiple times, but never without the ability to fight back.

I never wanted to be the weak little girl that was taken and abused again. I promised that for both mine and Cassie's sake, I would fight until the end. Yet when faced with my end, all I wanted was to close my eyes and accept my fate. Not because I didn't want to fight, but because it was pointless.

Asher staggers towards me and falls to his knees, gripping my face in his hands. "You okay, baby girl?"

He looks almost as bad as Zack. His face is bleeding and swollen, one arm lies limp by his side and he's barely holding himself against the table. I shake my head in response. I will never be okay again, not if my brother dies, not if I don't get my daughter back. Before he can say anything else all three Rebels burst into the room.

"What the fuck?" they yell in unison.

I don't get to respond before Ash speaks again. "Where is Cassie?" His tone is dark, harsh, and completely menacing, as his eyes plead with mine to put him out of his misery and tell him that she's fine.

I feel the stares of all four of them burn into my skin at his question. How can I answer a question I don't know the answer to? A question I fear the answer to. Where is my daughter?

I flick my eyes to Marcus and then back to Ash, the former looks fierce and ready to take on the world, the latter, so far past the edge of reason I doubt he knows the way back. I know they know the answer, they can see it on my grief-stricken face, but they need to hear it to know it's true.

"They have her. We're too late."

Ash collapses backwards like the words have impacted his full body. Panic and devastation staining his face, as a look I've only seen once before appears. In this moment he isn't the stealthy, cunning, and dangerous Asher Donovan that has been making moves against his family. No. He's a kid, just like me, defeated in a game played by awfully bad men. He is wearing the same shattered expression that I saw that night when I first came out of my drug haze. Heartbroken, anguished, and utterly helpless.

I wish I could help him, say something, anything, to make him feel better, but it's pointless. The despair he feels, I feel it too. I am living it right alongside him, and I know there is no relief in sight. My best friend is breaking apart right in front of me and I don't have the power to put him back together. He's been my rock for the last four years, and the one and only time he has ever needed me in return, and I am powerless.

The need to break down and give up is fucking paralyzing. But if I break, they win. If I break, we lose. If I break, my brother dies. If I break, we won't get our daughter back.

I can't break.

I have to ignore his despair and focus on Zack. I suck in a deep breath through my nose and wipe my cheeks against my shoulders to scrape away the tears.

"I need towels, alcohol, and the first aid kit from the kitchen," I shout out at the Rebels. None of them move, they are frozen to the spot taking in the scene.

The blood-soaked carpet, my blood-soaked dress, my blood-soaked brother, just so much fucking blood.

"Are you fucking deaf!" I scream. I don't miss the tears that continue to spill down my cheeks. "I need help!" My voice breaks on the last word.

Marcus is the first to spark into action as he disappears to find what I need. Jace remains frozen to the spot, like the sight of blood has cemented him in there, and Lincoln is looking between Zack, Asher and me.

"Get my phone," I yell at them both.

"Elle," Linc starts, but I cut him off.

"Lincoln, get my fucking phone." He picks up my discarded purse and pulls my phone out. "Dial number one on my speed dial and put it on speaker."

The dial tone fills the room, and it feels like it takes forever for someone to answer, before Arthur's voice fills the room.

"Hi, sweetheart. How was the pa--"

"GSW to the chest, no exit wound." My voice is unsteady as I struggle to hold in my emotions. I'm losing it. *I can't lose it.*

"Who?" he asks immediately. I wish I could keep it from him. Save him from the heart ache he is about to feel, but there is no way I can lie to him right now, not about his own son.

"It's Zack," I choke out through a sob, still barely believing that this is happening.

I hear his sharp intake of breath, like he just took a hit himself before he speaks. "Okay, you're gonna need someone to keep pressure on the wound. Go to my office and in the bottom drawer of my medical cabinet you will find a needle and a long tube." His voice is a lot steadier than mine, but I can hear the pain along with rustling and movement as I'm sure he exits wherever he is to make his way back here.

He continues to ramble off supplies and Lincoln stalks away, my phone still in hand to retrieve whatever we need. I feel Jace's presence as he kneels beside me and covers my hands with his. It isn't until I feel his touch that I realize I'm still shaking. "I got this, princess," he declares, but it lacks the confidence he usually delivers.

I look at him properly for the first time since he came in, he's staring at me with the most serious look I've ever seen on his face. He squeezes my hands tightly. "Let go, Elle. I got this. I promise." I slide my hands from beneath him as he closes the small gap.

Marcus comes back holding a stack of towels, a first aid kit, and two bottles of vodka, dumping them next to Jace. Lincoln is here in the next second with the stuff that Arthur listed off, as he continues to instruct them on what to do in order to keep my brother from leaving me.

I'm as cold as ice, goosebumps covering my entire body as I watch them fight to save my brother's life. Still slumped next to me, Ash looks just as lost as I feel as he watches Zack's blood with an unwavering stare, completely ignoring his own injuries.

How the fuck did we get here?

Marcus grabs my face, pulling until my eyes meet his. "Baby, what happened? Where is Cassie?"

My words are barely a whisper. "She's gone." I barely hear them, but I feel them. In my aching heart, in my crushed soul. My daughter is gone, and I don't know if I will get her back.

Chapter 2

ASHER

I'm empty. Hollow. Void. Completely, fucking desolate. The feeling of defeat has cracked through my steel shell. I can't breathe. I'm trying, but the air keeps getting trapped in my throat, never destined to reach my lungs. Is this what drowning feels like? What happens when you lose all hope?

I don't feel the terror that should be wracking my body. In fact, I don't feel anything. I must be in pain. My cheekbone is close to shattered, my wrist snapped, and at least three ribs are broken. I'm sure that when I finally wake from this nightmare, I'll be in a world of hurt. Yet none of it compares to the fucking gaping hole in the center of my chest. I'm fairly sure the assholes that jumped me didn't land any hits there, but it's the only pain I register right now.

I knew something wasn't right the moment I saw Greg at the party tonight, I felt it in my gut, in my fucking bones. But I did nothing. I let him remain there and for what? To cover myself from my own lies. Lies I told to protect the only things that matter to me. And to what end? I still failed. Failed Elle, failed Cass, failed myself.

It was all for nothing.

I thought the dread of finding Greg in a room with Elle would be the worst of it. I wanted to let it go, allow the rest of the night to wither away until I could get back home. Nothing is ever that simple though, is it? I saw it in his eyes, the sick little gleam of him knowing something I didn't. Of having one up on me. So, I followed him, thinking that the worst thing that would happen, would be to witness more of his fucking horrific crimes. I've seen enough of them to last a lifetime, but I could have handled them. I could have handled anything I would have seen, except this.

What I didn't see coming was the fucking thugs who jumped me as soon as I made it to the back of the parking lot. Four of them and I still held my own. I may be injured, but the way they came after me I knew I was meant to be near dead. In hindsight, I got off lightly. They didn't.

When I got rid of all four of them, I staggered to my car and floored it here as fast as I could, all the while praying for time. More time with Cassie, more time with Elle, hell, more fucking time with the four pieces of shit I just murdered in the parking lot. Just more fucking time.

Once again, I was too late. Just like I was too late to save Elle that awful night. Had I been a second later with my arrival, I would have lost her for good. Not that it matters. I've let her down again. My only salvation is the bullet I put in that fucker's head before he could do the same to her. Yet do I feel it? No. I feel nothing but defeat.

They took her. They took my daughter. My worst fear has finally come to light. We did everything right, tried so fucking hard and for what? They still got her anyway. Every careful step, every meticulous plan, all a waste of fucking time. My shining star has been engulfed in darkness and without her I am nothing. Feel nothing. An empty shell of the man that once existed.

I don't register anything going on around me, I can't. My very reason for breathing is gone and I don't know if I will ever see her again. What else matters?

A door slams open and a second later Arthur storms into the room followed by Helen, and when she locks eyes on her son she bursts into tears. Lincoln moves from Jace's side so Arthur can step in next to Zack and try to save him. Ironic isn't it, he isn't even his father, at least not by blood, and he would give his life here and now if it meant saving his son.

My father? He's just no doubt had a hand in the kidnapping of my daughter. Not to mention attempting to have the living fuck, kicked out of me.

What the fuck am I doing? Why the fuck am I still here? I need to get her back.

I focus and quickly take stock of the room. Marcus is comforting Elle and Helen, both of whom are laser focused on Jace and Arthur. Zack continues to lie motionless in a puddle of his own blood and Lincoln is typing away furiously into a laptop he got from lord knows where.

I push up off the floor and the pain overtakes my entire body, but in comparison to the void in my heart, it does nothing to stop me. I don't care about anything right now, not even death. I don't care if the grim reaper himself comes to drag me to the pits of hell, just as long as I get my daughter back to where she belongs first. Elle will take care of her brother, and I will take care of mine.

I manage to slip out of the room without notice and almost make it to the front door until I am being hauled back. The touch on my arm makes me hiss in pain, but his grip doesn't let up as he pushes me into the wall.

"Where do you think you're going?" Blackwell's voice is calm, like fucking always. It fucking infuriates me I can feel his stare boring into the side of my skull, but I can't look at him. At anyone. I don't want them to see the defeat in my eyes. The same truth is on repeat in my mind… *I failed them*.

I grit my teeth. "You know where I'm going."

"Alone?" he scoffs in exasperation. "I thought you were the smart one." His tone is harsh and dark, his grip tightening. "How far do you think you're gonna get? They will kill you before you even lay eyes on her."

"I don't care. I have to try." I try to push him off, but he grips me harder and finally I look at him. Instead of the disappointment I expect to see in his eyes at my failure, all I see is worry and slight annoyance. There isn't even a hint of pity, which I would have hated more than anything. I can't bear it, especially not from him. His expression eases some of the tension from my body. I can't allow him to comfort me, not after what I've done.

I force my gaze to look past him and grit out my next words. "Let. Me. Go."

"I can't do that, Donovan." I flinch at the use of my family name. A name I never want to be fucking associated with ever again. The hatred for my blood is strong, but it pales in comparison to how much I hate myself right now. I flick my eyes to him again and see the pleading in his to make this easy, but how can I do nothing when they have her?

"It's my house, I can go there if I want to," I snap back as the anger burns through my veins, it's so close to the edge I can practically taste it.

"Think," he shakes me with his hands, "just fucking think. How did they find her? How did they know where to get her and when?" His grip remains iron tight on me, as his words puncture my mind. "They were a step ahead of us for who knows how long, we need to be smarter now. Cassie needs you."

The mention of her name cuts through me like a blade. I push him off, ignoring the pain waging through my body once more. "I don't care, I don't fucking care, they took her." I scream, but it catches in my throat as tears appear in the corner of my eyes for the first time in years. The pain and anguish forces me to slump back against the wall. "They took her, Lincoln." I whisper, closing my eyes to let the weight of my failure crush me. "I let them take her."

His hand finds my shoulder again and I open my eyes, locking them with his. "I know."

I can't bear the compassion in his words. "You know nothing!" I hiss, pushing off the wall and shoving him away from me. "You think you know the sickness that burns through the veins of my brother and father, but you don't. I have a rapist and a murderer as my role models."

I crack my jaw back and forth to try to ease the ache there as I lean back against the wall to hold myself up.

I scrunch my eyes closed as I think back to the night, I saved Elle. "You didn't see what they did to her. What he did to her." I don't have to say Elle's name for him to know what I'm talking about. "Do you have any idea what it was like to overhear the things my father said about her and pray it wasn't true? What it was like to follow him to where he was keeping Elle and for him to think I was there because I wanted in on the action?" I grimace in disgust at just the memory.

"How Greg held his blade to her stomach on every thrust, laughing at every pained sound she made. How I had to stand there powerless, biding my time to help her." I shake my head, wishing for once I could forget the look on her face, wondering why I wasn't doing anything. Knowing that to truly be able to help her, I had to pretend I enjoyed it. To act like I was one of them.

"You didn't see the confusion and despair in her eyes. I did." I bang my fist against my chest at my words. "I felt her agony." *Bang*. "I felt her horror." *Bang*. "And I couldn't do anything." *Bang*. "And now that same sadistic fuck has my daughter. So, don't tell me you know."

"You're not the only one who knows what it's like to have a murderer as a father." His words give me pause as does the look on his face. It's unwavering, like what he's just said is the most truthful statement he has ever spoken. "I know what it's like to have someone you love taken from you, more than you know," he adds.

"I have to get her back before it's too late." I can hear the fight leaving my voice, but I try to convince him one last time.

The look in his eyes tells me he knows what it's like to be too late. He takes a deep breath before stepping towards me. "I know, but we fucking need you, okay? We need a plan, and we need you. All this?" He gestures with his other hand to me. "Lock it the fuck down until we need it."

He sees it, sees me. The line I usually walk, that I am so far away from now. The one thing that ties me to that line and kept me from slaughtering every fucking one of them is gone.

"What if we don't?" I whisper, letting my worst fear bleed out into the open. "What if we don't get her back?" The question tastes like poison on my tongue.

His other hand finds my shoulder, bringing him fully into my space and I no longer feel the desire to push him away. "I promise you; we will get her back. You have my word." His voice is smooth and unwavering. "I told you I would die for them and I will. I will get her back if it's the last thing I ever fucking do." His promise hangs in the air like a declaration of war.

I can't talk so I just nod, and his exhale hits my cheek before he nods back, straightening up. He releases my shoulders just as the front door slams open. His gun is in his hand with his body blocking mine in less than a second.

"Woah, baby, chill." Logan's flirty voice floats into the air and I see Lincoln visibly relax.

"Fucking hell, Logan. Where the fuck have you been?" Lincoln's voice is harsh, and his words are clipped.

"Oh, someone's needy. Been waiting for me, have you?" Logan continues to tease, clearly not reading the room.

"Lo," I step out from behind Lincoln, speaking his barely used nickname and his smile falters a little.

"Shit, psycho. Didn't see you - - what the fuck happened to you?" His smile changes to worry in an instant as he takes in my swollen and no doubt bruised face.

"Logan," Lincoln hesitantly steps towards him and I see Logan's glare flicker down to his bloodied hands. We don't even get a chance to say anything else before he rushes past us. Lincoln storms after him and I follow, getting to the room just as Logan's legs give out on him.

Lincoln manages to hold him up as he regains his footing and then he's trying to push him off. "Let go of me, Lincoln," he spits, trying to force Lincoln's grip off him.

Logan isn't as big as Lincoln so Blackwell doesn't even stumble as he holds him and responds, "You can't help them, just give them room to work."

"That's my brother. He needs me." I hear the crack in his voice as he lets the emotions take over.

Lincoln grips his face in a vice hold, forcing his stare to lock with his. "I know Logan, but you can't do anything right now. Come help me with Ash, yeah?" It's

38

the first time he has ever referred to me as anything other than Donovan or dark prince. It feels familiar and safe, but somehow wrong to be hearing it like this.

Logan turns his attention to me, his face pained, and as pale as a ghost. "What happened?" He moves towards me and grips my face so hard that I hiss, but the pain is welcome at this point. Nothing could hurt me more than the empty ache in my chest. I shuffle from foot to foot unable to keep still, desperate to run from this house and not stop until I have my daughter back.

"You know what happened." I rip my face from his hands and watch as realization dawns on him.

"Where is Cassie?" he asks me before swinging his gaze to Elle who is still sitting on the floor next to Zack's body. When she hears our daughter's name, she looks towards us. I thought the worst look I would ever see in her eyes was on the night she was raped, but that was nothing. She looked scared, confused, in pain, but there was still life there, still parts of her remaining no matter how small. Now though? Now she looks lifeless, like her heart has been ripped out and it's by sheer gravity that her body is still rooted here. It pushes me over the edge.

I push Logan away from me and scramble to get to the door and escape. Leave this fucking house and finish this fucking war. Kill every fucking person that gets in my path. Not resting until my daughter is home and my skin is soaked in the blood of my enemies.

Again, I almost make it out of the room, but this time I have two pairs of hands gripping me, still I fight.

For me, for her, for Elle. I have to get my daughter back, my girl. I will happily die trying.

I fight against both Lincoln and Logan as Marcus joins them in restraining me.

"Ash, look at me." Elle steps up between them and tries to talk to me, but I can't look at her. I promised her one thing, the only thing I could promise. That I would keep her and our daughter safe and I fucking failed. She is never going to forgive me, and I won't ever forgive myself either.

Chapter 3

ELLE

He's so far gone right now and I can't blame him. I feel his emotions like they are my own. Heartbreak, anger, despair, pain, they all flow through my body with a crushing force. My heart bangs against my chest rapidly, like it could just rip right out, and even with the goosebumps coating my skin, sweat still gathers on the back of my neck. The sick feeling in my stomach is constantly churning.

The look on my best friend's face is one I will never be able to unsee. Seeing him like this just reminds me of how our bond became so strong. How he was always there for me no matter what, and just how far we have come. Except I am not looking at my strong savior right now, instead he is the one breaking. He needs me, now more than ever and I have to show him we got this. That we are still in this together no matter what the odds are against us. I need to be strong for the both of us, for Cassie and for our family.

"Ash, look at me." I move Marcus aside to get to him, gripping his cheeks and forcing his gaze to collide with mine. His sparkling blue eyes aren't the ones I find, instead they are as dark as stone. He looks both like a murderous villain and a lost boy all at once, the mixture of the two jarring. "We prepared for this, Ash." I push the words past the bile in my throat, because yes, we may have prepared for the direst situation imaginable. But, experiencing it, living it, I could never have been ready for this feeling.

"Prepared for this?" he spits. "You think I could have fucking prepared for this?" I watch the lone tear track down his cheek before he wipes it away bitterly.

"Elle, I could never have fucking prepared for this." His admission hangs in the air as we all swallow his words. I watch his body succumb to his feelings as he stops fighting against the hold the boys have him in. I nod my head at them, and they release him. He slumps back against the wall as the weight of the situation we are now in takes hold.

Jace enters the hallway and I take in his blood covered appearance. He looks drained, which is exactly how I feel, and when I look back and take in the rest of the guys, they're just as bad. Five strong, powerful, and fearless boys, all brought to their knees in one night. One shitty, chaotic, fucking hell of a night.

I need to break. I need to forget everything and let the blackness inside of my heart take control, but if I do that who will bring me back? Who will protect my family? Who will save my daughter? No, I can't break, I just can't.

I take a deep breath, pushing down the sickness in my throat. "Come on, let's get you patched up and make a plan." My words sound confident, but that's not how I feel. What fucking plans do you make when a sick rapist cunt has kidnapped your daughter?

All the guys look at me and I wish it was just pain in their eyes, but I see the pity too. They feel sorry for me and it pisses me off. They all know me so well, yet clearly not well enough. I don't care. About anything or anyone that isn't my daughter right now. Arthur will look after Zack, I know that, so the only thing I have to worry about is who I am going to kill first. My list of targets is long, and I won't stop until every fucking name is crossed off in their blood.

I don't wait for the guys to respond before I turn and head back into the living area, knowing they will follow. Just as I enter, I see Zack is no longer on the floor and is instead lying on the huge dining table, he's hooked up to an IV and Arthur is working meticulously over him with Helen by his side. I fucking hate this, hate that I have done this to them. If it weren't for me, their son wouldn't be lying bleeding right now. Why did I let so many people get close to me when I knew it would put a target on their back? I should have done this how I wanted to from the start. Alone.

A phone ringing breaks me from my inner turmoil, and I turn to see all the guys standing just inside the entrance still with the same glib expression on their faces. Nobody is paying any mind to the phone.

The ringing is incessant and annoying. "Whose phone is that?" I snap.

They all look between each other and then Lincoln stalks towards the coffee table near where I found Zack, and retrieves a burner phone, I don't recognize from it.

I'm by his side in an instant and snatching it from his hands. I accept the call, immediately putting it on speaker.

"Do I have your attention now, Miss King?" Elliot Donovan's sickly voice purrs down the line.

"If you touch one fucking hair on my daughter's head, I swear I'll--." I start, barely controlling my rage, but he interrupts me.

"Oh, you mean my granddaughter. Why on earth would I hurt her? She's family." His tone is brimming with satisfaction. I wish I would have slit his throat in the graveyard when I had the chance.

I should have just stalked back into this town in the dead of night and ended them all at once. Why the fuck did I allow myself to get caught back up in anything else? I knew this would happen; knew I would paint targets on everyone I love. Did I try to minimize that damage? No. Instead, I added more names to the list of people I care for and increased Donovan's chance of causing me pain. Except they didn't need that list, they went straight for the one target that I will do anything to get back. My life is literally in their hands.

"You are nothing to my daughter," I spit back. "Bring her back, or you won't like the consequences."

"I think we're a little past your petty threats and retaliations, Elle." My name in his mouth makes my skin crawl. He says it like we are old friends catching up. "From what I gather you are lucky to even be alive right now. I have the upper hand here."

I hate how right he is. "Where is she?" The words barely get past my gritted teeth.

I can practically feel his smile when he responds, "Why, she is with her father of course." I feel the tears slip down my cheeks before I even know I'm crying. Usually when you imagine a child with their father, you would feel content, happy. But not me. Opposite ends of the earth wouldn't be enough space between my daughter and Greg Donovan.

"The only father to my daughter is standing right next to me." My words are laced with rage. Ash comes to stand beside me, gripping my hand in his. I feel the tremble though our connected fingers. He is barely hanging on. We are dancing in this anguish together. Once again bonded in the most horrific common ground.

"Ah yes, the little traitor. What a disappointment he turned out to be."

Ash snatches the phone and spits his words into them slowly, deliberately. "Listen here, Father, and listen well. Touch one hair on my daughter's head and you are going to wish I'd kill you quickly because when I get my hands on you, you will regret the day you were born."

His words don't deter Elliot in the slightest. "Well, I certainly regret the day you were born. You get your weakness from your mother." He sounds utterly bored as he brings up his ex-wife. I don't know much about her, except she left before they came here.

"I'm going to harvest every fucking one of your organs and feed them to that sick piece of shit you call a son. You know, the one you are proud of." Ash responds darkly and I can see that his control is clawing its way back into his body. That edge he usually has that keeps him on top of his game. He thinks this is his fault, I can see it written all over his face, but he's wrong. This is all our fault. Thinking we could take them on and win, how stupid were we? That stupidity has cost me everything.

"Is that my traitor brother? I thought four guys would have been enough, what a shame." Greg's voice comes across the line and I can't control my flinch. I see the guys look at Ash and take in his injuries again, now knowing that it was four against one. Fucking spineless cunts.

"How's our girl?" Elliot asks, the smugness pouring from him.

"Settled in her room, where she belongs." That arrogant, charming, devilish tone burns in my ears.

I snap, "You will pay for this. Even your pockets aren't deep enough for the fucking price I will make you pay." I am done playing games, these aren't petty battles of back and forth any longer. We are at war and it's time to take out the fucking General.

"That kind of talk makes me glad you're still alive. I'm really looking forward to fucking that attitude out of you, my queen." Greg purrs down the line and Ash's grip tightens to the point where I think he might break my fingers. A pain I'd welcome at this point.

I don't let the psychotic little prick get to me. "The only way you'd get to fuck me, is by dragging my fucking corpse to your bed, you sick fuck." I am fucking done. I snatch the phone back from Ash and stalk away. The guys follow me, but I don't stop until I get to my revenge room.

"Oh, so you wouldn't trade yourself for our daughter." His words halt me in my tracks as I enter. I don't reply, I can't, because I know the answer. He knows the answer. I would trade myself for her in a fucking heartbeat. I move inside and place the phone on the desk and load up the computers. I hear the door clink shut behind me as the guys come in after me.

I turn around as they take a seat at the table, staring at me blankly as Greg continues, "You can have her back, I just have one stipulation."

I cast my eyes across all the guys and find similar looks on all their faces. They look drained, scared, on edge. None of them have escaped Zack's blood, their black tuxedos rumpled, and shirts bloodied. A far cry from the beautiful boys that greeted me at the bottom of the stairs earlier tonight.

Marcus is the only one who will lock eyes with me, the rest glare at the phone as Greg speaks. When I reply my voice is flat. "Yeah, and what's that?"

"It's really quite simple. I don't want our daughter. I have no use for her, not yet at least." His words turn my stomach at the thought of what use he could have for her. "You however, you I have a lot of use for." I close my eyes, cutting off Marcus because I know Greg well enough to see inside his sick mind. I know what he wants before he says it. "I want a wife."

I feel River's flinch from across the room even with my eyes closed, as Ash snaps back at his brother, "Take your pick from your fucking hoard of kidnapped girls."

"Funny," he responds dryly, "But no. I don't just want any wife. I want the perfect wife. One born for this world, with her own fortune, blood on her hands and already willing and able to give me heirs."

47

I can't speak. Not one word. I open my eyes, but Marcus' gaze is hardened and focused solely on the phone.

"Willing?" he scoffs. "Fucking willing. What about raping a fucking child, screams willing to you? If you think that she is going to marry you then you are more fucking delusional than I thought."

That's the thing they don't realize though, he really is delusional. Greg's sense of reality is different. Elliot is an evil man; his crimes would make most men weep. His son, however, isn't evil, he's soulless. Doesn't feel anything, guilt, regret, remorse, love. None of it. A true psychopath living in his own world and that makes him more dangerous than anyone. Greg is the type of person to think that I belong to him, and is now more than ready to claim me, no matter what the cost.

"Really? Because her silence is deafening," Greg taunts and his words hit their intended target as every single guy turns my way. I see all of them take in my expression and the exact moment they realize the reality of the situation we are in. Right now in this moment, they see just how far I am willing to go to protect my daughter.

"I'll let you think it over, we can talk again soon. In the meantime, I will look after our girl." The line goes dead before I can respond, and the silence descends further into the room as we all let his words linger. We lost. The game, the upper hand, my daughter. All of it gone.

My thoughts are messy and unfocused, just like earlier when I found Zack lying on the floor, and look what that almost cost me. My daughter was gone, my brother lay dying and because I lost control, I almost ended up in my own blood next to him. I can't let that happen again. I turn and pick up the phone next to the computer and dial a number I know by heart from the secure phone we keep there.

"Z, my man, how are you?" His cocky, friendly tone hits my ear and I breathe my first sigh of relief as memories assault me from our time together. Grounding me in a way I so desperately need.

"Max, it's me," I croak into the phone, my voice wavering as the emotions begin to build again.

"Elle?" I hear his confusion, but he quickly adds, "Where's Zack?" I can tell from his change in tone that I have his immediate attention with my unexpected call.

Max is an old friend of Zack's, they trained together when they were younger. Him and his guys are all ex special ops who now run their own private security company. Zack pays them a lot of money for a variety of things. Max helped Zack with all my training and said he would always be here for us. I only ever use a couple of his guys for cleanup. We've never needed Max himself or his other services. *Until now.*

"He was shot in the chest, Arthur's working on him, nothing more I can tell you." I am blunt and to the point because I don't need him as a friend right now. He can't do anything to help Zack, except help me with what I need.

"What do you need?" I hear the unmistakable tapping of his fingers as he starts doing whatever he does before I even give him any instructions. I ignore all of the guys, Asher and Logan both know Max from the training we shared, but he isn't someone I would have ever told the Rebels about. His reputation precedes him, but that reputation doesn't include his real name or what he looks like. Just that he is lethal, deadly and always gets the job done. That's why I need him. Him and his guys are the best of the best.

For the first time since I came home, I push Cassie to the side of my thoughts as I try to think of everything, I need to keep everyone else safe. "Full security detail at the house, full house sweep for devices including vehicles. Access to a private, secure medical facility for Zack and a security extraction of Lily from college." I see Logan perk up at the mention of his sister's name, but I press on. "Safe house with full protection detail for Arthur, Helen and Lily, for however long it takes and a full arsenal of every weapon and tech you have on hand."

He blows out a breath. "This is a big job. It's gonna take all of my guys," he starts but I cut him off.

"You know money is no issue, offer them whatever it takes to get them here, and you will report to me and only me." My voice remains void of emotion, but that doesn't mean I can't feel the cracks in my throat, the pumping of blood in my veins. I am so close to snapping the thread of my control that I can taste it in the air.

"Roger that. We will be there in sixty minutes," he confirms.

"Make it thirty," I snap, only to be met by silence. His silence almost winds me, forcing me to take a deep breath.

"Elle?" He says my name carefully. "What happened?" It's the softest tone I've ever heard from him and if I didn't just hear it, I wouldn't think he was capable.

"They took Cassie." I barely let the three words linger before I am slamming the phone down and taking in another breath.

"Who was that?" Of course, Lincoln is the first to speak, unable to be in the dark about anything, but I don't have it in me to feed him the information right now.

"Backup," I reply simply.

I don't give any of them a chance to speak before I turn and focus my attention on the screens in front of me. I pull up the camera feeds and push back until I find what I'm looking for. I press play on the video, turning the sound on and we all watch. I watch as the van pulls up and the gate opens. I watch Greg and his men stalk after the few guards we keep on the property and shoot them. Nearly all of them point blank in the back of the head, before dragging their bodies into the trees. Then I watch them walk through the back doors, no key, no code, they just open for them and I also see why. One of the guards let them in.

I see Zack storming through the house to get Cass to the panic room, I see as he leaves her there, locked away safely. *Or so he thought.* I watch as he is stabbed, shot and left bloodied on the floor. But none of it fucking affects me the way it does to watch Peter walk back into the room with Cassie asleep in his arms. I watch in fucking horror as my baby girl is handed over to her rapist sperm donor. The Devil in fucking disguise. The absolute scum of this town. She sleeps soundly as she is carried off into my worst nightmare. I watch them climb into the van they came in and drive away in the darkness of the night.

51

I snap.

Chapter 4

MARCUS

The start of tonight was perfect. I had my brothers by my side and my girl on my arm. When she walked down the stairs in that red dress, she looked like the queen of hell itself, ready to take on the world. When I found her alone with Greg, I thought I couldn't get any angrier. The rage I felt when he was close to her, when he touched her, smelled her. It took everything in me not to kill him right there. If I'd had any idea how the rest of the night was going to pan out, I would have. Fuck the consequences.

Sitting in the car with my brothers as we listened to Jack talk about some business down at The Ring, was finally starting to relax me. He was going on about some of the members from the local motorcycle club, who had come to fight and wiped out one of our best guys. I had to admit I was impressed, but wary. Everyone knows as well as I do that the Hallowed Crows MC are controlled by Elliot Donovan. Whether by choice or force it doesn't matter, he still has them under his thumb, so we listened to what Hanson had to say intently.

The second I heard that gunshot my world fell apart. I've never experienced fear like that. The thirty seconds it took me to get from the garage to Elle were the longest of my entire life. The relief I felt when I saw her was wiped out in an instant when I took in the scene before me. Zack bleeding, Elle crying, a dead body and a broken Asher. All of it unbearable to see. The moment she locked eyes with me I knew we had lost. The sight of blood had me frozen to the spot. The last time I saw someone I cared about covered in blood, it was my father.

I saw the fear etched onto her face and the terror embedded in her very bones, but she didn't falter. She remained strong and in charge and battled against every emotion to stay in control. She's been trained for this, she's told me multiple times that she was, but it wasn't until the moment she was attempting to keep her brother's blood from pouring, that I truly understood what that meant.

She hasn't just been training to fight, she's been training to stay alive and keep those she loves alive too. No matter the cost. The second Greg offers Cassie in exchange for her, I feel it, I know I've lost her to her own mind. She will do whatever it takes, be whatever it takes, as long as it results in getting her daughter back.

I get it because I would do it too. If I could trade my life right here and now for Cassie to be back in her arms, I would. I would use my last breath to give my life for hers. To protect her, protect them, whatever the cost. But the consequences of losing them both? That would be unbearable.

I watch as the van barrels away from the house on the CCTV with Cassie inside. I flick my gaze to Elle just as the van goes out of sight and prepare myself. She finally breaks. Ripping the screen off the wall and smashing it to the ground, before reaching for the other to do the same. The third one, she launches across the room into her revenge board, shattering them both to the floor.

Anything she can get her hands on gets destroyed. Her rage uncontained and bursting, she isn't the Elle I know right now. The Elle I know, and love has ceased to exist, she stopped being her the second she walked into the house tonight and found her daughter gone.

I look at the guys and see them all watch her with the same broken expression as mine. Asher has the most powerful surname in this town. My brothers and I pretty much run the whole South Side, and Logan has the money to do whatever he wants. Yet all five of us are powerless. Metaphorically brought to our knees. Our fate entwined with that of a three-year-old girl and her mother.

Jace is the first to move to try to comfort her. He approaches her and wraps his arms around her waist from behind, ignoring her attempts to fight against him.

"Shh Elle, it's okay. I got you." None of us miss the crack in his voice, but still Ells continues to thrash. "Come on, sweetheart. I'm here, I got you, I promise."

She falters on hearing the word sweetheart, and I know immediately that she is thinking of Zack, he always calls her that. Her shoulders drop in defeat and he loosens his arms slightly to turn her around in his embrace until he is hugging her. The sight causes my heart to ache even more, not even my carefree brother can fix her now.

She finally reaches round to hug him back, a sob breaking out of her. She holds onto him so tight that her hands turn white against his back. I hate seeing her like this when I know I can't do anything. I look at them both in their bloodied embrace and feel nothing but pain and regret.

I move towards them, unable to bear being away from her any longer. Jace acknowledges me immediately, dropping a kiss to her head and moving to pull away, but she doesn't budge. I crowd behind her, letting her feel my presence as I put my arm around her shoulders. Locking eyes with Jace, I nod, and he moves with me so we can lift her until she lays in my arms. As soon as she feels the movement, she rips her arms from him and throws them around my neck and continues to cry.

I don't even stop to look at any of the other guys as I leave the room and move through the house. I avoid the living area and make my way upstairs to her room. Her cries never stop. Not as we walk through the house, not as we reach the bathroom, not even when I step under the hot spray of the shower, still fully clothed. She cries and I hold her. I don't know how long we stay there, huddled together under the water, but I can't stop. I feel like my arms are holding her pieces together and if I stop for even a second, she will truly disappear.

The only sound is the water, but I swear I hear her mutter a 'thank you'.

After I shower her and put her in some fresh clothes, she is silent. We have gone from one extreme to another. The screaming and crying have subsided and now I am left with an almost catatonic calmness. I think I preferred the crying, at least then I knew she was feeling something, letting her emotions out. Now there is nothing. No fear, no pain, no terror, just pure blankness.

I speak carefully, "It's okay to break, baby. I'm here, I promise I won't let the darkness take you." I know my words probably won't mean anything to her at this moment in time, but I can't bear the silence.

She finally looks at me and the usual sparkle of her eyes is nowhere to be seen. She gets up slowly and without a word, leaves the room. I have no choice but to follow. I follow her until we reach Cassie's room, and she doesn't hesitate to push inside. I expect the crying to start again, but still nothing. She just stands and stares at the crumpled-up blankets that haven't been made since Cassie slept here. It pains me to see them, so I know it must be breaking her.

We stand together in silence until she finally speaks. "What if we don't get her back?" she whispers, turning to look at me. "What if all this was for nothing? Because that is what I am without her, Marcus. Nothing." Marcus, not River. Fuck. I'm losing her.

"She is my reason for everything, my reason for breathing." She pauses, catching her breath, like she really can't do it without her. "She is the reason that I can handle that fucking awful night." No emotions cross her face as she talks, she is void of anything. "The reason that I can continue to live, the reason that I can fight, the reason that I can look into Asher's eyes and not remember the look on his face after everything he saw."

She says the words without the smallest sliver of pain in them, and yet every single one feels like a knife in my heart. "It was all for her. Without her I don't know if I can survive if I want to survive. She is my lifeline and now they have her. They have my baby, River."

A lone tear tracks down her face and I don't think she even feels it or realizes it's there. Her eyes remain vacant as she stares at my chest. I can't handle it, I grab her cheeks. "Listen to me Ells," I tilt her head back so she can't look anywhere but in my eyes. "You cry, you scream, you shout." I push my head against hers. "Whatever the fuck you need to do, but you do it with me. Whatever you need to do to keep fucking living. Because we are all fucking in, baby. For you. For her." I tighten my grip. "All of us together to the very fucking end."

I pull her into my arms until she is molded against my body fully, embracing her with everything I have. "I promise you we will get her back. I don't care if it fucking kills me. If it's the last thing I ever fucking do. I promise you I will bring our girl home to our family. Home to you."

She takes a deep breath as she processes my words. Pulling back, she looks up at me this time, she seems a little lighter and she goes to speak, but the door opens, stopping her.

"Max is here." Logan's voice is just as monotone and lost as his sister's. I can truly see the effects this will have if we don't get Cassie back. I look back to Elle and see the little light I saw spark back into her lifeless eyes, has disappeared once more.

She breaks out of our embrace and takes a step back, casting one last look around the room and then nods to herself before walking out. Logan and I both watch her leave without a word and then follow her, just like always. She is the center of all of us, the glue that holds us together. Yet now she is just as fucked up as the rest of us, and I don't know if she can do this on her own. My strong and beautiful queen is broken beyond repair and I don't have the tools to fix her.

Chapter 5

ELLE

Before Cassie, I would have said that the only person I truly lived for was my River. He and I have a long and complicated history, but one thing has always been a constant with him, he's always had my heart. I fell in love with Marcus Riviera before I even knew what love was. We went from children to teens and our relationship, although changing, was still a very permanent thing in my life. A bond like that would always be hard to break. It wasn't the bond that was broken, though. It was me. Broken beyond repair until I met my daughter.

Marcus' words almost work on me, they almost bring me back from the ledge I know I have to jump off. *Almost*. But even him, even his love, is not enough. I know what I have to do, and that is fucking anything. Whatever it takes to get my daughter back with me. If everything fails and I have to marry the fucking Devil just to do it, well, I'll book the fucking minister myself.

When I reach the main part of the house again, I follow the voices until I find them. Max Foster is standing around the large table in Zack's office with five of his guys, Elijah, Mason, Liam, Oliver, and Tyler. All of them I know and recognize from training with Max.

He runs a large operation, but these are some of his most trusted. Asher is standing directly between Max and Elijah barely holding himself up and still covered in blood. Jace and Lincoln are standing off to the side slightly. Their shoulders are almost touching as they hunch together against the wall, laser focused on the new guys in the room.

They all stop speaking when I enter and every eye hits me as I feel Marcus and Logan come up behind me. I ignore them all apart from Max. He is 6ft 3 with brown hair and blue eyes, built like a fucking linebacker, and covered in tattoos. He is wearing his usual fitted black t-shirt, combat pants and black boots like the rest of his guys. The only color is the embroidered logo that sits over his left pec with the words 'Infinite Security' underneath it.

Max storms around the table and I feel Marcus step even closer to me, but that doesn't faze Max at all, he doesn't even spare him a glance as he launches towards me. I catch his fist before it can connect with my face, twisting his arm and forcing his upper body away from me in one of the first moves he ever taught me. I bring the arm behind his back and grab the knife strapped to his belt and bring it around to his throat. I use my feet to swipe his ankles, so he falls forward to his knees. It only works because he expected it and allows it, but still, I appreciate the sentiment behind it. I hear a scuffle behind me as Marcus no doubt tries to intervene.

61

His men chuckle at the performance as I remove the knife and release his arm.

He stands, turning back to me with a big smile on his face as he ruffles the hair on my head. "Good to know my little warrior is still in there." I just about return his smile before he engulfs me into a bear hug, just like he used to at the end of our training sessions. Only this time we aren't playing at winning the battle, we are already knee deep in the fucking trenches of war and our opponent has the winning hand.

He pulls back and takes me in from head to toe before flicking his gaze over my shoulder to Marcus and Logan, before coming back to me. "Come on, let's all get caught up and make a plan."

I can't do anything but nod and follow him back over to the table. All the guys give me a nod hello with grim smiles as they gently give my shoulder a squeeze in greeting. I love these guys, aside from Cassie and my family, these guys are the ones who brought me back from the pits of despair and taught me how to fight. Not just physically, but mentally too. They repaired a part of me that I thought would be broken forever. None of the other guys in this room will ever understand the relationship that I have with Max and his team.

Max clears his throat before starting again. "I've got Zack on the way to a medical facility over in Lockstown. Arthur is with him, along with Alex and Seb. They will alert me when they arrive and are secured. I've also sent Owen and Josh to pick up Lils and they will bring her back here so they can grab Helen and move them to the safe house. They will be secured with them as well as Harry and Landon." I feel slight relief knowing Zack will be getting the proper medical attention he needs, but until Helen and Lily get to the safe house, I know I won't settle. Max knows that too, so he continues on.

"Us." He gestures to him and his guys. "Are yours for whatever you need, and I've got two other teams on standby if you need them." I stare at them all wordlessly. I don't know what to tell them because the compass of my life is gone and without her, I'm nothing but a lost wanderer. How can I guide them on the path of war when I've lost my own way?

When my silence lingers in the air Elijah speaks. "Ash was just giving us the rundown of the Donovan and friends security situation." He and Liam are making notes on the table in front of us. I see pictures of the Donovan estate, but I don't look at them, I don't need to. I could navigate round every inch of that house with my eyes closed. It's the first place I should have gone when I came back to this shitty town. I should have just gone in the front door and slaughtered every one of them and then left without looking back. If I did that I wouldn't be here. If I did that, Elliot and Greg Donovan would be dead. If I did that, I would still have my daughter.

I don't want to stand here and make fucking plans and look at fucking pictures. I want to tear their fucking limbs from their bodies and bathe in their blood. Every single one of them; Greg, Elliot, their fucking guards. I want them all bleeding at my feet.

I can hear Max asking questions, his guys coming up with ideas and even the Rebels chiming in here and there, but I ignore it all. I already know what I need to do. It's what I should have done from the start. I thought having my family, Ash and the Rebels was a good thing. I thought the more people I had on my side, the more I stood a chance at getting what I want. But with more people comes more attention. I teamed up with the most well-known guys on the South Side and thought I could still hide in the shadows. I may as well have dropped Cassie off at the Donovan estate myself with a white fucking flag in my hand.

Someone has been back to my revenge room and brought all the files up here so they can all go through them. I don't even bother giving them any focus, I could recite them all in my sleep. It's all stuff I've been over countless times. I don't need it, what I need is to kill.

"Okay, what we all need to do now is try to get some rest." Max starts looking pointedly at me before turning to Ash. "Get cleaned up." Then to the rest of the guys. "Fuel up and prepare for the next couple of days. They are gonna be hard. War always is, but we got this."

They gather everything up and start to filter out of the room, but I linger behind. "We'll catch you guys up." I grip Max's arm to halt him in leaving and I can feel Marcus' stare, but I can't look at him. If he looks me in the eyes, he'll see the lies within burning brightly.

I wait until the room is empty and then I move to close the door and turn around leaning on it before I speak. "I need your help."

Chapter 6

LINCOLN

I haven't felt this out of control in years. Not since I was a child. Not since I watched my father murder my mother. It wasn't the first time I saw him kill somebody, but it was the first time he killed somebody I cared about. Something in me snapped that day, broke, and it hasn't been the same since.

Now the girl I swore I would protect with my life is gone and I have no idea how to get her back. Well, that's a lie, I have plenty of ideas, but none with enough merit to implement. I trail behind Asher as he limps from Zack's office, he's a mess and there's nothing I can do to help him, either. All I know is that I want to.

Max told us to rest, clearly, he doesn't know me very well. I couldn't rest even if I wanted to. Which I don't. All I want to do is get myself alone in a room with Elliot and Greg Donovan. Dragging out every second as I show them all the skills my daddy taught me. I'm looked upon as the quiet one, the one you don't need to worry about. What they don't realize is that's exactly how I like it. I was forged in the shadows and it's in those shadows that I hunt and kill.

I watch as he staggers to the kitchen, grabs a bottle of vodka, some towels and a first aid kit before he slips away. I continue to trail after him until I find him in the guest room on the ground floor attempting to open the pack with one hand. I watch him as he seethes in pain, taking heavy breaths as he fights against it. Has anyone other than Elle ever been there for him? Has anyone ever just looked after him, offered him more than the fucking darkness that surrounds him? Elle would die for him without question, but his demons run deep. Even her unconditional love doesn't change who he is inside.

The dark prince of the Donovan name.

I stalk inside, breaking the silence. "Let me." I attempt to take the supplies from his hand, but he snatches them back.

"I don't need your fucking help, Blackwell," he spits at me while taking a step back, and I don't miss the grimace on his face in the effort it takes for him to do so. I know his anger isn't directed at me, not really.

I grip the wrist holding the first aid kit making him hiss in pain. He doesn't relent though, locking those dark, stormy eyes with mine. "You wanna fight me, Donovan? Then do it. You wanna hit me, then hit me. I'm not fucking going anywhere and believe me when I say that I can take it." He stares at me intensely until he sees I'm not going to give in.

He snatches his wrist back. "Fine."

I take the kit from him and start laying it out on the bed as he opens the bottle and takes two big gulps. I try not to watch his throat swallow them down, but I can't help it. Asher Donovan is a fucking masterpiece made to be looked at, explored, fucking worshipped. I can't help but admire him. He must be in agony. He took on four guys and came out on top, his daughter has been kidnapped and somehow, he is still fucking standing. He was brought up by a sadistic father and yet he has honor like no other. I won't let the darkness overtake him and win.

"First, take a shower, then I'll get you patched up." I nod to the bathroom behind him before adding, "I'll get you some clothes for when you're done."

I don't give him a chance to respond before I stalk out, leaving him there. I make my way back to the main living area. Max's guys are sitting around the island as Helen passes out drinks to them. She looks distraught but is still doing what she does best and taking care of everyone else. I can't see Max or Elle so they must still be talking, and my brothers are nowhere to be found. I head to my room and grab some gray sweatpants and a pullover for Asher to wear, we are about the same size so they should fit okay.

I'm heading back down to the guest room when I bump into Logan. "Shit, sorry. I wasn't looking where I was going." His voice is flat and nothing like the flirty tone I have become accustomed to. I can't even imagine what he is going through. His brother might die, his niece has been taken, and he's waiting for his twin to get here before she can be used for collateral too. What a fucking shit show this is turning out to be.

"You alright?" I ask even though I know the answer.

He looks up at me and I can see every single one of his fears right there on his face, but he doesn't speak, just shrugs. What good will words do at this point? We have been putting everything on the line for Cassie and Elle and we failed. I failed. How could I let this happen? I know better than this. I am better than this. I'm the one who sees everything, knows everything, and doesn't let anything slip past our fucking defenses. Yet Greg not only slipped past, but he also waved a fucking red flag while doing it. How? I've been keeping so many tabs on him, watching his every move, and dissecting his every bit of communication, so how the fuck did I miss this?

I should have fucking known when I saw him at the ball. Should have planted a bullet in his skull the second I placed my gun against his temple. Clean up would have been a fucking nightmare, but at least we would still have Cassie. Without her, I fear this thing we are creating here is all going to fall apart. This house is the only place that has ever felt like a home to me, yet now it's cold and tainted in blood. A family made by choice, now ripped apart at its center. I can't bear the look on Logan's face, the pain, the fear, it guts me to see it. Not just on his, but on all of their faces, Asher, Elle, Helen, Arthur. All of them barely holding it together.

Five months ago, I didn't know any of them, it was just me and my brothers. Now I would lay my life down for every single one of them. Die, if only to save that young girl. If that isn't true family then I don't know what is. It's not like I've ever had one. *Not since my mother.*

I take a deep breath and nudge him. "Come on, I could use your help patching Asher up." He needs the distraction and I need the help, he has more medical knowledge than I do.

He hesitates, thinking about my words before he nods and turns to follow me. "Yeah sure, okay."

We enter the room together but find it's now empty and I panic. Fuck. I should have known he'd leave, he's the loosest fucking canon here. "Donovan," I yell with a little bit too much force to be casual.

"Yeah?" He stalks from the bathroom in just a towel, and I falter. My gaze falls to the large angel tattoo on his chest that is still glistening with water from his shower.

"I erm…" I can't speak as I take in the dark coating of bruises across his ribs and the cuts to his face. None of it diminishes his attractiveness, but it does remind me that tonight could have been even worse. What would have happened if those guys got the better of him? We could have lost him as well. That thought churns my gut, harder than it should.

"Fucking hell Donovan now isn't the time to seduce us," Logan teases, but his voice doesn't hold the same hint of humor and sexual tension that it usually does. He's trying to pretend everything is fine, we all are. Asher barely glares at him and doesn't even bother to roll his eyes, nothing like his usual reaction. I know Logan is just trying to focus on anything other than what's happening and distract us, but it's not working.

He walks towards me gesturing to the clothes in my hand and when I still don't say anything, he asks, "Are those for me?"

"Yeah sorry." I hand them over to him and he nods in thanks before heading back into the bathroom, closing the door behind him.

"Is now an appropriate time to jerk each other off over what we just saw?" Logan asks, staring after Ash. I huff a small laugh which is all I can manage then cock my brow at him. "What?" he muses. "Don't act like you weren't thinking about bending him the fuck over, because I certainly was." He swipes his hands down his face and I can see that despite the attempt at flirting, he is breaking.

I clear my throat, ignoring the image he just painted in my head. "I think we can both agree that now isn't the time for that." I didn't wanna add that I don't think it would ever be the time for that. Logan might be down for the guys, but Asher seems uninterested in any human being, let alone have a specific taste in gender. "Let's just get these supplies sorted so we can sort Ash out and then make a plan."

"Thought Max was making the plans." He frowns rifling through the first aid supplies on the bed, and now it's my turn to roll my eyes.

"You really think I'm gonna leave the fate of Cassie's life in the hands of some fucking stranger who only just showed up?" I thought he was getting to know me a little, but clearly, I was wrong.

"Max isn't a stranger; we have known him for years." He tries to defend him, but I really don't give a fuck.

"Yeah, you have, not me. The only thing that concerns me is getting that girl back alive and safe."

70

"For once we agree on something, Blackwell," Asher responds in a flat tone. I don't even hear the words because I'm too focused on the sight of him. Asher Donovan in fucking gray sweatpants is not what I should be focused on right now, but I cannot pull my eyes away from him. Lord have fucking mercy on my black soul.

"Ugh don't start, Asher. You've never given Max a chance," Logan scolds him.

"Why would I give him a chance? The fucker hates me," Ash grunts in disgust.

Logan sighs, "He doesn't hate you, just everything you stand for. Your money, family name, upbringing."

"Yeah, well that makes two of us," he mutters under his breath in response.

"What's the deal with him anyway?" I ask, gesturing for Asher to sit on the bed so we can get his face cleaned up. Now that he's showered, the only thing that really needs attention that we can help with is a split eyebrow. His right eye is swollen, and the left half of his face is covered in purplish bruising already, but we can't do anything about that. I'm hoping Logan can set his wrist before any permanent damage is caused.

He flops down onto the end of the bed with a groan and Logan and I both halt. He looks at Asher, then me and I just know he is thinking about the sounds he just made as he sat down. Fuck, who made the dark prince of the Donovan family a fucking walking temptation?

"Zack knows him from school, I think." He groans again and it's clear that the vodka isn't doing much of a job of numbing his pain. I rifle in the first aid kit until I find some painkillers and toss them to him. He accepts them without argument and that's how I know he really is feeling the pain.

Logan huffs. "There's a little more to it than that."

"Well, it's fucking irrelevant at this point. As long as he doesn't get in the way of me getting my daughter back, I don't care." The deadly tone of his voice cuts us off effectively, silencing the room as he knocks back a handful of painkillers with a swill of vodka.

Logan takes a deep breath and then drops down to the floor at the end of the bed, silently starting to fix Asher's face. I see him start to relax slightly and I know what he took is starting to take effect.

Logan must sense it too because he breaks the quiet, "Told you, I'd be on my knees for you one day, psycho." He purrs with a teasing glint in his eye, clearly trying to ease the tension, I can still see the pain that hides there though. I see right through his defense mechanism, just like I do with Jace. They are one in the same. They use their good looks and jokes as a weapon to keep people from digging deep enough to uncover their trauma.

Asher smiles a dazzling, sinister smile as he flashes his eyes to me and then to Logan. "Yeah, well we all know how much you enjoy being a bottom, Lo."

I almost choke. Never in my life did I think I would hear something like that come from his mouth. I didn't even think him capable of being human enough to make a joke, let alone make one in a situation like this. I can't hide the smile it brings to my face, and as his eyes lock onto my mouth, I can't help but lick my lips before responding to the taunt.

"Does that make you a top, dark prince?"

His gaze flicks to lock with mine. "I'm a top in everything I do."

Neither Logan nor I know what to say to that. Mostly because he is right, but also because we know we would both drop to our knees if he asked. Not that he would. Lusting after Asher Donovan is like lusting after a celebrity. Unrealistic and unattainable. The only time they are ever in reach is in your fantasies. But what fulfilling fantasies they are.

He may not have the upper hand right now, but I still wouldn't bet against him. I know he is capable of getting his daughter back and I want to be right there to help him. That's the only thing that matters right now. Bringing Cassie home. I don't care who I have to kill or what I have to do. I won't fail her again. *Fail him.*

Chapter 7

ELLE

After my talk with Max I am feeling a sense of calm for the first time since I walked back into the house. Now that I know exactly what I need to do, I feel at peace. Max has disappeared with a couple of his guys to arrange what I asked for. The rest of his team are set up in Zack's office making other plans for the Rebels. None of them agree with my plan, not even Max, but it's irrelevant. They work for me now. A fact I was sure to remind them of. I told them it was my way with their support, or they could leave, and I would do it alone.

I'm sitting at the kitchen island with a large cup of coffee. It's past four in the morning, officially making this the longest night of my life. Zack is being taken care of for now, and I am making plans for Cassie. If I think about them any harder, I am going to snap, so I try to focus on everyone else. Marcus is brooding silently next to me as Helen scrubs the same patch of kitchen counter that she's been at for the last twenty minutes. I'm not sure where Ash, Lo, and Linc have disappeared to, but I'm most worried about Jace.

He's slumped on the sofa staring at the large patch of blood on the carpet. I know he's taking tonight hard, we all are, but Jace has lived this before. He's watched someone he loves be taken by the Donovan's before and never come back. I can't live in that reality right now. *Or ever.*

The laughing and carefree Jace is gone, his armor down and his heartbreak pouring out for all to see. I hate it, hate seeing him this way. I watched his facade drop earlier tonight, but for an entirely different reason. I saw his reaction when Taylor reached up and kissed him, he was totally surprised. It didn't matter that he's been flirting with her for weeks, trying to shoot his shot, he just presumed she was too good for him.

Jace has one of the kindest souls I've ever known, but he's the only person who doesn't seem to realize it. Instead, he hides his problems, never letting anyone close enough to know the real Rebel inside. It's going to take a special girl to break through the reckless mask that is Jace Conrad. I only hope when he finds the right girl, she's not cut by all his broken and jagged pieces. If that girl is Taylor, well, she has got her work cut out for her.

Lincoln is another story entirely, always so closed off and never letting anyone get close. Yet tonight I saw him, I mean really saw him for the first time. He was by my side with his gun to Greg's head before any of us registered him moving. A stealth and silence that can only be inherited, not taught. He was practically a ghost, and it makes me wonder again what happened to him. How did he become the dark and ruthless shadow he is today? And how do I become the same so I can take down my enemies?

I focus my thoughts. So much has happened, yet there is still so much to happen. I mentally recite every single person that is a main player in this sick twisted game of revenge. How they fit into the puzzle of this whole mess and how they have helped Elliot Donovan stay on top. I think of what they did and how they are going to die. Chanting their names keeps me focused on what I know I have to do, and it stops me from breaking down completely and giving up.

Rolland Atkins

Joseph Kavanagh

Carter Fitzgerald

The Hallowed Crows MC

Sarah King

Jonathan King

Elliot Donovan

Greg Donovan

Then the endless list of nameless lackeys who supported them. Every single one of them has had a hand in everything that has happened, one way or another. And every single one of them will pay.

The price? Their demise.

I will make them all suffer, regardless of who they are, what they do and whose blood they share. That includes my parents. Their blood means nothing to me unless it is being spilled in retribution for everything, they did to me.

Helen, finally throwing down the cloth she's nearly torn to shreds, breaks me from my thoughts. She stalks out of the kitchen, most likely heading to a private place to break down now that she can't focus on taking care of anyone else. She likes to be the strength in us all, always has been, but tonight is the time for her to fall apart. We all need it.

You have to break so you can be made again, better, stronger. The same mistakes you once made, left in the shadows of your old self so you can be reborn and move on. I felt lost earlier tonight, but I refuse to let myself drown in my own despair. I know what I need to do, and Max is going to help me.

My thoughts are broken when a commotion sounds from out in the hall that is soon followed by Owen and Josh dragging in an incredibly angry Lily. She's fighting against them with a bag on her head and I find myself smirking a little at the dramatics.

"Why the hell did you bag her?" I ask.

Lily stops struggling immediately. "Elle? Is that you?" Her tone is glacial, and I just know she will find a way to get payback on these two for the way they brought her here. I gesture towards them and they lift the bag, releasing her arms at the same time. She squints as the light assaults her eyes and then quickly takes in her surroundings.

"What the fuck?" she exclaims turning to look at her captors, and I find myself doing the same.

Owen is smirking like a crazy person whereas Josh is giving her the stink eye as he speaks, "We tried to extract her quietly, but she wouldn't cooperate." He brings his gaze to me and shrugs. "We had to get creative."

"Creative? Fucking creative." She moves towards him and I jump up to grab her back as she continues, "I'll give you creative, you fucking pussy."

"Lils," I say, putting my arms around her stomach from behind and pulling her towards me, stalling her movements. She huffs as I release her, and as she turns to me her face immediately drops.

"What's wrong? Why am I here?" She casts her glance to Marcus and then back to the security guys before coming back to me.

"Come sit down, Lils."

"No. I don't wanna sit down, what the fuck is wrong? Where's Logan?" Of course, her first question is for her twin. She's had this conversation before when someone ripped her world apart and told her that their parents didn't survive the car crash.

"Logan's fine." I hesitate, not sure how to even say the words at this point. "It's Zack, he was shot."

Her eyes widen in shock and I see her take a deep swallow as she tries to process what I just told her. Then she scrunches her eyes up as she assesses me from head to toe and once again looks at Marcus.

"What else?" She asks looking back at me, and I frown at her question. How does she already know there is more? When I don't respond she continues, "Elle, I've only ever seen that look in your eyes once before."

Logan enters the room as she speaks, followed by Ash and Linc, all of them look relieved when they see Lily.

"Lils, thank fuck." Logan crosses the room in an instant and crushes her into a bear hug and when he pulls back, she looks even more worried than before.

Owen and Josh slip away as Lincoln and Asher join us at the kitchen island and then to my surprise, so does Jace. She takes in each of our faces one by one.

"Where's Mom and Dad?" Her voice cracks slightly at her question. She likes to act tough and unaffected by everything. Has always been the most closed off of the Royton clan, but I know it's just an act. A way to try to keep people at arm's length so if she loses someone else, she loves it won't affect her. If only that was the way, it worked.

"They're fine," I assure her. "Arthur went with Zack to the hospital and Helen is here somewhere, she was waiting for you. The two of you need to go to a safe house."

"Where is Cassie?" Her question doesn't throw me, I expected it, but the sound of my daughter's name cuts me like a knife.

I continue, "I don't know how long yet and I know it's not ideal missing college, but until things calm down, we need to be safe." I move to the fridge and pull out a bottle of water, just to do something with my shaking hands.

"Where is Cassie?" she asks again, her voice laced with more anguish this time. She knows, but she needs to hear me say it.

"Don't worry, I will contact your tutors securely and make sure they send you work so you don't fall behind. With break coming up, it will be fine. Everything will be fine." I can feel every set of eyes in the room burning into my skin. How can you hold yourself together when everything has already fallen apart?

Lily crosses the kitchen and grabs my arm, her fingers bite into my skin. "Where is Cassie?" she demands.

"The Donovan's have her."

The words feel like they strike every person in the room. No one is immune to the situation and every single person here will feel the effects of tonight forever.

Lily stands dumbfounded as she tries to comprehend what I just said. She blinks a couple of times and I watch the tears escape onto her cheeks. She takes a deep breath and dashes them away quickly, but I saw them. Saw the love she has for my daughter. She looks back around the room until she finds Asher. She moves quickly towards him and out of nowhere, slaps him hard across the face,

"Lily!" I shout in protest. *What the fuck?*

Ash barely flinches at her attack. Given the injuries he has already sustained, I don't know how, but it's like he doesn't even feel it.

"I told you this would happen," she screams at him. "I told you that you being around her would be no good for her."

"Lils!" Logan cuts in. "Stop."

"Stop?" she laughs in disbelief. "They fucking have her, Logan. Don't act like we don't all know exactly what happened to bring her into this world."

She turns back to Ash. "What the hell are you still doing here? Go get her." She pushes him hard, and he allows himself to stumble away from her. Her words look like they have cut him deeper than anything else.

"Lily." Helen's voice cuts through the tension. "Enough." Her tone silences the room, but then Ash clears his throat.

"It's fine, but thank you, Helen--" he starts, but she cuts him off.

"Nothing about this situation is fine, but you will not turn on one another."

"Why? I'm a Donovan." He shrugs. "Their bad blood runs through my veins too."

"You are nothing like them!" Helen snaps back at him. "They are vile and filled with hate. That's not you, Asher. Don't let me ever hear you say that shit again."

He takes a deep breath, trying to absorb her words, but I know how much hate he will be feeling towards himself. "I should have done more to protect her; I know exactly what my father and brother are like. I should have done more. I could have done more for her."

"Ash," I move until I'm in front of him. "You did everything you could, you've risked it all for us for the last four years."

"Yeah, and it was all for nothing." His tone is flat, and I can tell he will blame himself for this forever.

"No, it was so our daughter could have a father. So, she could know love and joy, and what it means to have a daddy who loves her."

"We need to get her back, Elle." His words are barely above a whisper and I know he means we, as in me and him. There is a knowing look in his eyes that mirrors my own. We both know we will do whatever it takes.

I give a slight nod of my head and then step back. "We've all had a long night and there's nothing more we can do right now." I look each of them in the eyes. "Go, we will reconvene in a few hours with Max and the guys and start making moves to get our girl back."

No one moves, but I can no longer stand the tension and the pity. I leave the room at a quick pace and don't stop until I get to my room. Once there, I quickly grab the empty black bag from under my bed and start filling it with clothes. Anything that I think I might need to take on my retaliation. When I hear footsteps approaching, I quickly shove it back under the bed and climb into the blankets.

Marcus appears thirty seconds later with the permanent grimace that has been on his face all night. I don't want to speak to him right now. If he talks, I will break and confess everything. I can't do that. Not now.

"Come lie with me?" I ask before he can speak, and when he sees the no doubt empty look on my face, he nods and climbs in behind me. He curls his arms around me until we are one and then we just let the silence eat up the room.

It isn't long until his breathing evens out and I know the exhaustion of the night has finally got the better of him. I wish I could do the same, wish I could slip into the unconscious lull of dreams and pretend that this fucking chaotic shit show wasn't my reality. I am fairly sure the only thing keeping me awake at this point is the pure determination to bring my daughter home.

The sun is already starting to peek through the curtains, and I know I have to go before it's too late. I silently climb from the bed and slip into my wardrobe. I change into fitted black cargo pants, a long sleeve black top and combat boots, tossing my leather jacket over my arm and pulling my hair into a slick ponytail. Once ready, I move quietly back into the room and look over Marcus' sleeping form. He looks peaceful and I wish that could be the look etched onto his face forever. That this life stops tainting him and hardening his already brick exterior.

My phone lights up on the nightstand and I slowly reach my arm out to retrieve it. There is a text message from Max that simply says, *We're good to go.*

I take one last look at Marcus as I pick up my bag and open the door. I whisper into the night and pray he hears my words in his dreams.

"I wish on all the stars I make it back to you."

It's time to do what I should have done the moment I came back here. I am going after every single person who has wronged me and my family. Every single person who has had a hand in hurting me is going to die. I need to get my girl back, but before that I need to make sure it's safe for her to come back. This town is about to be shaken up until it isn't built on crime and dirty money.

I'll burn it all. Burn it until there isn't a shred of anything left and I will do it all by myself. A lone wolf is still a wolf.

Chapter 8

ELLE

The house is silent as I move through the shadows towards my escape. I use my code on the side door and slip out undetected until I reach the trees lining the side of the property where Max and Elijah are waiting. They both have stern looks on their faces as they watch me approach, they aren't happy with what's going on. They can join the fucking club because neither am I.

He doesn't say anything as he drops another black bag at my feet similar to the one slung over my shoulder, only this one is filled with weapons.

"You've got guns, knives, crowbars, knuckle dusters, even a couple of bats. I've added some useful syringes in there and then the usual rope, cable ties, chains, handcuffs, basically anything you need for prisoners. There is also some Kevlar in there, make sure you use it." He looks at me with a stern face before continuing, "I've put an untraceable burner in there with some other tech, call me for whatever you need, and I will send any intel we find."

I nod, not really knowing what to say at this moment in time. I know what I am about to do is stupid and reckless, but I have no choice. They went too far and it's time I ended this. It's me or them. My daughter or my family. I choose her.

I pick up the bag and he hands over the keys to the car I asked for. I go to move towards it when he grabs my arm. "Are you sure you wanna do this?"

I drag my arm from his grip. "I have never been more sure of anything in my life."

"You call me if you need anything, King. I mean it, I don't want another fucking midnight phone call when it's already too late to help you."

I fight back the burn of emotion in my throat. I know how close he and Zack are, how much he means to him. This night will be hard for him too. I step back and throw my arms around his neck and give him a hug.

"Remember your training, Elle. Panic--"

"Is what gets you killed," I finish for him.

He smiles into my hair as I pull back and swipe the tear from my cheek before he sees it. The words Zack spoke to me so often hit me right in the heart.

"Don't worry, I remember everything you taught me," I say with fake bravado because the last thing I feel is confidence right now, all I know is that I have to do this.

He nods and gestures for me to move past him. I put the bags on the passenger side floor and then climb into the driver's seat. I take one last deep breath before I start the engine, adjusting the mirror to take one last look at my home. The place that currently has most of my family inside, all safe and protected, and then I do the only thing I can do. I drive away and leave them behind.

I have one stop to make before I end all of this and that is to see the person who saved me once before. My brother.

The drive to the hospital is silent. It's weird. I used to love the quiet. Was never bothered by it. Now it just makes my thoughts scream louder in my head and reminds me of everything that I have already lost. I always think that Cassie saved my life, made me the person who I am today, and she did, but it wasn't just her. It was my brother too.

He was the person who held me in his arms while I cried night after night over what happened to me. He was there with a cool rag to wipe my sweaty forehead every time I woke up screaming from a nightmare. He made me snacks every time the morning sickness had me hugging the toilet for hours. He held me close when I found out about Michael Riviera. He was by my side through it all, he gave me a family, one I could count on, introduced me to Max, and most importantly, was just my big brother.

Zack knew what I needed before I even knew it myself. I first met Max when Cassie was a few months old, she had healed my heart in ways I never thought possible, but my mind was another story. I still woke every night from terrible nightmares, still had panic attacks every time I remembered what happened to me and would still flinch anytime I had to go outside alone. It was unbearable. I felt like I was barely alive in my own skin.

The day I met Max, he walked right over and tried to strike me. I was so terrified that I had a panic attack. Max left and Zack stepped in to comfort me. This continued every day for weeks. I would come across Max at different times of the day and every time he would attempt to attack me, and my body would shut down in terror. Every single time. Until, one day, it just didn't. One day, when he went to grab me, I grabbed him back. I pulled my hand away immediately, fearing his retaliation, but the only thing that hit me was his contagious smile, as he grunted four words at me.

"It's about time, King."

From that day forward, I met with Max every single day to train, as he and Zack taught me everything I know now. We started with basic breathing exercises, stretching, movement and even balance. Before moving onto kickboxing, karate and krav maga. We practiced with fake weapons, until I learned how to use real ones, did one on one combat until I could give just as good as he gave, and even scenario attacks with his team. Any fighting or protection technique he could think of, he taught me. I spent every single morning at his training facility, and every afternoon with Zack learning about hacking and coding, six hours every day for almost two years. Basically, any time I could get that wasn't with Cassie, I was training.

All that helped me turn into a girl who can become an emotionless killer, but it didn't make me. What made me is my family: Cassie, Zack, Helen, Arthur, even the twins. Being with them made everything better and then Max made me stronger. Healed my mind and made me into a weapon that everyone underestimates. I let myself forget.

I came back here for my vengeance and then locked eyes with Marcus Riviera. Drowned in my River and haven't come back up for air since. And with him came his brothers. Two more family members to call my own. All of them would risk it all for me. I know they will understand why I now have to risk it all for them, for her. I won't forget again. Not until I am standing on the graves of every single person in my way of a happy and safe life with my daughter and the rest of my family.

An hour later I make it to Lockstown and pull into the parking lot of the private medical facility there. The guy guarding the gate takes one look at me through the window and lets me straight in. Ignoring the security this place has, I reach into the bag and sheath a knife to my thigh and a handgun to my waist.

Once inside, a nurse leads me to the top floor where they keep VIP's. This place is made for celebrities, politicians, and anyone with a lot of money. She tells me Zack made it through surgery and they have just wheeled him from recovery back to his room. Once I reach his door, I take a deep breath and flex out my shaky hands, before grabbing the door handle and stepping inside.

Zack is lying motionless in the bed with countless tubes coming out of his body including one down his throat. He isn't breathing for himself. The fire of tears burns behind my eyes, but I am done crying. Crying won't help me, help him.

I feel a presence in the room, "I thought you'd be at the safe house by now." I declare.

I hear the slight smile in his voice when he answers me, "And I thought you'd be at home."

I turn to Arthur, he looks exhausted, "You really think I wasn't gonna come and see my brother on his deathbed."

He rolls his eyes causing me to smile, because if he can be playful then I can guess it means Zack is out of the woods, for now. "Such a dramatic little firecracker."

He moves towards me until he is standing by my side, and then continues, "I've been waiting for you." I flash my surprised eyes to him at that and he nudges me with a smile, as he continues, "What you think because I didn't raise you, I don't know you like you're my own?"

I blow out a breath at his brutal honesty and his endless love. "I don't deserve you, or him," I whisper, looking back to Zack.

"I don't know anybody who deserves more than the two of you." Arthur moves to sit in one of the empty chairs by Zack's bed as I perch onto the side of his bed and pull his hand into mine. We both watch him silently for a few minutes.

"He shouldn't be here," my voice is still charred with emotion, "this never should have happened. I should have just left him to live his life, not involve him in mine."

Arthur smiles a sad smile, "Elle, you didn't have a choice. From the moment he found out about you I saw the change in his eyes. He acted unaffected, appreciative of his family, but I know how important it was for him to have a blood relative."

"But I did this to him, he escaped the curse of the King name, only to be dragged back into it. And now he is lying here unconscious."

"He is gonna be fine Elle, I promise. Besides, being a King is the least of his worries, trust me."

"The Donovan's know about him, about all of you. What if Sarah tries to find him?" I would never let her anywhere near him, but still, I can't imagine what this must be like for Arthur and Helen to have to go through.

Arthur reaches out and grabs Zack's other hand, "I love him, and I will respect whatever he wants. He is my son, no matter what anyone says."

I don't know what else to say, so I don't say anything. We just sit in silence for a while, watching Zack until I know it's time to leave. I think about trying to make an excuse to Arhur as I get up to leave.

"Erm I should go and--" I start, but my voice trails off, unsure on what to say.

"Elle, I know you. I know you need this. That you deserve it, they deserve it, but be smart, okay?"

I nod as the lies purge off my tongue to appease him, "I know. The guys are waiting outside for me, don't worry."

He stares me down, before deciding not to question me and nods. "Go make them pay, firecracker, I've got our boy."

I smile, give him a quick hug, and then drop a kiss to Zack's head, taking in his motionless form one last time. It's time to play the big game. Greg taking my daughter has lit a rebellious fire in me that won't burn out until I get her back. The Donovan's are done taking from the people of this town, it's time to do what I should have done from the start.

It's time for the first act of war.

Chapter 9

MARCUS

She's gone. I know it before I even open my eyes. I knew it before I even went to sleep. I felt it in my heart. I knew the moment she snapped, that I had lost her. The second Greg said he would give Cassie in exchange for her, I knew Elle would be gone. From the moment I found out about Cassie, so many things about Elle made sense. Why she left, why she came home, why she pushed me away, why she pulled me back. Through it all, the only thing I knew to be true was that she loved me, but Cassie would always come first. I never thought I would resent that, never imagined I could hate the love she has for her daughter. *Until now*.

That kind of love, the unconditional kind, it's reckless, ruthless, completely, and utterly life changing. She won't let anything get in the way of that, not even her own happiness. Yet I also know she won't go down without a fight. If that was her plan, then as soon as the call with Greg ended, she would have left and gone straight there. I know she wanted to, how could she not?

I'd give anything to get Cassie home to her and she isn't even mine. That doesn't mean I don't love her like she is because I do. I will use everything at my disposal to get her home and get Elle back by my side. Even if I have to plant a bullet in Greg myself. I'd do it. Without thought, without regret and with a fucking smile on my face.

I don't move straight away, not even to alert my brothers or Asher. I just allow myself a few minutes of silence, to feel the dread of the situation crush my soul. Elle is gone and I don't know if I'll ever see her again. I don't know if I will be able to do everything I need to do before she hands herself over to them. Ironic that the last time she disappeared from my life, I never wanted her to come back, now I pray on every fucking star in the sky that that she does. I know why she's gone, why she has to do this, but it won't stop me from doing what I need to do either. She isn't the only one with a plan.

I take a shower and get dressed before I head down to the kitchen. Max and his guys are all standing around the island talking. When I appear the conversation halts. I know for a fact that Max is in on whatever Elle is doing right now, I saw it in the way they interacted yesterday, the way she commanded him. He would do whatever she asked, and I can't begrudge him for that, because so would I.

"Hey" Max says tentatively, like he is waiting for me to freak out. Well, not today. Today I am a man on a mission. I pour myself a cup of coffee and then join the guys at the counter.

"Where are we at?" I ask, taking a sip as I look at each of them. They might do this for a living, might be more experienced, but none of them will fight as hard as I will for my girl.

Max clears his throat, "Erm, we were just going over all of Donovan's real estate, see if we can find any hidden places, he might be keeping Cassie, if not at the main mansion."

I nod as he talks, "Good idea, any that need checking out? We could split up, I'll take my guys, you take yours, get through them faster." None of them respond and all continue to stare at me. "What?"

"Erm, Elle said we should expect you to lose it a little," Max starts but I cut him off.

"Why? Because you helped her slip out in the night and go after the Donovan's alone?" There's no point beating around the bush, that is exactly what happened, I'm sure of it.

"I work for her," he replies like it's just as black and white as that. Like this whole thing isn't the most dangerous situation we will ever fucking face. He's unleashed her on them. Yet, he doesn't really know the evils of this town, he can't. You don't know unless you are born in this city of chaos and raised in its insanity.

"Just because you trained her into what she is today, doesn't mean she should be doing this alone." I feel my temper slipping slightly, but I hold it back as tight as I can. I won't waste it on the undeserving, not when there are so many targets, I can take it out on.

"That wasn't my choice to make," he replies solemnly. His words mean nothing, if anything happens to Elle because we weren't there to have her back, I will hold him personally responsible.

"It wasn't hers either," I snap. "She isn't the only one in this anymore." Asher comes into the room as I speak, followed by Jace and Lincoln and I smile sinisterly at Donovan's presence. "Besides," I say smugly flicking my eyes back to Max, "I'm not the one you should be worried about."

"Brother?" Linc starts judging the situation, "everything okay here?"

"All good with me, brother," I smile in return as I look at Asher, "You good?"

He looks at me confused, like he is wondering if I am being serious or not. Not too weird of a reaction, we might be on the same side, but it isn't like we are friends. We never really were. What I am only just realizing, is that it doesn't matter if we're friends or not, because we're family. One made in desperate times, yet more important than any blood and thicker than any real family ties. I will have his back until the fucking end, and I know he will have mine.

"Fine," he replies in a clipped tone, looking around the room again, "Where's Elle?"

I feel excited as I respond, knowing I am about to poke the bear. I look at Asher and then to Max, "Max helped her sneak out alone to go get her revenge, she's probably been gone for hours." I say the words casually, but they still taste horrific as they roll off my tongue. I know Elle can handle herself, but she shouldn't have to. We should be fighting side by side.

The room turns deathly silent. Asher doesn't speak, not one word. His blue stare turning dark as he locks in on Max. I barely blink and he has moved from the entrance to in front of Max, swinging a fist at his face. Lincoln captures it just in time, but then before Asher can protest, he punches Max himself, surprising us all.

What the fuck?

Max takes the hit and I see his team are impressed by Lincoln's strength, and for the first time since the party yesterday, I see the ghost of a smile on Jace's face. This is what we do, what we are good at. We protect people, keep them safe, and now the person we care about the most needs us.

Asher frowns at what's just occurred, and Lincoln looks at him with a stern face, "You probably have a broken fucking wrist, how about you refrain from punching anyone?"

"I don't need the help," he spits his nickname, "fighting my battles for me." I roll my eyes. They're so alike it's comical. I don't understand why they don't get along better.

"Really? Because the help is the one who is gonna bring your daughter home," Lincoln fires back.

"Listen here Blackwell -" Asher starts, but I cut him off.

"Measure your fucking dicks later, we've got work to do," I grunt at them before turning to Max and his guys. "We," I gesture to my brothers and Ash, "are going to get Elle back and bring Cassie home, with or without your help. Elle isn't here so whatever she told you is now irrelevant. The only thing that matters to me is those two girls being unharmed. We all need to set our shit aside and fucking work together."

Lincoln and Asher remain in a stare off until Asher breaks it and shocks us all, "Agreed."

I nod, "Alright then, let's do this. Where should we start?"

Max cracks his jaw and then resumes the conversation, "Ash we were just going over all the property owned by your family, is there any helpful information you can think of?"

Asher moves in between two of Max's guys and starts inspecting all the paperwork they have laid out in front of them. He picks up a pen and starts writing stuff on each of them, varying from numbers and markers, none of it seems to make any sense to anyone but him.

Once done, he takes them and splits them between us, Max and his guys as he speaks, "X's represent the number of guards usually there, O's the number of staff and the squares are the security feeds. I have a couple of people on the inside I can speak to, but it will take some time to contact them."

Max nods along as he listens to him, while his guys look over the locations they were given. I'm not sure how he and his team usually do things, but me and the guys usually work as a unit. Lincoln takes out security and hacks into anything on the inside and then Jace and I go inside and do whatever we need. I doubt any of the stuff we do from here on out will be as simple as that. The Donovan's and their men won't be playing, so neither will we.

"My father's men won't think twice about killing you all, so be prepared." Asher confirms what I was already thinking.

"We brought enough weapons and ammo to support a small army, so that won't be an issue." Max adds, "Once you're all ready to go, you can go through them and pick what you are comfortable with."

I nod along with my brothers, we won't turn down weapons, that would just be stupid. "So how are we doing this?"

"How we always do it," Lincoln says, "together."

Max glares at him, before turning to Asher, "You go with Marcus and his guys." He nods his head at me, "but I'm taking Logan with me and sending Elijah with you."

I look at Asher who is giving Max the death stare, but manages to grit out, "Fine."

"Okay," I start. "We leave in one hour." I tell them.

Max and his team filter out at my orders with a few grunts, I wait for them to disappear before I address my guys. "Elle thinks she has to do this alone, that she is protecting us, but she isn't running from me, from us, ever again. Let's go get justice and go get our girl."

She thinks she can keep us out of it, keep us safe. She forgets we have been in this since the beginning. Since they put hands on our girl and my dad. I told her we were inevitable but it looks like I have to remind her.

It's time to show her exactly how I became king of the South Side. I'm coming for you baby and I've got a whole team of Rebels by my side.

Chapter 10

ELLE

I used to be afraid of the dark. Now I hunt in it. I was an innocent little girl dragged into the depths of an eclipse and expected to obey. My demise... warranted. My death... imminent. What they didn't expect is that I would escape the darkness and bathe in the pain until it coated my body like armor. I took the hurt and turned it into my catalyst to fight, and now it's time for my second act.

As soon as I left the hospital, I started making my plan. I can't go after my girl when so many of the people who help the Donovan's are still alive. They need to be wiped off the board first.

I am sitting in the office of Joseph Kavanagh, clouded by the shadows of the late evening. I knew he would be the first target from my list. He took his law education and has been using it to protect criminals instead of the victims. That stops now. The last thing I need is Elliot Donovan calling in his best attorney to save the day. I won't give him the chance to have any legal ties to my daughter.

It took me most of the day to put my plan into action, even though it's relatively simple. He is going to die. Slow, bloody, and fucking beautiful.

At lunchtime, I donned a brunette wig and some office attire to snatch a key card as I flirted with some unassuming intern. Then I spent my afternoon downloading every piece of evidence that Kavanagh has buried for his clients over the years. Every cop he paid off, every witness he discredited and every payment he took from the monsters who controlled him. All of it there in black and white. I also found a sick sense of glee as I used his own office printer to print them all off.

They now sit on his desk in a neat little pile while we wait for him to arrive. See, Joseph Kavanagh knows all about me, knows who I am and what happened to me. He will also know what I have been doing since I came home. But what he doesn't know, is that I know all about him too.

I know he has three ex-wives who all left him. A variety of reasons were cited in the divorce papers, but after some digging, I found multiple hospital reports from them and even a couple of police reports that had all been squashed. It seems our man of the law has a taste for rough fucking. Whipping, choking, fisting. You name it and he's into it. No wonder Elliot found himself right at home when he moved to town.

I also know that every Sunday he uses his office for some extracurricular activities. It wasn't exactly hard to hack into his phone and see the countless hookers he has booked every week, for the last two years. All of them with extremely specific instructions on what he likes, one of them being leather.

How convenient, Mr. Kavanagh. I like leather too. I'm wearing fitted black leather pants with a matching leather corset. They look perfect with my knee-high leather heeled boots and leather gloves. The perfect murder outfit, if you ask me. Have you ever tried to get blood out of clothes? It's not easy. Lucky for me, leather makes cleaning up much easier.

Next to the pile of evidence against him on his desk, I have some cable ties, rope, tape and a small bag of tools. Some for him and some for my plan. I have already taken care of all the cameras inside the building, on the street and in the surrounding areas. We are going to be spending some time completely alone and uninterrupted.

I hear the elevator ding and I smile. *Showtime.* Joseph Kavanagh stalks into the office how I'm sure he stalks into the courtroom, like a hunter ready to rip his prey apart. Little does he know, he's the prey tonight. His smile is predatory when he takes in my leather clad form. I am standing in front of the window with only the outside light silhouetting my frame. The perfect backdrop to show off my body, but not my face. Not that he would recognize me. I traded my fake brunette locks for a bright red wig. This piece of shit is getting sliced up by the fucking little mermaid tonight.

"Fuck, you're delicious," he grunts, "am I paying extra for such beauty?"

I smirk even bigger as I purr back, "Oh trust me, Mr. Kavanagh. My price is very high, only few are afforded it."

"And worth every penny I bet." His sexual tone makes me grind my teeth. I should just shoot him right now in the fucking head, but I have plans first. I want him to know how fucked he is before he dies, and not in the way he enjoys.

He moves to walk towards me, but I halt him with a hand in the air, "Clothes off."

"Thought I was in charge here," he teases me, and I roll my eyes in the dark. Fucking slimy prick.

I put on my best flirting porn voice as I beg him, "Please sir, I wanna play a game first." I see him turn giddy when I say that, and I want to gag.

He unbuttons his suit jacket, taking it off and folding it over the arm of the sofa in a way only someone who grew up rich would. He reaches for his tie to loosen it, "Okay I'll bite," he says with a sick smile and wink. "You can have a little fun, but then I'll have mine."

I feel the bloodthirst burning through my veins as I reach for a leather riding crop from his desk and his smile turns sadistic. "Pants off, Mr. Kavanagh. Show me what I get to play with tonight." I don't even have to fake the excitement in my tone as I think about all the ways I am going to make him bleed.

He wastes no time stripping the rest of his clothes until he is standing in nothing but a fitted white wife beater and grey boxer shorts. His body is toned and muscular and I can see how he fools so many girls into thinking his fake charm is real. He is attractive for an older man, it's how he landed himself three wives, I'm sure. They didn't see the devil lurking within, they were too bewitched by his smiling face. But his eyes, that's where the soul lies, and his truth appears. He's just another sick fuck with too much money and too much power. I am going to relish in making him atone for his sins.

He moves towards me, still trying to remain in control, just how he likes it, well not tonight Satan. As he nears me, I push back against him, leading him backwards until he falls into a chair behind his desk. I turn him so it faces back towards his desk and then slide myself on top of it in front of him. I can already see him hardening beneath his boxers. God. Men really do let their cocks rule them. If he just looked past me, he would notice the flat lay of weapons waiting for him. I part my legs so I can pull him towards me, and he licks his lips as they land on either side of where he's sitting.

Once there, I tease him, dragging my hands across his chest before reaching down to one of his arms and then cable tying one of his wrists before he can even register. He tries to protest, so I reach down and palm his cock until he hisses in pleasure.

"Want me to play with this?" I tease while thinking of how many times I am going to fucking sanitize my hands after this, even though I am wearing gloves. He nods profusely. "Then let me be a bad girl so I can be punished." He groans at my words and I have to refrain from rolling my eyes again. He allows me to cuff his other wrist and then I use my heeled boot to push him backwards. Once I have him where I want him, I slide off the desk and fall to my knees. I used to think my beauty was a curse, but when I see the lust in his eyes and how it's allowed him to be at my submission. I suddenly realize it isn't a curse at all, just another weapon in my arsenal.

I drag one of my hands up his thigh, bypassing his cock slightly and keep pushing it up his torso to his shoulder. My other hand reaches behind my back as I lean in and whisper into his ear, "The King sends her regards."

My words barely hit his ear before I plunge my knife right into his cock. I pull it back immediately and watch in delight as blood pours from his groin. He screams out in pain, but I shove a rag in his mouth to silence them into muffles.

When I look him in the eye, his cocky and lustful stare has been replaced with pain and panic. I smile as I pull the wig off and watch realization hit him.

"Tell me, Mr. Kavanagh. Was it worth it? All those criminals you defended; all those crimes that went unreported, unpunished. Was it worth it?" He can't answer me obviously, but I enjoy watching him try.

"Anything you had to say in defense stopped mattering the moment Elliot Donovan took his first victim right under your nose." I'm not even angry, in fact, I have never felt this calm before. There is no adrenaline rush, no worrying about taking someone's life. There is just peaceful contentment. This is what I have to do. To beat the Devil, you have to become a monster.

I track the blood as it slowly seeps down his legs onto the floor, he is panting hard, and his body is covered in sweat. I watch as he tries to control his breathing, his eyes panicked as I reach forward and pull the rag from his mouth now.

"What the fuck is going on?" he manages to stutter, and now I do roll my eyes at him. I mean it's pretty obvious what is going on. His crimes have caught up with him and it's time for his death. I thought he was smart enough to realize that.

I bring my knife back towards his face and he stares at it in fear. "How long has Elliot known about Cassie?" I ask him.

He looks between me and the knife a couple of times before his eyes lock on mine. Judging by his defiant glare, he's clearly decided that I won't stab him again while I'm questioning him. "I don't know what you're talking about," he starts, but is cut off when I plunge the knife in between his ribs. There is a spot where if you tilt the knife at the right angle, it will miss any vital organs. Painful, but not life threatening.

He grunts out in pain as I respond, "I don't like liars, Mr. Kavanagh." I hiss at him as I slide the knife back out and wipe the blood on his bare thigh.

He starts to shake. I think he realizes he isn't getting out of this alive, finally that legal brain of his is kicking in.

"Okay okay just stop. Please," he begs.

I pull back ready to listen to him. "When did Elliot find out about Cassie?" I ask again.

"A couple of weeks ago," he pants through the agony he's no doubt feeling. "Someone saw you; I don't know who, he didn't tell me. Whoever it was is close to

Greg and, well, you know what he's like." He grunts in pain, "As soon as he heard about her, he wanted her, wanted you and well, Elliot is all about family." He says the last part like he actually means it.

"After that he ordered a tail on you. He had eyes on you at school, had you followed. But you were always with those little South Side punks, the Riviera boy and his pals." He grunts, slurring slightly and I know it's from the pain and blood loss, but clearly, he knows I don't care because he forces himself to continue. "They tried to get you alone, but you were too well guarded. They worked out an opportunity with the ball and you took the bait, like they knew you would." He isn't smug in the delivery of his words, just factual. He is right, they found my weakness and exploited it. Between the need for revenge and the safety of my daughter, they found my Achilles heel.

I think about all the times I have been out with Cassie in the last month and I can pinpoint the moment they discovered her. I know exactly who told Greg and they have just landed themselves a top spot on my list. I take a slow deep breath in as I think about what I have just learned, and then ask my last question.

"Where is he keeping her?" My tone is as harsh as steel as I try not to let my panic show when I think about what could be happening to her.

"Ahh," he gasps in misery, "Greg will keep her close, but not accessible, he knows Asher is with you, so he won't risk it." Hmm glad to know they don't underestimate my best friend. I nod through his words as I try to think of where she would be. She has to be on the Donovan estate, surely. It's their most guarded location, aside from their fucking trafficking warehouse. I pray to all the gods she isn't there.

I have no further questions for him, so I start packing up my stuff. I see it, the moment he realizes there is nothing else he can offer me, nothing but his death as payment for his crimes. He doesn't even have time to flinch when I bring the knife to his neck and slice in one swift movement from left to right.

Watching someone choke on their own blood sounds like it would be satisfying, but in reality, it actually takes a few minutes for them to die. It's pretty boring, but I don't allow him the final satisfaction of being put out of his misery early. I patiently wait until I see the life drain from his eyes and the struggling gurgled breaths pant into silence. Then I wait some more. Once I am sure he is dead, I plant a bullet between his eyes. That one is for my own pleasure.

The hardest part now is getting one of his large glass windowpanes out of its frame. I had to watch a few tutorials and call Oliver to walk me through it a couple of times, but I manage to do it quite easily after that. Once it's done, I slide it carefully aside, before wheeling the carcass, slumped in his office chair closer. I cut him loose and tie a rope around his upper torso. It takes a bit of maneuvering but eventually, I get him how I want him.

I get the large piece of card I brought with me and scrawl the words on it in black permanent marker before I staple it to his chest. Have you ever stapled into someone's body? It's quite fun. Once done, I step back and inspect my handywork and can't help but smile. He looks so perfect.

Then I push him out of the window.

Chapter 11

MARCUS

We're outside yet another of Elliot Donovan's properties while Elijah does a perimeter sweep. On Max's orders we are waiting in the car like sitting ducks. Asher is riding shotgun next to me, and Lincoln and Jace are in the back. This is the fourth house we have attempted today, but I know in my bones we will be leaving just as disappointed as the last three times. Cassie isn't here and we are wasting valuable time. Every minute we spend searching leaves her helpless to those monsters.

I smash my fist against the wheel in frustration, the guys don't even flinch at my outburst and I barely feel the sting. I'm just fucking sick of this feeling in the pit of my stomach that has been present since I walked into Elle's house and found her covered in blood. I use the same hand to rub at my chest in rough circular motions, just trying to ease the ache of loss I'm experiencing. I just need to be doing more than sitting outside that rich pricks endless fucking houses.

"This place is too quiet," Lincoln's voice cuts into the silence.

"It's not like they're gonna be advertising that they rape girls and kidnap children," Jace scoffs in sarcasm beside him. The sight of the guys makes me feel even worse. Asher is acting emotionless, but I know him well enough to know how much he is dying inside. I am too. We won't rest until we get our girls back to us. I never thought I would welcome him with open arms into my family, but he completes it in a way I could have never imagined. My brothers are just as cut up, and their pain is my pain. We are like a unit of joint emotion. All drowning in a hole of self-destruction and pain, just desperate for some progress.

"Blackwell is right," Asher starts.

"I usually am," Linc snaps in retort, and Ash rolls his eyes.

"She isn't here, there would be more security if she were. My father wouldn't risk losing something with such a high value," the words are dripping in disgust as he talks, yet his words mirror my thoughts. We are extremely in tune with each other, both more than aware of all the sordid things his father is capable of. How Elliot Donovan birthed a son with such honor when he was raised in the same house as fucking Greg, will always astound me. He should know he is nothing like those snakes.

"He lost you," I say, without taking my eyes off the property in front of us and Asher scoffs a laugh.

"If you think I've ever held any importance to my father, then you're dumber than you look." I look towards him as he speaks, "Only heirs' matter in this society, second born are irrelevant."

I don't get a chance to respond as Elijah climbs back into the car. "The only person there is a housekeeper and from what I can tell, she looked like she wasn't expecting any company."

"Elliot only ever uses this place to entertain females he needs something from but are too well known to bribe." Asher responds to him in a bored flat tone as he looks back to the property. "This is a waste of time, the only place he will be keeping Cassie is close to him, which means she is being kept at my estate behind a 25 ft wall and countless guards."

"I agree with Asher, this is bullshit," Jace replies.

I don't bother responding, just start the car and leave, heading back to Elle's house. By the time we get home, it's officially Monday morning and all I want to do is eat and try to grab a couple hours sleep. I am beyond tired. Being out all day and night has worn me out physically. The constant ache of missing Elle and Cassie however, is what's causing true exhaustion.

We pull up and are barely out of the car when Max emerges at the front door, "You need to see this," he gestures inside and then disappears. I didn't miss the extra cameras on the gate on the way in, or the team of guards trickling around the property line. Something's happened.

We all make our way inside and follow Max into the living room where him and the rest of his team are all staring at the huge flat screen on the wall. I look around the room, but no one says anything. Their sole focus is on the news report playing on the TV. I turn my attention to it and see a crime scene being shown.

111

The reporter is standing in front of a huge office building and it's swarming with police. Max starts laying out documents on the coffee table as we watch, and I flick my gaze between the two. What the hell?

"The body of Joseph Kavanagh was found about an hour ago hanging from the window of his office," Max starts, as he picks up the remote and mutes the news report.

"He killed himself?" Lincoln questions and Max looks at him and then back to the rest of the room, before settling on me.

"Not exactly." He takes a deep breath as he gestures to Mason who starts to bring up pictures on the TV screen in front of us.

"He was stabbed multiple times before he had his throat slit. Then he was tied up, had a sign stapled to his chest and then thrown from his window." His words are emotionless, but I can see the undercurrent of panic and anger rolling off of him.

"What did the sign say?" Asher asks with just as little emotion as Max.

Mason swipes through a few pictures until he stops on one of the bloody sign that they must have pulled from his body.

'I PROTECTED RAPISTS!'

Holy shit. They really woke the demon in Elle when they came after her family. I'm not surprised, but everything she has done so far has been in the shadows. Now she isn't only stepping out into the light, but into the public eye. She might not have revealed herself, but no one is safe.

Mason clears his throat, "His office was also covered in evidence of his own crimes that he had buried over the years."

"She knows better than this," Max snaps, losing some of his cool and I snort, causing him to cut his eyes to mine, "Something to add, Riviera?"

"Yeah, you're a fucking idiot if you thought this would go any other way." I can't keep the smile off my face as I talk. We may be in a fucking shit show of a situation, but Elle always loved the dramatics.

"Elle knows how to cover her tracks," the quiet dude called Liam starts, but I cut him off.

"Sure, if it were Elle playing the game with her head on straight. But we aren't dealing with a rational Elle right now, are we?" I grit through my teeth, "We are dealing with loose cannon Elle. The one who walked in here and found her brother fucking dying and her daughter gone. If you thought she was just gonna go about things silently, then you don't know her at all." I am beyond fuming; how could they think this would be any different? She will do whatever she needs to do, if it means that she makes it to Cassie.

She is done covering up the crimes of this town, including her own. She isn't whispering into the ears of Donovan's minions anymore, she is shouting from the rooftops and slaying whoever is in her path. She needs us now more than ever.

I look at Asher and then to my brothers, "Come on, let's get out of here." I don't even wait for them to respond before I am stalking out the room.

"Where are you going?" Max calls after me.

"Where I should have gone from the start," I yell back.

I head to the garage towards Lincoln's SUV and pull out a smoke as I wait for the guys to follow me. I only manage a couple of drags before they appear.

As soon as Lincoln's within ear shot, I speak to him, "Call Jack and get him and all our guys to The Ring asap. Tell him it's a family emergency." I inhale another deep drag as he stares at me, before he nods and pulls out his phone to make the call.

"Where are we going?" Asher asks as I flick the cigarette to the floor and stamp on it.

"To the South Side." I climb inside the car and slam the door behind me.

The drive over is quiet as we all take the time to center our thoughts after what we just saw on the news. By the time we pull up at The Ring I can see most of my guys are already here, which is good, it means no more wasting time. The South Side is officially joining the war against the Donovan's and to do that they need the truth. All of it.

"Hey man," Jack greets me with a fist bump and then nods to Jace and Lincoln. I don't miss his eyes popping out of his head as Asher rounds the car. He looks at him and then back at me with a confused frown, but I just ignore him and head straight into The Ring. I climb through the ropes and look down at the small crowd gathered here. My brothers and Asher join me, and I look to Ash before I speak. His face is set in a tight grimace and I know he knows what is about to go down here. He gives me the slight tip of his head, which is as good as I will get from him, so I take it.

I look back to the crowd and speak loudly, "This town is run by criminals, sick twisted murderers and rapists who have been running free for far too long. That stops now. These people took from me, took from my girl and they will pay with their life. From here on out, we are at full scale war with Elliot Donovan, and anyone associated with him."

There are a few murmurs within the crowd as I see them look between themselves and then between Asher and me.

"What the hell is the son of the enemy doing here then?" one of my guy's spits, and I see a few others nod in wonder along with him.

Jack steps forward, "I hate to be a prick Marcus, but he's right. Your first rule to all of us was never trust a Donovan."

He isn't wrong, I was clouded by pain and grief when I started this crew, hurting the Donovan's was my only endgame. I have since broadened our mindset to helping others who need it, but my main target has always been Elliot. My boys know this and to explain the trust I have in Asher, would mean revealing the truth to them all. I contemplate what to say next when Asher beats me to it.

"My father is scum. The Devil. He's hurt people. People important to me and people important to Riviera.

It's time he paid for his sins. I may have done things for him that I will never be proud of, but I'm not on his side, I'm not even on yours. The only thing that matters to me is that I get to put Elliot Donovan in a fucking grave. I will do that with or without your help." His wicked tone silences them all.

I feel the tension rolling from Asher as he looks at me, he knows there is no love lost between us, there never has been, but he saved my girl's life. He was there for her when I couldn't be when I chose not to be. For that I will be forever in his debt and he will forever be family.

I look back at my guys, "He's one of us, always has been, always will be."

Chapter 12

ELLE

The whole town has been swarming with police officers all day. They're all calling the murder of Joseph Kavanagh a shocking and isolated incident. I don't think I could snort any harder at that. This town is built on more blood and bones than I can count and run by more criminals than the local prison. Yet apparently, the slaying of a corrupted law official is a tragedy. Fucking ridiculous. I pasted the walls of his office with enough of his crimes that they would have been able to incarcerate him for the rest of his life five times over. But apparently that isn't as newsworthy as his murder.

He was only the start of my list. I have a lot of names and not a lot of time. I really need to keep moving, but I'm also not stupid. I need to eat and rest a little, and with the police crawling all over town, what better time than now.

I drive over North Hill, pausing in the mass of trees behind the Donovan estate. So close to where I know my daughter is, yet still so far. All I want to do is push through the branches, scale the giant wall, and slay every fucker in there until the house drowns in their organs. Then set it alight and watch it fucking burn with Cassie safely back in my arms. But I can't do that. Not until all the other pieces of this game have been taken.

I drive a little more and reach a house I know better than any other. The King mansion, my home, well, my childhood home. I wonder if my parents are inside. If they ever regret the terrible things they have done. If they know how much they are going to pay for their sins.

I remember when I was a little girl my mom told me I could be anything I wanted to be. I bet she never thought I'd grow up to be an avenging angel covered in blood. I didn't dream of this path for me either. She played her part and for that she will suffer in the darkest depths of hell. I don't doubt the Devil has a chamber on reserve for my parents, but tonight isn't the night I send them there.

I keep driving, looking for a place I'm sure I will be safe for the night. The Riviera mansion remains empty to this day. No one wanted to live in the house that Michael was murdered in, and then Elliot had it condemned. I think that was his last fuck you to Michael for what he did. It's all boarded up and empty, such a sad end to a house that was always filled with love and happiness. Until the night it was ruined by the curse of the Donovan's.

I pull over into a thick wooded area and then move a few branches around to cover my car. There won't be anyone coming out this way, but it's better to be safe. Climbing the fence into the backyard where I spent many of my summers, is like climbing into the past. I remember the way like it's engraved on my very soul. Past the pool, over to the left of the rose bushes and twenty steps past the Oak tree.

Once I clear the tree, I see it. Mine and River's treehouse in all its glory. It looks a little worse for wear since the last time I was here, but that isn't surprising since Michael isn't here to look after it anymore. If we make it to the other side of this. I'd love to do it up and bring Cassie here. She'd love it.

Just thinking my daughter's name causes a sharp stabbing pain in my heart. I press my hand firmly against my chest, like I could ease the pain, but it's impossible. I can't stop thinking about her, worrying about what they might be doing to her. Elliot and Greg have no fucking morals or sense of good, but I pray even they aren't twisted enough to hurt a child that young. She is the only thing that is keeping me going, her and the promise of the euphoric feeling I know I'll get when I gut them.

I push my bag fully onto my shoulders, grip the ladder at the base of the tree and begin the climb I have done hundreds of times. The steps creak more than I remember, but I suppose I'm bigger than the last time I was here. I push the door with only a little resistance and it slams open against the wooden flooring.

I push myself up into it and then close the door after me. It's pitch black and if I didn't have this place memorized, I would probably trip up. But stepping up here is like stepping into my childhood. It reminds me of my other life, my life before, when everything was simple and the only problem I had was waiting for my best friend to kiss me again.

I find the old lantern we used to use for our late nights here and I'm pleasantly surprised to find it still works. It lights up a thousand memories that this place still holds. I feel the cracked pieces of my heart threatening to slice through my chest and leave me bleeding out, but I fight against it. That is all I can do now. Just fight. Fight and pray that everything I do will be enough.

The treehouse is built out of beautiful recycled oak wood, the only way in is through the trapdoor in the floor, and there is a large window that overlooks the back of the Riviera property. During the day you can make out a river that's flows far deeper in the forest. But the most magical thing about this place is the deck carved on the top. Marcus and I would watch the stars anywhere we could, but this was our favorite place. It was just ours.

I take a seat on the old sofa in the corner and cough slightly when the dust dances up around me. I waft it away and grab the plastic bag from my rucksack that contains now cold Chinese food, a donut, and a large bottle of water. Grabbing this stuff wasn't necessary, but keeping my strength up is. I didn't realize how exhausted and hungry I am until right now.

As I eat, I continue to recite the list of names over and over in my head, never forgetting every little thing they have done and why they deserve to die. Growing up I always thought if someone killed another human that it made them a bad person. It was a very black and white way to think about things, especially when the world we live in is painted in multiple shades of gray. I do still believe that killing someone is bad, but what if the person you kill has hurt so many others? And in taking them out you would save countless other lives? Does that still make you a bad person? I can't help but wonder if in this sick twisted town of corruption and lies, *am I the hero or the villain?*

I don't know what time I fell asleep, but by the time I wake up there is sunlight streaming through the window. I check my watch, it's 6.32am. Usually at this time, I would be waking up in Cassie's bed, or she would be diving onto my head to drag me from sleep. I would give anything to have another day like that. I will give everything to make sure that happens again.

Standing up, I stretch out my stiff limbs and force myself into a few yoga poses to loosen myself up. I need to remain as limber as possible, it will be one of my advantages. In the daylight, the cabin brings back even more memories. I smile when I see a few polaroid's stuck on the wall from a few summers ago. There is one of Marcus and I on the top of a Ferris wheel from a carnival we went to on vacation. We look happy and carefree, which I guess we were. I think we are about thirteen in it and you can see by my face just how much I already loved him, even back then.

There's another of a younger Taylor and me, she hasn't changed much, just has shorter hair and bigger boobs. We are posing by Hallows Waterfall with our arms around each other and tongues out. The falls are so close to where I was taken from and I can't help but wonder how many other girls faced the same fate.

Then there is a third one of me, Marcus, and Ash from the last summer we all spent together. Marcus is sitting on the huge log we had in my backyard, I'm in his lap and Ash is by our feet. Marcus has his arms fully around my waist and all three of us are pulling a goofy face. We look like we are having the best day ever. Just kids enjoying their childhood. I still had my innocence; Marcus still had his dad and Asher still had his pure heart. Looking at this picture, you could have never predicted the nightmare we were all about to endure.

The photos show all the people who made my life so perfect back then. All they do now is remind me of how many more people I have in my life that need me. That I care about. If anything happened to any of them because of me, I wouldn't be able to forgive myself.

I cast my gaze further round the cabin and see a few textbooks in the corner that we were using to get us ready for Hallows Prep. There are some drawings on the wall, some board games on the shelf and even one of Marcus' hoodies folded over the beanbag in the other corner. It's like a time machine back to that summer, back to when we clearly thought we would come back again. I wonder if Marcus ever came back here after I left.

Thinking of Marcus being here reminds me of the secret spot we used to share. No one else ever came into the treehouse without us here and even then, Asher and Taylor only ever came up here a handful of times. Still, Marcus thought we should have a hiding place that no one else knew about.

I smile as I find the loose board and think about the amount of times Marcus and I hid stuff in here. I can't even remember when it started, but I do remember how often I would find things in here from him. From notes to chocolate and candy and even flowers he stole from the bushes at the side of the pool. We never spoke about what we left here or thanked each other. It was just one of those things we did, a thing I didn't realize how much I appreciated, missed even, until right in this moment.

I finally manage to pull the board back and my heart catches in my throat when I see a note wedged in there. It's covered in dust and a little mold. Fuck, how long ago did he put this here? I take a deep breath in as I reach in and pull it out, blowing the dust off so I can see it clearer. I unfold it and expect to find a dirty drawing or a silly poem like he used to leave for me. But that isn't what I find at all....

Find Beth. She has the answers you need.

This isn't Marcus's handwriting. In fact, it looks like Michael's, but I can't be sure. Did Michael leave this here before he was killed? Who did he want to find it? And more importantly, who the hell is Beth?

Chapter 13

MARCUS

It's been a week. A fucking week since we lost Cassie, and Elle went rogue. Every day without them is like a fucking knife, right to my gut and I know everyone feels the same. We all wonder if Cassie is being kept safe and if Elle is ever going to come back to us. I've officially lost count of how many of Elliot's lackeys keep mysteriously disappearing before showing up dead. I know the blowback from Joseph Kavanagh's murder means Elle has set her sight on lower targets for now, but that won't last long. There are too many key players that she blames for everything that happened.

We have her list of targets and some of Max's guys are tracking them. They are looking out for any unusual activity, but mostly just waiting for Elle to turn up and kill them. I can see Max regretting his choice to let Elle go every day. I know he was just doing what she wanted, what he was asked and paid to do, but deep down he cares about her as more than just a client. She is family to all of us and without her we are all a little lost.

I haven't slept more than a handful of hours here and there and I've barely eaten. Every second I spend not doing everything I can to find them makes me feel like a failure, and I'm not the only one. Asher is so far gone he has no human emotion left in him, he barely had it before, but this is different. His whole persona is just void of anything. His self-control is shattered beyond repair and I fear for anyone who gets in the path of his destruction. It's weird, because as far gone as he is, I have never felt closer to him. Like he was always meant to be here, part of us. Elle knew it from the moment she met him and now I am finally catching up.

Jace is barely sober, he has slipped back into his old ways very quickly. The first couple of days they were gone he was here, present. But every hour that ticked by without them coming home was another bit of control he lost. He's the same Jace as the one I first met, lost, detached, and completely struggling with his emotions. I knew how to help him back then, but how can I help him now when I feel exactly the same? I could spiral just as easily as he has, but I have to keep my faith. Faith that we will find them and faith that Elle knows what she is doing.

Lincoln is more frustrated than I have ever seen him. I can see the guilt eating away at him, at what he thinks he should have prevented. He blames himself for not knowing the Donovan's plans before they were executed and is punishing himself daily. He hasn't taken more than a thirty-minute break all week. He hasn't slept and only steps away from the laptop to shower, change and inhale a few protein bars before continuing whatever the fuck he's doing on there. Lincoln has always been the most closed off of my brothers and I, but now it's like I can see him bleeding from the inside out. He is my brother in every sense of the word and we are sharing this pain like we are connected as one.

Logan's still here too, he refuses to leave, and I can't say I blame him. Between Cassie being taken, Elle gone and Zack in a coma, how he is still coping is beyond me. Helen and Lily went to a safe house located near the medical facility that they are keeping Zack in, and along with Arthur, they move back and forth between the two every day. All of them are scared, on edge and desperate for Elle and Cassie to come home.

Max and his team are quiet, but they haven't stopped either. From stakeouts to recon to even fucking flying drones over the Donovan mansion. Anything they can think of to try to get more information on how to get in and out without Cassie getting hurt. We still haven't been able to come up with a solid plan, but if that doesn't happen soon, I'll fucking snap. Walk right in the front gates and blow the head off anyone who gets in my way. I need my girls back, for all our sakes.

We have all exhausted every little thing we can think of, and aside from doing what I wanna do and going straight in the front door, we haven't really got anything. I can't stand this feeling of fucking defeat. It's the same feeling I had the night my father was killed. I knew something was off, it had been for weeks since Elle left town. Obviously, now I know why, but back then I was just a punk who thought I knew best. My dad was gone all hours of the night, and days at a time, never telling me where he went or when he was coming back. The night I walked into my home and it was dark, it wasn't really

126

anything new. I had become accustomed to finding the house empty, save for a few staff, what I didn't anticipate was stumbling along his body and that of our old housekeeper, Margaret. Both of them bloodied and cold.

It's a sight that will haunt me forever.

I did what any normal person would do, I called the police. It wasn't long before the house was swarming with cops and paramedics, until eventually a coroner came. I was questioned a little, until Captain Baizen showed up and everyone started to filter out. He was the one who told me to pack up so I could go to emergency care. I didn't think anything was weird about it at first. I mean of course, my dad was dead, I had no other family. My mom died giving birth to me and we had no extended family, so it was always just me and my dad. It wasn't until I was sitting on the steps of my childhood home that Elliot Donovan pulled up. I'd never liked him; he was just a grown-up version of Asher to me. Quiet, weird and had the members of the King family under some kind of spell.

Every other person that night looked at me with pity in their eyes, but not him, the only thing lighting up his eyes was glee. I was too fucking out of it with grief to collect my thoughts, but I will never forget what he said to me.

"You can thank Elle King for the death of your father. She's the reason I put a bullet in his skull."

I was too stunned to even respond. Everyone I had ever loved, gone and everything I had ever known, shattered. My hatred for Elle had already begun to burn at that point. A small flame flickering inside of me, but with Donovan's words it turned into an uncontrollable inferno that didn't burn out until I realized the truth. Now all of that hatred exists for Elliot and his fucking vermin son. Ironically, not the Donovan son I hated as a kid. Now Asher is my biggest ally. I know my brothers would do anything I asked of them, same as my crew, but I know Asher won't let anything stop him from saving them both.

Thinking about them causes a tightness in my chest. I miss my dad every day. Thought I knew what living without someone was like. But every day without Elle by my side and Cassie in the hands of the Devil, is another day where I realize I won't survive if we don't get them back. Whenever you go to the doctors in pain, they ask you to rate your pain out of ten. I always thought seeing my dad's body was a ten, but it wasn't. My ten would be seeing Elle's and I can't let that happen. No one will make it out of that wreckage.

I am still lost in my thoughts when Asher finds me. He looks rugged and run down, far from the Asher I knew and hated. I wouldn't say we have magically become friends, but we have reached some sort of alliance in working together to get our girls back. I think of all the times I was ever jealous of him, even as kids. Every time he had Elle's attention, I would be sick with envy, thinking he wanted her the same way I do. Now I know him, know the true face of his family, I understand their relationship much more. Even before that night, he just wanted some light in his life, and that light was Elle. I am glad he is still there for her and Cassie. We are all just one big fucked up, barely functioning family, but that's what makes us work well together.

"Hey man," I tip my head at him in greeting.

"Hey." He pats my shoulder as he sits down next to me with a sigh.

I'm sitting on the back porch staring at the tree Elle and I had sex under a couple of weeks ago. The night she told me she was scared; it turns out she had every right to be. I imagined multiple ways the party could go wrong, but Cassie being taken wasn't one of them. Or at least wasn't one I was willing to admit.

"I miss Cassie," I admit freely. Missing Elle is obvious. She was a constant part of my life for so long, even when she was gone. But Cass was something unexpected and she's easily slipped into my heart.

Asher's hands grip his knees tightly. "I miss her so much it physically hurts," he confesses. His honesty is brutal.

"Do you think she's okay?" It's a question I have been scared to ask for so many reasons. The answer might just kill what bit of hope I have left.

He doesn't answer for a while and I almost think he isn't going to. "My father has a sickness that turns my stomach," he starts slowly. "But he has always cared about Greg. Loved him." I'm not really sure where he is going with this, but I remain quiet. "Elle is different for them, for him." He doesn't have to say which him; he means. "I saw his eyes that night, the obsession in them, he wanted her, but it was more than that. Possession, ownership, craving." He huffs a long breath before

129

adding, "Cassie will be an extension of that for him. They won't risk hurting her."

I'm not sure if his answer relieves me or makes things worse. I just reach out and grip his shoulder, giving it a light squeeze. Letting him know I am here for him, whether he needs me to be or not. I think about how many times I worried about Asher being in my way when it came to Elle. Not once did I ever think I was looking at the wrong Donovan. Now he is going to be the one to help save them with me.

"What are you doing out here anyway?" He changes the subject.

"I was just thinking about how much I hated you when we were kids." I don't know why I tell him that, but it's that or we sit in the deathly silence of our failures.

He huffs a laugh slightly. "Just as kids?" he asks with a small smirk.

"Yeah, now I know that you don't want my girl, you're slightly more likable." I grin as I shove his shoulder with mine.

He rolls his eyes as he leans back against the sofa, we're on. "I never wanted her, at least not the way you always did."

"Yeah, yeah. I know that now, you prick," I lean back next to him, "but what was I supposed to think about another teenage boy hanging around her."

"I wasn't just hanging around her, you were there too." His words give me slight pause, I never thought about him trying to be my friend too.

"Oh, come on, you were barely my friend," I scoff.

130

"Yeah, that's because of your dumb ass, not mine. Me and Elle always made the effort to include you." He rolls his eyes again and I kind of want to punch him a little for being insufferable.

I sit up to take a sip of my drink. "Yeah, until you both used to hide from me, and I'd spend half the day looking for you both before giving up and going home." I smile a little at the memory, "Where the fuck did you always go anyway?" I ask, turning to look at him. He's sitting up straight with a stern look on his face.

"The tunnels," he whispers, "the fucking tunnels. I can't believe I forgot." He stands abruptly and starts to walk inside before turning to look at me, "Come on we need to find Max, now!"

What the fuck are the tunnels?

Chapter 14

ELLE

Rigging the last wire makes me miss Jace, his pyromaniac ways made for the perfect accomplice on things like this. But I can't make myself wish he were here. This is one of my riskier plans and I don't want to put him in danger. Whatever it takes, really means whatever it takes. Once I attach the last wire, hoping it looks good enough, I cover it with a bit of tarp and then sit and wait.

The clubhouse is quiet, not what I expected when I decided to come here, but a pleasant surprise. It isn't long before I hear the familiar rumble of motorbikes and immediately think of Marcus. He hasn't been on a bike since he lost his when Elliot burned the loft down, I make a mental note to get him another one when I get back to him. *If I get back to him.*

I hear the click of the lock before the door bangs open and the sound of shuffling feet and cocky voices fills the air. I take a deep breath and pray I haven't just walked into a fucking den of lions, and when I look up, I meet the surprised eyes of the President of the Hallowed Crows MC and three of his men.

The one to his left, who I notice is wearing the VP patch, immediately draws his gun when his dark eyes meet mine. "Who the fuck are you?"

I hear the click of the safety get flicked off, and I smile chaotically as I pull the tarp off the small bomb I rigged up before they got here. "I'd put that safety back on if I were you."

All of their eye's flick to the device at my feet and the receiver in my hand. Crazy idea? Definitely. Necessary? Absolutely. We aren't playing the small game anymore, it's all or fucking nothing.

Another one of them huffs a smile, "You set that thing off and you die too."

I flick my eyes to his, returning his smile, "I'm not afraid to die, Ezra." The use of his name startles him, but he barely lets it show. I know all of their names and I'm sure they know mine. You can't go to war without knowing everything about your opponents' armies.

President Connor O'Sullivan finally speaks, his Irish accent curling around his words. "What are you afraid of Miss King?"

I smile big, but roll my eyes at the same time, "Ah, my reputation precedes me." I can only imagine the bullshit that gets spread around about me.

His face sets into a firm grimace, like he is trying to act unaffected, "I take note of all the girls Elliot Donovan has his eye on."

"Yeah, I'll bet. Just not enough to protect them though, huh?" I shake my head in disgust. How can this many men be this fucking corrupt.

"Don't presume to know anything about me." He snaps his words at me, losing that cool edge he was going for, and I see the anger lining his features.

"No? Connor O'Sullivan, born in Belfast in October of 1973. Moved to the States as a teen after a stint in juvie. Your parents wanted a better life for you, so they sent you to live with a family friend. Except he was President of the Hallowed Crows to which you became a prospect for, almost immediately. You worked your way up until the day he was shot and killed by an enemy club and it was at that time you were voted in as Prez yourself. Now you've got Aiden here," I nod to his VP, "and then my man Ezra, and let's not forget about the infamous Killian," I add gesturing to the final man of the group. "Wanna talk about reputations? Because damn, his is impressive."

All of them look furious and unimpressed with the information I have on them, and I can feel the tension rolling off all of them. "Very skillful I see," O'Sullivan replies dryly.

I sit forward until my elbows lean against my knees and spin the knife I had hidden, round the tip of my finger. "No, skillful is how I could take out all four of you without breaking a sweat. It's high past payment for your sins, don't you agree?"

"And what sins would we be paying for exactly?" Killian asks in a deadly tone that makes me want to shudder. He is the kind of guy only spoken about in dark alleys with no one around. The stuff he's said to have done is enough to fill anyone's nightmares.

I push my fear aside and remember why I'm here, "Every single one you have committed while being in bed with the Donovan's."

Aiden snaps first, "We are not in bed with that piece of shit!"

"No?" I fake disbelief and intrigue, "Then why are you still running his guns and drugs every month?"

"Those shipments are ours; he just takes them for himself," Ezra barks in disgust, and I can tell I have hit a nerve with him.

"What, and the big bad Crows can't stop him?" I'm being sarcastic as fuck, but I'm beyond caring. Their alliance with the Donovan's is one of the only things I have never been able to work out. Why do they yield to him constantly and do all his dirty dealings, allowing him to keep his hands squeaky clean?

They all remain silent until Connor blows out a deep breath, "We have no choice."

That pisses me off. "There's always a choice," I spit back. "You're just making the wrong one. Just like him. And like him, you will pay."

I stand up and flick open the device in a last attempt to get some truth. Aiden, Killian, and Ezra all raise their guns at me as I go to press the button.

Connor shouts, "He has my daughter."
I immediately pause, "What do you mean, he has her?"

He looks at me with a grimace as he responds, "You know better than anyone, exactly what I mean."

Fuck.

I drop my arm and they all visibly relax. How did I miss this? I dug up every part of his life and nowhere did I come across him having a daughter. He must see the thoughts on my face because he answers them without me voicing them.

"I kept her well-hidden, her Ma was some club whore I had a one-night stand with many moons ago. She turned up here when Bex was still a toddler. Had a meth problem and wanted money in exchange for my daughter. I paid what she wanted and then some, ensuring she would fuck off for good. Then I moved her to the other side of town with a trusted friend, where she grew up untainted and safe. But it seems you can't control teenagers as well as kids, when she got older, she came sniffing around here." He glances to the guys next to him, but none of them so much as flinch as they take in his words. *Interesting.*

"It wasn't long before she was seen here, and someone started asking questions, and as they say, loose lips sink ships." He looks in physical pain as he speaks about her and I can only imagine what he is going through. My daughter has only been gone a week and I'm losing my mind.

"How long?" My voice is struggling to remain unaffected.

"I haven't seen her in two years." His words are barely loud enough to penetrate the empty room the five of us stand in, yet somehow they pierce the air with their impact.

Fuck. Two years. Two fucking years. I can only imagine what she has endured during that time.

"Do you know where Elliot is keeping her?" I don't know why I ask, I shouldn't, I definitely don't have time for anything other than getting my own daughter back. But two years is a long fucking time.

He snorts in disgust, "Oh yeah, I know exactly where she is, she's the guest at the residence of Carter Fitzgerald, more security than the fucking Pope."

Fuck. His daughter is with the Mayor of fucking Black Hallows. The most powerful name on my list and in the eyes of the law. He just became a bigger fucking priority.

"What if I get your daughter back for you?" I ask boldly, even though I haven't got a fucking clue how I am going to get to Fitzgerald yet.

Killian scoffs at the very idea, "Yeah you and whose army princess?"

I smile at the underestimation of my skills. "I don't know. I didn't have an army when I took down Captain Baizen and Joseph Kavanagh, maybe I'll just improvise." I shrug my shoulders casually and see all of their surprised faces at my admission.

Connor is the first one to step closer to me, "You bring home my Rebecca and you will have the full charter of Crows behind you. No questions asked." Every word is delivered with force and determination, like he is really ready to join the war against Donovan, it makes me giddy.

Standing, I pick up the bomb, smiling as I see each one of them tense up, "Chill out, it's fake," I say like it's no big deal, when really it was the craziest idea I've probably ever had.

"You just walked in here with a fake bomb and nothing else?" Aiden asks, looking slightly impressed,

137

even though I know he would never admit it, and I shrug again.

"I didn't need anything else." I move to walk past them but pause as I stand in front of O'Sullivan. I offer him my sweetest smile and then launch the knife in my hand across the room to the dartboard hanging there. I don't have to look to know it hit the center. "Bullseye." I smirk. "I'll see you soon Mr. President." I toss him a wink, and then walk out leaving their shocked faces behind.

Chapter 15

JACE

The pain is paralyzing. I'm not bleeding, at least not on the outside. No, my affliction is purely psychological. Grief, it's a fickle fucking emotion, can creep up on you at any time and take over your fucking life. I was getting better, or better at handling it, hiding it. Yet now, I am drowning again with no air in sight.

The day I met Marcus everything changed for me. I had forgotten the feeling of friendship, trust, family. Rachel left a hole in my heart so fucking deep that I thought nothing would ever matter again. I tried to fill it will alcohol, weed, fucking coke, but all that did was numb it for a while. Until numb was all I was. Marcus rescued me from a deathly fate that we don't admit to. Not out loud anyway.

Now, that feeling of pure helplessness is back. I feel lost, weak, completely fucking useless. The fact that I can still feel anything at all is the worst bit. I don't want to, would give anything not to. I just want to turn off every fucking emotion in my body and exist as nothing.

I think about the weeks running up to Rachel's death. She was different, running with an older crowd of girls, out of the trailer a lot, acting strange. Nothing like the big sister I had grown up with. I remember one night in particular, a couple of days before her body was found. She came back to the trailer crying, mascara running down her cheeks and her hair and clothes disheveled. Our asshole parents weren't home, they never fucking were, so the only person to comfort her was me. She hugged me so tight that night, told me that Black Hallows was an extremely dangerous place and that one day she would get us out of here. Three days later, she was dead.

The day I was pulled out of school by the principal and told there had been an accident, was the worst day of my life. An accident, a fucking accident. That was a funny way to describe a murder. Rachel's body was found out in the woods by a pair of hikers. She was naked, beaten, and bloodied. I barely had time to register what happened to her before I was being hauled off into the foster system.

My parents didn't even give a fuck about Rachel's death, so they didn't care about me leaving. One day, I was barely surviving them with Rachel by my side, and the next, I was in a home full of strangers with a box of stuff. Some of it Rachel's. I only had a notebook, a blanket she stole for us and a strip of pictures from a photobooth. Inside the notebook were words I will never forget.

Jace,

If you are reading this then I'm sorry I didn't protect us better. I tried. I really did but I didn't stand a chance against them. This town is a dark place and I hope you escape it. Go live your dreams somewhere else.

I love you always bud,

Rachel xoxo

P.S. Don't trust the Donovan's.

I didn't know much about the Donovan's, at that point. I was just a poor kid from a trailer park. I didn't think anything of them until Marcus moved into the home, I was in. He was very vocal about his vendetta against them and hearing their name brought back the memories of the note. I listened to what he had to say, learnt what I could, and then we started making money together. A couple of well-timed stake outs and a few bribes allowed me to piece together what happened to my sister. The day I met Elle; I saw the same look in her eyes that I had seen in Rachel's. Cold, distant, determined. It was like I was drawn to her, like I knew her from another life. We bonded immediately and that only grew the more I learned about her.

It's how I know she won't come back to us, not without her daughter. Maybe not at all. Maybe I will lose them both like I lost Rachel, and that pain will be unbearable.

I snort another line at the thought. I don't even know where I am or how long I have been here. I'm outside, I know that at least, except the world looks weird, on its side. Nothing where it should be. I wish I could just end this feeling. Maybe coke isn't the vice I need. Maybe I should pump some heroin, that always seemed to do the trick for my parents.

I try to focus on something, anything that isn't this awful feeling inside. My vision is blurry as a dark angel wanders towards me. Maybe death has finally come to put me out of my misery.

Jace.

The black-haired siren calls out to me. It's angelic and laced with the offer of peace, but they aren't within reach. Not to someone like me. I am not worthy of such gifts.

Jace.

I smile as the voice pierces my bones offering me slight comfort. Maybe death is the right choice, maybe I have nothing left to offer this life anymore. I am nothing but a reckless and damaged playboy with too many vices. I couldn't protect my sister; couldn't protect my best friend's girl and I couldn't protect Cassie.

Jace.

This time, it isn't just the angel's voice that touches me. This time, I feel their grip on my shoulder, it's so life-like. I reach my hand out to clasp theirs and smile at the silkiness of it. The afterlife is going to be good for me. The slap comes out of nowhere.

I groan drunkenly, "I didn't think angels would hit so hard."

"Jesus' effing Christ. Conrad, you're a mess." An annoyed, tired tone hits my ear.

"Does that mean I won't be accepted into heaven?" I wonder aloud.

Two small hands grip my face and drag it to theirs, "What the hell are you on?" A fraction of recognition flows through me.

"Taylor?" I grumble in questioning.

"Yeah, it's me. What the hell are you doing out in the park in the middle of the night?" she scolds me in accusation, as she takes in the empty bottle of whiskey on the floor beside me, the stubbed-out joints and the discarded bag of coke. *Empty bag.*

I try and fail to stand as I slur back, "Fucking dancing how about you?"

"I was running," she replies simply.

"From who?" I slick my gaze around, determined to find her tormentor.

"No one," she frowns. "I run recreationally, like when I'm stressed and shit." She shrugs like that is a totally normal explanation for why she is out. Who the fuck runs for fun?

I snort, "Sounds terrible."

"It's about as bad as getting high in the park alone." Her scold is slightly playful, and it warms me on the inside. It's a feeling I want to grab onto and never let go.

143

"Touché," I say with a smile, lighting up another joint.

"Is everything okay?" She gives the mean eyes to the joint in my hand as she talks to me.

"Fucking peachy!" I snap.

"Why aren't you answering your phone?" She points to it, and when I look down, sure enough, I watch a call that I didn't hear go off, and then the phone lights up with twenty missed calls and eleven text messages. My keepers no doubt trying to bribe me into another waste of time bullshit mission. I ditched my tracker and turned the location app on my phone off, before I started my little pity party.

She huffs at my response and when the phone starts ringing again, I actually hear it this time, she snatches it off the ground before I can protest.

"Hello," she snaps in irritation, "Marcus?" She listens for a second and then adds, "It's Taylor, yeah he's here." She looks around and then back at me, "we are in Riverside park, yeah by the bike course." She continues to listen to whatever the fuck he is saying before she finally replies, "Yeah sure, see you soon."

"They're coming to get you," she says matter of factly.

"Great," I drag out sarcastically. I can't wait for whatever fucking lecture I am going to get.

I finish the joint before snorting the final line of coke I had lined up. Even a hot girl in yoga pants won't change how I fucking feel right now. God, I bet Donovan would fucking love her, tear her apart until she was begging and bleeding. The thought turns my stomach. I jump up and grip her wrist tightly.

"Ow," she cries out at my tight grip, but I don't relent, I can't. She has to know exactly what kind of fucking town we live in.

"Promise me you will be safe, that you won't let them take you!" I plead with her, trying to use every ounce of convincing I possess.

"Let *who* take me?" She tries to pull her arm back, but I don't let up.

"The Devil and his disciples, you're just their type." I release her wrist and she pulls it back, rubbing it with her other arm, as I start to pace.

"It just got all fucked up. I finally found a family, a place where I felt loved and at home and now it's been taken from me again." I stop in front of her and her eyes lock with mine, "I just want it back Taylor. Why does everyone always leave me?" Her eyes soften at my words.

She reaches out and palms my cheek and I close my eyes at her soft touch, "No one is leaving you, Jace. You have amazing friends and even me, I'm your friend too."

I drop my head and pull her into my arms, just needing to be close to someone. Just to feel a little less alone in this fucked up world. Her arms come up around my waist, she can barely reach. We stay embraced like that until headlights break the moment.

When I look up, I see Marcus storming towards us, with Linc not far behind him. He doesn't stop until he is right in front of me and grips my jaw in his fist. "Fucking

145

high as a kite," he sneers, but I can still see the relief in his eyes.

"Hello to you too." I toss back.

He is so angry right now, "Hello? Fucking hello? Do you not think we have enough fucking shit going on right now without me having to be out looking for you too!" He yells in my face, and then shakes his head in disappointment.

"What's going on here?" Taylor asks and I can see her trying to work out what the hell is happening.

Marcus ignores her as he sighs and grabs the back of my neck, "Don't fucking do this man, I've lost enough, we've lost enough. We can't lose each other, not now. Not with so much on the fucking line. Lock it down, okay?" His voice is serious, but I can practically feel the pleading in his words, his desperation.

I want to answer him, to tell him I'm sorry and that it won't happen again, but I can't. I am many things, lost, broken, wild, but I'm not a liar. I don't say anything.

I don't need to look at Lincoln to know he is wearing that same impenetrable mask as always. Cold and ruthless through and through. If you didn't know him well, you would think nothing affects him. But you'd be wrong. He looks at me and then to Taylor.

He sighs gesturing to the SUV, "Come on, Taylor. We will drive you home."

I feel her look at me, as Marcus and I continue to burn our stares into one another. I know he's right, but he also knows why I am in such a state. He finally shakes his head one last time and stalks back to the car, getting inside and slamming the door.

Taylor slips her hand in mine and I finally break my gaze and look down at her. "Come on, Conrad. Time to go." She says it casually and with a small smile, but it feels like so much more. It feels like everything I needed to hear at this moment. That's the last thing I remember before I pass out.

Chapter 16

MARCUS

'm fucked. I can't keep doing this. I need Elle, my Ells. I need to see her, hug her, kiss her. Just fucking breathe her in and never let go of her again. Six months ago, she was a ghost of my past that I pretended didn't exist. If someone had told me then that not only would she be back in my life now, but I'd be ready to fucking die for her. I would have laughed in their face. I didn't let her walk back into my life, I fucking dragged her, kicking, and screaming. She wanted nothing to do with me and I pretended the same. God, I was fucking stupid. I wasted so much time. Time I would quite literally kill for.

I'm lying in her bed, it's the only place I feel close to her. This isn't even my home, but with her scent surrounding me I can pretend that everything's okay. Even if only for a few moments. I haven't been to Cassie's room. Here in the house, or even her other one in the guesthouse. I can't bear it. Can't stand to look at her tiny clothes, her toys, her books. All of it just a reminder of how small and innocent she is, and of where she is now. Is she okay? Does she understand? God, I hope not. I hope that her contact with the Donovan's is minimal. I just keep praying for her, to what god I don't fucking know. All I know is I feel helpless.

I think about Elle, what will happen if we don't get Cassie back. She's already lost too much, dealt with too much. Losing Cassie isn't an option, we have to bring her home, no matter what. If we can't, well then, I might as well put a bullet in my own fucking skull, because life without those two girls wouldn't be worth living. And I know I'm not the only one who feels like that.

I have spent more time with Asher in the last nine days than I have since I met him. He's become one of us in every sense of the word and I can't imagine what this would be like if he weren't here. We seek each other out more than either of us would care to admit, both of us spiraling without our center here to keep us grounded. He finds me when I fight back tears in the garden, and I grip his shoulders as he breathes through his panic attacks in the guest bathroom. Neither of us speak a word to each other, just offer that silent hand of friendship and brotherhood to one another.

I know exactly what it's like to lose your family, your status, your wealth. I remember the bitter feelings I had about it when I first moved to the South Side, but I see none of that in Ash. He just wants to burn his whole family, fortune, fucking name, until there isn't a shred of the Donovan legacy left. And I want to be right by his side to help him do it. I want us all to rise from the ashes and become who we were always meant to be, destined to be, a family.

149

As if my mind conjured him up, he appears. "Hey," he says with a deep sigh. He barely enters her room, like he can't bring himself to. He won't even look around it, his sole focus on me alone. I know he's spent many nights in this house, in this room, sharing time and life with my girl. Looking out for her when I didn't. I have always been the jealous type when it comes to Elle, yet seeing the love he has for her, what they all have for her, it brings warmth into my life. Now I am man enough and secure enough to understand the differing levels of love we all have for one girl. I have never appreciated them more.

I sit up and push myself forward until I am sitting on the end of the bed, "Hey man."

Neither of us bother to ask if we are okay, we know we're not. We are just in a constant state of nothingness while we hunt, make plans and then hunt some more. All of it pointless, until now.

"Is it time?" I ask, not missing the pleading tone in my voice.

He smiles for the first time since this all started, and I find myself smiling back. "It's time."

"Are you sure you are okay with this?" I know he isn't because I'm not.

He huffs a little laugh which is completely humorless, "I'm not okay with any of this," he replies solemnly, moving until he stands in front of me, offering me his hand. I take it and he pulls me up until we are face to face. "Whatever it takes."

I offer him another grim smile and nod. "Whatever it takes." I repeat back, before we both turn to leave the room. We won't set foot in this room again until we have Cassie back.

We move in unison through the house until we reach the den. Lincoln and Jace are already here, as is Logan. They all offer us both grim smiles as we enter, and I see Max and his guys going over the map of the Donovan estate for the hundredth time today. We all know it down to every square inch, but it doesn't stop us from going over and over it in case we missed anything.

This is about to be the riskiest thing we have ever done and if we can pull it off without getting caught, then Cassie will be back with us in just a few short hours. I know how desperate we all are for that reality. With Cassie comes Elle. If we can bring home, her daughter then it will help us in getting her back to us too. A lot has happened, more than she knows and as broken as she is going to be with everything, Cassie will keep her intact.

I look at everyone here, at the men who are going to save my girl's life and I hope we all make it back here tonight. For once, we look like we belong together. We are all fitted out in black combat trousers, long black sleeve tees with Kevlar vests. Black combat boots and a weapons belt. Each of us have an array of weapons supplied to us by Max, along with lessons on each in preparation. We have been working on this plan for the last three days.

Max is pissed that Asher came up with it, but none of us care, we just want Cassie home and Elle back. When Asher remembered the abandoned tunnels underneath his house, we wasted no time in looking into them. Lincoln brought up historical blueprints for the mansion, Oliver came up with routes we could take to access them and then Max and Liam spent yesterday checking them all discretely to see if they were still viable. Once we had everything we needed, we had to come up with a plan. Which is pretty simple really, get in, get Cass, and get out.

We have all agreed that this needs to be as quiet and stealthy as possible. No matter how much we want to go in there guns blazing and slaughter every one of them. Our only priority is getting Cassie. That being said, we know we are also working under the shoot first, ask questions later policy. Anyone associated with Donovan can't be trusted to not raise the alarm. Meaning anyone we come across needs to be killed or put to sleep. It doesn't matter. As long as we get to Cassie without anyone alerting others to our presence.

"Okay does everyone remember what they're doing?" Max's voice booms around the den and we all nod our agreement.

"My inside contacts said to be there for 10pm. There is a guard shift change at nine, so it gives them a chance to swap, leave and get settled," Asher replies, and I see the flex of his hand as he forces himself not to fidget. The loss of control for him is something he isn't accustomed to.

"That's good Ash, keep us posted if anything changes," Max responds.

"Lincoln will take a bug to freeze the feeds as they pass them. I'll run interference from the van and keep a look out for anyone on their tale." Liam adds as he taps away on his laptop, and I see Lincoln nodding along as he reads whatever's on there over his shoulder.

"Great. Remember what I said, in and out as quiet as possible and stick to your planned routes. Recon has both Elliot and Greg at the Mayor's house for his annual bullshit Christmas party, which means Cassie should be where Ash's contact said."

I take a deep breath, digesting all the information I've already heard and just pray we have done enough. Nothing can go wrong. It just can't. When we all nod in silent agreement, he continues.

"Okay, well there is only one thing left to do then." He adds solemnly and we all grimace at that. "I am comfortable with doing it, I have known both of them a long time, they are my friends, but I can keep it short and to the point."

"Yeah, I'm sure that will help." Asher snorts in disgust. He thinks this is the worst possible thing to do. Thinks we shouldn't, but we have to.

"We have no choice; we need her to come home." Mason adds quietly.

"This is going to break her." Jace replies bitterly.

"She's already fucking broken." I boom and they all quieten. This is probably the worst thing we are about to do to Elle. We are about to rip her world apart even more than it already is. Max says it's the only way.

Logan breaks the silence, "I'll do it," we all look at him. "I'm their brother, it should be me." His tone is full of despair and I know how much pain he is in. How much pain I am in and how much pain Elle is about to be in.

153

Max nods, pulls the burner phone from his pocket, and walks across the room to meet Logan, "Make the call."

Whatever it takes.

Chapter 17

ELLE

I am covered in sweat and blood. The guy in front of me is someone I have wanted to kill for an exceedingly long time. Brett Buckley. He is one of three men who held me down while Greg ruined me. I have never forgotten his face, his laugh or the feel of his fucking fingers digging into my skin. None of it. From the potent smell of cigars to the stench of his sweat. All of it has been engraved into my mind since that night. Greg might have been the only one to rape me, but that doesn't mean the others aren't just as guilty. They all deserve to bathe in the Devil's flames for what they force girls to endure. I aim to cause them just as much pain in return.

I relish in the sound of my knuckle duster smashing into his cheek as he screams out in pain. The more time that slips by without Cassie, the more I am losing control. I could have just put a bullet in his head and moved on, but he needs more than that. I need more. That's how we ended up here. In my torture cabin in the middle of butt fuck nowhere as I beat him bloody. I picked him up at his house, drugged him, threw him in the trunk and then dragged him in here.

For the last hour. I have taken my time in learning all about what makes him scream. Most guys would love the thought of me getting to know their bodies intimately, certainly sounds appealing. But not how I do it. First, I shattered his kneecap with a hammer, then I cut off all of his toes. When his cries got louder, I sliced open his forearms. There is blood everywhere. It's fucking beautiful.

I punch him again and the burn of the exertion makes me feel fucking alive, reminds me why I'm here and what I'm fighting for.

"What's the matter Buckley, not a fan of the screams when they're your own?" I taunt as I drag the blade in my other hand down his cheek. He cries out again. His face is a mixture of tears, sweat and blood. Something I know he has seen on countless victims, but he still thinks he can defend himself.

"I didn't even touch you. Greg wouldn't let us; you were too important to him." Does he think that makes it better? Like, is he that fucked up, he thinks I would accept that as his defense?

His answer pisses me the fuck off and I stab my knife right into his hand. "So, whose fingerprints bruised my legs as they held me down, whose laughs haunted my nights? Did I just make all that up?" I scream at him as I fight back my own tears. I won't allow him to bring out that weakness in me again.

"You're scum. You think just because you didn't penetrate me with your disgusting dick that it's okay?

How many times did you watch Greg take someone against their will? How many girls were given to you to keep you quiet and compliant." I laugh in disbelief at his audacity. "There's a special place in hell for men like you and it's time you went there."

My ringtone blares from my bag and I frown at being interrupted, but Max said he would only call me if it was an emergency. I've heard from him a few times by text. He's sent me information, warnings, bullshit. This is the first time he is calling. I huff, but move to the table, drop my knife, wipe my hands on my pants and then pick up the phone.

"Yes." I answer in a no-nonsense tone. This might be an emergency but I'm kind of fucking busy right now and in case he hasn't noticed, I sort of have my own def con one kind of shit going on.

"Elle?" My name is barely a whisper, "it's me." Logan's guarded voice filters down the line and it pulls me from the murderous edge I have been on for the last week. It's so familiar and safe that I feel like it can't be real. It feels as if I haven't heard his voice in months.

I pull the phone from my ear and check the screen, I see Max's number lit up and pull the phone back, "Logan?" I ask even though I know it's him, "everything okay?"

He takes a deep breath, going silent. After a couple of seconds, I hear Marcus murmur next to him, "This is bullshit. Give me the phone." Just a few words and they crack my already shattered heart. I miss him so much. I miss them all. Regret so many things between us, but I know he understands. I can tell from the stern tone he just used on Logan. He isn't falling apart without me; he's fighting for me.

Just like I knew he would. Just like I needed him too.

"Logan?" I push again as panic starts to creep through me, and he sighs again.

"It's Zack..." He pauses like he is trying to think what to say before he adds, "he's gone Elle, we lost him. You need to come home."

I barely breathe, I grip the phone so tight it burns my fingers. Zack is dead. The words blow my already broken world apart. I'm too late. He didn't make it. My brother is dead.

"Elle, we need you to come home." It's Max's voice I hear this time, his serious and bossy tone gutting me further. I lost my brother; he lost a friend. We fucking lost.

I can't do this, not anymore, not without him. He saved me and I failed him, he saved me, and I lost him, he saved me, and he fucking died. He's dead. I feel my heart beating out of my chest, the only reminder that I am still alive. Alive, while my brother is dead. Alive thanks to him. How do I ever repay him when he is no longer here? How do I survive when I no longer have my hero here to guide me? I collapse into the chair by the table as tears start to coat my face. How can I ever go home? That wasn't my home, it was our home, mine, and Zack's and now he's gone.

"Home, home to what?" I bite back and the echo tells me I'm on speaker phone. No doubt all of them are listening in. "My brother is dead, and my daughter might be too, for all I know. Fuck coming home. There is only one place I need to go now."

The tears spilling down my face aren't going to do anything for me. I let them fall but I won't let them control me. The empty crater in my chest has burst wider than ever before. There is no going back now. I pick up my Glock and stalk back towards Brett with the phone in my other hand.

Even though I know they can all hear me I don't speak directly to them. I can't, "tell Marcus that I love him and Ash and the guys that I'm sorry."

"No, Elle, stop." Max starts but I cut him off.

"Thank you for everything Max. I wouldn't be who I am today without you, without Zack." My voice catches as I say his name and I can barely hold back my sob. "Truly, thank you. Goodbye."

"Elle wait!" Marcus roars.

"Where are you?" Max shouts.

"Hells Bells!" Asher screams.

Everything has fallen apart around me. I have lost too much, and this has gone on for too long. I got to as many of them as I could, but time has run out. Now I have to take the next step, take out Elliot and Greg. Getting to them won't be easy, but I will. Even if I have to become Elle fucking Donovan to do it.

The bang of my gun is the last thing they hear before my phone goes dead.

I shoot Brett three times. One in the head and two in the chest. One for me, one for Cassie and one for Zack. The brother I am never going to see again. I won't ever see his smile or hear him call me sweetheart. We won't shoot guns at the range or take that trip to Vegas that he promised me for my 21st birthday. He won't get to walk me down the aisle, won't get to find the love of his life, have kids of his own. Everything we talked about, everything he deserved, gone and all because he was my brother. A blessing and a curse. We already lost so much time together and now we can't make it back. The bullet that took him from me is never going to stop impacting my life.

I breathe in through my nose and out through my mouth. Over and over again, just trying to calm myself and push through the pain. I have come too far to stop now. I owe it to Zack, and I owe it to myself. I meant what I said to Max, there is only one place I need to go now.

I stalk through the cabin grabbing my stuff as I go, I will send word to Oliver for clean up, but to be honest, I am beyond caring. Let someone find his body, let anyone find it. Because there isn't going to be any hiding the fall out of my brother being murdered. They are going to need to a build a new fucking graveyard for all the bodies I plan on slaying.

Once in the car, I push down the accelerator until it hits the floor. Nothing is going to get in the way of what I need to do next. I don't know exactly how I am going to play things when I get to the Donovan estate, but I do know one thing. They want me alive and that is the only ace I have to play. I could try to take out some of their men when I get there, but they would just be replaced with others.

Lord knows what they will do to me once they have me, but I can't think about that now, the only thing I can think about is seeing my daughter again, protecting her and avenging my brother. Greg wants a compliant wife, but he's getting an avenging queen. I won't be silenced again.

I drive so fast that it isn't long before I approach the estate from the back. I dump my car there and waste no time grabbing my bag of weapons and moving towards the direction of the gates. I stop every few meters and stash weapons anywhere I can. Memorizing each stop for future reference, only keeping my Glock at my waistband and my knife at my thigh.

My thoughts are chaotic, and I struggle to stay in control, but I need to lock it down. My mind is the only weapon I will have once I enter their pits of hell. They will strip me of my weapons, my family, and my freedom, but that won't stop me. Nothing will. The sight of Zack bleeding out in our home is the only thing in my mind. They did that to him, they murdered him in cold blood just to get to me. I can't see the times he taught me to drive or the first time he took me to the gun range. I can't see every time he made me breakfast, or all the times he sat through Disney marathons with me and Cassie.

No, all I can see is his blood, his panicked and desperate eyes as they locked with mine. I didn't know then that it would be the last time I would ever see them, I didn't let myself face that reality, I couldn't. But now, as I make my way to the gates of hell, it's all I see. That look I last saw on his face will haunt me forever, and that's just one more thing the Donovan's will pay for.

Once I clear the tree line it's a short walk to the gravel path that leads towards the gates. As soon as I hit it, they will know I'm here and everything will change. I ignore every branch snapping beneath my feet and every rustle of leaves by my side. The cold December air bites into my skin and the hard thumping of my heart continues to beat against my rib cage. All I do is breathe and walk. Just in through the nose and out through the mouth. It's time.

I step forward and aim my gun at the first guard before he even spots me. Yet before I can take the shot, I sense the presence behind me. The gun is knocked from my hand before I can even turn around and a gloved palm covers my mouth. I fight with everything I have got, but then another person joins the fray and when I feel the prick of a needle pierce into my neck, I know I'm done for. I continue to fight but my limbs become heavy and slow. I see a blur of movement surround me as I'm thrown around and carried away. The gates of the Donovan estate are the last thing I see opening before darkness claims me.

Chapter 18

MARCUS

The adrenaline is pulsing through me like a drug. My breaths are coming in quick but steady pants as we move quickly through the tunnels underneath the Donovan estate. It's dark down here and extremely dusty, but that isn't what's causing my short breaths. No, that's the anxiety flooding through my veins. I'm filled with apprehension about what we are about to do. Over how we might get caught, how many people might get in our way, and what state we might find Cassie in. All of it causes the blood in my body to feel as cold as ice as it pumps through my body at a rapid pace.

We've split into two small teams of four, but also picked a partner to stay with and cover. Jace is with Max, Logan is with Elijah and Mason is with Oliver. Liam is back in the van running the tech alongside Ash who is at a safe house doing the same. He wasn't happy about being left behind, but the last thing we need is any of his father's men catching sight of him.

I'm with Lincoln, and we are tasked with going straight to where we believe Cass to be, while the rest of the guys keep our route clear. I'm scared, I think we all are, but I'm not afraid to die. No, I'm scared of what we might find when we get to Cassie. I know exactly what Elliot Donovan and his sick twisted son are capable of, and I just hope that sickness doesn't extend to hurting their own flesh and blood. It's the main reason I didn't want Asher here with us, he would have been an asset for sure, but he also would have been a liability. I dread to think what his father or brother would do to him for betraying the family legacy. He didn't give a fuck about that of course, but he knew deep down he was needed more on the outside of this.

It's just me, Linc, Max and Jace in this tunnel, Logan, Elijah, Mason, and Oliver are entering through one further round the side of the estate. We want to cover as much ground as possible and as quickly as possible. Ash's contact, one of the maids who has worked for them since he moved here, told him Cassie is being cared for by another one of the maids and is being kept in an east wing bedroom. Which is right above where we are entering the house, so it should be simple to get to her. I just hope the information is correct and we aren't walking into the biggest trap of our lives.

We slow our pace as an old rusty gate comes into view. From the information Asher gave us, I know the entrance into the house is just round the corner. Max signals for us to stop, while he moves forward and checks the gate. Once he's happy there is nobody here, he makes quick work of picking the lock and opening it so we can all get through.

"We're approaching the door," Max says quietly.

Ash's voice follows in all our ears, "Okay you are all clear to enter, swapping to fake feeds in 3 2 1." We hear the tapping of keys as Lincoln steps forward to stand by Max with the camera device in one hand and his gun in the other. Donovan's security was unable to be hacked, but Liam gave him some tech that will allow us to freeze the cameras as we come into range with them. Asher has entered Greg's passwords into the system, so it won't raise an alarm. At least, we hope not.

Max unlocks the cellar door with ease, and pushes inside, gun raised. We follow behind him quietly, all with our own weapons drawn. Max looks at ease, he must have done this kind of thing a thousand times, Lincoln strangely looks as comfortable as Max and I find myself, again wondering how he became how he is. Jace looks on edge and I don't miss the shake of his hand slightly as he palms his own gun. He's sober, for the first time all week. I suggested he sit this out, but he told me that wasn't an option. That he was sick of not fighting back, so here he is. I'm calm, or at least calm enough that my hand holds the gun steady. Inside I am burning through fear, panic, relief, longing. All of them clashing together as my heart bangs against my chest.

We move through the cellar until we come to a set of stairs that I know leads up into the main house. Once at the top, Linc silently opens the door and pushes the device against it waiting for the light to turn from red to green, signaling that the cameras are paused. We don't wait more than a few seconds before we see the green light, and we move inside the door. It leads us into the downstairs corridor of the east wing. From studying the floor plans, all we have to do is move to the end of this hallway, enter the foyer, go up the stairs and get to the third room on the right. Simple right?

Or at least it would be if this house didn't belong to the biggest fucking criminal in town. Even with the blocker device, I still find myself tracking every camera I can see and sticking close to the walls as we move through the house.

When we come to another door, it's Liam's voice, we hear this time, "Two heat signatures just beyond that door." He confirms, and Max signals for us to stand back.

He opens the door, slipping inside and he is barely out of sight before I hear two muffled shots and a thud. He comes back through the door dragging two guards by their collars. Two very dead guards. Now we have spilled the first bit of blood, time really is of the essence, it won't be long until someone stumbles across them, or us. We have to keep moving.

When we reach the bottom of the stairs, I am holding my breath so hard that if the adrenaline wasn't so potent within me, I would pass out. Max swings around checking everywhere constantly, as he speaks.

"Bottom of the stairs. Going up." He states and swings around as a door on the other side of the stairs swings open. An arm sticks through it with a thumbs up, and he relaxes slightly as Elijah's head follows it. With all eight of us now here, the four of them surround the foyer in the shadows, as we begin to ascend the stairs. Moving as one until we reach the top. As agreed, Lincoln and I will be the ones to grab Cassie. She has spent more time with us recently than Max and we want her to be as comfortable as possible. Especially considering we have no idea what state she is going to be in. Is she going to look like the same little girl I have come to know and love? Will they have hurt her or worse? Is she tied up? Have they fed her? The disgusting images barrel into my mind before I can stop them, and I shake my head like I can physically toss them out of there. Whatever state she is in doesn't matter. All that matters is getting her home. I need to rescue the princess so the queen can be whole again.

Lincoln signals for me to move and I go ahead as he steps up behind with his hand on my shoulder. Both of us have our guns raised.

It doesn't take us more than thirty seconds to reach the room we believe Cassie to be in and I waste no time in entering. I palm the handle and take a deep breath, before silently pushing it down and opening it as slowly as I can. The room is dark with the only light coming from a small lamp on the bedside table. I immediately spot Cassie sitting on one side of a huge bed and my heart rate quickens. Flicking my eyes to her left, I see a woman sitting beside her, reading a book, but as soon as I speak into my mic she looks up.

"We got her." I say, and I hear Asher's sigh of relief loud and clear.

Taking me in, the woman's features are shrouded in fear, but she doesn't scream, run, or even try to reach for something to use as a weapon. She just freezes, the panic forcing her body to shut down, as she stares at my gun. I lower it slightly and when she still doesn't move, I take a slow step forward.

"I'm not going to hurt you; I just want the girl." For how nervous I am, my voice comes out calm. Cassie is so close, her sleeping form snuggled down under the blanket. We could actually pull this off, all we have to do is grab her and get back out of here undetected.

The woman still doesn't say anything, so I continue, "We are taking the girl home, with or without your cooperation." I can see her shaking from across the room, but she nods ever so slightly. She looks young and is probably being forced to do all sorts under the employment of Elliot Donovan.

Lincoln enters behind me, but I don't risk looking at him as I move closer to the bed, until I reach the side Cassie is sleeping on. I breathe a slight sigh of relief that she appears to be unharmed and as Lincoln stalks across the room to deal with the maid, I gently pull the blanket from her causing her to stir.

Her sleepy eyes open and lock with mine and her surprise is instant, "River?" She wonders aloud in a tired tone.

"Yeah baby, it's me." I say with a soft smile. I barely have time to register her moving before she dives at me and flings her little arms around my neck. I don't think I have ever felt such instant happiness. The comfort of finding her here, and from what I can tell, unharmed. It's the best I could have ever hoped for.

"I missed you so much," she whispers, and my throat burns with the pain of emotions as I place my gun back into its holster and cuddle her back.

"I missed you too." I reply, rubbing my hand up and down her back, watching as Lincoln ties the maid up with ease and drags her into the closet shutting the door. Once she's secured, I pull back from Cassie, "are you okay?"

She nods enthusiastically, "Is my Mommy here?" She asks and the hope in her voice cuts me. Four words and I can tell how much she has missed her mom, probably just as much as Elle has missed her.

I sigh slightly, knowing I am going to disappoint her, "No princess, just me and the guys, but we are taking you home to mommy, okay?"

She takes in my words, then notices Lincoln as he moves into her view, "Superman!" she yells excitedly, and I am grateful for the distraction.

Lincoln drops to his knees by the bed, so he is eyeline with her, "Hey princess, miss me?" he asks with ease and she nods again with a huge smile on her face. The sight causes my heart to ache for a whole new reason. I wonder if she will grow up realizing how many people love her and would die for her in an instant. So much more than what Lincoln ever grew up with. Seeing him offer her such instant comfort makes me grateful to have him here with us.

"Good because I missed you too, but I'm gonna need you to be quiet, okay?" His tone is the softest I have ever heard from him, and I can tell he is trying his hardest to stay calm and in control for her.

"Like the quiet game?" She asks him and he nods.

"Exactly like the quiet game, remember what mommy told you about me protecting you?" She keeps

169

nodding, "Well, this house is a very bad place for little princesses so we came to take you home, but to do that we need to get back to our car as quietly as possible, can you do that for me?"

"Yes." She says and then immediately throws her hands over her mouth nodding dramatically and I can't help the little laugh that slips out of me.

"That's perfect," Linc praises her, "now let's go home."

He looks at me and nods, before he stands and tosses the bag, we brought with us at me. I pull out the extra Kevlar vest along with one of her pink blankets from home.

"Okay, I am going to carry you little one, but I need to wrap this around you alright?" She nods once more, and I waste no time wrapping her up until the Kevlar covers as much of her body as I can manage with the blanket securing it in place. I move my arms to support her back and then stand lifting her as I go. Just the feel of her tiny weight in my arms makes my heart ache. So small, so innocent, so fragile, I will not stop until we get her out of here safely.

Lincoln moves towards the door and I follow close behind him, slipping the gun back out from my belt with one hand, while keeping Cassie secured tightly against me with my other arm. Her little breaths tickle my neck, and I am glad to feel that they are as steady and as normal as they could be, considering the bizarre situation we are in.

"Secured and leaving." Lincoln speaks into his mic as Jace speaks into our ears.

"We got company."

Lincoln curls his arm around the handle, just as shots are fired and we all tense as Cassie lets out a little squeak. I can tell she is scared and trying her hardest not to make a sound.

I lean my head back so I can look down at her, and her little sparkling blue eyes lock with mine, "You are safe with me okay princess? Pinky promise." Lincoln grabs my gun so I can bring my finger to hers and curl them together. "Just hold on tight and don't worry about any loud noises or shouting alright?"

"Everyone here is loud." She replies, and I grind my teeth and I see a muscle lock in Lincoln's jaw. Neither of us want to think about what she may have seen or heard while being here.

"Ready brother?" he asks, and we lock eyes, knowing no matter what happens we will do anything to ensure we get Cassie out of here.

"Ready."

He opens the door just as a guard is about to enter and before we are even seen Lincoln puts a bullet right into his skull. Cassie clings to me as tight as possible and I tighten my hold on her. As if keeping her as close as possible will make everything okay.

We don't stop for even a second, stepping over the dead guard and moving out into the hall. Gunshots continue to go off from downstairs and we look at one another.

"Plan B?" he questions, and I nod my head.

"Plan B." I agree, and we both turn left instead of going back the way we came.

"Talk to me." Ash barks into our ear.

"Taking the secondary route, down the back stairs and through the kitchen." Linc responds to him as we move quickly down the hall.

"Alright you have four heat signatures currently on that path." His voice is tense, but it doesn't scare me because I hear something else. He has just become the prince. The master of his darkness. On edge, but completely in control and prepared to do whatever is necessary for his daughter.

"Heard." Is all Linc replies as we continue on our path.

We make it down the hallway and stairs without incident, as the gunshots either die down or are now too far away to be heard. As we make it to the bottom, we hear footsteps coming towards us and ready ourselves. I crush my body into the wall as much as I can giving Cassie as much cover as possible. Lincoln then covers us both, as he stands and waits.

The first guard doesn't even make it round the corner before Lincoln kills him. Without hesitation, without fear and without regret. My silent and brooding brother is deadlier than even I thought. His shot lands with precision and he is already moving to shoot the second guard, before the first one even hits the floor. Lincoln's second shot misses the kill slightly, only hitting the guard's shoulder as he moves to raise his own gun, but the next one hits him in the center of his chest.

Again, we don't hesitate and quickly move on our way to bring ourselves closer to our escape. I keep a tight hold on Cassie, praying this is the last time she ever has to face something like this. She is being quiet, and I want to praise her for handling this so well, she is tough and resilient, just like her mother.

"Two down." Lincoln states simply, and I take another deep breath, so close yet still so far.

I follow him as we continue on, but a sound behind us has me whipping around and I shoot at the same time the guard does. His bullet flies past me, but I hear Lincoln grunt slightly as I kill the guard with a bullet to his chest, before he can shoot again. I don't wait for his body to fall before I turn around to check on Lincoln.

"You okay?" I question when I see him standing there rubbing his arm.

"Just a graze," he grunts, and I sigh in relief.

"Okay let's keep moving." I say quietly, checking on Cassie once more, but she has her eyes scrunched tightly closed.

Lincoln passes an alcove ahead of me and before I can warn him someone is kicking his gun from his arm and aiming their own. Linc is quick to disarm them, and he goes into hand-to-hand combat with him. They move quickly and I'm not able to get a clear shot. Not until Lincoln throws back his elbow and then ducks, giving me a clear aim. I fire at the guard, but not before he's able to plunge a knife into Linc's back causing him to cry out in pain.

"Fuckkk!" he ruffs out as the guard drops next to him.

"What the fuck is going on?" Asher barks into our ears at the same time Max speaks.

"Who's hurt?"

"Lincoln just took a knife to the back," I say, moving towards him as he begins to stand, "You okay man?" I ask and he nods.

"Fine" he grits through his teeth, but I can tell it hurts and the panic begins to swirl through my body even more. This isn't good.

"You know you're not allowed to die on me, right?" I ask only slightly teasing and he huffs a humorless laugh.

"Is that an order, boss?"

"You bet your fucking ass it is." I toss back and then cringe slightly remembering Cassie in my arms, but there are worse things to worry about other than cussing right now.

We knew the risks in coming here, all of us more than willing to take them, but as I stare at the knife, I feel sick. His black clothing stops me from seeing the blood I know will be soaking there, but I know it's there. My brother's blood might as well be my blood. I can't lose him. I won't lose him.

I push my fear aside as I step towards him to check it out. "Want me to pull it out?"

"Don't even think about it," Logan's voice startles us both as it comes from behind us instead of in our ear as him and Elijah round the corner.

I see he has a bloodied lip and Elijah seems to be limping slightly, but apart from that they both appear unharmed.

"Uncle Lo?" Cassie asks tentatively and Logan immediately zones in on the bundle in my arms.

He moves towards me until he is close enough to peek inside the blanket, "Hey little one, you alright in there?" He asks with a big smile on his face.

"You got boo boo?" She asks and he reaches up and wipes his lip.

"Just a little one, but don't you worry about me, us Roytons are tough, aren't we?"

"Tough as nails," she replies, and he smiles widely.

"That's right, now let's go home, everyone has missed you." He tucks the blanket securely around her and nods at me.

Elijah speaks, "Let's get out of here."

Logan moves to Lincoln checking the knife sticking out of his back, you okay?" He asks as he steps in front of him bringing them face to face and Lincoln nods.

"I'm fine." He says in exasperation, not enjoying any attention as usual.

Logan smirks, "you certainly are."

"Just get the fuck out of there," Asher snaps into our ears and Logan smiles even wider.

"Yes sir," he replies before tossing Lincoln a wink, "don't worry baby, I'll take care of you when we get home" He purrs at him and I don't miss the slight tip of Lincoln's mouth at Logan's words.

"Let's just get out of here alive," he grits back through his teeth and I can see he is panting through the pain from his wound.

Elijah takes the lead as I follow right after him, leaving Lincoln and Logan at the rear. We hear grunts and shots every so often through our earpieces.

Numerous threats being dealt with by the rest of the guys, but thankfully we make it back to the tunnel the others entered through, without coming across anyone else.

As soon as we enter the tunnel, we all break into a run, we have probably been inside the house for no longer than ten minutes, but it feels like a lifetime. I don't think of anything other than putting one foot in front of the other as I cling on to Cassie with everything I have. Almost there. When we get to the entrance of the tunnel Elijah halts us all.

"Leaving the nest with package in hand and three allies." He says into his mic and waits for a response. Max responds almost instantly, "moving through the west tunnel with all remaining allies."

We all collectively breathe a sigh of relief as we exit the tunnel and move into the trees at a quick pace, not stopping until the van is in sight. Liam flings open the door as we approach, and we all climb inside awaiting the others. It isn't long before they clear the trees on the other side. Oliver jumps back into the driver's seat as Mason slides in next to him and Max, and Jace dives in the back with us.

The van doors close behind them and Oliver tears out of there like a bat out of hell. I look at each of the guys ensuring everyone is okay and apart from the knife in Lincoln's back it seems that there isn't more than a black eye or busted lip between us.

I shake my head in disbelief at the feel of Cassie in my arms and all of us back here and alive. I lean down into Cassie and take comfort in the fruity smell of her hair.

We did it.

Chapter 19

ELLE

I feel weightless, like I am floating towards consciousness, but not fully there yet. I push myself to try to open my eyes, but they feel as if someone has glued them shut. What the fuck? My head is pounding, and I feel the nausea swimming around between my stomach and throat. I am probably going to throw up any minute, but I can barely move. My limbs feel awkward like I don't have control over them, and I begin to panic.

No. No. Please. Not again.

The first thing I remember is that Zack is gone. He's dead. The grief slams into me all over again and suddenly I don't want to open my eyes anymore. I don't want to wake up and exist in a world that my brother no longer breathes in. But I have to. My brother may be gone, but my daughter isn't. She is still here somewhere, and I need to get to her.

I know the Donovan's want me alive, want me as a fucking Donovan, but I know them too well. I know they don't really care about my wellbeing or her's. I know Greg is beyond help and his sick twisted mind knows no bounds. Wanting me as a wife is just another way, he thinks he can torture me again. I think of the soulless smile on his face as he fucked me, the bruising grip on my arm from his buddies and the stench of blood filling the room as I tried to block it all out. I was helpless then, didn't have the power to fight back, the will, but I'm not the same girl I was back then.

I hear a door open, and I know it's time to fight again, I'm so tired, so weak, but that won't stop me. I can't let anything stop me. I have come too far, gotten so close. It's time.

I force myself to open my eyes and the unfamiliar room confuses me. It is not what I expected at all and that is when I register that whatever I am lying on is comfy and warm. Nothing like the last place I was in when I woke up from a drug induced haze. Guess I hold more value to the Donovan's now, no longer a whore for sale, but an heir producer. I want to laugh, but I don't have the energy.

I move to roll onto my side and am pleasantly surprised that my body obeys my mind's intent. That surprise ends when I lock eyes with the last person I was expecting.

"Ash?" I scrunch my eyes closed and then open them again to clear my blurry vision until it's back to normal, yet it doesn't change what I'm seeing.

"Yeah, Hells Bells, it's me." He smiles a relieved smile as he stalks towards me and drops to his knees at my bedside.

I'm so confused, "Where am I?"

He sighs, "We're at a safe house."

His answer does nothing to ease my confusion. The last thing I remember was going to the Donovan estate, did I make it there? I'm almost sure I did. How did I go from there to wherever I am now?

"How? Why?" My words come out a little slurred as the effects of whatever's in my system continues to flow.

"We had to take some precautions so they could go get Cassie."

I gasp, "What, who?" I'm in full on panic mode right now. Is he even serious?

"Everyone. Marcus, Jace, Lincoln, Logan. Max and his team. They've all gone to get her." He delivers the words casually, but I can see the undertones of panic in his tense shoulders and clenched jaw.

I force myself up and my fear allows my rapid movements, even against my body's protests. "They can't do it alone, they're gonna get themselves killed."

He laughs, "Oh, kinda like you were, you mean?" I can tell from the bite of his words that he is angry with me, but I don't have time to deal with that right now.

"Greg doesn't want me dead!" I snap loudly and it hurts my head.

He doesn't back down, "He isn't stable enough to know what he wants!" He yells back at me. It's the first time he has ever raised his voice towards me, but he is past caring, as he continues. "He never has been. My brother is a fucking psychopath that would have relished in having you again and yet you were about to walk right back into his fucking hands."

I feel the tears on my cheeks, but I ignore them as I force myself to stand up, "of course I would, he has our fucking daughter Ash!"

"You don't think I know that? That I haven't been suffering with that truth every fucking day!" He screams back, "I know more than anyone what my family is capable of."

"Told you she'd be pissed." Another voice cuts into our argument and my legs almost give out when I hear it. It can't be.

I turn around and a shocked cry bursts out of me as I say his name in disbelief. "Zack?"

He smiles from the wheelchair, "Miss me, Sis?"

My legs move before I can even tell them to, like my body has taken over everything and I find myself in front of him in a second as I launch myself at him. He grunts as I throw my arms around him and sob into his chest.

When I remember his injuries and register his grunt I try to pull back, "Oh my God. I'm sorry."

He hugs me tighter to him, "Don't be, the pain of your hug is a very welcome one indeed, sweetheart."

The word sweetheart molds around the shattered pieces of my heart like it could piece them back together in one swoop. A word I never thought I would hear again from a voice I never thought I would hear again. My lungs burn as my heart races faster than I have ever felt, I think I could go into shock, but Zack begins to rub his hand up and down my back, like he knows I need the comfort. He's here, my brother is here.

I don't know how long we stay in each other's embrace, but I do know it could never be too long. Not when I know what it feels like to think I had lost him for good. I don't want to ever know that feeling again for as long as I live.

I pull back and look him over, checking every inch of him like I can't believe he is really here. When my disbelief still doesn't subside, I choke out one word, "How?"

Asher answers first, "You can thank your precious Max for this one." He grits out, and I can tell there hasn't been much improvement in Ash's opinion of Max while I've been gone. He continues, "When we set on a final plan to get Cassie back, we needed a way to bring you home. He thought telling you Zack was gone would bring you back. Clearly, he doesn't know you well enough. They got to you just in time before you ruined our whole plan."

The mention of Cassie jolts me from my relief about Zack, "Cassie" I say, barely above a whisper. "I need to go get her." I stand up on shaky legs and stumble from the room with Asher quick on my tail and Zack wheeling further behind.

Ash grips my arm and drags me back, "They've got it handled, Hells Bells, leave it be."

I rip my arm from his, "Like hell." I push away from him and continue through the unfamiliar surroundings. I reach the living room, but it's empty and when I see the curtains pulled back, I notice how dark it has gotten. Fuck what time is it? How long was I out? How much time have I wasted?

I keep moving until I find the front door and move towards it, throwing it open, but Ash's hand finds my arm once more. He pulls me back until he has me blocked in against the open door. I fight against the dizziness trying to cloud my eyes and the nausea swirling in my stomach.

"Are you done being reckless and stupid." He asks in exasperation.

I struggle against him, "How could you?" I shove him off me, "how fucking could you let them go?"

The beeping of the gates startle me as soon as the last word leaves my mouth. Heart pounding, my head whips round as it opens, and headlights shine brightly across us both. The van speeds inside before the gates even fully open and stops a few meters from the porch.

I inhale a sharp breath as the back door opens, Jace steps out first, followed by Liam and Elijah. Max climbs out next and then stops to help Logan with a pale looking Lincoln, and then finally, Marcus.

I don't hear anything, see anything, feel anything, until the small bundle of blankets in his arms moves, and the top falls down, revealing a small mass of blonde curls.

As soon as she feels the cool air brush through her hair, she whips her head around, her gaze finding mine with ease. Then I hear a sound I have been praying to hear every second since I walked back into the house after the ball.

"Mommy!"

Chapter 20

ELLE

She's here, she's really here. I fall to my knees at the sight of her wriggling free from Marcus' hold as she rushes to get to me. She doesn't look hurt or traumatized, only tired and happy. The impact of her body slamming into mine is a feeling I won't ever forget. I wrap my arms around her, and it feels like I inhale the first real breath I have taken since she's been gone. The grogginess from whatever Ash gave me and the anger I felt at the whole situation just moments ago, now completely forgotten. My baby is home.

I can't hold in my sob as I snuggle her tight into my arms. I don't even know what my tears are for right now, happiness at her being back, fear of what could have been or relief that she seems unharmed. The truth is, it's everything. I never should have become a Mom at fifteen, but there isn't one second since the day she was born that I have ever regretted her. She fixed my broken heart and has held it together every day since. Every moment in the last week that has passed without her felt like a lifetime. Nothing would have ever healed my severed pieces if I didn't get her back.

All I can do is hold her and cry. Her tiny hands gripped around my neck and her little legs curled around my torso. I bury my face into her curls and inhale her sweet scent, allowing everything about her to overtake my whole being and soothe my crushed soul. I haven't stopped fighting, surviving, barely hanging on, just to try to get her back, and now she's here.

Asher drops to his knees beside us and pulls us both into a crushing embrace. I feel his deep exhale as he lets himself have a moment of raw love with us. She's here, she's safe. We are still a family. We came so close to losing everything, that I thought I would never have this again, not without giving myself over to the enemy. But we are here, together, and safe.

Cassie finally pulls back, looking between the two of us with a tired smile on her face, "I missed you so much Mommy Daddy!" She exclaims and it just causes me to cry more.

She frowns, then reaches out to wipe my cheeks to get rid of the tears, "It's okay Mommy don't be sad, I'm here now."

I take a deep breath as I force the words out that are locked in my throat, "I'm sorry, baby, I just missed you so much." I try to stop, but my emotions are getting the better of me. It's like I have held them all in until this very moment.

"Mommy is just so happy to see you little angel, we both are. We missed you." Asher replies as I continue to cry. I can hear his own emotion lacing his words and I see a lone tear track down his cheek. The only time I have ever seen him cry is the night I woke up in the warehouse. At least his tears are for better reasons this time.

I try to force myself to stop crying, but it just starts a fire in my throat, but I don't want her to see me upset. I want her to know how happy I am that she is here and safe.

"Grandpa Elly said you'd come get me and he was right." The smile that follows her words is big and bright. I force one onto my own face, even though her statement chills me to the bone. *Grandpa Elly.*

I take another deep inhale as I look at Ash briefly, before focusing on her again. I don't want to ask my next question; I don't even want to think it. "Did Grandpa Elly hurt you baby?" The words taste like poison on my tongue, and I'm not sure I want the answer, but I have to know.

She scrunches her nose up in confusion, "No," she says sweetly and then smiles, "he gave me ice cream and candy and let me play every day." Her words as usual are rushed and slightly mispronounced, but the tension eases in me ever so slightly.

How? How can she have survived a week in the Devil's mansion, and be here now unscathed?

"Are you sure baby? Did he…" I pause as the bile rises in my throat, "did he touch you; did anyone touch you or hurt you, it's okay, you can tell Mommy."

The smile drops from her face and my blood runs cold as I prepare for her answer. "No everybody was nice. I played with Elly and Greggy and a nice lady named Sarah came by, but she was sad."

The mention of my mother's name jars me, I dread to think of all the things she must have been told. "And what did they say to you about why you were away from Mommy."

She smiles again, "they said you were having a little think about what you did." She pauses before asking, "what did you do Mommy?"

Not enough. That's what I want to tell her, but her innocence would never be able to comprehend it, so I settle on, "I trusted the wrong people and got a boo boo."

"Oh no, are you okay?" She reaches out to touch my forehead as if to check my temperature and my heart bursts with love for her gentle kind ways.

Tears continue to coat my cheeks, "I'm all better now that you're here."

"Greggy said you were coming soon. That you are his queen and soon we would all be together." Her childlike wonder makes it sound like a dream when in fact it's my worst nightmare. A nightmare I almost allowed. A nightmare I almost walked right into and would have if the guys didn't get to me first. So fucking close.

I go to ask her another question when she casts her gaze over my shoulder and her eyes widen in delight,

"Grandma, Grandpa, Uncle Zaaaa." She screams, struggling to wriggle from my arms. I don't want to let her go, I don't want to ever let her go, but I know I'm not the only one who has missed her.

I release my hold on her and Ash and I watch as she rushes towards Zack who has Arthur, Helen and Lily standing behind him. I didn't even realize they were here; they must have been sleeping. I guess that this is the safe house Max put them all in from the start. She does the same thing I did and dives into Zack's arms without a care for his injuries, then again, she doesn't know anything about them. He doesn't seem to care as he pulls her in tight and looks as if he never wants to let her go. Every time I see them together, I am thankful to have Zack in my life, even more so, now I almost lost him.

Zack reluctantly let's her go as Helen steps towards them and Cassie leaps into her arms for a cuddle. I don't hear what she says, but it causes tears to pour down all their faces as they bask in her presence. I pull my attention away from them, but only so I can keep my own tears at bay.

I turn to Ash first, "she's back." I whisper, still in disbelief and he pulls me into his arms.

"She's back." He repeats back to me, "we did it," he adds in a soft exhale like he still can't quite believe it himself. I know I can't.

I pull back and wipe the tears from my cheeks again as he does the same. I reach out and squeeze his hand and take comfort in the strength of his grip in mine. We are still here, still fighting.

My daughter is back, and my brother is alive. The Donovan's came for me, again, and failed, again. This time they got too close to my utter destruction. I should have never come back here, never given them the chances they've had, but then who would make them pay? I have my family back together. Do I run and never look back, or fight harder than ever before?

Chapter 21

MARCUS

She's here. My girl is here, and more importantly, our girl is here too. We did it, we got them both back and managed to do it relatively unharmed. We all risked our life to rescue the princess from the twisted castle she was being held in. Elle turns from Ash towards me, and our eyes collide, but only for a second. Her gaze drops instantly, like she doesn't want to look at me before it comes back a second later. I think she is going to say something, but then she looks at my brothers and her frown is instant.

She moves slowly towards Lincoln who is being held up by Logan, "Oh my god what the hell happened."

He tries and fails to shrug considering the knife poking out of his back, "I got stabbed."

She huffs slightly, "I can see that. Are you okay?"

He smiles, "Elle, I appreciate that you care, but I'm fine honestly, go be with your girl, she needs you more than I do."

"Don't sweat it sis, I got him. Go give the little monkey extra cuddles from me." Logan adds and I can hear how genuine he is. I know it must be killing him to have Cassie back and not immediately go to her, but he knows she doesn't need anyone but her mom and dad right now.

She pauses, taking in his words before she accepts them with a slight nod. She turns to walk away before turning back and stepping forwards to engulf Lincoln in a tight hug.

"Thank you." She whispers on the verge of tears again. Pulling back, she glances between all of us still not lingering on me, but it doesn't matter. All that matters to me is that her and Cassie are both here and safe. "Thank you, I don't know how I'll ever repay you." She chokes a little on her words and I feel the emotion pouring from all of us at her vulnerability. Elle King isn't someone who needs people to rely on these days, but she has to know how many people love her and have her back.

Max steps forward, "You don't say thank you to your family." He says with a small smile and ruffling her hair.

She glares at him and then out of nowhere punches him in the stomach. "That was for your stupid fucking plan." She grunts flexing out her fist.

He takes the hit silently and then moves past her and gestures at his guys to follow.

She takes one last look at the four of us left standing here before she turns and heads back towards the house, scooping Cassie back into her arms and going inside. Asher remains in front of us watching her until she is inside and it's only us guys left outside.

He turns, locking his eyes on Lincoln first, "how are you really?" He grills him with the hint of worry in his tone and it sounds weird coming from him towards anyone that isn't Elle or Cassie.

Lincoln smiles again and honestly, it's the most I've ever seen him smile, it's weird. Maybe he's delirious with blood loss. We really need to get him inside.

"You worried about me, dark prince?" He asks him with a teasing glint in his eye. When Ash doesn't respond he adds more seriously, "I told you I'd die for her if I had to." Even in his struggling state I can feel how much he means that. We all would.

Asher huffs a laugh, "Yeah well, I never knew you meant that so literally. Thought you'd be better at handling yourself."

"I handle myself just fine," Lincoln jokes and it's clear that Ash doesn't know how to respond, but thankfully Logan is happy to jump in.

"Does it take almost dying to get your attention my little psycho, if so, somebody fucking stab me." He teases, lightening the awkward tension that was beginning to build. It just shows how much comfort those two girls inside bring us all. We've barely been able to take a breath without snapping at each other in the last week.

Asher just shakes his head at him, before turning to me. "Marcus," he takes a deep breath, pausing like he isn't really sure what he wants to say. "I don't even know what to say man, just thank you. I couldn't have done it without you." He offers me his hand and I stare at it bewildered at first, but then I realize he wants me to shake it. I put my hand in his and he grips it in his own.

It feels silly and awkward to just shake his hand after everything we have been through, with everything we still need to go through. I use the grip of his hand to pull him into a one-armed hug and pat his back with my free hand. "You don't ever have to say thank you to your family." I say, repeating Max's words, pulling back, squeezing his shoulder slightly before letting go. We have come a long way in the last few weeks, and I don't know what is going to happen, but I do know he is an important part of my girl's life, therefore he's an important part of mine.

"Now go inside and be with your daughter, she's missed her dad." I add with a content smile. He nods, casting one last look at the others before turning and heading inside.

I watch him go before turning to the guys, addressing Lincoln first, "You go get that seen to before you die of blood loss." I'm only half joking and I'm glad he doesn't fight me on it, but he doesn't really have a choice.

"Come on, let's go find my dad and get him to fix you up." Logan adds and they both move inside slowly as he supports Linc.

I turn to Jace, having not really spoken to him all night and see the grimace on his face. I know exactly how it felt to be inside the devil's house and not stay and kill them. I felt it so I know he did. For what they did to Elle, Rachel, Cassie and all the other nameless girls we know nothing about but deserve just as much justice.

"You okay brother?" I don't know why I even ask when I know the answer.

He looks at me and offers me a tight-lipped smile, "I'm okay, tonight was just…" he pauses slightly trying to find the right word, "a lot." Understatement of the century. He killed someone tonight. That someone might have been our enemy, but that is still a line you can never return from once you cross it.

I nod knowing exactly what he means, what he feels. "Come on," I throw my arm around his shoulder in a side hug, "let's go grab some food and sleep and enjoy just a few hours of peace. The girls are here and they're safe, we're all safe."

"Yeah, for now." He whispers.

"Now is what matters most." Is all I respond before we head into the house.

Once inside, everyone seems to have scattered. Max and his guys are debriefing in the office, Lincoln has gone with Logan and Arthur to get fixed up, and Jace grabs a bottle of Jack and heads to bed. Elle is sitting on the sofa with Cassie curled up in her lap, Asher to her right and Helen and Lily to her left. They all look beyond exhausted, but content enough to just be sat there. I should shower, eat, change, do anything that isn't just standing here staring at them, at her. But I can't help it. She left. We came so close to never seeing her again and the feeling that's left inside of me will be with me forever.

They all talk back and forth, telling Cassie, tales of happier times until she falls into a slumber. Once she goes, it isn't long before Lily says goodnight and then Helen too. It's just me, Elle and Ash, now left with a sleeping Cassie. We all sit in silence just watching her sleep. Like just her presence alone is curing us all, I'm sure it is. Eventually Elle falls asleep with her and Ash and I continue to watch them. Just completely zoned in on them and what we came close to losing. So fucking close.

Ash is the first to speak, "we should get them to bed." He says quietly and I nod, standing up and stretching out my limbs. He gently pulls Elle's arms from around her and softly lifts Cassie into his own, protective embrace. Once he has her, I lean down and scoop Elle. She shifts in my arms until her head lands on my shoulder, her scent drifts up to me and I finally feel like home again.

I follow Ash until he gets to the room they set aside for Cassie and he places her in the middle of the bed and then I put Elle in next to her. We both stare down at them and then Ash sighs slightly, as he starts to move away, but I stop him with a hand on his arm.

"You stay." I say quietly.

"No, Marcus, it's fine." He starts to argue but I lift my hand halting him.

"Ash, that's your daughter, she's been gone, and she deserves a night with her Mom and Dad, so just stay okay." I want him to know how okay I am with this whole situation. He will always be Cassie's dad, no matter what is happening with Elle and me. Do I wish things were different? Of course, I do. But if they were then they wouldn't have Cassie and that is something I would never wish for them. That girl is the light in both their lives, and they need it. Hell, I need it too. Now more than ever.

He looks at them before turning back to me and he nods, "thanks man."

"Anytime." I say turning to leave, but then he speaks again.

"I will always look after our girls." He replies and the way he says our girls hits something right in my gut because that's what they are. It may not be normal or conventional to love someone this much, this young. But I do and with her comes her daughter, her daughter's father, and I wouldn't want to share them with anyone else.

I turn back and offer him a smile, "then I know they will always be protected." I reply before leaving the room and closing the door behind me.

It's not that I don't want to be in there, near them, near Elle, but they need each other more than they need me right now and I'm man enough to admit to that. They have endured trauma together before and it brought them closer. They know how to lean on each other without question and without words. That's what they both need right now.

I head back into the main part of the house and find myself at the door of the office. I go to speak but a phone ringing stops me. I look at the couple of people left in the room. It's just me, Max and Elijah. The latter is the first to speak as he picks up the ringing phone which I recognize to be Elle's from before she went rogue.

He grimaces, "It's Greg Donovan."

I move before I even realize it, snatching the phone from his grip and answering before he can protest, but I notice he immediately starts tapping away on his computer.

"Evening, wifey. You left me quite a mess to clean up. I'd be pissed if I weren't so impressed. If this is your idea of foreplay, I can't wait to go another round with you." His arrogant and psychotic tone purrs down the line making my skin crawl.

I can't control my temper, "The only foreplay you're going to enjoy is my gun down your fucking throat." I snap.

Like the true psychopath I'm sure he is, my words don't deter him. "Ahh Mr. Riviera. Sorry I didn't realize I was in the presence of Royalty." He drawls sarcastically, "how is the delightful South Side of town these days?"

I have no time for his bullshit games. "Listen here you sick fuck, you lost, you are gonna keep losing and you would do best if you crept back into the demonic hole you were birthed from and fucking rotted there. We are done playing your games."

"But you know how much I love to play, especially when it comes to our girl."

The way he says our girl makes me want to fucking reach down the phone and gut him where he stands. A stark contrast to how I felt just a few minutes ago when his brother said it. "Keep fucking playing asshole, the last thing you are ever going to see is me slitting your fucking throat."

He laughs wildly like he is genuinely enjoying himself. "We'll see about that. Give my fiancée my regards. Bye for now."

The phone disconnecting is the last thing I hear and all I can think is, this is far from over.

Chapter 22

ELLE

I wake up to the best sight I could ever wish for. Asher is facing me with his arms curled around Cassie, both of them flat out and snoring softly. They look peaceful, happy, safe. It takes everything in me not to burst into tears again. We got her back, she's here, with her family, exactly like she should be. Safe and completely protected.

I try my hardest not to think about the nights she has spent away from us. Did she cry? Did she have nightmares? Did she wonder why we weren't there? Fuck just thinking about it makes me want to rip her from Ash's arms and pull her into my own and never let go again. What would have happened if the guys didn't get her back? If I walked right into the den of lions that awaited me and gave myself over to them? I was fucking stupid, no, I was fucking desperate. I would have done anything.

I don't know how long I lie here in the dark staring at them, could be minutes, could be hours. It doesn't matter, I just want to be lost in the feeling of having them here, alive, and just with me. I think about how close we came to losing her, how bad, no, how fucking awful this whole thing could have been. Even a bond as strong as ours wouldn't have been able to save us from the tragedy of losing her.

It's not easy pulling myself away from them, but my bladder has other plans. I roll out of the bed as silently as possible and move to the en-suite off to the side of the room. Once I'm done, I come back into the room and note the time from the clock on the bedtime table: 4am. I thought with everything that has happened I'd be able to sleep a lot longer, but I guess my little drug induced nap hindered me. I stretch out my limbs which feel kinda stiff and I know it's probably the effects of whatever Ash pricked me with yesterday. I know I won't be able to go back to sleep, I'm still too on edge and reeling from all that's happened.

I take one last look at Cass and Ash and smile. I'll just go grab some coffee and come back. I leave the room as silently as possible, but when I close the door behind me, I find Marcus sitting on the floor against the wall opposite with his head down. When the door clicks shut, he looks up at me.

"Hey," I whisper, unsure of what else to say at this point. It's not like I avoided him earlier, but I truly didn't know what to say to him. It was like the day I came back to town and set eyes on him for the first time since I left. So much between us, yet I left it behind, just like I did three years ago. But he has to understand how much I am willing to risk to protect my daughter. She's everything.

"Hey," he offers me a soft smile and then stands up and gestures for me to follow him.

I know we really need to talk and there is no escaping it now, so I move down the hall to follow him. We reach what I presume is his room and he steps inside, and as soon as I'm in he shuts the door behind me.

His grip finds my throat faster than I can comprehend as he slams me into the door and pushes his body against mine kissing me with everything he's got. Totally not what I was expecting. This kiss is unlike any we've ever shared. It's rough, urgent, animalistic. Like he is living for every breath he can steal from me. Like I am his only lifeline and without me he will perish.

His mouth leaves mine as he trails kisses across my jaw and down my neck, nipping me slightly as he grunts, "You forgot."

"Forgot what," I say breathlessly as his teeth sink into the curve of my neck, causing a moan to rip from my lips.

He pulls back, tightening his grip slightly, "that you're mine, that I'm yours, that we are in this fucking together." He grits before kissing me again, forcing his tongue against my lips until I open my mouth and let it tangle with mine.

Everything is just teeth, tongue, and hands as he drags his grip over my body. I need to see him, feel him. I drag his top up and over his torso revealing the Kevlar vest he's still wearing. While he rips off my own black top and discards it on the floor. I make quick work of dragging the zip down his vest and pushing it off his broad shoulders before he reaches round and rips my bra from my chest.

He palms my breasts roughly, squeezing until my nipples harden into tight points. Then he leans down and sucks one into his mouth, lapping at it with his hot tongue then pulling at it with his teeth. It's so sensitive I feel I could come from this alone. His gaze locks with mine as he continues to suck them into his mouth before dropping to his knees in front of me. He drags my pants down and I lift each of my legs to help him get them off and my thong quickly follows.

His mouth reaches my pussy without pause, and I can't contain my moans as my back arches. I push against his tongue as it finds its way to my center. He laps at me like a starving man devouring his last meal, sucking my clit into his mouth, and sliding a finger inside me, reaching that delicious spot.

"You were going to sacrifice yourself to him." He grits, finger fucking me at a torturous pace.

"I had no choice," I manage to gasp out as he curls his finger and brushes it against my g spot. My orgasm starts to climb, and I would give anything to reach it.

He grunts, "wrong answer, little King." His finger begins to fuck me furiously and at the same time he bites down on my clit hard, not letting up until I am on the very edge of my orgasm and then he pulls back.

"Fuck!" I snap as my back slumps against the wall in anger and desperation and he smiles.

"You did something very bad, and you need to be punished for it, baby." He doesn't give me time to digest his words before he grips both of my thighs and throws them over his shoulder so he can feast on me again. His tongue circling my clit over and over and I can't help but ride his face. He drags it down until he can fuck me with it, and I claw at his hair, pulling it tight, desperate to come. Marcus doesn't stop, just continues to dip his tongue in and out of my hole and when my moans turn to cries all River does is drag his mouth down to my other hole, licking at the tight bud of my ass. It sends me over the edge, and I come with a silent scream, my legs shaking, clamped tight around his face.

He pulls back while I try to catch my breath and wipes his face against my thigh before he bites his way back up my body. Licking, sucking, nibbling anywhere he can touch. He kisses me again and I taste myself on his tongue as it swirls with mine, then he pulls back, "time to show you who you belong to."

He drags me from the door and pushes me down on top of the dresser next to it, knocking a lamp to the floor in the process. He drags my hips down until my ass hangs over the edge slightly before stepping between my thighs and dragging his cock up and down my wetness until it's covered in me. I don't even get a second to think before he slams into me and I cry out. Fuck, I barely catch my breath before he pulls out and does it again. Pounding into me as hard as he can, hitting my clit with every thrust and I can already feel the chase of another orgasm beginning.

I reach up and curl my arms around his neck and hold on tight as he continues to fuck me with deep, long strokes. My nails digging into his back as I bite back my moans. He must feel me start to clench as my orgasm builds.

"Yesssss, that's it, baby," he hisses. "Fucking give it to me, Ells. I want you fucking dripping on my cock, I'm not stopping until you've fucking drenched me, baby." He grits his words out through clenched teeth as he slams into me over and over, hitting that perfect spot until I can't hold back. I come hard, throwing my head back, as his hand smothers my mouth in a tight grip, muffling my screams of pleasure.

I'm panting hard as I come down from another mind-blowing orgasm, but he doesn't relent. Instead, he pulls out of me and drags me down, flipping me, before bending me over and pushing my face against the dresser. "Lift those hips for me, baby," he purrs, grabbing me and lifting them towards him before I can even move.

He drags his cock between my folds and up across my ass, coating me in my own juices. "You're fucking mine, Ells." He grunts desperately, his hand joining his cock as he strokes himself. His fingers sliding through my dripping pussy before he sinks his dick back inside me. He starts to fuck me slowly from behind as one of his wet fingers presses against my other hole. Fuck the intrusion shouldn't feel so tempting, but it does, and when I gasp in pleasure, I feel him swell inside of me. He wants this. *I want this.*

I start to push back against him, meeting his thrusts, as Marcus slowly slides a finger inside my ass, I instinctively clench around it. Holy fuck, it burns yet feels fucking deliciously sinful at the same time. My eyes roll into the back of my head as he fucks both my holes, feeling him hot and hard inside of me. I can barely catch my breath and my vision blurs to the point where I can barely see, as I come close to yet another orgasm.

"Baby, you're so tight back here. I can feel my own cock sliding inside of you." His words are raw and dirty, they push me close to the edge as I clench again. He groans, "Ells, keep doing that for me," I do it again and he moans louder. "Fuck Ells, you like me fucking both your holes?"

"Yes, God yes" I pant out and he picks up the pace. "Fuck Marcus, don't stop, I'm so close. More, please." I beg fumbling over the words in my pleasure induced haze. He doesn't make me ask again, and as he slowly adds another finger into my ass, I almost pass out in a mix of pleasure and pain. It hurts, yet I want it, want the pain, want the pleasure, want it all and I want it from him. Want to feel everything he's got to give me.

"Who does this pussy belong to?" He asks, but I can't form any more words, I just moan, but that isn't good enough for him. He begins to thrust his fingers harder into my ass as he fucks me even harder, "who's are you, Ells?"

He thrusts his fingers one last time before dragging them out and I come hard with a loud cry, "yours!" I shout as he moans loudly, and I can tell he almost came himself. He grabs both my arms and pulls them behind my back, holding them in place with one of his hands, as he pulls my torso towards his chest. His other hand comes around to grip my throat as he delivers fucking punishing hard thrusts into me as he chases his own release.

"Don't. Ever. Fucking. Leave. Me. Again." He speaks each word with a brutal thrust before he spills inside of me.

Another weight lifts off my chest as we both fall forward onto the dresser, panting and breathless and perfectly satisfied. I honestly didn't know if I would ever get to have this again. Not just the sex, but feeling him, holding him and just being with him. It's all I want, time with him, time with Cassie, time with my family. Yet I can't help thinking that, as long as Elliot and Greg are still out there, we are living on borrowed time.

How do you live when so many still need to die?

Chapter 23

ELLE

When I wake up again, I am back in bed spooning Cassie. Marcus is curled around me, and Asher is sitting on the other side of Cass, with his laptop open, tapping away. I feel even more settled than I did when I woke up earlier. Three of the most important people in my life are all within touching distance and I feel happier than I thought I could, especially given everything that's gone on. I sigh in contentment and Ash's eyes immediately find mine.

"Hey," he whispers with the same sad tortured expression I have become accustomed to back on his face. It doesn't matter that Cassie is here with us and safe. He will wear that expression until he chases his father and brother into the pits of hell.

"Hey, how'd you sleep?" I ask and I'm greeted with a slight teasing smile.

"Not as good as you, apparently." He wiggles his eyebrows at me, and I can't help but laugh at him as I hide my blush. It's a gesture I've never seen on his usually serious face, but it's certainly a welcome one.

"Ash." I squeak back and he laughs at my awkwardness.

"What? Maybe keep it down next time, Hells Bells, some of us were actually trying to sleep." He teases and I can feel the burn of my embarrassment all over my face.

Marcus groans from behind me, "maybe keep it down now because some of us are still trying to sleep."

"Sorry, Riviera," He snorts in response, "I didn't realize how much beauty sleep the King of the South Side needed."

"Eurghhh, I remember why I hated you when we were kids now." Marcus grunts in response. My embarrassment quickly turns to shock as I listen to their light, back and forth banter. When the fuck did they stop wanting to completely kill each other?

I don't get a chance to ask before Marcus sits up slightly and snuggles into my neck, planting a kiss there. "Morning, baby."

"River?" Cassie asks as she stirs awake.

"Yeah, it's me, little one." He replies without pause and she smiles wide rubbing her tired eyes.

I'm still so wary, just waiting for her to cry or break down and tell me something awful happened, but she seems completely fine. Like she just went and had a little vacation. The most dangerous and anxiety-inducing vacation ever.

"Did we have a sleepover?" She asks and Asher snorts again. I give him the death glare as Marcus laughs behind me.

"Yeah, princess, we all had a sleepover because we missed you so much." I say brushing her hair from her forehead and leaning down to give her a kiss.

"So fun!" She exclaims excitedly as she sits up, "can we do it again when Santa comes?" She pleads and I falter.

Fuck. It's almost Christmas. I didn't keep track of what time it was, let alone what day, while she was gone. Shit. We have so much fucking work to do. I need to make sure this is the best Christmas she has ever had.

Marcus doesn't miss a beat, "of course we can, whatever you want."

Her eyes widen as she looks at me, "really Mommy?"

I smile, "whatever you want baby."

She throws herself at me cuddling me just as tight as she did last night and once again, I breathe her in. I will never allow myself to take one cuddle for granted, when I know what it's like to be without them.

A knock on the bedroom door breaks our moment and Asher yells that the door is open and a few seconds later, Arthur pops his head round. If he's surprised to find us all together like this, he doesn't show it.

Just smiles and says, "just thought I'd see if my little spitfire wanted some chocolate chip pancakes."

"Yesssss!" She screams, bouncing off the bed and running towards him. He scoops her up and cuddles her. A huge smile plastered on his face, he's happy our family is whole again.

He focuses back on us. "Anything for you guys?"

"Yeah, we'll be out in a minute." I say with a nod moving to sit up and he offers me a mock salute and shutting the door behind him as he leaves.

I huff as I flop back down covering my eyes with my arm, trying not to panic at letting Cassie out of my sight, which is absurd. She is literally with her Grandpa in the next room, but I can't help the anxiety that crawls across my body like a bunch of spiders.

"I feel it too." Ash whispers. I move my arm to look at him and he continues, "the fear, wanting to keep her right next to me where I can see her. Even though she is perfectly safe. Yeah, I feel it too." He exhales deeply and I'm glad I don't have to be alone in my feelings. I think we will probably feel like this for a while or at least until there is no longer a threat against her. Question is what do we do about that threat?

"Should we leave?" I ask, not really aiming my question at any one of them in particular. "Do we just take her, run and never look back."

I feel Ash shrug, while Marcus remains silent, "It was a close call." Ash says. Yeah, real fucking close. "But does leaving really solve anything?"

"She'd be out of danger." I shrug back.

"Could you really do that? Leave behind your revenge and move on, knowing they're still out there?" Ash replies.

"Yes." *No.* I don't know. All I know is I almost lost my daughter thanks to my revenge, but hundreds of others will continue to lose theirs if we do nothing.

"What do you think?" I focus on Marcus and he looks shocked that I would direct my question at him,

He looks to Ash, then back to me, "I think my opinion on it doesn't really matter." It's the first time I've ever seen a hint of sadness in his eyes, while he's been thinking about Cassie. He doesn't realize how serious I am about us. He is it for me, and if he's a part of my life, then he's a part of her's too. Always.

"Please don't start being a whiny bitch again. I thought we were past it." Asher huffs at him and I have to smile. "I'm family, you're family, we are all fucking family, everyone gets a vote." He adds on and I don't miss the shock on Marcus' face that Ash sees him that way. It's how I've always seen the two of them but having them both here now. My best friend and the man I love. It's everything.

"I think leaving isn't as easy as it sounds." Marcus shrugs.

"Why?" It isn't so much my curiosity that asks the question, but my feelings. Would Marcus not be willing to leave his hometown?

"Zack." He glares like the answer is obvious, but when neither Ash nor I say anything, he continues. "Clearly the Donovan's know you are with him and well he's Zack Royton, tech billionaire. It's not like he can go into hiding."

He's right. Of course, he is. Zack isn't someone who can just go and disappear. He has a company and people that rely on him. Even if we ran, how far would we have to go for someone not to recognize him.

"Zack isn't the only issue," I muse out loud. Having Cassie back reminds me that someone else is still missing their daughter. "Elliot took the President of the HCMC's daughter. That's how he keeps them in line."

Ash frowns, "Connor O'Sullivan?" He questions, and I nod. "I wasn't aware he had a daughter."

"It was a well-guarded secret; her name is Rebecca." I tell them "she's at the Mayor's house."

"Fuck." Marcus curses and it's my exact thoughts too. Getting to her, would be the hardest thing to do.

"She's not our responsibility," I argue without much value, because I know how much I want to save her. But is she worth risking us all?

"That's a big fucking risk." Ash huffs, mirroring my thoughts. "Leaving doesn't sound so hard now."

"It would be hard, but if we had help." I think about the note I found in the treehouse.

"What help could we possibly require that we don't already have?" Asher questions but before I can answer there is another knock at the door.

This time when I shout, 'come in', we are greeted with Logan as he whistles, "Damnnnn, sis, this is my kind of party. Where was my invite?"

Marcus pretends to grab me possessively, "watch it, Royton."

He rolls his eyes. "Calm down, lover boy, I'm hardly gonna mack on my own sister." He purrs, tossing me a wink, "besides, I'll take my little psycho over here any day." He adds gesturing to Asher and for the first time ever I'm sure I see a slight blush on Ash's face.

He covers it quick enough that I can't be sure before replying, "in your dreams, Logan."

"Every damn night, dark prince." He purrs back using Lincoln's nickname for him and I can't help but laugh.

He switches his attention to me, "don't know what you're laughing at King, we all heard your late-night activities, loud and clear."

He starts motioning thrusts and I almost die of embarrassment. I throw a pillow at his head before stalking to the bathroom and slamming the door to block out the chorus of laughter coming from all three of them. *Fuckers.*

Chapter 24

MARCUS

We spend the rest of the morning together as a family. One huge, dysfunctional yet somehow perfectly fitted together family. Arthur and Helen put on a huge spread of food and we are kept entertained by stories of Zack and the twins' childhood and what it was like when Elle joined them. Max chips in with stories about his school days with Zack, and me and the guys add our own stories about some of the foster homes we were housed in together. It's a perfect morning after the terrible week we've all endured.

Elle keeps Cassie in her lap the whole morning as they eat, laugh and play. Asher never leaves their side for more than a minute. I catch him multiple times just staring at them with a concerned look on his face. A look that tells me this isn't over, not for him and I can't help but feel the same. We almost lost both of them and the threat to them is still out there. How can we settle when we not only know that, but also know they won't stop until that they have them. Not unless someone else stops them first.

The rest of the day is spent turning the house into Santa's grotto. There are multiple trees and decorations everywhere. I have no idea where it all came from or how it got here so fast, but I can only presume from the smile on Helen's face that she is used to pulling off the impossible to keep her family happy. It isn't long before a few of Max's security guys pile back into the house with boxes and bags filled with gifts. Max, Tyler, and Liam will be staying with us for Christmas, but the rest of his guys leave tomorrow morning to spend Christmas Eve and Christmas Day with their families. The house isn't on Donovan's radar and it's completely secure. Mix that with us all staying here together under the best security system money can buy, well it's safe to say we feel protected enough to relax a little.

Elle hasn't spoken about anything other than having the perfect Christmas for Cassie and I don't blame her. I don't know what is going to happen once Christmas is over, but for now I am happy to just be here with her, with everyone. She tucked Cassie into bed and then came to my room, where we proceeded to rip each other's clothes off. We fucked hard and fast in the shower, then long and slow in bed, and once my girl was finally satisfied, she left to go back to Cassie. I was only in bed an hour before I found myself creeping down the hall and quietly opening their door, only to find Asher shaking his head at me with a smile, as I climbed in on the other side of them.

When we wake up the next day it's Christmas Eve and it follows a similar pattern to yesterday. We have a big family breakfast and then us guys are all put to work in the spare room, wrapping presents and building toys. My Christmas Eves usually consisted of sneaking out of whatever foster home I was in and heading to my dad's grave to get drunk. Last year was a little better as I had the guys with me, but this year is completely different. I'm sitting building a dollhouse while my brothers build a bike. Something I didn't think I would ever see, at least not for another ten years. But here we are, and I have never felt more at home.

Elle and the girls are in the kitchen making gingerbread houses while Helen preps all the trimmings for tomorrow's dinner. Everything feels so mundane and normal, just family stuff. Yet the ache in my chest has never felt such relief. I haven't been this happy in years and when I lost my dad, I didn't think I would ever be this happy again. It really is the perfect day.

When evening comes, I go in search of the girls and find the cutest sight I've ever seen. Elle is sitting in the center of the huge corner sofa with Cassie in her lap, they are wearing matching red pajamas, and both have their hair braided. Lily is on Elle's left with Helen next to her and are both wearing exactly the same outfit too. It's like the picture-perfect family photo. I can't help but smile at them.

Cassie is the first to spot me and she dives off Elle's lap running towards me, "Look, River." She stops in front of me and does a little twirl to show off what she is wearing, "Christmas jammies." She squeals and my cheeks hurt from how big I smile.

"You look beautiful princess," I say, scooping her into my arms and heading towards the sofa, dropping down next to Elle on her right. "Just like your mom." I add, leaning in to give Elle a kiss on the cheek causing a blush to coat her cheeks. Doesn't matter that I've seen her naked, covered her body with my mouth, every time I give her a compliment she still blushes.

"We're watching Frozen." She squeals and I laugh. *Of course, we are.*

We wait a few more minutes for everyone else to arrive. Asher is the first to find us, coming right over and sitting next to me, and then Arthur comes in and drops down next to Helen. Lincoln enters with Logan trailing behind him and I don't miss the way Asher tracks them across the room. I have no idea what their dynamic is about, but there is definitely something there. Zack wheels himself in with Max and Liam, they help him from the chair to the sofa and give him some pillows to ensure he's comfy.

Jace is the last to arrive, looking around the room before he slinks over to a lone chair by the window and slumping into it. Tyler joins him and they quietly pass a bottle of whiskey between the two of them.

Elle hits play on the movie and by the time Elsa sings *Let it Go*, Cassie is fast asleep, so we switch the movie to Elf, giving us all something to laugh about. We have hot chocolate courtesy of Helen and homemade cookies that the girls made earlier in the day. It's the perfect Christmas Eve.

Once everyone is in bed, I help Arthur bring all the presents out of hiding and place them under the tree ready for morning. He told me I didn't need to help, but I can't help it, I have this energy burning inside of me, like I

216

just need to be doing something. I rearrange the presents three times after Arthur leaves to go to bed and that's where Zack finds me.

"I thought everyone was asleep." I look up from the box in my hand and shrug.

"I'm not ready yet." I can't help but feel like the words mean more than being ready for sleep.

"Me either." He replies simply, as he rolls his shoulders, wincing slightly at his injuries.

"How are you?" I ask awkwardly, realizing we haven't really spoken much.

"Sore, relieved, fucking pissed." He shrugs and I huff a laugh.

"What do you think is going to happen now?" Greg shot him, or one of his lackies did, wanted him dead, yet here he is, alive and well.

He looks at me, like he is gauging my reaction to whatever he is about to say, "I think this is far from over. I think that Greg will stop at nothing to have her." We both know the *her* he is talking about isn't Cassie. "I think he's a fucking psychopath that needs to be executed."

I laugh, I don't know why, I just can't help it and then he laughs too. "I never thought I'd have things in common with a girl's older brother." I say and he laughs harder, wincing again in pain.

"Fuck, I needed that," he adds when he finally stops. I smile again because I know exactly what he means. He moves to leave but stops first to add, "don't stay up too late, the girls will have us up at the crack of dawn." He says with a smile of his own and I nod as he leaves.

I finish up moving the presents one more time until I am happy with them, then take a drink of the milk and bite of cookie that Cassie left out for Santa before heading to bed. On my way back to the room I see someone pass in my peripheral heading down the hall towards the door. Instinct has me following before I can even think about it and when I round the corner, I find Asher reaching out to grip the handle on the front door.

"Going somewhere?" I ask and he startles slightly before sighing and turning round.

He's dressed head to toe in black with a Glock secured at his waist and bag in his hand. I raise my eyebrows at him, and he scowls.

"I just have a couple of things to take care of." He says hesitantly and I can tell he's on edge. More so than usual.

"What and those things need doing on Christmas Eve night when everyone is sleeping?" I want to make sure he knows how stupid that sounds.

He snaps, "Yes, they do," he moves to leave again before pausing and looking at me, "Do you wanna come with me?"

That is literally the last thing I expected him to say, but I take in his stance and attire again. The all black and the gun, the tense set of his jaw and his hunched together shoulders. Wherever he is going is somewhere dangerous. I give him a sharp nod, turning to run to my room, grabbing shoes, my jacket, and then a gun of my own, before heading back out to him. I follow him silently to one of the cars parked outside. We climb inside and drive away from the house. From our family.

We've been driving in silence for about twenty minutes, when I finally crack, "where the hell are we going?"

The corner of his mouth tips up in a cocky smile, "I knew you'd crack before we got there." I roll my eyes, "we are going to pay some old friends a visit." The way he spits the word friends tells me everything I need to know.

By the time we stop in front of a house just off of Riverside I can feel the tension rolling off him. Like it's taking everything in him to hold himself back. I don't recognize the house, so I wait for him to say something.

When he doesn't say anything or even move, I ask, "whose house is this?"

He snaps his gaze from the house to mine, "inside that house live two men, two of my brother's friends. Ken Andrews and Adam Kirkland." Their names don't sound familiar to me, so I still remain just as confused. Who the hell are they and why are we here?

When I don't say anything in response he continues, "Kirkland held both her arms down in a vice grip, he held them so tight he left bruises." His words turn my stomach, fuck I know exactly why we are here. "Andrews." he laughs, "Andrews is the one who dragged me into the room after my father found me, the proud look in his eyes still knocks me sick. He said he was glad I had found out on my own and that Greg would show me the ropes. Andrews laughed every time she cried. I got there too late, it only lasted for a couple of minutes, but it felt like a lifetime. And I couldn't do anything, nothing, but just stand there and pretend I was enjoying it. Now though, now I can do everything."

The fire starts to burn in my veins, the tension pulsing through my entire body. I know why he's here. I know why he invited me. Cloaked in black and armed with guns, ready to bring death on the men who hurt our girl. Vengeance happens tonight.

We move in unison as we exit the car and walk towards the house, both of us looking up and down the quiet street. It's dark and deserted like the reaper himself cleared our path for us, awaiting the justice we are about to serve. I can tell that Ash knows exactly where he is going and that we aren't just going in blind, because he pushes up towards a side door, quickly producing a lock picking kit. Fucking hell is everyone I know just a walking talking serial killer in the making? He quietly, and efficiently picks the lock, and gently pushes the door open.

I move in close behind him as we enter and we are greeted by complete darkness, but I trust Asher enough to follow his lead. We find both Ken and Adam passed out on the sofa with the soft glow of the television lighting up their ugly faces. I look to Ash and he is staring at them intently, like he can't quite decide how to make them suffer. He grinds his jaw before looking at me and nodding.

We step towards them and I raise my gun, but Asher moves before I can pull the trigger and cocks one of them with the gun startling him awake. He shoves his gloved hand across his mouth to muffle his scream, but it still wakes up the other guy. He startles, but I aim my gun at his head to ensure he doesn't move.

Both their eyes flare in recognition when they look at Asher and he removes his hand allowing the scum to speak.

"Asher, what the fuck man?" The one he hit says, but I can see the fear in his eyes already. He may be the youngest of the Donovan clan, but even I've heard the stories about the people who cross him. They disappear without a trace.

"Long time no see, Andrews." Ash drawls in the deadliest tone I've ever heard from him. Which means the guy I'm aiming my gun at is Adam Kirkland.

"What the fuck, Donovan. Does Greg know you're here?" Adam barks and I have to laugh, they really think they have an in with the heir to the Donovan name. I can tell from the look of the house they are staying in and their lack of knowledge about Ash, that they are exceptionally low on the food chain.

Ash smiles a sinister smile, "I will get to Greg eventually, but tonight is about you two." He says leaning down to get in their face and I watch Ken gulp.

"Remember how funny you found it, Kirkland? How you laughed as the tears ran down her cheeks? How you begged Greg to have a turn?" He grits each word out with such wrath, yet his whole body is completely calm, like he is completely at ease doing this.

"Wait, this is about King?" Adam asks in panicked confusion. "Fuck you care about one of your brother's whores for? Jealous?" He smiles thinking Asher will find it funny.

Asher smashes the gun into his face. "Like anything that disgusting piece of shit could ever do would make me jealous." He grits at him as Adam coughs, spitting out some blood. "But you were jealous, weren't you Kirkland? I remember how desperately you pleaded."

"Look man, you saw how Greg was. She belonged to him, no one else. His plans for her changed as soon as he had a taste of her."

Ash grits his teeth at his statement, but before he can react, I shoot Adam right in the stomach. His words setting fire to my fucking rage.

Asher does laugh now, sadistically, and loud before doing the same thing to Ken Andrews. Then shakes his head looking at me, "who knew you could be so much fun." His grin is infectious considering where we are and what we are doing.

He opens the bag and pulls out a little saw and my eyes flare wide. *What the fuck.*

Both the guys are gurgling in pain as the blood pours from their stomachs. Ignoring them, Asher quickly secures both of their wrists with cable ties, before injecting them with some shit that makes their bodies stop moving. I can see from their eyes they are still awake and aware, but completely fucking helpless. Asher steps back admiring his work and then he pulls out two little plastic bags. I panic as I remember back to when he said he would gift jars of cocks to Elle. Thankfully, he only cuts off one finger from each of them and drops them in the bags.

When I eye him, he shrugs tucking them away in his bag and packing up everything else apart from his guns. When he's satisfied, he looks at me with a nod and I know we are done here.

"For our girls?" He asks and I smile mirroring one of his own sadistic grins and reply with a nod, "for our girls."

We raise our guns at their heads, completely in sync. We look at one another and nod, both of us pulling the trigger at the same time and clocking them right between the eyes. See you in hell, fuckers.

Chapter 25

ELLE

Last Christmas I never would have imagined I would be here now. Celebrating not only with my family, but with Asher and Marcus here too. I would have laughed at just the thought of it. Yet here we are all sitting around a beautiful tree surrounded in gift wrap and presents with the happiest little girl in the world. We've been at this for hours now because every time she opens a gift, she squeals thank you and cuddles whoever gave it to her. I don't care if we sit here all day, all fucking week. Just as long as I get to see the smile on my baby girls face.

When she picks up a small blue box, she scrunches her nose up and I know she is wondering what is small enough to fit in it. My eyes flare wide when I spot Tiffany's packaging. I have no idea who it's from, but then Marcus speaks up.

"That's from me, princess, it goes with this one for your Mom." He says pulling a box from behind him and passing it over to me. I almost choke on my breath as I take it from him, and I can feel every eye in here on us.

"You're not planning on proposing are you, because I still think she is still too young for that." Zack jokes and Asher snorts a laugh. I give them both the death glare as Marcus looks at us in confusion.

I don't have time to explain as Cassie squeals, "same, Mommy!" She pushes through paper so she can come sit by me on the floor. I look at Marcus and smile and then hesitantly start to open the box as Cassie opens hers.

What I find brings tears to my eyes. Inside is a delicate silver chain with a little star pendant that has the words 'make a wish' engraved on it. I swallow trying to clear the lump in my throat but it's no use.

"Wow, that's beautiful honey." Helen says as she leans in on my left to admire it.

I look back up at Marcus, "River, I don't know what to say. It's beautiful, thank you."

He smiles, glancing at Zack quickly, before looking back at me, "just something to remind you I'm always with you." I smile and just for a moment, I wish it were just the two of us so I could tell him how much this means to me, but he seems to understand.

"Wow!" Cassie gasps and I bring my attention to where she is holding a small, roped bracelet with a little star hanging off it. The only difference is hers is engraved with the words 'pinky promise'.

"Marcus you really didn't have to do this." I say in awe at how much these must have cost him.

Cassie isn't of the same attitude as she runs across the room and throws her arms around his neck, "thank you, River." She says into his neck and he pats her back in response.

"Anytime, little one. Yours is to remind you that I will always come for you."

She smiles, "you're a superhero just like Daddy and Linc." She beams at him and his smile is so carefree and easy towards her that it reminds me of when we were kids.

"Wow, burn little rascal." Jace replies and we all laugh.

"Don't worry, Conrad. We are just too pretty to be superheroes." Logan offers him with a wink, and I roll my eyes.

The rest of the day is just as perfect, all of us eating and enjoying the most amazing dinner. It's the best Christmas I've ever had and tucking in my girl is the icing on the cake. She's snuggling a brand-new orange unicorn from the guys and an embroidered blanket from Asher. She doesn't realize how protected she is going to be, even more than before. After staring at her for a while I give her one last kiss and turn to leave only to find Lily standing in the doorway.

When she sees me, she smiles awkwardly like she didn't want to be caught here. We've always had a weird relationship, she isn't an incredibly open person and is not someone that is easy to get to know, but we found common ground in Cassie. I know she would have been distraught when she was gone.

"You okay, Lils?" I ask.

"Yeah, sorry. Didn't mean to barge in, just wanted to check in before I go to bed." She rocks from foot to foot, and I can sense her anxiety.

"How about I kick the guys out tonight and you have a sleepover with us." I ask hoping she will give in and accept.

She scrunches her face up and it reminds me of how Cassie does it, it's probably where she learnt it. "A sleepover? What are we twelve?" She snorts a laugh.

I roll my eyes, "no, we're sisters and that's what sisters do. Besides Cassie would love to wake up next to her aunt Lils." I see straight away that my words impact her, she loves the Roytons, always has, but she still always lingers on the outside. Like she doesn't deserve to be happy after what happened to her parents. It's such a familiar feeling, one I know well. I want us to be better than we are now, especially with everything that is going on.

Her face softens and I know the mention of Cassie is what will have persuaded her. "Yeah, alright then." She smiles before adding, "but you better tell the guys, because if I wake up with Ash's dick against my ass, I'll be the one getting stabby". She huffs and we both laugh.

"Did someone say Ash's dick?" Logan pops his head in and then Lily and I both laugh even more. He looks confused having never seen us share a joke, "everything okay?"

"Yeah, we are just arranging a little girls' night." I say.

"Right," he drags the word out, "well don't start now, the adults have all retired to their rooms for the night so I thought us kids could play a few drinking games." He waggles his eyebrows at us, and I can see he's hiding his own anxiety just like Lily was. She just needs some comfort, and he just needs some fun.

"Sure, sounds great Lo." I reply and he beams at me before holding both his arms up for us to grab.

"Well let's not keep the little psycho and the Rebels waiting ladies."

An hour later we are all relatively buzzed as we sit around the huge corner sofa just laughing and having fun. It's the perfect end to a perfect Christmas and I thank every star in the sky for how this week has turned out.

I'm practically sitting in Marcus' lap as he curls his arms round my waist from behind, occasionally nuzzling into my neck and kissing me there. Lily and Jace are sitting on the floor looking moody as they pass a bottle of whiskey between them without speaking. Logan is sitting next to Lincoln where I see him keep whispering stuff into his ear, causing a slight smirk to tug on Lincs mouth. I don't know if they are becoming a thing, but they do seem to be getting closer and I know I'm not the only one who has noticed. Ash keeps glaring at them which just makes Logan do it even more. I have no fucking idea what that means.

Eventually Ash slams his glass on the table and stalks away. I see Lincoln frown and looks as if he is ready to follow him, but Ash soon comes back holding a black box in his hands. He walks right over to me and places it on the table in front of me, before sitting back down.

"Erm, this for me?" I am confused because we already swapped Christmas gifts this morning. He nods, "Ash, you got me enough already."

"Trust me, you will want this more." He says and I feel Marcus tense slightly behind me. I frown and then move forward until I am sitting on the end of the sofa. I reach out and pick up the box, it feels light, like it might be empty, and it only adds to my confusion.

I slide off the lid and inside is a small black envelope with a card inside, I pull out the card and there are just two words on it '*never again*'. I frown looking at Ash, but he is just staring at the box. The tension in the air thickens as everyone seems to sit up to try see what's inside. I put the card on the table and then pull apart the tissue paper and find two human fingers.

"Christ, Ash!" I startle at the sight and then gag at the smell, "Who the fuck do these belong to?" I don't even want to ask how he got them.

"Ken Andrews and Adam Kirkland are dead." He says and I watch his eyes flash to Marcus before he adds, "I couldn't find Brett, but I will and when I do, I'll kill him too." I sigh and go to speak, but he holds his hand up to stop me. "I know you're done Hells Bells and I understand why. Just like I know you'll understand why I can't be done. Not until they're all dead."

I sigh because I do know. I know that he can't be done just like I know I can't be done. This won't be over until they're all gone. I sigh, "Brett is already dead." His eyes flash to mine and then he smirks with a glint of pride in his eyes. "I shot him three times."

"Of course, you did. I'm sorry I didn't bring those two to you, but I needed to do this," he looks at Marcus again, "we needed to do this."

I turn to Marcus and see him looking right at me waiting for my reaction, "you helped him with this?" He nods slowly and then picks up the card that Asher left in the box, smiling as he reads it.

He passes it back over to me, squeezing my hand as he does. "Never again, Ells."

"So now what?" Lincoln asks and I want to laugh. Superman is always swooping in and needing the answers to everything. I look at the rest of them and they are all looking at me. I know they will go along with whatever I decide, even Lily has a determination on her face like never before.

"They won't stop." I start, "I know Greg, more than I'd like to and I know he won't give up, he will just keep coming, even if I do run." I turn the card over and over again in my hands just to settle my nerves. I keep thinking about the danger I put Cassie in by coming back here, but even if we left now, she wouldn't be safe.

"This is more of a game to him now." Ash agrees. "I knew the moment I saw the look on his face that night, that things had changed. He wanted more, craved it."

I nod at his words, he's right. "Look at what they have done." I shake my head as memories assault me, "they raped me, beat me, shot my brother, stabbed my friend, kidnapped my daughter and that's just the tip of the iceberg." I list their crimes against me, reciting it like it's nothing but a grocery list. "That doesn't even include every other crime they have committed. How many girls have there been? How many were raped, or killed?" I look at Jace and see the glisten in his eyes as the tears for his sister threaten to fall.

I think of her and Rebecca O'Sullivan. I know they are just two of many girls, but they aren't just nameless pawns. It's too late for Rachel, but not Rebecca. I can't forget her. If I ran, her face would always be in my mind taunting me.

"I can't leave. Not while they stay." My words aren't much louder than a whisper, but their impact is felt by everyone in the room. All of them nodding and sitting up a little straighter. Like they are readying for our next move.

"Where do you want to start?" Ash asks and I start to tell them everything I did while I was away. How I killed Joseph Kavanagh, my run in with the HCMC and the full story of what I did to Brett. They all listen and none of them seem surprised, well apart from how I handled the Crows.

"Where did you sleep?" Marcus asks, and I have to smile, all of the dark and twisted things I have just told him, and his main concern is where I laid my head.

"I didn't really," I don't want to admit how little I was looking after myself, "I did spend one night in our old tree house though." He smiles in wonder and then I remember what I found there, "oh shit, hold on a second." I rush from the room and dig out the jeans I was wearing that night from the bag I still haven't emptied and pull out the note I found.

I walk back into the room and hand it over to Marcus, "I found this in our spot, I'm pretty sure it's from your dad."

Marcus scrutinizes it closely, "yeah that's definitely my dad's handwriting, but I have no idea who he's talking about. I don't remember anyone named Beth."

"Beth?" Ash questions with a gasp holding his hand out for the note. Marcus reaches out passing it to him and he snatches it up, reading and rereading it multiple times.

"Ash do you know who the note is talking about? Do you know Beth."

He drags his gaze up to mine and exhales, "Yeah, I know Beth."

Chapter 26

ELLE

I have no idea where we are going. Ash is driving, I'm sitting next to him and Marcus is in the back. Max and Elijah are following in the car behind us for extra security, but none of us have a clue where we are heading. Asher has been cagey ever since he read the note from Michael last night. He said he knew who Beth was and then he got up and left the room. None of us knew what to do and I didn't see him again until this morning when he walked in the kitchen with Max and Eli saying it was time to go. It's the first time we have left Cassie and I didn't want to go, but I could tell from the look in his eyes he needed me. So here we are.

We drive for about two hours and when we pull into a gated community, I sit up straight, knowing we must be close. Asher shoves a wad of cash into the hand of the security guard, and he waves us right in. Money really can buy fucking anything. We stop in front of a beautiful white house lined with trees and a big blue front door. I turn to ask Ash more questions now we have finally arrived, but he is already getting out of the car. I look to Marcus who mouths 'what the fuck' before we both get out and follow him.

We have to rush to catch up to him and by the time we make it to him the door is already swinging open. It's a woman who looks to be in her early forties. Beautiful and blonde, dressed in a casual pair of linen pants and a denim shirt. She's got a pair of oven gloves folded in her hands like she just took them off and when her gaze lands on Asher her face falls.

She looks like she has seen a ghost. "Asher?" Her voice is barely audible as she chokes out his name.

"Hi, Mom." He replies.

My eyes nearly pop out of my head. Beth is Elizabeth Donovan, Asher's mom. She has never been in the picture and I didn't dig up anything about her, I just presumed she was dead. Nobody ever spoke about her, especially Ash, yet here she stands. I have never been more confused and when she swings her gaze to me and Marcus, I see recognition flow through her.

"My god, you look just like them." She looks between us, "you both do." That's when it hits me that she means our parents. She must have known Michael and Sarah.

"We're not here for a trip down memory lane, we need something. Can we come in?" Asher snaps and his shortness is even sharper than usual. The tension between them is thick. The bitterness in his voice cuts me deep.

She looks at him hesitantly, before looking over our shoulders and no doubt eyeing the guards we came with. "Where is your father? Does he know you're here?"

234

She asks and I can hear the undercurrent of panic in her tone.

"Elliot knows nothing about where I am." He bites back and she softens slightly and nods. She steps back and welcomes us into her home.

I look over my shoulder and offer a nod to Max and follow the guys inside. She leads us to a living room and gestures for us to sit on the sofa there. The room is decorated in soft creams and golds with plants giving it a pop of color. I notice there are no pictures or personal effects anywhere, and when I bring my gaze back to her, she is staring intently at Asher. He is still standing and gazing around the room with a scowl. I can't imagine what is going through his head right now. All I can think is why did he never talk about her? Has she been here all this time? Why did she leave? And more importantly why didn't she take Asher with her when she left?

"Can I get anyone a drink, some iced tea? Coffee maybe?" She's standing in the entrance which I guess leads into the kitchen, looking like she would rather be anywhere but here.

"How did you know Michael Riviera?" Asher barks at her, not wasting any time to get to the point and she sighs, coming into the room fully and sitting down. She looks at him until he sighs too and comes to sit next to me and Marcus.

"Michael and I grew up together, before my family left Black Hallows. We lost touch for a while, but he was always there for me and Sarah." She looks at Marcus, "how is he?"

Marcus grimaces slightly, looking at Asher before admitting solemnly, "he's dead. Almost four years ago now."

"Elliot murdered him. Shot him right in the head in the foyer of his own home. Leaving Marcus to find his body." Asher bites out in disgust, and I see her thick swallow as she fights against her emotions. A lone tear tracking down her cheek.

"I'm so sorry. He was a good man. The best man." She whispers.

I reach into my bag for the note, "He left this behind, we only just found it."

She takes it and inhales a deep breath as she reads it. She stands on shaky legs leaving the room and then returning a few minutes later with a big brown box. It's slightly worn, like it has been used or touched multiple times. She sets it on the coffee table in front of us.

She puts her hands on top of it, gripping it like it's a lifeline before she locks eyes with Asher. "I know I should have taken you with me, I regret that decision every day."

"I'm not here to cry about why Mommy left me," he spits bitterly, "I'm here to protect my best friend and our daughter."

The words cut right through her and she stutters out, "you have a daughter?" She looks between me and Ash and then takes in Marcus' arm around me and I see the confusion. She has no idea of the dynamic here.

When Asher doesn't respond I jump in, "her name is Cassie, she's three." I pull my phone out and show her a picture.

"She's beautiful." She hesitates and I can practically hear the questions she wants to ask so I answer them before she has to ask.

"When I was fourteen, I was kidnapped and raped. The result was my daughter." I pause reaching out to clasp Ash's hand in mine. "Our daughter."

"It was Greg." Ash adds in a cold tone, "in case you were wondering."

She closes her eyes like she's in physical pain. Putting her hands on the box again. "Your father is an extremely sick man. Always has been. I didn't see it until it was too late. By that time Greg was already following in his footsteps." She shakes her head, "I didn't know what to do. There had already been so many girls that I'd missed."

Her admission should shock me, but I think I am numb to anything I learn when it comes to the Donovan's.

"So, what you did nothing?" Asher snaps in disgust.

"I did the only thing I could do. I took this and I ran." She sounds ashamed and I want to feel sorry for her, but I can't imagine ever leaving a child defenseless against a monster like Elliot. She left Asher behind, left him to be surrounded in darkness and grow up to become who he is now. How different would his life have been if he'd have escaped with her?

"My dad helped you, didn't he?" Marcus interrupts my thoughts, and she nods.

"I didn't know who else to turn to. Michael was still in Black Hallows and I knew he had helped Sarah out years before, so I knew he would help me too."

"How did he help my Mom?" I interrupt, but she ignores me and focuses on Ash.

"I watched your father for weeks. He was taking you boys everywhere. It's like he knew what I was planning. I waited until you were all out of the house and I broke into the cellar." She stops closing her eyes like the memories are haunting her, "what I saw I won't ever forget. I found this." She pats the box, "then I planned my escape. I knew Elliot would let me go, especially when he knows I have this. But I knew he would never let you or your brother go. So, I made the hardest decision I've ever made. I ran and left you behind."

"What's in the box?" Is all he responds.

She sighs pulling the lid off and pulling out a huge binder, "evidence." She mutters before handing it over to him. He takes it flipping through it and all I see are newspaper clippings, missing persons posters, and what look like bank statements.

"What is all this?" He questions as he takes in every page.

"It's everything I could find." She shrugs, but I can see how long she has been holding onto this. "We moved around a lot, Elliot said it was for work and I guess for him it was. I didn't realize it at the time, but whenever he felt the heat got too much, we moved. But he kept this box, like a sick little box of trophies of all the girls he'd sold."

Asher continues to flip through it but I can't bear to look at it any longer, there are so many pictures in there. Elliot has kept track of every girl he's ever fucking taken. I shouldn't be shocked, but this is sick even for him.

"These all look like girls without families or runaways." Ash muses and I know we had already come to that conclusion, that prior to me, he only ever seemed to take girls that nobody cared about.

"Safer that way," she mumbles and then sighs, "from what I gathered he would use Greg to lure in the younger girls his age and they would do whatever with them and then they'd disappear."

I fight down the bile as I remember what they did to me and what has been done to hundreds of others. All without justice. I can't ignore that. There is just too much to let it go and it's worse now, before he got away with it because it was girls nobody gave a fuck about. Now he gets away with it because he found his people. Just as sick and fucked up as he is and with power like he wouldn't believe. He thinks he's untouchable.

"So why ruin that by taking Elle?" Marcus wonders aloud.

"That was personal." Beth responds mindlessly before I see her eyes widen like she's said too much. She knows more, more than I ever could have anticipated. Ash doesn't miss it either and calls it out straight away.

"Why do you think Elle was so important to them? She was just a fucking kid and a King. Taking her was reckless even for him."

She blows out a breath and I know she doesn't want to tell us, but I also know she can see how much of

239

a force her son is. He won't let this go. "It was never about her," she replies looking at me now, "this was set in motion before she was even born."

"That doesn't make any sense." I quip back.

"Not to you. It all comes back to Elliot and Sarah."

I frown, "Impossible. They didn't even know each other until Elliot moved to Black Hallows."

"Trust me, they did. Sarah comes from a powerful family. You know that better than anyone. She was wild, never did what they said. They went away one summer and when she came back, she was different, quieter, calmer. I barely saw her and then a year later she was being forced into an arranged marriage with your father."

"What has any of that got to do with Elliot, or Elle for that matter?" Asher questions and she glances at him before looking back to me.

"Elle was payment. A child for a child." She says the words slowly like they are going to make any sense, but none of us pick up on whatever she means.

"Stop speaking in fucking riddles!" Asher shouts and I can see the anger in him rising. Being here is not good for him, it's digging up too much of the past. We need to go.

She takes a deep breath and then says four words that change everything.

"Zack is Elliot's son."

Chapter 27

ASHER

The drive back to Hallows is silent. None of us know what to say. We thought we knew everything; was so sure we had all the pieces of the puzzle. Turns out we have been playing a game we didn't even know the fucking rules to. No wonder we were never a step ahead of them, this has been in the making longer than we thought.

My father raped Sarah King when she was sixteen. They met on vacation and because my grandparents had just come into their huge fortune, they were trying to rub shoulders with old money families to gain status. Elliot spent the week chasing her and when she refused, he decided to take her anyway. When she went home, she tried to forget about it, until she realized she was pregnant with Zack. She turned to the only friend she had left, Michael Riviera. Michael told her he could send Zack to a nice family and nobody would ever know. That family just so happened to be Arthur and Helen. They hid the teenage pregnancy scandal and then Sarah was forced into an arranged marriage with Jonathan who took her powerful name.

She knew, knew how depraved and evil he was, yet became friends with him anyway, or was she forced? Jonathan King is the mystery here, did he know about what Elliot did? Did he care? Does he know about Zack? So much information and still so many unanswered questions.

All of that and the only thing I can truly think about is that I have a brother. A good brother, a brother that isn't a total fucking psychopath. A brother that my fucking other brother tried to kill. Zack is the one who found a way to reach out to me after Elle disappeared from town. He let me know she was okay and safe and thanked me for getting her out. We've gotten on well all this time and now I find out he's my older brother, my eldest brother. Fuck. The thought hits me like a bulldozer. Zack Royton is the true Donovan heir.

"That's why Greg tried to kill him." I mutter smacking the steering wheel, I should have fucking known.

"Huh?" Elle asks swinging to look at me.

"Zack's the oldest," I say, and she looks at me in confusion, "he's the heir." I confirm and her eyes widen as I conclude what she hadn't yet put together. "That's why Greg wanted him dead."

"Fuck!" She shouts and I know she understands now more than ever. This isn't over, it can't be. They won't stop, so we can't stop.

The rest of the drive is silent and I'm grateful, I have too many thoughts swirling around in my head, too many plans. Greg and our father have been ten steps ahead for too long. It's time we take the upper hand. We already have, we got Cass back. She's safe, Zack's alive and we're all together. I don't even register getting into the gates of the house, pulling up and getting out until Elle speaks.

"I'll go inside and gather Zack, Arthur and Helen." She says squeezing my shoulder softly before heading towards the house.

"Get the twins too." I say back to her and she pauses and gives me another nod before disappearing inside with Marcus. I know they need to know, so might as well tell them all at once. We are all in this together.

I don't know how long I stand there, but apparently, it's long enough for the help to find me. "Everything go okay?" Lincoln asks and I close my eyes in frustration, the last person I want to see me freaking out right now is him.

"Fine," I grit out.

"You don't look fine," he starts, and I open my eyes and glare at him, "I mean you always look fine," he adds and then he pulls a weird face, I scrutinize him closely, but can't put my finger on it. He huffs, "what I meant to say is you look stressed."

I take a deep breath, I don't see the point in hiding it, he's going to find out. Elle trusts him, fuck even I trust him at this point. "Elliot is Zack's father."

He frowns and I watch as he tries to put the pieces together, trying to get to the conclusion of what I just told him. Good luck, I've got most of the answers and I still don't know how we fucking got here.

"Hmm," he finally says, and I snap.

"Hmm? What the fuck does hmm mean?"

He laughs a little, in that way he always does with just a little tip of his mouth, "Nothing, it's just I can actually see it. You and Zack being brothers."

"How is that even possible. We didn't even grow up together, we don't look alike."

He shakes his head, "strong, caring, loyal, would do anything for the ones they love. Ring any bells?"

I hadn't really thought about Zack and I being similar, never had a reason to, but now I am it makes my chest feel a little lighter. I always thought everyone in my family was a piece of shit. My mom left us, and my father and brother are literal murderers. Yet I have a brother who is smart, compassionate, and completely devoted to his family.

I offer him a slight smile as thanks and head into the house to find Elle and the others. They are all sitting in the living room and by the time I enter I can feel the thick tension in the air. Arthur and Helen are sitting with their hands clasped, Lily is in the corner with her usual frown and Logan is lying across two cushions like nothing is a big deal. Zack is in his wheelchair next to the sofa where Marcus and Elle are sitting.

He looks between them and me and then sighs, "you know about Elliot?" He asks and Elle's head snaps towards him in surprise. "About him being my biological father, I mean?" Now it's Lily and Logans turn to look shocked, but I note Helen and Arthur don't look surprised.

"You knew about this?" She asks in disbelief.

"I suspected." He confirms, looking at me warily.

"Since when?" Elle demands.

"Since the night Greg shot me." He shrugs slightly, "he said something about family resemblance and at the time I thought he meant to you. Then a few other things made me realize he was referring to himself."

"You are nothing fucking like him." She cries, "don't even think that for a second."

"I know. When I woke up, I had Liam dig into Sarah's past and I found a crossover with Elliot from when they were teenagers. Didn't take much to figure out the rest." I can see he's had time to digest this. Well, I haven't.

"And when were you planning on telling us?" I blurt, breaking my silence.

"Honestly? I don't know." He sighs and I know he means that. "This changes everything."

"It changes nothing." Arthur says, "you are our son, always have been, always will be,"

"That's not what I meant, dad. You know you guys are the only parents I will ever recognize, but we all thought this whole thing started because of what happened to Elle. But we were wrong."

"What does this all mean?" Marcus asks and I see the flash of Donovan DNA across Zack's face then for the first time ever.

Zack sits up straight looking at Marcus, Elle and then eventually me, "It means we're going to kill them, all of them. Before they kill us."

Chapter 28

MARCUS

E very single time I think the Donovan's and their sick list of crimes can't get any worse, they prove me wrong. Monsters like Elliot and Greg aren't made, they are born. That pathological need to hurt people ingrained in them from the very beginning. I want to end them, stand over their dead bodies in victory and fucking cheer. I need the thrill of making them bleed, the one I got with Asher on Christmas Eve as I watched the life drain from those two bastards that helped Greg. I understand now more than ever why Elle came back, why she had to do all of this. It's the only acceptable justice.

Zack Royton. Zack King. Zack Donovan. Not once since I met Zack had it ever crossed my mind that Elliot Donovan could be his father. A King and a Donovan. What a toxic fucking mixture. A child for a child, that's what Beth said. So that means Elliot found out about Zack years ago and instead of looking for him like a normal fucking human being, his solution was to kidnap his little sister and use her to punish Sarah. We all thought that night triggered a chain of events that would change everything forever but turns out this was all in motion before we even existed. Zack Royton, Elle's brother, heir to the fucking Donovan throne. What the fuck do we do with that?

I think it's safe to say we have all undoubtedly decided that this isn't over. We are moving forwards with Elle's plans for revenge and hopefully this time we get no more surprises. We are completely off radar at the safe house, but school starts again in a week and then what?

We are all together in the living room including most of Max's guys who have made it back after taking Christmas with their families. The only people missing are Cassie and Lily who went to bed a couple of hours ago.

"Are we going back?" Lincoln asks and everyone looks to Elle.

She huffs a long slow breath, like she is still thinking about her response, but we all know her answer. We knew it the moment she got Cassie back, the moment she saw Lincoln's blood, the moment she found out she wasn't the first King to be raped by a Donovan. The moment her fourteen-year-old innocence was stolen in the black of night. It isn't over until she says it's over.

"Yeah," she sighs, "we're going back. We aren't letting them win. If Greg wants me, he can come and get me. I'll be armed and waiting."

"The twins will have to stay here. They can't be that far away without protection." Arthur says with a no-nonsense tone and I see Logan's nod in agreement. College isn't even on his mind right now. He wants revenge just as much as Elle. She smashed into their lives and changed the course of it forever. Family is everything to them.

"That's the best plan, this is the only safe place for any of us right now." Zack agrees as he rubs his hand over his chest where he took the bullet. His wounds aren't even healed, and he is ready to go headfirst back into the trenches for his sister.

"Okay then." Max starts, "we need to do a full security sweep of the school and get some extra measures put in place." he says without pause looking at his guys, "I want every inch of that school under surveillance."

"Principal Lock is an old friend, none of that will be an issue." Elle replies absentmindedly, I can tell she is already knee deep back in mission mode, ready to take out her next target.

"So what? We're just supposed to go back and act normal?" Jace asks bitterly, taking another swig of whiskey from the bottle that is permanently in his hand these days.

"As opposed to what?" I ask with warning in my tone, he might be my brother, but Elle is my girl, and we are all in this together. He just huffs in response, taking another drink.

"We put on a united front, watch each other's backs and act like we aren't spending our nights violently murdering the scum of the town." Elle responds to him with a glare, but I can tell she is worried about him. This is the side of Jace she hasn't seen before.

She watches him a little longer before she brings her gaze to Asher who is silently listening in the corner, "what about you?"

He flicks his eyes to hers. "What about me?" He asks.

Elle glares at him now, "What are you going to do about school? I presume you won't be returning to Hallows Prep, not unless you have a fucking death wish." I refrain from rolling my eyes at her statement, because if anyone has a death wish, it's that psycho. He'd walk into his home with no weapons and murder his father and brother with his bare hands if Elle would let him.

"I can easily hack into your files and transfer you to Hallows High with us." Lincoln interrupts before Ash can give Elle an answer.

He looks at him now and smirks, "no thanks help, I try to avoid the masses where I can. I'll just stay home with Cassie and do some work." He cocks his brow at him, like he is daring Lincoln to challenge him.

Of course, Linc takes the bait. "What sort of work?"

"The kind that's none of your business Blackwell." He snaps at him, effectively ending their conversation.

Elle cuts in before their little sparring can continue, "that's great Ash, she will love it." He offers her a small smile and then silence descends again.

"Okay aside from setting you guys up to go back to school, what's the next priority?" Max asks zoning in on Elle.

"Rebecca O'Sullivan." She replies simply.

"The MC President's daughter." Liam confirms with a nod as he starts to furiously type into his laptop.

"Yeah. We get her then we get the whole of the Hallowed Crows MC on our side. This war isn't about numbers, but they sure will help" Elle adds.

"We've had eyes on Fitzgerald since we got here, but there has been no sign of any girl. We've all got her picture, so for now we keep watching. Get his routines down and see if we can track down where he is keeping her."

"If he even still has her. If she is even still alive." Jace mutters in contempt.

"I can't find any evidence that he does or doesn't, but there are several purchases from high end boutiques that only retail women's clothes and lingerie and he doesn't appear to have any other woman in his life." Liam continues to tap away as he talks, but his words don't offer comfort. What the fuck has he been doing to her if he still has her. Elle said that her dad hasn't seen her in two years. I can't even imagine what she's endured.

"We don't give up until we know for sure." Zack says looking to Elle who nods in response, I imagine she is thinking the same as me. She suffered for one night, but that must seem like a walk in the park compared to two years with one of these sick fucks.

"Nothing more can be done tonight." Helen says, speaking up, "Max and the boys have the house secured, Cassie is sleeping and you all should be too." She scolds and I know she hates all this talk. I can't blame her for that, everyone she loves is deeply involved and she almost lost her son because of it.

"Helen's right," Elle smiles, "it's getting late, we can talk more in the morning and decide on next steps."

250

She stands up stretching and it prompts everyone else to follow.

Arthur and Helen come over and give her a hug before heading to bed, Max ruffles her hair and Zack kisses her forehead. Jace storms away without a word and Linc offers us a grim smile before he follows after him. Asher settles in on the sofa opening his own laptop making it clear he isn't done for the night and once Logan is done staring at him, he makes his way over to Elle.

"Lils in with Cass?" He asks and she nods. "Mind if I join them," he looks to me and back to her, "give you guys the night alone."

"Sure Lo, that'd be great, thank you." The tone in her voice doesn't sound like she is happy about it, but I know she is trying her best to let Cassie go back to normal and be surrounded by her whole family and not just be smothered by her and Ash.

Once they say goodnight, she follows me to my room and flops down onto the bed with a sigh. She is still wearing the same clothes we went to see Beth in. Dark colored jeans and a thick cream sweater, she got rid of her shoes, but her feet are still covered in fluffy socks. Her hair naturally messy with her tousled waves. So, fucking beautiful, even with the worry lacing her face. I take in the grimace that's still permanently etched there, and bypass her heading right for the en-suite. I start a bath and pour in some lavender smelling bubbles, letting it fill until it's over half full. Once done I head back into the room and dip down, picking her up and throwing her over my shoulder.

"Marcus!" She squeals and that tone is the only time my name ever sounds good coming from her mouth. "Put me down." She pleads.

I don't oblige until we are standing in the steam filled bathroom. "Time to relax, baby." I cup her cheeks and kiss her gently, but when I go to pull away, she circles her arms around my neck and presses her body against me. I let her devour my mouth before I pull back and take in her now lust filled stare. I slowly lift her sweater up and off, and then lower myself to drag her jeans down her legs, discarding them on the floor. I pull off her socks until she is standing before me in nothing, but a lace cream set of lingerie. I groan at the sight of it.

"Fucking hell, baby, I don't know what I did to deserve you, but I'm glad you're mine." I run my hands up the back of her legs as I slowly rise, watching as goosebumps break out onto her skin as I trail kisses up her body. I stand, cupping her ass and pulling her against my hardness. I place more kisses across her jaw and down onto her neck, as she pushes into me. When I bring my mouth backs to hers, I kiss her again, devouring her taste. "Promise me you won't ever leave me again, baby."

She looks at me as she responds, "never again, River." I know she had already said it to me, but I needed to hear it again. Every day with her is like a fucking miracle I don't deserve, but I won't waste. "This is far from over, but I won't do it without you anymore."

She pulls my shirt over my head and she presses kisses across my chest like she is trying to force her words to imprint on my skin. She fumbles with my zipper before she slips inside and grips my hard length in her hand giving it a small squeeze and I feel precum leak from my tip. She isn't satisfied with that though and when she drops to her knees in front of me, I groan again as she looks up at me, pulling my jeans down with my boxers freeing my cock. She licks her lips and I slide my hand in her hair.

"You look so fucking good on your knees for me, baby."

"Only for you." She purrs back, those blue eyes meeting mine as she sucks me into her hot, wet, mouth, humming around my tip. It takes everything in me not to slam myself to the back of her throat. She continues to look up at me as her tongue darts out and lashes against my slit as she laps me up. I can't bear it. I use my hold on her hair to drag her mouth deeper onto my cock and she hums appreciatively. Bobbing back and forth, taking me deeper each time, pushing her limits. Fuck, she's pushing mine and when I hit the back of her throat I almost come on the spot.

She feels my grip in her hair tighten even more as I try not to spill down her throat and she fucking smirks around my cock. Hollowing her cheeks and forcing me even deeper down. Her eyes are watering as she practically fucking deep throats me and when she reaches out with her hand to play with my balls I can't hold back. I pull her hair as I thrust into her, again and again, fucking her hot mouth with my hard thrusts until I can't take any more.

"I need to be inside you now."

I pull her back and drag her up at the same time, flipping her round and pushing her against the counter

253

until her ass is in the air and she's completely at my mercy. Our eyes lock in the mirror and hers are slightly red and still watering and her mouth is slick with saliva. I almost rip the underwear from her body as I rush to get her naked. Not offering any warning before I line myself with her and sink deep inside in one hard push. Slamming all the way in until I fill her completely.

"Fuck!" She screams as she takes me.

She is ridiculously wet and tight, and I grow even harder inside her as she clenches around me. The feel of her is fucking unreal. Like my wildest fantasies couldn't even compare. She is fucking everything. Drawing back again and again. Fucking her with deep, hard thrusts, chasing both our releases.

She watches me in the mirror as I fuck her raw and the desire that coats her skin is fucking stunning. I grip her hips and pound into her. My fingers are gripping her so hard that I'm afraid I might hurt her, but I can't stop. The look of pure desire in her eyes as she holds my gaze, let's me know that she doesn't want me to either. She grips the counter with both hands and pushes back against me, taking everything, I've got to give. Watching her take my cock is fucking hypnotic, I reach around finding her slick core and rub her clit in hard fast circles and she immediately starts to shake.

"Fuck, River, don't stop, right there," she cries, and I don't let my fingers falter, giving her exactly what she needs.

I'm close, so fucking close, "come baby, I need to feel you on me before I come." I grit out through my teeth.

She clenches around me as she comes with a loud moan and my pace becomes animalistic. I fuck her harder and faster until I am groaning my own release. Our sweat slicked bodies fall into the counter. I kiss her shoulders, neck, cheeks. Anywhere I can reach as she tries to catch her breath. I will never get enough of her.

She laughs, "okay now I am definitely ready for a bath." I laugh with her, pulling out of her. I scoop her up and move until I can step into the bath with her in my arms, holding her against me as we sink down into the hot water.

Chapter 29

ELLE

Once again I don't recognize the girl, no the woman, staring back at me from the mirror. The black satin gown hangs by two silver straps and flows completely to the floor, hugging in at my breasts and waist. My hair is styled in a messy bun with a few tendrils escaping on either side of my face and a simple wing liner and red lip combo completes my look. The silver stilettos finish off my ensemble perfectly, all ready for a family celebration. It's New Year's Eve and in spite of everything going on, Helen insisted on a family dinner and instructed us all to dress for the occasion. So here I am, dressed and ready to go, so why can't I force my feet to move, to turn around and leave this room and join my family to celebrate even if just for one night.

It just feels stupid to celebrate something so mundane and regular, but that's what I'm fighting for right? The chance to live, the chance to survive, the chance to just be a normal eighteen-year-old girl with no enemies. Yet all I think about is the last time I got dressed up like this. All I can see is my brother's bloodied body and my daughter being carried away by the enemy.

But this isn't like last time. Zack is here and alive, Cassie is here and I'm here, nobody can find us, we are safe.

For now.

We won't truly be safe until I finish this and wipe everyone else off the board.

But what's one night off war?

My thoughts are interrupted when my door swings open and I lock eyes with Zack in the mirror. He's here, he's safe, he's alive. He's dressed in a fitted grey suit, paired with a dark pair of loafers and a silver tie. God, it warms my heart to see him like this. He almost looks like himself now; the handsome, young CEO that could conquer the world. Yet, the reminder that he almost died is still there, in the way he holds his shoulders and the slow limp he does as he moves towards me. That makes the warmth in my heart fade, as anger and desperation burn through me instead.

"You look beautiful sweetheart." He grips both my shoulders and drops a kiss to the side of my head.

"You look pretty handsome yourself, Z." I feign a smile, but he sees right through it.

"You okay?" He asks and it's a loaded question, I haven't been okay for a long time.

I exhale a slow breath before I whisper, "I'm nervous." Admitting that out loud to him makes me feel weak, but I am so sick of being strong all the time. Too much has happened. I lower my eyes to the floor so he can't see the shame I feel in admitting that.

"I know. I feel it too." He replies and my eyes snap back to his in the mirror. "It never stops," he goes on, "it plays on repeat in my head, I just watch her get taken over and over again while I lay there helpless."

My frown is instant, "you were bleeding," He has got to believe that none of that was his fault.

"Exactly!" He snaps causing me to startle. Zack can be harsh when he needs to be, I've seen it, but never with me. "I vowed to protect you, both of you and when it mattered most, I failed. I'm sorry."

I turn to face him, "don't you ever apologize to me again, if anyone should be sorry, it's me. You were never supposed to be a part of all this."

He shakes his head in disagreement, "all of this is because of me." He disagrees. "I won't fail you again."

"You could never fail me Zack, you're my brother, you'll always be my hero."

"You're your own hero Elle King, you always have been." He smiles softly and I can't bear it. I throw my hands around him and take comfort in his embrace.

I should wish that I never laid eyes on Greg Donovan, that he never did those awful things to me. But without them I wouldn't have Zack, I would still be living blissfully ignorant in a jail I called home with parents I thought loved me. Now I am surrounded by a family that I would die for, but more importantly, I would live for.

"We are going to end this, and all make it out alive and in one piece, right?" I ask, but it comes out muffled against his chest.

He pulls back and looks down at me, "Right," he agrees, and he almost sounds like he believes it. Almost. "Now come on, I was sent in here to get you, everyone is waiting. Let's go."

I nod, turning to take one last look in the mirror before smoothing down my dress and then following him out of the room.

As soon as I make it to the living area my eyes immediately zone in on Cassie. She's here, she's safe. She's also surrounded by five beautiful protectors: Marcus, Lincoln, Jace, Logan and Asher are all with her, dressed in beautiful black suits and listening intently to her like she is the center of their whole world. I know she's mine.

She's wearing a beautiful black dress with a silver bow attached to the back, the skirt puffs out a little and stops at her knee. Someone has braided her hair and fixed a little crown to her head. She looks perfect and it looks like our dresses were made to match. I had one of Max's guys pick both of them up from Robert in Havensgrove yesterday just for the occasion. Jace is saying something back to her when he glances up and spots me, stopping mid-sentence. They all look to see what got his attention.

"Damn, sis! Looking hot!" Logan calls out from across the room.

Asher groans, "I really wish you wouldn't make it sound so creepy when you say shit like that."

"Would you prefer I compliment you, baby?" He winks at him and Ash as usual rolls his eyes before stepping towards me and kissing my cheek, always the gentleman.

"You look beautiful, Hells Bells." He smiles softly, but I can see the darkness flaring behind his stormy blue eyes. He is just waiting for his next chance at revenge.

259

I move towards the guys, Logan first who pulls me in for a hug, Lincoln next who smiles, "you scrub up well, King." I kiss his cheek and then turn to Jace. He is still staring at me intently and I know why. Just like me, he's thinking of the last time we were all dressed up like this.

He clears his throat and shakes his head like he wants to rid the thoughts in there, "beautiful as always, Queenie." His smile is forced and lacking his usual care and I can't help myself. I hug him, hard, like I can heal him with just my arms around him. He doesn't say anything, neither do I. He just hugs me back, letting this friendship we have built, this family, flow through each other, giving us both the strength, we need to get through this. When I pull back his smile is a little more genuine and he offers me a wink. Better than before so I take it.

By the time I turn to Marcus, he has scooped Cassie up into his arms, a sight that makes my breath falter. Never in my life did I imagine I would feel this type of love this young. The unconditional kind, the die before losing it kind. It's almost too much. Almost. The smile he gives me makes my knees go weak. The strong and powerful Marcus Riviera, leader of the Rebels and King of the South Side. Still, when he's here with me, all I see is my best friend, my first love. My only love. Holding my daughter, accepting her. Loving her as much as he would if she were his own and making it all the easier to love him.

She jumps down from his arms and almost leaps at me as I pick her up and cuddle her close. "You look beautiful," I say into her hair and she pulls back with a huge smile as she struggles to get down from my arms.

Once she does, she gives me a twirl showing off her dress. "Wow so pretty."

"Daddy says I'm the prettiest princess." She replies just as Asher comes back over and we both smile.

"Daddy is right."

"I usually am," Ash teases as he picks Cass up, "now come on dinner is almost ready." He takes her and they all move to head towards the dining area as I focus on Marcus.

"You look fucking stunning, Ells. The dress is beautiful." He drops a kiss to my lips, which is far too quick and light for my liking, but I suppose considering we aren't really alone, this isn't the time or place for anything more. He leans in until his breath tickles my ear, "I can't fucking wait to see what's underneath it later." My blush is instant, and I don't miss the smug look on his face as he pulls away. Not wanting to let him have the upper hand I smile as I think of my comeback.

I place my hand on his chest and give him another quick kiss on the lips, before leaning up to whisper, "the only thing I'm wearing under this dress is my knife." He groans, as I pull away, and immediately tries to grab me back, but I skip out of his hold and make my way into the dining room.

"Fucking little tease." He mutters following me, but apparently, he wasn't quiet enough.

"Swear jar!" Cassie yells and I can't help the laugh that bursts out of me as we make our way to our seats at the table.

Dinner is perfect, the food is amazing as always when Helen has been in the kitchen and it's nice to have everyone together to celebrate. The drinks flow and the conversations are light and easy for a change. Marcus's arm never leaves my thigh, and mine and Asher's gaze never strays too far from Cassie. Both of us offer each other the occasional smile. I haven't felt this content in a long time. This is what we are fighting for.

After dinner we all head to the living area to relax. Arthur and Helen are dancing to some jazz music he put on, Z is in the corner with Max and the guys sharing stories. Logan and Lincoln are trying to best each other at a game of chess and Lily has wrangled Ash into playing cards. Cassie is in his lap, excitedly yelling out the numbers on his cards, making him lose and Lily for once has a huge smile on her face.

Jace is sitting alone by the Christmas tree, looking out the window where strangely enough, a dusting of snow has started to fall. I'm worried about him, but I know he wants to be alone, he isn't smoking or even drinking, just lost in his thoughts. Just when I think I might go over to him and make sure he is okay I am grabbed from behind and pulled into a hard body.

"Time to show me those knife skills, little King." Marcus purrs into my ear, nipping it slightly and I feel his touch searing through my dress where he holds my waist.

I look around the room, seeing if we could really get away with sneaking off. Everyone is occupied enough and when I let my gaze travel across them all, the only person to catch my eye is Ash. He zones in on Marcus's grip and smiles, shaking his head and then offers me a nod towards Cassie. I know he is signaling for me to go, have fun and not worry and for once I can let myself. Because we are all here, together, and safe and I know nothing bad is going to happen, at least not tonight.

I turn and Marcus loosens his hold, allowing me to spin until I face him, His dark stare is lustful as he gazes down at me, "come on, little King. I've been imagining ripping this fucking scrap of dress off you all night." He leans in licking a path up my neck to my hair, "let me show you how fucking hard I am for you."

His words burn through me and I don't even think twice about grabbing his hand and leading him from the room, I don't stop until we make it inside his room and lock the door. The soft rumbles of the music filter through the walls and I know nobody will hear us in here, no matter what we do.

Whenever he looks at me like this, all I can think about is how he makes me feel, how he makes me forget everything. The high I feel when he worships my body is one that will never fade. Now I am craving that high. The need for him is ever present and lurking. Like a buzz beneath my skin. I am obsessed. No, I am fucking addicted, and I need my next fix.

I push him until his legs hit the bed and he drops down onto it, looking up at me. I take a step back and slide the straps of my dress off my shoulder, letting it slide from my arms, revealing my bare chest. His gaze devours my tits as he licks his lips, like he is thinking of all the wicked things he wants to do to me. I grip the dress and slowly drag it past my waist until it gives and completely drops to the floor. Leaving me in nothing but my stilettos and the black strap attached to my thigh. I wasn't lying when I said my knife was the only thing I was wearing. Any underwear I tried on earlier left lines on the dress, so I had to skip it, but I never skip my knife, even when I know we are safe here. My fingers dust down my body until I find the strap and go to remove it.

Marcus reaches out, halting my movements, "leave it on." He stares up at me with a depraved fucking smile on his face and I smile back.

I let my hands fall from the strap, but his remains. He drags it around my leg, brushing against it all the way, until he reaches my ass. Grabbing it, he pulls me closer to him, before he continues to drag his hand back down to my thigh. Still gripping the strap, he uses it to pull my leg up onto the bed, so my pussy is completely open to him.

"Do you have any idea how fucking sexy you are," he purrs bringing up his other hand and letting it trace along my seam. I can't hold back my shudder. He's so close. "How many times I fucked my hand thinking about you?" He pushes his fingers a bit further, "how many times I came just thinking about this fucking pussy." he grazes my clit. "Fuck, how just one look at you had me coming even after the worst fucking blow job ever." He presses my clit hard, and I gasp. His words should make me jealous; I shouldn't want to hear about other girls, remembering how I found him that first day of school, but all they do is spur me on.

Because he's here, he's mine. His finger starts to make miniscule circular movements and every slight friction pushes me further into my desire. "How I wanted to fucking kill every guy that lusted after you on that first day of school, including my own fucking brother." He slides a finger inside of me, "how I wanted to fuck the defiance out of you when you didn't react to what I got them to do to your car." He fucks me with his fingers, his thumb finding my clit as I climb further towards release.

"Fuck, Ells, that first time I kissed you, I knew. Knew one taste would never be enough." He works his fingers faster inside me as he fucks me roughly with them. I start riding them, chasing the high only he can give me. "Let go baby, give it to me." His words send me over the edge and I'm coming with a scream as he continues to fuck me, wringing out every last bit of my orgasm. He pulls his fingers from me and they glisten with my cream. He stares at me intently as he brings them to his mouth and sucks them clean. "Fucking perfect," he groans.

I reach out and unfasten his shirt, ripping open each button as fast as I can, sliding it off his broad shoulders. He unfastens his belt, pulling it off, before letting his pants and boxers follow, until we are both naked. His hand flattens against my stomach and pushes up between my breasts until it closes on my throat. He uses his grip to pull me down towards him and I follow his lead, spreading my legs wide, as I straddle him.

"Ride me, baby." He says leaning up to kiss me. He pushes his tongue to dance with mine as he lines up his cock. I push him back bracing both my hands on his chest before I sink down on it making us both groan. "Fuck, Ells."

Slowly, I rise again, before pushing back down with a little more force. He leans back up, gripping my neck again and forcing my mouth to his. We kiss like it might be the last time and fuck like we are gonna live forever. The perfect fucking mix of passion and pure lust. I take him deep inside and ride against him and he meets me thrust for thrust. My clit brushes against his groin with every swipe of my hips and I throb. Pushing me closer and closer to another release. I need it, crave it and he knows exactly how to give it to me.

"Oh fuck, Ells, yes just like that." He moans, gripping the back of my neck as his other hand finds my ass. He squeezes it tight in his hand as he keeps up the momentum of my movements. When he keeps hitting the perfect spot inside me, I rush towards my orgasm. "Oh, fuck baby, come on, come for me. You feel so fucking good clenching around my cock, Elle." I fuck him harder as sweat drips down both our bodies, but nothing matters right now apart from the way he feels inside me. I slam down onto his cock one more time before I am coming so hard, I almost black out, but he doesn't stop. He grabs my hips in both hands and continues to pound into me, the sounds of our bodies hitting against each other, filling the room.

I wrap my arms around his shoulders and hold on tight so he can keep fucking me, I know he's close, I can feel him swelling inside me and I want him to find the same pleasure I feel so I lean in and whisper, "come inside me, River, I want you dripping out of me." He groans, picking up his pace even more until he is leading me into another release, "fuck, Marcus. I'm gonna come again." I barely get the words out before he rips another orgasm from me as he finds his own with a loud groan.

His hand grips my cheek and drags me to his lips, "fucking perfect." He's right it really is perfect. I just wish everything else was.

Chapter 30

JACE

I fucking hate New Year's Eve. All that new year, new me bullshit, when in reality everyone continues to be the same shitty cunt they always are. People talk about resolutions and new beginnings, no one ever thinks about the people who won't get to start a new year. About the people who are no longer here to celebrate such trivial things. My hands are itching to feel the weight of a bottle or the tip of a cigarette, my nostrils burning for the taste of coke. All of which, I'm ignoring because I don't want to be like this. A reckless fuck up that people need to look after. I want to be better, stronger, just more than this fucking waste of space I am now.

I'm in a room full of people and I have never felt more alone. I don't fit in here, everyone has a purpose, everyone but me. Even my silent and brooding brother seems to have found a spot for himself. Our King won his Queen, and me? I've fallen back into the depths of despair, constantly worrying about Donovan and his sick fucking ways, and trying anything possible to forget all about my past. I reach for the joint in my pocket, just as my phone vibrates next to it. I pull that out instead and find one new message from the last person I thought I would hear from, especially after my last drug-fueled run in with her.

TAYLOR: Hey Conrad, you at Riverside tonight?

I had heard through socials that there was a big party happening there tonight. I mean there always is, but this would have been bigger than most. Everyone puts their differences aside to ring in the new year. I couldn't think of anything worse, yet anywhere is better than sitting here alone. I let playboy Jace take the reins.

JACE: I could be persuaded *wink emoji*

I don't know why I even try to flirt with her, she is miles out of my league, and we have nothing in common, but she makes me want better for myself. Mix that with what a fucking knock out she is and well, I can't help myself.

TAYLOR: Fancy a jailbreak? Stuck at the parentals party listening to their work buddies talk shop. Send help *praying hands emoji*

I contemplate my options: Staying here and sulking alone or going to get a pretty girl from a party. Looking at the time, it's not even ten yet, but it would take me at least an hour to get to her and that's if I managed to sneak out. In fact, there is no way I could sneak out, the house is too secure, everyone too on edge. That means I'd actually have to ask to leave, like I'm a fucking child. I've never had to ask permission for anything. I scoff just thinking about it, but then the thought of staying in this house one minute longer makes me want to fucking die, so fuck it.

I get up and move towards Max, him and Zack are chatting in the corner, while the rest of his guys that are inside are playing on the Xbox. He looks up at me as soon as I approach, and Zack follows his gaze.

"I need to go out." Simple and to the point, I don't see any reason not to be blunt. He eyes me slowly, not saying a word, but managing to completely unnerve me with his unwavering glare.

Eventually, he sighs. "Take Tyler with you." Is all he responds before he turns back to Zack to continue their conversation. That could have been worse, and out of all his guys, Tyler is the one I get on with the most.

Max spoke loudly enough to get Tyler's attention and he moves towards me, grabbing his jacket off the chair, "where are we going?" He asks with a smile and I relax slightly when I realize none of them are going to bust my balls about it.

"Party." Is all I say, before we turn and leave. When we reach the garage, he tosses me a set of keys to signal that I'm driving and I climb into the car. It feels good to be behind the wheel again, to be leaving the inside of these gates. I never thought I would ever look forward to going back to school, but at this point it can't come quick enough.

I shoot a quick response to Taylor to tell her I'll be there in an hour, and then we set off. We drive in silence until we reach the outskirts of Black Hallows.

"Are you armed?" Tyler asks suddenly, and I frown.

"Should I be?" I retort and then it's his turn to frown.

"Thought you grew up here? You should always be fucking armed." He snaps, pulling his jacket aside and showing the two guns on his waist.

I roll my eyes, "I've got a knuckle duster in my pocket." Is all I respond, because it's the only weapon I have on me and it's the only one I've always used. I try not to think about the fact I killed someone, that I took a life without regret. I shouldn't feel bad, they deserved it, but I am still responsible for the death of someone, and I haven't fully decided how I feel about that yet.

When we finally make it to Taylor's estate, the gates are open, and her long driveway is lined with cars. When she said her parents were throwing a party, she really meant a party. There has to be at least a hundred cars here. I drive past them all until I am swinging in front of the fountain in the middle of her drive. I roll my eyes at the ridiculous amount of wealth here, I will never get used to it, no matter how much time I spend with Elle and her family. I fire off another text to let her know I'm here, and then I wait.

A couple of minutes later, she stumbles out of the door. Seems she already started her party. As I climb from the car, an older man follows her out of the house. He's staying in the shadows, but clearly he's following her. When he steps into the light, he spots me and freezes. His face is vaguely familiar, but I can't place him. He looks rattled to see me there and begins backing up immediately. I have the strange urge to follow him, but then Taylor trips and almost falls, and I rush towards her.

"Woah, princess, careful." I take her arm and steady her as she swings her gaze towards me. Her pupils are wide, and her eyes look glossy, her cheeks filled with a blush despite the cold air.

"Jaceeeeee," she says excitedly, dragging my name out as she tries, and fails to throw her arms around me.

"Started the party early, I see." I say teasing her and she frowns.

"What? No. I had one glass of champagne off Dr. Asshole a few minutes ago, that's it." Her words slur slightly, and I frown. There is no way she only had one glass, she's almost completely out of it.

"Who's Dr. Asshole?" I ask with a slight grin, and she huffs.

"He's here," she turns to where I just saw the familiar looking man, but the space is empty. She shakes her head. "He was right there. He was the one who told me I should come out and get some fresh air. Said he would help me."

Her words make the grin fall from my face, why would she need to be outside, in the dark, for him to help her if he's a doctor. "What's his real name?"

"Rolland." She slurs, "Rolland Atkins." Then she collapses into my arms.

272

Tyler jumps out of the car and rushes towards me, "What the fuck happened to her?"

I can't answer him, all I can hear is Rolland Atkins' name on repeat in my mind. A name I have seen countless times, for years. He's the owner of the biggest pharmaceutical company in the state, one of Elliot Donovan's closest friends, and a target on Elle's murder board. He also happens to be the name on Rachel's death certificate. Taylor isn't drunk. I believe her, she only had one glass, given to her by the trusted and respected Dr. Atkins, and I know exactly what was fucking in that champagne.

"She's been drugged." I bite out bitterly, "we need to get her out of here, now!" I move Taylor so I can pick her up in a fireman's hold, and head back towards the car. Tyler opens the door and helps me lift her in safely, before he jumps into the driver's seat.

"Where are we going?" He asks, and I know he won't like my answer, but right now I don't care about anything but her.

"Home, she needs to see Arthur." His gaze collides with mine in the mirror before he turns and looks at Taylor, sighing, he nods, then floors it out of there. I can see him keep checking the mirrors as he makes sure no one is following us. Smart man.

He saw me. Looked me right in the eye with enough recognition that he backed off. Does he know who I am? Who I'm with? Have I just put a target on her back without meaning to? I push those thoughts aside and concentrate on the only thing I can control right now, and that's helping Taylor. I look down at her passed out

273

on my lap, and wonder if this is what it was like for Rachel. Tricked by someone she thought she could trust. It makes my skin crawl. I reach out and brush a black strand of hair away from her face, and for a moment, I pretend. Pretend that we are the same, that we have lived the same kind of life, and that we are just a regular couple who could have 'it'. That thing that people dream of, that Marcus and Elle have already found. That I say I don't want, but secretly crave. I pretend, and it feels good.

I watch her breathe in and out and wonder if it's possible. Wonder if, given the chance, could the right girl break through all my shit and make it all better. Make me better? I don't know if it's possible or if Taylor could even be the right girl, but just for a moment, here in this car, she is, we are, and life doesn't feel so bad.

By the time we make it back to the house, the new year has come and gone. Tyler took a long route home to ensure we weren't followed and as we move through the gates, the house is a lot darker than when we left it. He pulls into the garage and turns off the engine.

He turns, "I'll go alert Max and get Arthur ready for her." He doesn't wait for me to respond, just gets out, opens my door for me and leaves. It's like he knew I needed a minute longer to just pretend. But I can't anymore, not in the light of the garage. This isn't pretend, this is real life, my life and I just dragged her into it when I should have pushed her away. Elle is probably going to freak out that I brought her here and I'm sure Donovan and Marcus will have something to say about it too. But I can't worry about that right now.

I slip out of the car and slowly maneuver her back into my arms and carry her inside until we reach my room. I get there at the same time Arthur does, and I don't miss the flash of disgust passing over his face, or the way he locks his jaw when he sees the innocent girl, passed out in my arms. I place her on the bed, and he starts checking her vitals.

I don't know if she is going to be okay, If I'm going to be okay, but I do know who needs to die next and I know I have to be the one to do it.

Chapter 31

ELLE

It's a new year and I'm waking up in River's arms feeling perfectly rested and satisfied. So much has changed in the last six months, so much has happened. So much blood and death and almosts, I can barely keep up. But I'm here, we're here. We're safe. Marcus and I stayed in bed curled up in each other all night. Ash popped his head in on his way to bed with a sleeping Cass, and for once, everything just felt right.

I stretch out, careful not to wake Marcus, who is still snoring softly beside me and head to the bathroom. I go to the toilet, wash my hands, and then look at my reflection in the mirror. There are marks across my chest and up my neck that remind me exactly what we did last night, and I can't help but smile. Being with him is like being free. Free from my demons, the weight of the world and everything I still have to do. He makes me weak in the best kind of way, reminding me of who I truly am at my core.

I head into the kitchen to find coffee, which I desperately need, and find Jace pacing. He halts as soon as he spots me, grabbing the already brewed coffee pot and pouring me a cup, and silently handing it over. He looks anxious and on edge, and I start to worry slightly. He's just in black sweats leaving his tattooed torso completely on display and when he reaches out and absentmindedly touches where I know his sister's name sits, I really start to panic.

"What happened?" I put my mug down and lean on the counter across from him.

He sighs, "I have a situation." Is all he says, and I frown.

I pick up my cup again and take another sip, blowing it a little. "Okay," I drag the word out, "want to tell me what that means?"

"Taylor Kennedy is in my bed." He blurts out, and my eyebrows nearly hit the roof as I slam my coffee back onto the counter. "Before you yell, I can explain."

"Yell?" I scoff in disbelief, "I wouldn't even know how to yell right now, do you know how reckless this is? Cassie is asleep right down the hall, Jace."

"I know, Elle, I know, but I couldn't leave her, she was in a bad way."

My senses immediately go on high alert, "what do you mean?"

He takes a deep breath as he launches into the explanation, "Taylor texted me last night, asking if I wanted to go to a party. I spoke to Max and he said I could go, but that I had to take Tyler." He shrugs and I smile a little at the fact that this 6ft tattooed Rebel had to ask permission to go to a party, "she said to pick her up from her house, but when I got there, she stumbled out. I thought she was drunk."

"She wasn't?" I ask to confirm, and he shakes his head.

"When she came out, I saw a man I recognized, I couldn't place him, but Taylor confirmed his name."

My spine straightens as I prepare for whatever name he's about to say. "Who was it?"

"Rolland Atkins." He grits his name out in disgust and his earlier pacing now makes sense, he must have been stewing on this all night. He tells me what happened, what he saw and how he brought her here so Arthur could take a look at her. She is fine now, she was given something to make her pass out, but all her vitals are good.

I huff out a long breath. I should have expected this. Dr. Atkins has been on my list from the beginning, and it seems my disposal of his friends hasn't deterred him in any way. He needs dealing with and soon. I need to know how much Jace wants Taylor to know. She's here, and when she wakes up, I'm sure she is going to have a lot of questions.

I consider my words carefully before I ask, "are we bringing Taylor into the fold?" I have no idea what is going on between them, Jace has been so closed off so it's hard to tell where the playboy Rebel starts and my soft and caring Jace ends.

His shutdown is immediate. "No. She doesn't deserve to be dragged into this, especially not by me."

I soften at that, "Jace," I start, but he cuts me off.

278

"No, Elle. I won't put her life in danger. I only brought her here last night because I had nowhere else to take her. It won't happen again." His words are final, and I nod in agreement.

"It's fine, she's my friend, don't worry we will work something out." I have no idea what we will do, but I know it has to be something. She already has a target on her back regardless of her association with me or Jace.

"As long as she's safe." His tone breaks my heart a little. Such a beautiful, broken Rebel.

I want to throw my arms around him and comfort him, tell him everything is going to be okay, but I don't know that. I sigh and roll my eyes trying to break the serious tension in the air. It's clear he likes her, but apparently, we aren't admitting that today, so I just smile and say, "you're insufferable."

"But you love me, right?" He smiles for the first time, throwing in his signature, flirty wink, making it impossible not to smile back.

I don't hesitate this time, rounding the counter and pulling him into a hug, "too much for my own good, pretty boy." I whisper into his chest, as he hugs me back.

"We need to take him out." He whispers into my hair.

"I know, but we need a plan," I pull back and stare up at him, "we can't just go after him without a plan."

He gives me a look as if to say he doesn't believe me, "since when was that a rule?"

"Since I won't risk losing any of us again, we've had too many close calls and I don't want anymore. We're all in this together, right? Whatever it takes?"

He nods, "Whatever it takes, Queenie."

I nod and move to leave, but he grips my arm, "I wanna be the one to do it, the one to kill him."

"Jace," I start, wanting to tell him he doesn't deserve that kind of stain on his soul, but we are interrupted.

"Elle?" Both our heads snap to the entrance of the kitchen at the sound of Taylor's confused voice.

I look at Jace who is just staring at her and then turn back to her, "Hey Tay, how are you feeling?

"Like a truck ran over my head repeatedly." She says rubbing it slightly before looking at Jace, "what happened last night? Where am I?"

I look at Jace again, unsure of how much to even tell her at this point. Jace said he doesn't want to bring her in, but Rolland went after her which means Elliot went after her. That and the fact she is standing in our kitchen, how can we not bring her in?

"You're at our place." I say and her frown deepens, which is understandable, it's not like it's been broadcast that the Rebels were burned out of their home, and I was bloodied out of mine. "Look there is a lot of stuff to tell you and a lot of stuff we can't tell you, but I need to know that you won't tell anyone anything that you learn."

She gives us both a questioning look, "anyone like who?" I think she is asking a genuine question, but when I go to answer, she goes on, "it's not like I'm bursting at the seams with friends."

Her words hit me in the gut because I know what it's like to feel alone and like you have no one, but I was never alone. I've always had someone. I can't say that to her so instead I settle on, "This is life or death Tay. So, are you in or out?"

I feel Jace's glare piercing into the side of my head as I give her the ultimatum and Taylor looks between the two of us again, before she speaks at the same time another voice enters the kitchen.

"In."

"Mommy!"

Cassie bounces into the kitchen with Ash right on her heels, and his eyes flare wide as he notices Taylor. His gaze snaps to mine straight away. I catch Cassie as she leaps towards me pulling her into a hug, all the while watching the shock embed itself onto Taylor's face. This was my biggest concern when Jace told me she was here. Not what almost happened to her or everything else she could find out, but this right here.

"Morning, baby," I brush her curls from her head as I kiss her cheek. Then gesture across the kitchen, "meet my friend, Taylor." Cassie immediately turns her head and flashes her the cutest smile.

"Wow she's so beautiful." She gasps waving at her while Taylor still remains in shock.

"Jace sure seems to think so." I smile smugly and he groans at me, but of course it goes right over Cassie's head.

"Nice to meet you." She isn't fazed by Taylor's silence and just turns back to me to proudly add, "Daddy is making me pancakes."

I slide her onto the counter, "oh is he now?" I say eyeing Ash as Taylor's head snaps to him, and I think she goes into even more shock, if that's even possible, "well Daddy better make some for Mommy too."

Ash is still glaring at Taylor, both of them locked in a stare off as he speaks, "like I would ever risk your wrath and not make you some, Hells Bells." He says calmly, but I know he is probably plotting out every way this situation could turn out. Which is ridiculous, I have known Taylor almost my entire life, and Ash has known her since halfway through middle school. She isn't some stranger, ready to sell our secrets to the highest bidder. She's our friend.

The tension thickens the longer she doesn't speak, so I break it, "great, you boys do that while Taylor and I go have a girly catch up." Hearing her name, she looks back towards me as I turn to Cassie, "stay with Daddy, okay? Mommy will be back for pancakes."

"Okay, Mommy." Cassie smiles, completely oblivious to any of the tension surrounding her.

I don't wait before I grab Taylor by the arm and drag her from the kitchen. I hear Ash snap, "you fucked up." and then Cassie shouts, "swear jar." But I don't stop, I just pull her down the hall. We pass Marcus on the way as his eyes widen. I reach out and give his arm a little squeeze as we pass, but I don't stop until we get to my room. I pull her inside and over to the bed, until she slowly sinks down on the end of it.

"I," she starts, staring at the door like she can see all the way to the kitchen and then stops, "how," she pauses again so I stop her.

"What you have just discovered and what I am about to tell you is not only a secret, but it's also dangerous, do you understand that?" She stares at me like I have grown two heads, before nodding slowly so I continue. "I have a daughter. Her biological father is a very perverse and dangerous man who raped me. That's the reason I left Black Hallows."

I expect the flinch that leaves her at the word rape, but then instead of pity in her eyes, I see confusion, "You weren't at boarding school?" She asks and I shake my head slowly.

"That was a lie to cover up what happened to me. God, forbid I soil the King name." I roll my eyes in disgust, taking a seat on the bed next to her. "What happened led me to having Cassie. I didn't want her to know her real father, so Ash became her dad." It sounds so simple when I say it like that, so very black and white. If only.

"You guys never?" She asks trailing off.

My eyes widen, "Lord no. We're close, but we have never been that close." I say with a slight laugh.

"I don't even know what to say." She admits, which is understandable. I've had over three years to adjust to my reality, I can't expect her to digest it in one morning.

"Honestly." I blow out a breath, "that's probably for the best. I wish I could tell you more but trust me when I say it's safer this way."

She takes a deep breath, looking round the room. I can see her trying to digest what I just told her before she swings her head back to me, "what does all that have to do with me being here?"

She was always smart, that hasn't changed. "The man who raped me, works with a lot of sick men. He didn't just want to hurt me, he wanted to sell me." I can't think of a better way to put it and I wait for the words to sink in.

She shudders as they wash over her and she realizes what I mean, "they tried to take me?" She says panicking as her hands start to shake.

I reach out and clasp her hand in mine, "I'm not sure, I think maybe they were planning on it, but Jace was there. You passed out and he brought you here." I try to stay calm as I talk, but it's hard. The rage I feel whenever I think about what fucking sick crimes those bastards commit could blow up the world.

"Why can't I remember anything?"

"We think they put something in your drink, Arthur checked you over and said other than that you were fine."

"Who's Arthur?"

I huff a laugh, because what I have just told her is the tip of the iceberg, "not important, what is important is that you can't tell anyone you know where I am, or who I'm with okay? I promise I will keep you safe, but I need you to do this for me."

She takes in the no doubt serious look on my face before she nods, "of course Smell, anything for you." She smiles, squeezing my hand, which has remained in her grasp, this whole time.

We spend the rest of the day catching up and she gets to know Cassie. We have tea parties, a movie marathon and just hang out like friends should. It's a perfect day, reminding me exactly why we were so close as kids. Jace comes by a couple of times, trying not to linger, but the attraction between them is clear as day. I

284

understand him wanting to keep her out of this, but I can't see how we can. She's here, she knows, that puts her in it whether we like it or not. Another innocent person caught up in this fucking war. We can't wait anymore; we need to end this once and for all.

Chapter 32

ELLE

We shouldn't be here. Every other normal high school senior is preparing to go back to school tomorrow. Probably catching up on forgotten homework, texting friends to arrange catch ups and picking out the perfect back to school outfit. But not me, not the Rebels. No. Instead, we are spending our last free day before school starts, breaking and entering, stealing, and killing. So many fucking crimes I can barely keep up anymore. My moral high ground no longer exists, not when it comes to the Donovan's and their band of sick little helpers.

Right now, Dr. Rolland Atkins is sitting inside his mansion. A mansion he got because he made money off of people's suffering. His pharmaceutical company was miniscule, a blip on nobody's radar until he met Elliot Donovan. He created a drug named Atkaprazole. It is known for treating heart disease, but what people don't talk about is the fact that when you inject it into the system the side effects include loss of consciousness and being unable to move. All it takes is the right dosage and you have yourself a docile little victim, ready to play with. It doesn't matter if you inject too much and it kills them, because all that will show up on an autopsy is a heart attack, which when they find heart related drugs in your system doesn't seem unrealistic. Helpful, lethal, and completely profitable. By day he heals people of their heart problems and by night he knocks them out to pass over to Elliot Donovan and his son. When Arthur ran my blood work the night we met, he could never make sense of what he found. Not until we started digging up everything on Elliot and his men. That's when things started to slot into place.

All of that and more landed the esteemed Dr. Atkins a place on my revenge list. So here we sit, watching, waiting. Readying ourselves for the next step of revenge. Max and his team are getting ready to break into the building of Atkins Incorporated. They are going to burn it down until it's nothing but ash. Elijah and Lincoln have already hacked into his accounts and rendered his insurance policies useless. Not that he is going to be alive to know any of this. The burner phone buzzes in my pocket and I know it's showtime.

I look to Marcus and nod and he does the same. We push up and over the wall, followed by Lincoln, Jace and Tyler. Asher is our distraction tonight, he, like the absolute fucking psycho he is, just drove through the front gates. When he told me his plan, I thought he was insane, but it's actually kind of genius. It doesn't matter what he has done, in this town he is still a Donovan. Royalty by name and nature, meaning when he knocks on Rolland Atkins' door, he will swing it right open, giving us the chance to slip in the back, undetected.

We make it easily and quietly to his back porch, where he has conveniently left his patio doors wide open. Dare anyone have the audacity to try to break into his house. I note the cigar in the ashtray and the empty tumbler on the table. Like he was having a pleasant quiet evening that has just been interrupted by an unexpected visitor. Isn't that nice? I love ruining someone's night and their fucking life. We slip inside silently and hear Asher's voice filtering from the next room.

"My father doesn't know I'm here."

"I thought as much," Rolland responds. "What can I do for you, my boy?" My lips curl in disgust at his tone. Patronizing fucker.

"It's what I can do for you actually," Ash replies coolly.

I follow their voices to Atkin's office; the door is slightly ajar, giving me a clear sight of Asher. Sensing my presence his jaw tightens, and his hands clench into fists. He's holding himself back, stopping himself from ending Atkins by his own hands. He knows I can do it, that I want to do it, but he still thinks I shouldn't have to. He would take pleasure in taking out every one of my enemies without remorse and so would the guys beside me.

"And what's that?" Atkins asks and I can hear the smile in his voice, like the thought that Asher could possibly offer him anything, is laughable. We shall see who's laughing soon.

I push the door open, letting it bang against the wall, alerting him to my arrival. His head snaps around as I reach behind me and pull the tranq gun from my waistband. Watching his face fall from smug arrogance to recognition and fear thrills me. I lift the gun and shoot it directly into his thigh before he can even move. It's got a small dose of his favorite drug, not enough to knock him out completely, but it will keep him compliant enough until we can get him tied up.

The guys filter in behind me as Asher catches Rolland and lowers him into his chair. Lincoln moves to help him before he pushes past them to hack into his computer, no doubt downloading everything. Ash makes quick work of tying him up just as Marcus opens the plastic sheeting and spreads it across the floor. Jace and Tyler stand silently watching us work in unison. Once we have Atkins where we want him, we wait. Only a couple of minutes pass before he is pretty much fully lucid again.

When his eyes collide with mine, I offer him my most sinister smile. "Dr. Atkins, we've never officially been introduced, I'm Elle King." His eyes track my movements and I note him taking in the wall of muscle behind me, He knows he's fucked, but they always try anyway right?

"What the fuck is this? Don't you know who I am?" He slurs out and I laugh. It's always the same. I pull my knife from my thigh and run my fingertips along it as I settle my other hand to lean against the gun on my side. His eyes flare wide and his bravado from a second ago begins slipping as I step up in front of him.

"Anything you want, just take it." He manages to stutter out and I can't help the laugh that bubbles out of me again.

"Is that your life motto Dr. Atkins? Anything you want you just take?" I spit out dragging my knife lightly down his shirt. Not enough pressure to do any damage, but enough to have him squirming in his seat.

"I never meant..." He starts, but I hold my hand up to stop him.

"You can save the excuses and the lies. I know everything. Every sordid little thing you've ever done. From the bad batches of drugs that killed people to the type of fucking porn you watch. So please don't annoy me further by lying to me. This isn't an interrogation."

"Then what is it?" He asks nervously again looking at the guys over my shoulder. I wish he would stop that. The real threat is standing right in front of him. The lack of respect pisses me off, so naturally, I stab him. "It's retribution," I grit as my knife plunges into that spot I love so much in a man's thigh. He screams out in agony and it releases the tension in my shoulders. I really needed this.

"This won't be bloody, she said," Tyler snorts from behind me and I flash him a grin.

"Oops?" I say with a shrug and he just laughs. "You're right though, we should get a move on." We don't have the luxury of time on our hands tonight. Once his building is set alight it won't be long before someone comes looking for him. Not that they'll find him, but still, it's best to be quick. I pull the other tranq gun from my waist and don't hesitate as I slam it into his other thigh. This dose a lot deadlier than the last.

I watch his body react and my grin gets bigger. "I imagine right now you feel your legs and arms getting heavy, you want to move them, but you can't. Your head will get fuzzy soon, you'll start to slip in and out of consciousness, until eventually you blackout. Don't worry though it won't kill you." This would have scared him more if he weren't already bleeding out, but oh well. What's done is done.

He grunts as his body starts to shake, tears and sweat pouring down his face. "What's the matter Atkins? Don't you love the rush? Aren't you getting off on it? Or is the high not the same when you are on the receiving end of it?" I purposely bait him as his eyes begin to roll back into his head. He's fighting it, or at least trying to.

I watch as his body slowly starts to shut down, but I can't let him die. I hold my hand out to Marcus and he hands over the syringe I asked him to bring. This one is filled with adrenaline, and I pump it straight into Atkins. Time may be off the essence, but I like my enemies to suffer too much for a quick death. I don't deserve this death, but so many others do. So many people have been hurt by him, he probably doesn't even realize how many. The adrenaline takes root, and his eyes flare open as his grip tightens on the chair. I can practically see his heart beating out of his chest.

"People like you deserve to die. You deserve pain and suffering. Not just for what you do to all those girls, but for what you do to the people who get left behind."

He gurgles as he tries to talk, but it's just gibberish that makes no sense, getting lost in the choked sob he lets free.

"Pathetic." I want to end him. Want to take my knife and sink it right into his fucking chest until it meets his heart. The only thing stopping me is the resentment and grief I can feel burning through my back. He deserves this more than I do. I shake my head giving Atkins one last look before I turn and walk over to Jace and hand him my gun. "He's all yours."

He looks at me as he grips the gun, clasping his hand around it. He doesn't have to say anything, I can see all the thanks I need right there on his face. This isn't going to heal him, help him get over losing Rachel, or lessen the grief he feels. It will just allow him the pleasure of knowing he took out one of the people responsible for her death, If there is only one thing I could ever offer him, this would be it.

I leave the room just as the gunshot echoes out behind me, and instantly feel overwhelmed with a sense of pride. Jace didn't even hesitate to pull that trigger, and that's how I know that he's going to be OK. We all are. One way or another, we will make it through this, together.

Chapter 33

MARCUS

After how we have spent the last three weeks, going back to school just seems so ridiculously normal. Lincoln is driving, Jace is up front, and Elle and I are sitting in the back. She had worried about leaving Cassie every day, but she knows that Asher has her, no matter what. They're staying home with Zack, Arthur, Helen, and the twins. A couple of Max's guys will stay with them too, while the rest of them are already waiting for us at school. They've gone back and forth with Lock and managed to get security cameras fitted fucking everywhere. Excessive, but necessary. Elliot Donovan isn't playing, and neither are we. Mix that, with his fucking psychopathic son thinking Elle is his, it's safe to say we are all on edge. We know a pushback is coming, we just don't know when. When they inevitably get the news of Rolland Atkins' disappearance, I know they won't sit and wait any longer.

We've been off radar for weeks and this is the first time we will be doing what is expected of us. The hour drive to school has been spent mostly silent, but the nerves are practically screaming from our bodies. Elle got Lock to change our schedules, so all our classes match up, which eases some of my fear. I should be scared, I am scared, but not for me, for Elle, my brothers. I can't lose them. We have come too far. I just want all of this to be over so we can actually live our lives.

"Starbies?" Jace breaks the silence.

"What the fuck does Starbies mean?" Lincoln asks, his tone even more blunt than usual. He has left no stone unturned as we prepared to come back, and I can tell it's taking a toll on him. He still hasn't forgiven himself for allowing Cassie to be taken, he thinks it's his fault. I get it, I do, I feel so much guilt about what happened to her and Zack, we should have done better. I should have done better.

"I think he means Starbucks," Elle answers from beside me, "and the answer is no, pretty boy." Her tone is slightly teasing, but I can tell it's forced, we are all still reeling from the events of last night.

He huffs in annoyance, throwing his feet up on the dash and sulking the rest of the way to school. Out of all of us, he is the least excited about the plan to continue as normal. He thinks we should have stayed in hiding, but that isn't what Elle wanted. As we pull into the parking lot, he rolls his window down and lights up a joint. Is it too much to ask for him to tackle today with a clear head?

"Seriously?" His eyes snap to mine in the mirror as soon as I speak.

"Just cause you're too pussy whipped to get stoned, doesn't mean I have to be." He replies, slowly puffing out a wave of smoke.

He looks at Elle as soon as he says it and I see his regret. "Real nice, Jace," She sighs, shaking her head before getting out of the car and slamming the door.

"Fuck," He mutters, swiping a hand down his face.

"Look brother, I know you are going through some stuff, but she doesn't deserve your shit." I don't need to tell him. I can tell by the look on his face he already knows.

"I know," He huffs, throwing the joint out of the window and leaving to run after her.

Lincoln watches them before turning to me. "Are you ready for this?" I nod and he continues. "Nowhere alone and anything out of the ordinary is checked out."

"Agreed." We exit the car in unison, both of us swinging our gaze around the lot. The fence is now brand new and there are cameras attached all along it. I can hear people commenting on the changes as they make their way across to the steps.

All hands-on deck really means, all hands. So, as we catch up with Elle and Jace we are also joined by a few of our main South Siders, Jack, Kai, Malcolm, and a few others. They haven't been told everything, just briefed enough to know that we are on high alert. I see all of them eyeing Elle, they're still not used to being around her. I can't help myself. I pull her in by her waist and see them immediately avert their eyes.

"You ready, baby?" I drop a kiss on the space where her neck meets her shoulder, and she leans into it.

"I'm ready," she sighs, "I just want to get all of this over with and…" she cuts off mid-sentence as she tenses up. "This fucking cunt," She mutters, before pulling away from me. She storms off and all our eyes follow to see what has snagged her attention. When I find what she has spotted, I curse inwardly. *Fucking Cherry.*

I follow after her quickly, but not quick enough, and before I can even take a couple of steps, Elle's fist is already cracking Cherry's nose. Her dramatic scream of pain draws so much attention, that a lot more people see the second punch to her jaw. Someone shouts, 'girl fight', and all hell breaks loose. We push through the crowd and they part to let us through. I see a few people already recording.

"Phones away now!" I boom to the crowd and Lincoln moves to confiscate the ones who had already started filming, and the rest of my guys push the crowd back. Elle continues to beat on Cherry until she falls to the floor.

I grab her waist and pull her away. "Elle, what the fuck?" I know she hates her, but a public display like this is bad.

"It was her," she replies without looking at me, she just stares down at Cherry on the floor.

"What was her?"

"She led them to Cassie. I saw Cherry that day we went shopping in Havensgrove, I thought I was seeing things at the time as she disappeared quickly." She's panting heavily, the anger burning out of her body. "I could never figure out how Greg found out about Cass or how he found the house and got to Peter. Then I remembered Cherry. With everything going on, I forgot about it again. But it was her, Marcus. She's the reason."

My hold on her releases immediately, no hesitation. Not after what she did. I wouldn't care if Elle killed her right here and now. This is all her fault. We had the upper hand, had everything under control, until that night. Cherry almost ruined everything, almost cost us everything. The guys have pushed the crowd back far enough that they can't hear what we are saying, but I know they still watch our every move. Elle steps back towards her, bending down next to Cherry until she is crouched by her head.

"I told you not to make me come for you, but you didn't listen, did you?" Elle lifts Cherry's head by her hair. "Did you think he cared about you? That he would protect you? You're as insignificant to them as you are to me." She lowers her voice so that I barely catch the next bit. "Tell Greg to watch his back, I'm coming." With that, she stands and releases her head, and it smashes back into the ground.

Elle turns to me, flexing her fist out, examining the blood coated there, before eyeing everyone in the crowd. For a moment, I think she might slink back into the silent and stealthy Elle, but she proves me wrong. "Nobody touches her. Trash belongs on the ground. Help her out and you'll join her there." Her voice is loud and clear, and I see everyone looking at her in a new light, including me. She's never looked hotter.

I smile at her as I allow my voice to echo around the lot. "Everyone, fuck off to class." They scatter immediately as Jace and Lincoln join us again.

"Fucking hell, Queenie." Jace starts lifting her bloodied fist for inspection and she snaps it away from him, eyeing him with a cocky smirk.

"It was her or you, pretty boy."

He bursts out laughing, "Nah you love me too much for that, even when I'm acting like a dick." He slings an arm around her shoulder, as she shakes her head at him.

"Someone's got to, Conrad." Her tone makes me smile, in a few short, albeit drama filled months, they have grown so close. I've never seen him let his guard down the way he does with her. I imagine this is what he was like before Rachel. Before her murder tainted his soul. It's the same with Lincoln, he has his own demons that he never talks about, his darkness always on show, but with her, he is somehow lighter.

"You alright?" Lincoln asks her and she nods.

"All good, Superman. Sorry I know you said to keep a low profile." Her tone is genuine, and I can tell how much she means that.

The corner of Lincs mouth tips up. "If you didn't do it, I would have." Even with the ghost of a smile tugging at his features, I can still hear the seriousness of that threat.

She smiles big at him. "That's why you're my favorite." She pushes away from Jace and links her arm with Lincoln instead.

"Ouch, Queenie," Jace says at the same time as I say, "What about me?"

She just laughs and they both turn and walk away. I look to Jace and he shrugs and moves to follow them. I turn and look at Cherry. She is crying in a ball on the floor, and I feel zero sympathy for her.

I use my foot to roll her on her back, and then bend down as she looks up at me. "Come for my family again and I'll finish what she started. Are we clear?"

She nods, and, feeling semi-satisfied, I get up. Cherry may have been just another fucking pawn in the Donovan's weaponry, but she took it too far. Her mistakes need to be paid for. Elle may have started it, but I'm not afraid to finish it if I have to.

I turn and head off into school, leaving her in the dirt where she belongs.

Chapter 34

ELLE

Considering how the week back at school started, the rest of it has been quiet in comparison. I haven't seen Cherry since I delivered my less than obvious message on Monday, and I have no doubt the Donovan's are aware of my return to school. I'm still awaiting their retaliation. Not for what I did to Cherry, I know they don't give two fucks about her or her wellbeing, nobody does. She's lucky she landed the role of spy and not 'whore for sale'. No, I await retribution for all my other crimes. The ones I haven't stopped committing against them ever since I got back to town.

I am simply waiting. I know they'll be planning something, it's not like they will have suddenly grown morals and decide to let me be. That was never going to happen. I know too much, have done too much. The price they will want me to pay is astronomical, which is why I have to fight harder than ever. If they get me again, I won't survive.

I know they'll be pissed that we got into the estate and got Cassie back. Well, at least Elliot will be. Greg probably got off on it. He thinks we are playing a game of cat and mouse, just toying with each other until I'm his again. That's just how his sick, twisted mind works. But I'm not playing, not anymore. I want their deaths and nothing less, which is why, while they continue to hold back, I'm pushing on. Dr. Atkins was an unplanned but welcomed mission. Yes, he was a name on my list, but I hadn't decided when or how to deal with him, not until he went after Taylor. I can't help but worry about her, she spent most of Saturday at the house with me and the guys, even though I refused to answer most of her questions. It was nice to just have a friend, one that isn't tainted by my crimes. I've had Owen, one of Max's guys, keeping an eye on her all week, he hasn't reported anything unusual.

We're attempting to cover all our bases, but that still leaves Carter Fitzgerald as my biggest issue. As far as we know, he is still holding Rebecca O'Sullivan somewhere and we need to get her back. If we get her, then we get the Hallowed Crows on our side and the balance of power in our war against the Donovan's, will tilt in our favor. I'm slowly taking their world apart piece by piece and I won't stop until there is nothing left.

Max has Elijah tracking Carter's every move. He spends his weekdays at the Mayoral offices and his weeknights at numerous restaurants across town. Saturdays are spent at the golf club, and Sundays at Church. Yet, it's his evening weekend activities that interest me most. He spends every Friday night at the warehouse on the corner of Middleton and 5th. Lincoln and I followed my father there once, or we tried to, but were interrupted. We have since learned that it's a very exclusive club called 'Crimson', whose members have, what you would call extremely specific tastes. Doesn't take a genius to figure out what that means, when their members include the Donovan's, Carter Fitzgerald, and my father.

We have managed to dig up enough information to know that there are three levels. First floor is a nightclub, where members can drink, and watch beautiful young men and women dance on poles and in cages. Top floor is a BDSM club, where members can explore the life of dominants and submissives, and then there is the basement. We don't have any information on what happens down there, but I think we all can guess just how fucked up it will be.

Unsurprisingly, Mayor Fitzgerald is a remarkably busy man, constantly surrounded by people and yet, not once has anyone laid eyes on Rebecca, until now. I'm sitting on the back patio with Marcus, Linc, Jace, and Asher when Max and Elijah come out, with Zack not too far behind. As soon as I see their expressions, I know something is up. I'm immediately grateful that Cassie is already in bed.

"We got her. She's on the move with Fitz, destination unknown at present." Elijah starts and then he looks at Max, before concentrating on me, "but it's Friday." He doesn't have to say anything for me to catch his meaning. We know where he spends his Fridays. *Fucking Crimson.*

"How do we know it's her?" I ask them, concentrating on Max.

"Seb IDed her from her picture. It's definitely Rebecca O'Sullivan." he confirms and my stomach flips in excitement. She's alive. *For now.*

"Well, come on, let's go." Ash stands without hesitating; he's been so on edge about Rebecca. It's easy to look past all the girls being hurt by his father and brother when they are lost in a sea of nameless faces, but when you can put a face and a name to it, it becomes real. He sees her as me, imprisoned against her will and probably being broken beyond repair.

My frown is instant, we haven't yet been able to find a way into the club, short of becoming a member, so we don't really have a plan. "How are we going to get in?"

Ash just smirks that deadly Donovan smile, "through the front door, they'll let me in." He's that confident in his name, and in this town, I can't say I blame him. He doesn't wait for my response before he pushes past Max and heads inside. Max just shakes his head but follows after him anyway. Well, alright then, looks like we are going out.

It isn't long before we are armed to the teeth and spread across two black Escalades as we speed toward Black Hallows. Seb has since confirmed that the club is where they headed, and they have been inside for around ten minutes. Already too long if you ask me, especially considering that even with the speed we are going we still aren't close.

Twenty minutes later, we arrive. I exit the car with Asher, Marcus, Jace and Linc. Leaving Max and his guys to check out other entrances as we move towards the front door. It opens easily and when we step inside, we find an elegant lobby area. There is black satin covering the walls, a large black gloss desk and a plush rail of black material. We agreed on our way over that Ash would do the talking and I would act as if I were there as his party favor. Leaving Marcus and the guys to act as Asher's security. The guard eyes us immediately.

"Members only." He states before any of us even have a chance to speak. Not shocking considering we don't exactly look like their usual clientele.

"Asher Donovan." Ash responds and I see the recognition in the guard's eyes at his name. He flicks his eyes down to his tablet and taps away before looking back to him.

"Sorry sir, but I only have two Donovan members registered and you aren't one of them." I hold in my eye roll. Just as his hand goes to his ear as if he is about to communicate with someone, something flashes past me. I don't even get to recognize what it is before Lincoln has the guard unconscious on the floor.

Speechless, we all stare at him, but he just shrugs. "What? He clearly wasn't going to let us in." I mean what can we say, he's right.

He picks up the guy's tablet and taps away on it as Asher swipes some black cards from the desk. I look at the rail and realize that the black material that I thought made up the wall, is actually a row of cloaks. Fucking rich people shit, like this is just some kind of fucking rapist get together, complete with uniform. It disgusts me, but I'm not stupid, putting the guard down is bad enough, we need to blend in. I grab one for each of us, then pass them out to the guys who shrug them on without question.

Ash uses the black card to swipe us through the first set of double doors and as soon as they open, the pounding of music greets us. We enter right into the nightclub, the music is blaring, the lights are flashing and there are people dancing everywhere. There is a stage in the center of the room that has multiple cages on it, all filled with naked women dancing along to the music. To anyone else, it would look like they are having the time of their life, but the dead, vacant look in their eyes tells me otherwise. Fuck this is worse that I imagined, and I know this floor isn't even the worst of it.

From the intel we gathered, I know we need to move to the back of the club. The entrance to the top floor is over to our left, but we won't find what we need there. What we came for, I'm sure awaits us in the basement. We push through the gyrating bodies until we get to the other side, and Ash again uses the card to swipe us through. As the door opens, another guard appears and moves to grab me. He's quick, but I'm quicker. I dart back from his arm at the same time as I kick out my leg, hitting him in the stomach. Another guard steps up to help, but I know the boys have my back.

Lincoln and Jace tackle the other guard, just as Marcus drags back the one on me before I can do anything. I huff, "I had him River."

Marcus smiles, as his fist connects with his face, "I know baby, just let me, okay?"

I roll my eyes and he laughs. Once both the guards are down, we quietly make our way down the

305

stairs. I expect to come across more guards, but it seems to be strangely quiet. Shivers dance up my spine when we reach the bottom, because this place is like a maze. There are a few doors in front of us, and then numerous hallways, leading only the lord knows where. We all exchange a look knowing that until Max and his guys find us, we need to split up.

Before I can even say anything, Lincoln hauls Jace to his side and nods, "we got this," he says gesturing to one of the hallways, "you guys go." He taps his ear and I nod, turning on my comms and watching as they take the first hallway, leaving one for us and another unmanned. I take a deep breath and pull my gun from my waist and Marcus does the same. Asher looks between the two of us and then heads to the third hallway.

"Ash, what the hell?"

"Don't worry about me, Hells Bells, I'm the only one they won't kill on sight." He gives me a sadistic smile before turning and heading out of sight. I would be worried, but I know we all have our earpieces in to alert anyone if something goes down.

Marcus and I move down the hallway, and when we reach the first door, he presses up right behind me, "don't make me have to punish you again." He whispers into my hair and I smile, even though he can't see me.

"You wish, Riviera." We kick open door after door, coming across empty rooms and men in the middle of acts I won't wish to recall. When we get to the sixth door, I push it open and nearly choke on surprise, when the first eyes I meet are that of Rebecca O'Sullivan. She is slumped in a chair, wearing nothing but lingerie, and a

306

silk nightgown that's open, showing off her tanned physique. She looks slightly out of it, but still her stare widens as she takes me in. A guy turns towards me, raising his gun just as Marcus shoots him right in the head. Carter moves quickly, grabbing Rebecca by the throat and dragging her body to cover him. Gun to her head.

When I see there is no one else in the room I focus on him. He's handsome, brown hair that is tousled perfectly and brown eyes that are warm like chocolate. Even the smile he offers me now seems kind and friendly. That perfectly, polished, practiced face of a politician. Oh, he's good. His three-piece suit is clearly designer and tailored to perfection, and his shoes look freshly shined. Always putting on a public show.

"Miss King, you just ruined my business meeting." His voice is calm, controlled and completely lacking any fear. I sense the same relaxed nature in him that I get from Greg Donovan. Like they know they are completely untouchable. If the gun to her head scares Rebecca, she doesn't show it. In fact, her hand curves around the grip he holds to her throat. *Interesting.*

"I'd apologize, but I don't like to lie." I toss back and his smile widens. I knew it. Just like Greg, they get off on defiant women, but only on their terms. They would never fully relinquish control. I know it, he knows it. He won't let her go without a fight.

"Greg said you were exquisite," he purrs, his grip pulls Rebecca further into his body, she doesn't even react. Like this is completely normal behavior for him. He whispers into her ear loud enough for us to hear, "She's beautiful, isn't she, my little rose." She flinches slightly on the word rose, but it's gone so quick that I don't know if I even saw it. "I wish we had time to play." He says talking to me again now, "but seems like the fun is over." His finger tightens on the trigger, Marcus mutters my name, but I ignore him, keeping my eye on Carter's hand.

"Hurt her and I will kill you." My voice is calm and steady which is the exact opposite to how I am feeling right now.

He smiles the most genuine smile I've seen on him yet, dark, with a hint of evil. "I believe that, Miss King, you are your father's daughter after all."

The way he delivers those words sparks my interest. He wants to talk. Men like him always do and if I keep him talking, maybe I can distract him. "What do you know of my father?"

He smiles again, taking the bait, "I know he wanted a son, a son to be just like you." His gaze travels over my body, up and down. He pauses on the knife at my thigh and groans, "he'd be so proud of everything you've done." He takes his time dragging his eyes back to mine. "If it weren't for that cunt between your legs, that is. Jonathan King never knew how to treat a woman. Stick around in one of these rooms and I'm sure you'll find out."

My father's here. That is the only thing that sticks in my mind, but I don't want him to know how much his words are distracting me. Instead, I snort, "yeah and because of this cunt everyone presumes I'm a pussy."

Just as my words echo into the room, the fire alarm begins to blare. It startles me, as sprinklers spray out immediately and, in a flash, Rebecca is thrown to the floor and Carter disappears. What the fuck? I rush towards where he was standing and find a slim line in the wall, indicating a secret entrance. I push against it, but nothing happens. Fuck.

I turn and see Marcus looking at me as he wraps Rebecca in his black cloak, before lifting her into his arms. Her face is still a blank mask, like she has perfected the art of no emotion. Two years with that sick fuck, I can't imagine what she has had to endure. But there is no time to worry about that now. We need to get out of here and fast.

I ignore my drenched clothes as we leave the room. There are men in suits rushing past us, some alone and some dragging along half naked women. We follow them down the hall through the rain of the sprinklers, but just as we are passing the last door before the stairs someone grabs my arms. I whirl around raising my gun, but find Lincoln staring at me and I sigh in relief.

"Why is the fire alarm blaring?" I ask him, raising my voice slightly to be heard over the commotion.

Jace steps up beside me, completely wet and dripping, and shrugs his shoulders, "because there's a fire." He says it so casually that I almost want to laugh, almost.

I huff muttering, "of fucking course there is." I shake my head slightly, and then look between the two of them, wondering where Ash is. "Now what?"

Lincoln smirks and it's the biggest smile I have ever been gifted from him. "Now we do this quickly and get out of here before we burn."

I frown, we already have Rebecca, what more can we do when Carter has already escaped. "Do what?"

He ignores me and instead looks to Marcus, "you and Jace get Rebecca out of here, we will join you in a few." He eyes him with a serious look, knowing that Marcus will want to fight him, but before he can, Linc adds, "don't worry brother, I got your girl."

As my eyes meet River's I let him see the plea in them. He has to go. He has to get Rebecca out of here before someone comes for us, "I'll be fine."

Instead of arguing, he maneuvers so he only has one hand holding Rebecca, and he uses his other hand to drag me by the neck so he can claim my lips in a quick, searing kiss. "Don't make me come back for you Ells." His tone is dark and filled with filthy promise, his lips curling into a sinful smile, making sure that I know just how serious he is. He looks to Lincoln then, "ten minutes." is all he says before Linc nods. Jace and Marcus disappear into the crowd of people and we watch them go.

Turning back to Linc, I give him a playful glare. "What trouble are we getting into now, Superman?" I tease with a smile, and he laughs, shaking his head slightly to clear the water from his face.

"Only your favorite kind, you stabby, little King." He ushers me inside the room he appeared from and when he closes the door and steps out of my eyesight I am greeted with a shocking turn of events.

Cherry Daniels is strapped to a table. Naked, beaten and bleeding. Asher is standing behind a chair in the middle of the room and tied to the chair is the one man who could have stopped it all. Jonathan King.

Chapter 35

ELLE

A father is supposed to be a girl's first hero. The man she will measure every other man in her life against. The man who loves her unconditionally and protects her fearlessly. The man who teaches her how to be strong and independent. The man who doesn't let anyone hurt her. The man who gives her the world and everything in it.

My father is not that man.

Jonathan King is cold, calculating and completely heartless. It's something I saw growing up but was too young or naive to fully understand. He never spent any time alone with me, was never interested in anything I was doing, and didn't pay any attention to me until the summer I was taken. At the time, I was thrilled. I felt excited that he was finally taking an interest in me. Inviting me to join their elite parties and constantly introducing me to his friends. He would brag about how well I was doing in school and all my extracurriculars. It never crossed my mind to think it was anything other than fatherly love.

I was an idiot.

Jonathan King cares for one person and one person only. Himself. When he sees me, he laughs maniacally, "What? You expect me to be scared of her?" He shakes his head like this is all a big joke, but when he sees he is the only one laughing, he stops, straightening up.

"What's the matter, Father? Not up for some daddy, daughter bonding time?" I ask as my lips curl in disgust.

"Not unless you want to replace your friend on the table there." He tosses back without pause, and the sick thing is that he's completely serious.

Unable to stop myself from wanting an answer to the only question that has ever truly mattered, I step forward and ask. "Why'd you let them do it, Dad?"

He rolls his eyes in disappointment but answers me anyway. "Your mother was supposed to be mine, but when I got her, she was already tainted."

I can't hide my anger at his words, "Yeah by that sick fuck, you call a friend."

"Semantics." He waves his hand in dismissal. "Women like her are only good for one thing. I wanted an heir, and she was going to give me one. Only, I got you instead." His words sting, but I don't let it show. "I was a man, surrounded by powerful men with sons set to take the reins and all I had was a pair of pussies living under my roof."

"That was a good enough reason to sell me. To let your friends' rape and butcher me. Just because you wanted a son?" My words are laced in disbelief at what I have always known, but still hurts to hear. I can't stop the lone tear as it tracks down my cheek. Asher sees it and steps closer to my father, but I shake my head slightly, as I wipe it away.

Jonathan doesn't miss it though, and he scoffs. "You're pathetic, just like your mother, only good for one thing and you couldn't even do that right."

"I was a fucking kid. I wasn't supposed to know what's right. You were the parent, you were supposed to protect me, yet someone else's father had to be the one to save me." The tears continue to stain my cheeks, but I don't let the cry escape my throat.

"You think you are above us, yet you used your body to gain Michael's attention. Leading him to ruin his life and mine." He shakes his head, "it should have been simple. I found out about the boy your mother abandoned and I went straight to Elliot. He wanted revenge and I wanted power, so I gave him you."

"What power could that have possibly given you?"

"God, Elle, I thought some of myself would have rubbed off on you, but you're just as weak and naive as your mother. You'd be surprised at the price someone like you can fetch. You'd have made us both a lot of money and gained us a huge amount of favor. But Michael just couldn't resist being the fucking martyr."

"My brother would have ruined your plans." Asher speaks up from behind him, "he wanted Elle from the moment he had her, and Greg always gets what he wants."

"Even better." Jonathan spits, "you were too fucking stupid to make a move on her and bring the families together. I had no other choice."

314

"There's always a choice." I answer bitterly. He really thinks the only way for him to gain power was to hand me over to them. His own flesh and blood tossed away like trash, just because I wasn't an efficient heir.

"We don't have much time." Lincoln interrupts from behind me and I startle, having been unnerved by the interaction with my father. From the emotions he was evoking in me. What the fuck am I doing? I am Elle King. Not the heir he wanted, but the heir he fucking got. It's time he got to know exactly what kind of daughter he has.

I slowly walk towards him, as I speak. "You think your words have any effect on me daddy? That you can cut me down." I shake my head with a humorless laugh, "I've already been down, further than you can imagine until I bathed in the pits of hell. You thought I was an easy target. Just a lamb you could send off to slaughter?"

I glance at Cherry as she silently watches us with fear in her eyes. She is already fully acquainted with the Elle King that stands in this room. It's time my father is too.

I bend down until I can look him right in the eye, hand slipping to my thigh, but he is too focused on my words to notice.

"But I'm not a lamb, Daddy, I'm a wolf."
I slice his throat before he can even take his next breath. Letting his blood splash onto my skin. I don't know when the sprinklers stopped, but it's now that I register that we are no longer being showered in water.

I look at Ash, who stares silently until a proud smile spreads across his face. He looks past me to

315

Lincoln and when I do the same, I find an eerily similar expression to Ash's on his face.

Lincoln shakes his head slightly before saying, "we really need to go."

"I know." I reply turning to where Cherry still lies, "just one more bit of business."

I stalk towards the table and check her over, the injuries she sustained from me are still evident, but clouded in fresh ones. Blood pours from her neck and stomach where there are two fresh wounds and the bruising around her thighs tells me exactly what was going on before we got here. I should feel sorry for her, but I don't. I can't bring myself to feel one ounce of compassion at her being in this state.

She almost cost me everything. She took the thing that mattered most to me and handed it over to the Donovan's. without a care in the world. She doesn't deserve anything from me, but I give it to her anyway. I lean over untying her wrists and then move to her ankles. I can feel Asher and Lincoln's stares on my back as I free her, but I don't look their way. Once she can move, she sits up and pushes to the side of the table. She moves to stand, and I help her, as her legs almost give out on her.

When her eyes meet mine, she opens her mouth to speak, but I beat her to it. "If you dance with the devil then you are going to get burnt." I plunge my knife into her side. Right between her ribcage and straight into her heart. She's dead instantly, her eyes barely reacting to the shock. I push her body off mine and let it drop to the floor, as I meet the guy's widened eyes.

I wipe my knife on the table and place it back on my thigh. "Now we can go."

Chapter 36

MARCUS

I can't stop my knee from bouncing up and down as I wait for Elle to come outside. It's been seven minutes, three more and I am going in. I put Rebecca in the front passenger seat and strapped her in, she is still yet to say a word, her vacant stare constantly scanning the surrounding area. Jace is pacing back and forth outside, furiously smoking a cigarette. Just as sirens start to blare in the distance, I see Max burst out of the side door, followed by Mason and Liam. I hold my breath, but then Max turns and ushers out Elle, with Linc and Ash quick on her tail. As soon as I see her my whole body relaxes.

As she gets closer, Jace rushes over to her, gripping her by the shoulders and checking her over, like he just needs to reassure himself that she's okay. She smiles, saying something I don't hear, and nods her head towards the car Max and his guys are heading to. He fist bumps Lincoln and they both follow Max as Elle and Ash make their way over to me. Asher opens the door for her, letting her climb inside before he joins me in the back. Elle is covered in blood, but I say nothing as we speed off into the night.

She eyes us in the mirror and nods, and we head off in the direction of the South Side. With the speed she is going it doesn't take long for us to get to the Crows clubhouse and when we approach, I think she is going to slow down, but instead, she presses down on the gas and crashes through the gate, without warning.

They burst open and before I know it, she slams on the brakes and jumps from the car, just as men pour out of the buildings, guns raised. It isn't long before their President pushes his way to the front. When his stare lands on Elle, he frowns, swinging his gaze to the car, as Asher and I step out. I move towards Rebecca's door and pause waiting for them to lower their weapons.

Connor waves his hand, and they all drop their arms, as he speaks, "you really are as fucking crazy as they're saying." He eyes the blood covering her but doesn't comment on it.

A slight shrug is the only reaction she has to his words, and with a nod from their President, all but three of the Crows, head back inside. Not before they all let their stares linger on Elle, as she stands there with her clothes clinging to her body thanks to the water and blood covering her chest. Once it's just the four of them, Elle turns towards me and nods. I pull open the door and go to help Rebecca out, but she bats my hand away. Stepping out alone, head held high. She is wrapped fully in the black cloak from the club, and looks almost regal as she brings her gaze to her father's.

"I held up my end of the deal." Elle says calmly, as Connor O'Sullivan stares at his daughter in shock before stalking towards her and engulfing her in a hug. She doesn't react at first, but then her arms slowly curl around his waist and a tear slips down her face.

Connor looks over her shoulder to speak to Elle. "Whenever, wherever, call us and we'll be there." He says, and one of the guy's lips curls in distaste at his words.

Elle nods at him, as he turns to one of the guys standing here, "Get Frank here now!" He snaps before turning and taking Rebecca inside. She halts, turning to look towards us before leaving her father's arms and slowly approaching Elle.

They stare at one another until Rebecca steps up to her, close enough so she can whisper in her ear, as she grips her arm. All six of us just watch them, unable to hear what she said, but when she pulls away Elle smiles and nods her head. We all watch her leave with her dad and then I notice Elle's focus has moved to the three men still standing here.

"What?" The one wearing the VP patch snaps, as he pulls out a cigarette and lights it up, blowing the smoke out.

Elle shrugs, "Nothing, Aiden. Just thought you guys would be a little happier at Rebecca being home." She cocks her head to the side as she surveys them. "Or was her being gone better for you? Did one of you fuck her and you don't want daddy to know?" There is a teasing glint to her voice, but I can tell she is serious as she watches them all closely. The one on the left huffs slightly and she zones in on him, "was it you Ezra? Did you take a taste of Daddy's little princess and thought you could take it to the grave?"

"None of your fucking business." Aiden shuts her down, and she smiles like she got the reaction she wanted.

"Interesting. Well, you're welcome."

Ezra breaks his silence, "what's the matter princess? Want us on our knees, ready to taste that sweet cunt in thanks, like every other man in this town?"

"Watch it." Ash snaps, stepping forward before I can, and the third one's eyes flash in delight as he takes his turn to speak.

"How's that brother of yours, Donovan?" He purrs.

Ash smirks, taking the bait, "not nearly as dangerous as I am, Killian."

"I'll bet." Is all he responds, flashing him a grin of his own.

"Where's the Mayor?" Ezra asks, and Elle looks at him.

"Running, if he knows what's good for him." She responds, and he frowns.

"You let him go?" He spits, out and I swear if he moves an inch towards her, I'll fucking end him right here.

"It was him or her." She replies, simply and he grinds his jaw as he realizes what she means. All three of them stare at her intently with furious expressions until Aiden brings his gaze to mine.

"I'd take your girl home now, Riviera." I can't help the laugh that bursts out of me.

"I don't take my girl anywhere." Is my only response and Elle flashes me a smile over her shoulder, before she looks at them and slowly backs away.

321

"I look forward to seeing you again very soon, boys." Her tone and the way she handled them has me hardening in my pants. Doesn't matter when or where, whenever she takes control like this it gets me hot as fuck. She moves towards the driver's side, but I snag her by the waist and drag her to the back door, opening it and pushing her inside. Asher rounds the car without complaint and gets behind the wheel to get us out of there.

I ignore the blood coating her as I grab the back of her neck and slam her lips to mine, and she gasps in surprise, allowing me to slip my tongue right into her mouth. Her hesitation doesn't even last a second before she is kissing me back, devouring each other's mouths like we are both chasing our next breath from the other.

I pull back, planting my forehead against hers as we both try to catch our breath, "do I even want to know whose blood this is?" I ask, only slightly jokingly, and she huffs a little laugh.

"It's Jonathan King's." Is all she says, and I can't keep the surprise off my face.

"And Cherry Daniels'." Asher adds from the front, and I groan.

"That shouldn't turn me on, but it does." I whisper and she laughs like I'm crazy. Fuck it, I am. Totally and insanely crazy, and all for her. She presses her hand to my thigh so she can shift closer to kiss me again. When her fingers graze against my hard cock, she pulls back in surprise. Her eyes dance with lust of their own. "It's going to take a very long, hot shower to get my baby clean." I tease, and she grins. I move to whisper in her hair,

322

leaving a trail of kisses as I go, "all of them wanted you, looking at you like you aren't mine." I say, thinking about how every guy let themselves check her out.

She tilts her head to the side giving me better access to her neck, "too bad I am all yours."

Her hand squeezes me over my jeans slightly and I groan again, nipping her ear before gritting out, "that's right you are."

"Please don't fuck on the back seat while I'm here with you. It's bad manners." Asher's voice halts us both in our tracks, freezing like a pair of naughty kids. We look at each other and then burst out laughing,

"Sorry, Ash." Elle says, with a laugh.

"Yeah sorry, man." I add, and he just shakes his head and mutters 'insufferable' under his breath and we both laugh again. I turn back to Elle and lean in to whisper one more time, "later," is all I say and the wicked smile she gives me in return tells me how much fun we are going to have when we get home. I look forward to that shower.

Chapter 37

LINCOLN

What I saw tonight, is the closest I have felt to my childhood in a long time. I killed so many men tonight. *Too many.* Yet somehow, it will still never be enough. There will always be more, sick depraved men who use and abuse people for their own pleasure, until their playthings become useless. Only then are they discarded and sometimes, not even then. I neck the whiskey, letting the burn slide down my throat.

I can't relax, can't settle. There were just so many girls. Young, naked, fucking abused, and broken girls. I'm here with a team of guys looking out for Elle and Cassie, but who's looking out for all of them? These girls have families or homes, or at least they did, at some point. Who's watching out for them? Who's missing them, waiting for them to come home, even though some never will? How is that okay? It's not. Someone should be doing something. I should be doing something, more than I already am. Elle opened my eyes to a world of crime happening right in front of me, and I can't sit and do nothing. I need to help them.

I hear the door open and a minute later, Marcus is marching through the living room with Elle slung over his shoulder, muffling her laughs into his back. "Brother," he nods at me before they disappear down the hallway towards their rooms.

I frown just as Asher enters after them, "where are they going?" I ask, even though I suppose it's pretty obvious. I just didn't expect it after what she did tonight.

Asher rolls his eyes as he joins me at the counter, pulling his own tumbler from the cupboard. "To fuck each other's brains out like always, I don't know how they aren't sick of each other." He huffs. helping himself to a healthy serving of vodka.

I can't help the slight smile that ghosts over my face when I think of the difference in Marcus, since Elle came home. He's not the same boy I met in foster care. No. That Marcus was cold, calculating and lost in his grief and pain. The brother I have now is an entirely new man. Elle brings out the best in him, like they are two sides of the same coin, destined for one another, always.

"When you have chemistry like that, you can never get enough." I answer him, Marcus and Elle are drawn to one another like a moth to a flame. That won't change, no matter how long they spend together. Their connection is so deeply rooted with one another that even their trauma couldn't break it.

I take another burning sip as I continue, "When you have that kind of connection, why wouldn't you wrap yourselves in it?" With all the shit we are facing, they are still somehow managing to find happiness in each other. That's the kind of thing that will keep them fighting.

325

"They're happy and they please each other." I shrug, feeling the tension in the air and wanting to disperse it. "And from what I hear, it isn't easy to please a woman." I smile at my own little joke, which I'm sure went right over his head, and just when I think he will ignore me he responds.

"And what do you know of pleasing a woman? I thought the male specimen was the only thing that interests you. Or should I just say Logan?"

He eyes me expectantly, and I take a slow sip of my drink as I contemplate how to answer. He smirks slightly behind his glass, thinking he has silenced me. "Oh, a lot of things interest me, dark prince. I just don't act on them." I ensure my tone is laced in innuendo, but of course he ignores it.

The look in his eye turning more serious if that's even possible, "this is a now or never kind of life, Lincoln. You should know that by now." His words have my spine straightening, does he think I could ever forget that after what we all just went through, what we still have to go through?

"I know that better than anyone," I snap, adding more whiskey to my glass and downing it again. The taste on my tongue forces me to speak more freely than usual. "I just know now isn't the time to indulge in the fantasies in my head."

He smirks again, and my eyes transfix on the dimple that appears on his left cheek, "And is it your fantasy to please a woman?"

"Is it yours?" I toss back, watching his fist clench around the glass in his hand, but he remains silent. I think

326

he is going to leave, but instead he drops into one of the stools and sighs.

I don't know why I start talking, but the words leave me before I can stop them. "My father was a serial killer." His head snaps in my direction as soon as I speak, my focus remaining on my now empty glass.

When he doesn't react more than that, I continue, "there were so many women." I pour another drink and take a healthy sip, I need it. My father would bathe them, dress them, do their hair and makeup, and then pose them. Then once he had indulged himself in his sick fantasy, he would murder them.

Asher remains silent yet, his full attention is on me as I speak, "I helped him. It was our little game, our little secret." I have never told another soul what happened that night. Not the police, my social worker or even my brothers, so I don't know why I tell him. I just feel like I should. I don't tell him how scared I was or how wrong it felt, I don't want his pity. It's why I've never told anyone else. They would say things like 'you were just a kid' or 'you didn't know any better'. But they'd be wrong, because I did know better, I was just a coward.

"My mother was his final victim." My spineless behavior and fear of my father left me blind to protecting her. If I would have just stopped him, told someone, she would still be alive. Her death was my fault.

"None of the others screamed." I recall, they were all so silent and docile, but not my mom. She begged him, pleaded with him, she cried so hard her voice went and he just ignored her. He said he would let me say goodbye, that it was his gift to me, and I should be grateful. Then he strangled her.

"He killed her right there in front of me. Then I killed him"

The silence following my admission should be awkward, deafening yet I find nothing but comfort. Like a weight has been lifted off my chest at my admission. I can feel Asher's stare burning into me, but I can't bring myself to look at him. To allow my darkness to mix with his, it won't change anything. I don't know how long we sit there, but for the first time in a while, the silent company feels nice.

When he finally breaks his silence, I don't expect what comes out of his mouth. "That's how you knew how to trust Elle right from the start. Why you had her back, no questions asked. You saw the look in her eye. The one that only comes from a specific type of trauma." He knocks back the rest of his drink and I am once again transfixed by the masterpiece that is Asher Donovan, as he swallows it down.

"Isn't it funny how one night, one moment, can just change the course of everything." He says, staring down into his own glass, thankfully, completely oblivious to my stare. "I still remember her eyes, the way they were before. I had never seen eyes as blue as hers, or a smile as big. I envied Marcus when we met." He admits, and it's like he senses my raised brow because he shakes his head. "Not in the way people always presume. I envied their friendship, their closeness. I'd never had that. We moved around a lot, never settling in one place for long. When we got to Black Hallows, and I saw the bond they had, the friendship they'd built. God, I wanted that." He shakes his head, like the memories are just barreling into his mind.

"You have that." I tell him solemnly. I see the way he and Elle are with each other. They have each other's back no matter what. They have killed for one another and would die that way too.

"Yeah, at what cost?" He snaps. "My friendship with Elle led her right into a pit of fucking snakes." He grips the tumbler so hard I don't know how it doesn't break, and I can't control myself.

I storm around the counter until I am next to him, "No. It led her to an unbreakable friendship, to the father of her child, and to a family she adores. Don't ever forget that. You are not your father's son, Asher."

His stormy blue eyes lock with mine as he digests every word I say. His body turning towards mine, bringing his knees against my outer thigh as he replies, "neither are you, Lincoln."

He stares at me intensely, and the way he says my name has me thinking ungodly things. I feel like we have broken through the invisible barrier that always seems to sit between us. He's looking at me and finally seeing the real me, like no one else has before. The connection like no other I've ever felt. He looks like he wants to say more, do more, but that can't be right. Just as I open my mouth to ask, someone else beats me to it.

"What's going on here then?" Logan's flirty banter breaks us apart. I watch as those Donovan defenses slam back into place. That barrier rising back up, never to be brought down again.

329

"Just talking shit," Asher responds without taking his gaze from mine, before he finally breaks it, grabbing his glass and slipping off the stool. "It's late, I'm gonna head to bed." He doesn't look at either of us as he rinses out his glass, and then leaves without another word.

I can feel Logan staring at me, but my gaze trails after the unattainable and forever out of reach dark prince.

"Don't let yourself sink, Lincoln." Logan says, stepping up beside me.

I turn to look at him, letting myself appreciate the beauty that is Logan Royton. We have been getting closer these last few weeks, but neither of us has stepped over the line we crossed in the gym again. "I'm not sure what you mean."

He sighs, "I know better than anyone what it's like to be caught in the tsunami that is Asher Donovan. I've drowned in it for years, and trust me when I say, it doesn't come with a life raft."

He looks at me one more time and I detect a hint of pity in his gaze, before he shakes his head and returns back the way he came, and I remain where I always do. Alone and in control. Ignoring the temptations, they both have to offer. I won't ever be like my father and take something that doesn't belong to me, no matter how much I want it.

Chapter 38

ELLE

I wake up to Marcus' hands roaming across my naked body. I don't know how many times we fucked last night, but I do know I lost count. Against the bathroom counter, still covered in blood, in the shower as it washed down the drain and multiple times between these sheets. Just endless hours of pleasure, riding the high and adrenaline of the night before. I should feel something, guilt, grief, remorse? I don't. I feel nothing but peace and pleasure.

The only sins I will think about are the ones I committed in this bed with my River. I won't think about my father, about Cherry. I won't feel any sort of regret. Not for him or for her. They both got what was coming to them. I think Marcus was expecting me to break, distracting me with his body so I could do nothing but be consumed by him. He didn't need to do that; it happens without him even trying.

That's why now, instead of worrying about the bodies that were dropped last night, I think about the way his hands grip my waist possessively, the way his stubble covered mouth grazes up my neck. The tug of his teeth on my earlobe, the pads of his fingers as they slip between my legs and cup me. The groan he releases when he finds me wet for him, is fucking unholy.

"Mmm, morning, little King." He mumbles into my ear, as his finger sinks between my folds, brushing against my clit.

"Morning," I moan out breathlessly, as he swipes his fingers around my sweet spot, my toes curling in response. Fuck. It doesn't matter how many times he fucks me. I always want more. My hips start to roll against his hand, and I feel his smile on the curve of my neck.

"Does my baby need something?" He asks, letting his teeth sink into my shoulder as I muffle my moan with a pillow, pushing my hips back into his groin.

"Marcus, please." I beg, and the hand that still grips my waist tightens.

"I fucking love hearing you moan my name, Ells." He grits through his teeth, as his hand moves to grab his hard cock, as he lines it up between my ass cheeks, slowly letting it slip down until he finds my entrance.

"And I fucking love you." I hiss, as he slams inside with a loud moan.

"I love you too, baby." Using his free hand, he lifts me up and rolls us over, so I'm on top with my back to him. "Now ride me, Ells, show me how much."

I reach out and lean my palms onto his thighs so I can rise up and then I slowly sink back down. His hands fly to my hips again tightening around me. He pulls me down even further and holds me there, so I am feeling him deep inside. When he squeezes me, I start to slide up again and he uses his grip to slam me back down. We do this over and over until we are fucking each other relentlessly, moaning and panting and desperate for more. When I find a rhythm, he sits up, leaning back on one of his hands and using the other to reach around to rub my clit. We fuck slow and hard, until Marcus can't hold back. Pushing me forward, he slips out so that he can reposition me on my knees before he comes up behind and slides back inside. He fucks me hard and fast, hitting that perfect spot inside.

"I'm getting close," he grits out. "Touch that pussy for me." I slide my hand between my legs and press my fingers in quick circles around my clit, feeling myself clenching around him as my orgasm begins to build. "Ah, fuck, Ells, just like that." One hand grips my side as the other slips into my hair pulling slightly and the moan I let out is fucking porn worthy. "Fuck!" He groans, as I come around his cock. He thrusts a few more times before I feel him spill inside me. Both of us fall forward, breathless and sweating, and then he rolls me over, pushing my hair from my face. "So, fucking perfect. I love you" He kisses me again and I can't get the smile off my face.

"I love you." I repeat back to him and now he smiles.

"Pinky promise, you'll tell me that forever." He grins cupping my cheek and kissing me again.

I bring my pinky into the air and he laughs as he curls it with mine, "pinky promise, River."

After we have both showered for a second time, we quickly get dressed and make our way into the kitchen. Only Helen and Cassie are in there and both smile wide when they see us.

"Mommy." Cass greets me, and I move towards her.

"Morning princess, you okay?" I ask, dropping a kiss to her head.

"Yes. Grandma said we can have slumber." She tells me excitedly, and I look at Helen with a smile. It's something we haven't done in ages, yet Cassie loves it. We did it at the old house. We would drag mattresses into the living room, pile them with blankets and pillows and have an on the floor sleepover with all the family. We'd eat pizza, watch movies, and Arthur and Helen would even show old family photos. We all love doing it and I know we are long overdue for it.

"Sound's perfect baby, I can't wait." I say, smiling as Helen hands me a coffee and I thank her.

"Can River come?" She asks with her pleading tone, and I laugh.

"Of course." I say, sitting down next to her and leaning close, "how about we invite daddy and all the other boys too?" I ask, and she gleams up at me before throwing her arms around my neck.

"And Taylor too?" She adds, and I can't turn down her cute face, so I agree to invite her.

"Yayyy!" She practically screams down my ear but seeing the happiness on her face is worth the deafness she might have just caused me. Mom life, hey.

We spend the rest of the early morning making breakfast and reading books to Cass, not even once thinking about my father and the fact that I just killed him.

334

I just think about how I will do everything in my power to be the parent to her, that I should have had growing up.

Once Cassie gets distracted by Logan playing Mario Kart, I leave her and Marcus and head off to see where everyone else is. I haven't seen Ash, Lincoln or Jace yet this morning and I want to check in and catch up after everything that went down last night.

I find Lincoln busy at work with Elijah so leave him be, and Zack tells me that Asher is sparring with Tyler out back. I shake my head at that and then head off to hunt down Jace, texting Taylor on my way to invite her over.

I find him at the back of the garden, where he has dragged one of the sun loungers. He is lying down staring up at the sky with a lit joint hanging from his mouth and he doesn't sense my presence, until I flop down between his feet.

"Stalking me, Queenie?" He asks, without looking at me.

"How did you know it was me?" I ask curiously.

His eyes find mine and he smiles, but it's nothing like his real smile and I frown, "you're the only one who would ignore my silent brooding and come check on me." He says matter of factly.

"Ah, so you admit you are brooding," I tease, hoping to turn that fake smile into a real one, but he just shrugs. I know how hard he is finding things. How much of the past is being dragged up by being here with me. I hate that he is caught up in this. "Well snap out of it, we're having slumber night."

"Should I know what that means?" He inhales another drag of his joint and I can't help myself when I grab it and toss it away. "Hey!" He protests, but I ignore it.

"Slumber night is Royton tradition and I'm calling mandatory attendance." I stand, trying to enforce my fake authority and he glares up at me as I add, "sober."

He rolls his eyes, pushing himself into a seated position, "I'll be there." He grumbles, and I note he is still wearing last night's clothes.

My phone vibrates in my pocket and I pull it out, reading the new message from Taylor that says she wouldn't miss it, with a smiley face. I can't help my smug tone as I say. "Yeah, well so will Taylor, so I suggest you take a shower."

I don't linger for his response as I turn and head back to the house but smile when I hear him shuffling along behind me. He might not admit it, but she's definitely already one of us and I can't wait for both of them to realize it.

I spend the rest of the afternoon helping Helen set up for the slumber. We get the guys to push all the living room furniture up against the walls and then drag a few of the mattresses into the center. Max sends one of his guys out to get a big projector with a screen, and Lily adds a few fairy lights for ambience. By the time Taylor arrives, the whole room looks like a giant bed, filled with pillows and blankets.

Cassie is bouncing excitedly between Arthur and Helen on the sofa, as she yells out higher and lower to Zack and Max as they fix the projector to the wall.

"Wow, so when you said sleepover, you really meant sleepover." Taylor stands awe struck at the door, as she takes in the room.

"Tay, you made it." I greet her with a hug, and it feels good to be doing something so teenage like.

"Yeah, Owen gave me a ride." She eyes me curiously like she's waiting for me to expand on Owen's presence at her house, but when I don't, she continues. "This place looks insane."

I laugh, "yeah well, what my daughter wants, she gets." I shake my head at the thought. I'm not usually the kind of Mom to give her things on a whim, but after everything that happened, I can't help it. I realize how precious time with her is.

She smiles, clutching her bag tightly. "I still can't believe you have a daughter."

"You get used to it." Marcus curls his arms around my waist from behind.

"I can't believe you got used to it. That's the most unbelievable part." Taylor jokes, and I can't help the laugh that bursts out of me.

"Miracles can happen." I jest lightly, and that earns me a nip to the neck from River.

"Watch it, little King." He murmurs into my ear, and I can't keep the wide grin from my face. These are the kind of nights I want. Fun and light-hearted, surrounded by my friends and family. Nights like this make it all worth it.

"Where should I set up?" Taylor questions.

I nod for her to follow me. "You're over here by Cassie and I. Come on."

I get Taylor settled and then we join Lily in the kitchen to make fruit mocktails for Cassie. Surprisingly, Lily gets on really well with her and it's nice to see a little friendship forming with them.

We watch two princess movies, eat more popcorn than I care to admit and have taken part in more Disney karaoke singalongs than I thought possible, with so many guys here. Tonight, is what we all needed, a reminder as to why we are doing any of this, a reminder of what we could lose.

A couple of hours later, Cassie is snoring softly beside me, tired out from all the fun of the slumber. Everyone seems to have settled in their own little groups. Max and Zack are playing Call of Duty, while a few of his guys watch. Ash is sitting in the corner tapping away on his laptop, Lily is sitting by him and she keeps pointing to things on the screen and he keeps batting her hand away.

Marcus, Lincoln, Jace and Logan all sat by the sofa, they're laughing and joking and every so often I watch Jace's eyes float across the room towards Taylor and I.

"You think he would make it less obvious." Taylor grumbles.

"What?" I'm guessing she has noticed the same thing I have, but I want to be sure.

She huffs, "Conrad and his lingering eyes, way to make a girl feel flustered." She fidgets with her empty mocktail glass and pretends like she isn't looking back.

"You like him." I tease, bumping her shoulder with mine and I see the blush against her pale skin.

"What's not to like? Look at him! He's a freaking walking temptation." She slowly flicks her eyes his way, then huffs again when she catches him already staring at her. "No eighteen-year-old should be that attractive. It's unnatural."

I follow her gaze towards the guys and grumble my agreement. Because she is right. Marcus with his dark brooding eyes, Jace and his tattooed torso, Lincoln, and his little corner of the mouth smirk. Hell, I can even appreciate the sharp line of Logan's jaw. All of them are ridiculously good looking, yet more than that because they also have personalities that rival their looks. A dangerous mixture for anyone who gets too close, they're hypnotic.

"So, what are you waiting for?" I wonder. I know Jace doesn't want her in this, but she's already in it whether he likes it or not. I mean technically she was one of us before he was.

"A cold shower," she mutters under her breath before adding louder, "I thought after the dance, when I kissed him." She shrugs, "I don't know, that he would make a move."

I flinch at the mention of that night. Fuck. To be normal and be worrying about something as mundane as kissing a guy and him not reacting to it. She doesn't even know half of it. Jace probably forgot all about it.

I sit up on my knees and grab her hand, "look, there has been a lot going on, but I know Jace likes you more than he is letting on, so if you like him, then you should tell him."

She looks at me and then back to him before she also shifts to her knees. "You know what, you're right!" She agrees, her face setting into determination. "What's the worst that could happen?" She adds and then before I can say anything, she stands and makes her way across the room to the guys, and I have no choice but to follow.

Because she's right... What's the worst that can happen?

Chapter 39

LOGAN

I have never liked it when we did slumber night. All it does is remind me how lucky I am. I have an amazing family, I know that. I could have landed in a much worse place than I did, but when we do stuff like this. All it does is remind me that I only got this lucky because both my parents died.

Everyone is sleeping. Well, everyone that is here, but I am wide awake. I can't relax. Not that I have ever been a good sleeper. It's something I've always struggled with. Lily helped when we were younger. We used to sneak into each other's rooms all the time, but that stopped as we got older. She's the same, doesn't always sleep great and I worry about her now. She never talks to me, not like she used to. She was doing better at college, seemed happier, but then everything happened, and now here we are.

It was nice to watch her get along with Elle and Taylor tonight. Watching the three of them bond over their love of Disney karaoke and then The Vampire Diaries. They're all team Stefan apparently, which is fucking stupid. Everyone knows it should be team Klaus.

I can feel the anxiety practically crawling through my body, I need to do something, anything. I slip out of the mattress I'm on and eye everyone else. My mom and dad are sound asleep on one side of me and Cassie, Elle, Taylor and Lils are on the other side. Marcus is on another mattress next to them, like he can't bear to be away from Elle. Zack is on another, a tight grimace on his face even while he sleeps, never escaping the pain from what that piece of shit Greg did to him.

I don't know what's worse, the fact he almost killed him, or the fact Zack is a fucking Donovan himself. My brother, my first friend, tied to the enemy in a way I never could have imagined. I shake the thoughts from my head and quietly tiptoe from the room. I decide to head to the gym, hopefully try and burn off some of this energy. It always helped when I still lived at home. I quickly change into sweats and a tank, and then make my way there, only to find someone has beat me here.

"Fucking hell, Conrad, you're the last person I thought I'd find in here."

"I can't sleep." Jace grumbles, as he pushes himself up on a leg press.

"Me neither." I respond pointlessly, because clearly being in the gym at 3am shows I can't sleep. I watch his form, taking in the tension in his shoulders and the tight set of his jaw. He's brutally stunning and it's easy to see why Taylor has been drooling over him all night.

"Wouldn't have anything to do with that little temptation in the silk pj's would it?" I tease, attempting to break the seriousness, but all it does is rile him up more.

342

"Watch it." He snaps, and I smile, knowing I've hit the nail on the head.

"Hey man, no threat." I hold my hands up in mock defense, moving to sit down on the floor so I can lean against the mirror. "I'm just saying, if I was trying to hit that I wouldn't be able to sleep either."

"I'm not trying to hit that." He grits out.

"No?" I question, because I watched them flirt furiously with each other all evening.

He huffs, slamming the leg press back into its resting position and climbing off. He wipes the sweat from his brow before coming and flopping down beside me. "I can't hit that." He adds quietly.

I frown, "problems downstairs?"

He scoffs, "No, you fucking dick!" He swipes both hands over his face in distress. "I don't want her anywhere near any of this, near me. It's not safe to be around us." I don't have to hear the silent 'me', he added onto that in his head.

I soften at his confession because I know first-hand what it's like to be in this world. I remember the night I woke up to my mother's cries and discovered a distressed and bloodied girl in my father's office. Our life was so disgustingly perfect. Elle changed that, changed all of us. I was blinded by my pristine fucking everything. Forcing it all to be flawless, as I tried to forget about the destruction my parents' death left behind. It would have been easier to keep my rose-tinted glasses in place, but at what cost? Elle isn't the only girl out there who was hurt. Thousands of people are abused, trafficked, and murdered every single day. It would be wrong to ignore that.

I want to help people. It's why I'm following in my dad's footsteps and studying to go to medical school. I want to become someone worthy of helping those people when they need it most. But I still want to live my life. The situation we are in right now is dangerous, but it won't be like this forever, right? It can't be. We can't put our life on hold just in case something bad might happen.

"Shouldn't it be up to her to make that decision?" I ask, because I see the way she looks at him, if he doesn't see how far gone, she already is for him, then he's dumber than he looks.

"Sometimes we have to make decisions that no one likes but are for the greater good." He responds, and I look at him and take in the sadness that coats his face. Elle told me what happened to his sister and I can't imagine what that must have been like. The rage I felt that night, when Zack told me who Elle was and what she had endured, it was like nothing else I have ever experienced. She was a stranger, yet also family. All I wanted to do was protect her, protect Lily. Jace didn't even get that chance, but with Taylor he does.

Understanding dawns on me. "And this is one of those times." It's not a question, but he answers me anyway.

"Yes." He breathes out solemnly, before plastering the fake smile that I know all too well on his face. It's the same one I have perfected for myself. "Besides, she probably just wants a night with the playboy Rebel."

I can sense his desperation for lighter topics, so I offer him a wink. "Don't we all." I nudge his shoulder again suggestively, and he smiles more genuinely this time.

He ignores my attempts at flirting and adds. "Besides, girls like Taylor are unattainable to someone like me." I want to call bullshit, tell him that isn't true, but the words die on my tongue as my own realm of torment enters the gym, pausing when he spots us both.

"Trust me I know all about the unattainable." I mutter in response to Jace, as Asher Donovan crosses the threshold.

"Mind if I work out?" He asks, ever the perfect, polite, fucking, annoying gentleman. I don't know why he bothers with that perfect, well-bred facade when we all know how many skeletons are in his closet.

"Didn't think the deadly, Donovan, had to ask permission for anything." I tease, and I hear Jace muffle a laugh beside me as I taunt Asher.

"I don't ask permission for anything. I was just trying to be polite." Ash tosses back, and I smirk, loving when he takes my bait.

I rise to my feet and move towards him as he grabs a towel from the rack, "Oh my little psycho, I love it when you talk dirty to me." My words land me with that signature eye roll of his, that I love so much.

I didn't really see much of Ash when Elle first came to live with us. Lily and I attended a private boarding school and were away from home during term time. After graduation, I spent the summer before college at home, and that is when the quiet and menacing

Donovan caught my eye. Since then, he has become a fucking thorn in my side. A sexy, infuriating, fucking thorn.

"Want to spar so I have an excuse to hit you?" He taunts back, and I can't hide my smile, he wants to fight me, then let's fucking go.

"You never need an excuse baby, just a time and place." I wink at him again, as I reach for the wrapping and start to tape up my fists. He grabs it from me and does the same.

I turn to Jace, "Want to spot us?"

He shrugs, "not like I'm doing anything else."

We go a few rounds, both of us pinning the other multiple times until we are panting and sweating. The anxiety from before is long forgotten, as I watch Asher move. I can think of a variety of ways I'd like to see him breathless and hot but considering this is the only one he would allow, I take it.

When I pin him for the third time, his irritation flares. "Get the fuck off me." He grunts.

"Get off you, or get you off?" I bite my lip suggestively, and instead of an immediate rebuttal, I watch his eyes drop to my mouth. *What the fuck?* Two years of over-the-top flirting and suggestive taunts, and not once has he ever hesitated to tell me to fuck off in one way or another.

I don't get a chance to linger on that thought when the gym door opens again, and Zack looks down at us. "Do I even want to know?"

I get up off of Asher, holding my hand out to help him up, as I respond to Zack, "just sparring big bro, no big deal." It's only when I refer to him, using that name, that I remember again that Zack and Asher are also brothers. Looking at the two of them side by side, you can see it, see where the resemblances are.

"Looks like we all had the same idea." Zack grunts, as he moves across to the treadmill and gets on, setting it to a slow walk. He is still trying to exercise his leg while recovering from the stab wound.

I crick my neck as I watch him, stamping down on the anger that flares up in me, every time I see him struggle. I note Asher is watching him too, and I wonder if he feels the same. I hate it. I'm just so sick of the morbid feeling that lingers in the air all the time lately.

My go to defense mechanism, slams back into place. "Guess we can't fuck now you're my brother's brother hey, psycho." I joke, and the tight clench of Asher's jaw, has me preening in delight.

"You and Zack aren't blood." He grits out, and my smile widens.

"I know that, just wanted to see if you did too. Sounds like you are trying to find ways to fuck me, I always knew you wanted me."

Asher picks up his towel and wipes the sweat from his neck and chest, "if I wanted to fuck you, Logan, I would. Go wake the help and have him see to your needs instead." He doesn't allow me to respond, before he stalks from the room.

Zack grunts through his pained breaths, "you never give up do you?"

"Quitting is for losers," I say, looking at him, "isn't that what you always taught me?"

He just shakes his head in exasperation, and Jace comes and stands beside me, as my eyes return to the spot Asher just vacated. "You have the worst taste in men, Royton."

"Nah," I shrug, "I have the best taste, they just haven't realized it yet."

Chapter 40

ELLE

The next week at school is quiet. Too quiet. Everyone outside of our group gives us a wide berth, since what happened with Cherry. We are still yet to face any backlash from the Donovan's. You think I would be relieved, but I'm the opposite. The longer they don't retaliate, the longer they have to make plans. Whatever they do next, is going to be something big. We need to be ready.

My hand runs along the knife that rests in its usual place, on my thigh. The steel of the gun tucked in my waistband, a constant reminder that I've got my back. It's the period before lunch and Marcus, Lincoln and I are heading towards Biology. Jace stopped to talk to Jack, but now, as the second bell goes, I can't see him anywhere. The hallways begin to empty and as the boys enter the classroom, I linger at the door. When I still don't spot Jace, I start to worry.

"I'll be right back." I tell the guys, but Marcus grips my arm.

"Elle, nowhere alone remember." He moves to follow me, and I halt him.

"Mase is just down the hall." I nod towards where Mason lingers, and Marcus nods in acknowledgement. "He'll come with me," I assure him.

"Five minutes," he warns, and I smile, leaning up to give him a quick kiss.

"I love you." I whisper, dashing away, but not before I hear him say I love you too.

I don't have to think that hard about where I might find Jace and nod for Mason to follow me. We move through the empty hallways until we reach the back double doors and I push out of them. Mason checks around the area, hand on his gun, as we head towards the bleachers.

As soon as I'm close, I spot Jace's relaxed physique laying across one of the benches. If I weren't so pissed, I'd roll my eyes. I storm towards him and when I'm close enough, I yell out to him.

"What don't you understand about nowhere alone, pretty boy!" I huff, annoyed that I even need to remind him.

He sighs loudly, sitting up to watch me march up the stairs, "Elle." He greets me.

My name on his lips sounds sad and full of grief. Fuck. I drop down next to him, nudging his shoulder, "everything okay?"

"Just needed to breathe." Is all he says. His stare fixed on the woods in the distance. The same woods I was taken from. The same woods Rachel's body was found in. I'm not stupid, I've seen the darkness clinging to him. The same darkness I sensed in him early on, but he never let it fully manifest. It's been swirling close to the surface. He needs snapping out of it.

I stare into the woods with him, until an idea hits me. I bring my gaze back to him and smile, "wanna sneak out for Starbies?" I offer him and for the first time I see the tug of that real Conrad smile.

"Won't we get in trouble?" He asks, and I laugh a little.

"Pretty boy, we are always in trouble. Come on." I drag him down the bleachers towards Mason.

"Hey Mase." I say sweetly, and he smiles eyeing us both.

"Elle." He nods his head, "what can I do for you?"

"Coffee run. Wanna grab everyone a little pick me up." My smile is casual as I hold my breath, awaiting his response, I expect pushback. With everything going on, running out for a coffee isn't exactly essential, but that's what having the extra security is for.

He eyes me before speaking, "you armed?" He asks, and I scoff.

I flash my weapons, "aren't I always?" I say, cocking my brow at him and he laughs.

"Come on then, take your car and I'll follow you." His response is quick, as he turns on his heels and walks away from us.

Hmm, that was easier than I expected, I guess I forget that they do, technically work for me. I'm just so close to them, that they always feel more like extended family than employees. I smile and toss Jace a wink and he laughs as we both move across the open school grounds and head to the parking lot.

351

I let Jace drive and before I know it, we are slipping through the gates with Mason on our tail. We drive silently and aimlessly, both of us lost in thought and enjoying the pretend freedom we feel, from just being able to drive. No mission planned, no killings warranted, just two friends heading for coffee.

We pull into the first Starbucks we come across and skip the drive through, to park up. I call Mason and ask him what he wants and once I have his order, Jace and I head inside. It's relatively quiet considering it's the middle of the day, and we slot in line and wait our turn, joking back and forth while we pretend our problems don't matter. Once we have placed our ridiculously oversized order, since I tried to remember to get a little something for everyone, we snag a table and wait.

Jace focuses on his phone with a frown, "something wrong?" I ask and he shrugs.

"Not sure," he starts before sighing, "I haven't heard from Taylor." He adds, and then it's my turn to frown a little. He made it perfectly clear he didn't want her involved.

"Were you expecting to?"

"Yes. No." He sighs again, and I laugh. "She asked me out," he admits, and my eyes widen in shock, "I said no and told her she should stay away from me."

"What and now you're mad that she actually listened to you?" I'm only half teasing him, but he shakes his head with a laugh anyway, tossing his phone onto the table.

"No, this is a good thing. It's what I wanted." There isn't a hint of the playboy Rebel everyone knows, here with me, and my heart hurts for him. Then in true Jace style, he shuts it down and offers me that panty-melting smile of his, "just think of all the girls that will have missed me by the time we finish with our little problem." He winks.

I scoff, "our little problem, is that what we are calling it these days?"

"Of course, Queenie, the Donovan's scream little dick energy." He's completely serious and I can't help but laugh at him.

"Don't let Ash hear you say that. He will probably cut your little one off." I tease. and he scoffs.

"Nothing little here, Queenie, don't make me prove it." He winks. and I throw a napkin at him.

"Then I'll have to cut it off." I give him my best sadistic grin as I pat my concealed knife. and he shudders. Our banter is cut off when the barista finally calls our names, and we move to pick up our order. It takes two trips for us to secure all the coffees into the car and when we are finally happy, that they won't spill all over, we climb inside.

Jace pulls back out onto the road, and as we drive, I notice Mason isn't behind us. There's a black truck behind us, but it's not what Mase was driving, so he must be behind that. Jace keeps driving, as my eyes dart to and from the mirror looking out for Mason, but when I don't see him, I start to panic.

"I don't see Mason." I say out loud, and Jace eyes me before checking his own mirror.

"Maybe he's behind that truck." He says, sounding like he doesn't believe that for a second.

Keeping my eye on the truck, which is maintaining a close distance to us, I direct Jace, "take the next left."

"But that isn't the way back to school." He starts, but I cut him off, "I know Jace, just do it."

He doesn't hesitate to cut across two lanes, so he can take the next left and I hold my breath as we round the corner. Nothing. And then the black truck takes the corner and comes back into view. Fuck.

I pull my phone out, dial Marcus and it connects to the Bluetooth system in the car. He picks up after a couple of rings, and I can tell from his strained tone he was already worrying. "Hey baby, where did you go?"

"We're being followed." I cut to the chase and I know from his pause, that he's confused. He probably hadn't even realized we'd left school grounds yet. Jace takes another unplanned turn and thirty seconds later, so does the truck.

"Jace and I slipped out for coffee with Mason, we were on the way back and we've lost Mason and a black truck is following us."

"Where are you? I'm on my way." He snaps in response. I shake my head even though he can't see me and then grip the door handle as Jace takes another turn, at speed.

"No!" I shout, "You go straight home and don't leave Cassie's side, no matter what, River. Promise me. You and Asher stay with her, don't let her out of your sight."

"Baby..." He tries again, but I cut him off.

"Promise me, Marcus."

"Fuck!" he curses away from the phone, muttering quietly before coming back to me, "I pinky promise, baby. Max is coming, okay? Linc is locked in on your location, just stay on the phone, okay?"

"Okay." I respond, as Jace takes another turn, then speeds down the road to take another one, before the truck can see what direction we went in. I take the gun from my waistband, check it, and then pull off the safety. My eyes don't leave the rearview mirror as I wait.

I can feel Jace looking with me, and after a few agonizing minutes, he releases a breath, "I think we lost them."

I think he's right and I turn towards him just as the truck comes into view again, "Jace, look out!" I scream, but it's too late.

It smashes right into the side of us at full speed, Jace's side taking the force of it and in an instant, we are rolling. Everything feels like it starts to happen in slow motion. The car spinning, the windows smashing, the coffees spilling, the blood pouring. I feel the gun slip from my clenched fist as my body is forced in all directions and my head smashes into the glass at the same time it shatters. The impact of the crash wracks my entire body with instant pain. I think I black out, I'm not sure, but I hear voices outside and Marcus' distorted voice still coming through the speaker.

A voice I don't recognize comes closer, "we got her, she isn't alone." There is a pause before the unfamiliar voice continues, "the one with the man bun." He adds. I look over to Jace and immediately wish I hadn't. He's unconscious and bleeding and I feel the fear and tears claw at my throat instantly. This is it, they found us. I reach for the phone in my pocket, as the voice outside speaks again.

"Boss says to bring them both." He says calmly, and the crunching of glass tells me they are getting close.

I press the button on my phone that disconnects the Bluetooth, as my vision starts to blur, "River." I gasp out.

"Elle!" He screams, "Elle what the fuck happened?" He sounds so far away yet I can feel his desperation as if he's next to me. I can feel myself starting to fade and I know without a doubt we are about to be taken. "Ells, talk to me please."

A gas canister is thrown through the smashed window and I push out one last word before the darkness and the Donovan's, both take me.

"Crabsticks..."

Chapter 41

MARCUS

Can the sound of someone's screams imprint onto your soul? I doubt there will ever be a day that I forget the sound of crashing metal, shattering glass and the way Elle screamed for Jace to look out. I felt the impact as if it crashed into my heart. My voice almost lost from crying out her name, begging her to answer me. When she said my name, I had hope, it was quiet and weak, but at least it was there. She was alive, armed, and I knew she would fight. She wasn't alone, she had Jace by her side and I knew he would die for her, even if she wouldn't let him.

Then just one more word left her lips, one that changed everything. *Crabsticks.*

Crabsticks. Fucking crabsticks. The dumbest fucking word in the entire god damn universe. Yet when her broken voice muttered it down the phone, after we all listened in horror to that fucking smash, it cut through me like a knife. They're gone. Elle and Jace are gone. Lincoln and I remained silent as we stared at the disconnected phone. We didn't move, didn't speak, didn't fucking breathe. They're gone. The Donovan's have my girl and my brother and this time, I don't think we will ever get them back.

Lincoln burst into action before I did, dragging me along as he called Zack and relayed what just happened. Every guard on the school grounds met us out front and before I even knew it, we were speeding away. Some of Max's guys went to Elle's last location, but we went straight back to the house. When we arrived, Max was shouting orders. Zack had already sent Arthur, Helen, and the girls into a bunker, I didn't even know was there, and Logan was checking weapons with Asher.

I watched them all move in unison, every single one of them doing something to get ready to help get my girl back, and all I could do was stand there. My phone still gripped in my hand. Was that the last time I'll ever get to speak to her? The last time I will ever hear her voice. Was this morning the last time I will ever touch her, kiss her, love her?

Hour's pass, I don't know how many, but the ache in my chest grows by the second. This isn't like when she was gone before. No. Then I knew she was in control, had her guard up, and her wits about her. This is different. She didn't leave, she was taken, and we have no idea where.

"What do you fucking mean you can't find them?" I snap at Elijah as he taps away on his laptop, Lincoln right beside him.

"Exactly what I said, Riviera. They're gone, like they disappeared." He replies calmly, making me want to smash that fucking laptop right into his face.

We are all spread around the living room, dressed head to toe in tactical gear. I've got more weapons strapped to me than I ever have before, and all we need now is a direction to point them in.

"Then what was the purpose of the fucking tracker in her necklace if we can't use it to find her." I snap back at him furiously. Yes, I wanted to gift Elle with a beautiful, sentimental necklace for Christmas, but that wasn't its only purpose. It's fitted with a state-of-the-art tracker, as is Cassie's bracelet. After what happened, I wasn't taking any chances.

"They must have broken it. The signal is completely gone. It's weird." Is all he can come up with, and I swear he really is about to get a broken nose via laptop.

I look to Lincoln, but his eyes don't lift from his own screen, I can feel the anger burning off of him. This isn't just Elle, but Jace too. We can't lose them, we won't survive. Logan has positioned himself at one of the windows, gun in hand and his stare never leaving the front gates. Max's guys are spread around the house, awaiting instruction, while still standing guard, and Asher silently broods in the corner. He looks two seconds from killing us all and going after them in the only way he knows how. Alone. His gaze collides with mine, as if he sensed my stare and I see his jaw clench as something comes to his mind.

"What happens to it, if there aren't any towers to pick up the signal, like if they were in the middle of nowhere?" He asks Elijah, and I turn towards him to await his answer.

Elijah shrugs, "I guess it just wouldn't appear, but it would still give us a last known location unless something had blocked it."

Asher closes his eyes and cricks his neck from side to side. "I know where they are."

My head snaps back in his direction, "where?"

"Where this all began." He only says four words, but they turn my stomach. *Where this all began.* They've been taken to Donovan's playground in the woods. The huge compound they have there, that has more fucking security than Fort Knox. The one place we have avoided at all costs, because we know it's almost impenetrable. We need a fucking miracle.

Zack looks to Max who nods, pulling out his phone and stalking from the room. Doesn't take a genius to know he's calling for backup. I doubt he knows enough people to get us out of this one, but we can't not try. I promised Elle I wouldn't leave Cassie's side. How can I keep that promise and still save her?

Two hours pass, it's 8pm, they've been gone for eight hours and we have nothing other than a location. A location we don't know if they are definitely at, but does it even matter? Even with definitive proof we have no way to get in there. Lincoln hacked a blueprint and with Asher's help, they have printed us a pretty accurate layout of the place and all it does is reinforce the fact that we are fucked. So many entrances, so many guards, so many fucking cameras. We'd need a fucking army to get in there. As soon as I think it, it clicks in my head.

"Linc, call Jack and get every guy here. I don't give a fuck what they're doing. They are needed here." He looks up at me as I grab my jacket from the back of the chair and throw it on, pocketing a set of keys.

"Where are you going?" He asks, and I see Asher's eyes on me too.

"To pay President O'Sullivan a visit." is all I respond before I spin on my heels and walk out. I feel someone following, but I don't pause, just continue on my way, only stopping at the office to pick up a burner phone before moving through the house. I don't stop until I am climbing into a car and then the passenger door swings open too.

Asher climbs inside without saying a word and when I don't immediately move, he looks at me, "we doing this, Riviera?"

I smile, "you bet your fucking ass, we're doing this."

I barely register the drive over to the Hallowed Crows MC, but my knuckles ache from the tight grip I have on the wheel all the way there. I won't smash through the gates like Elle did, but only because if I did, I wouldn't stop there. The rage inside me burns through my veins and I need to channel it in the right direction. When I get my hands on Greg Donovan, I am going to fucking rip his limbs from his body. There won't be enough of him left for anyone to ID him. From the silent seething of Asher beside me, I know I'm not the only one thinking such things.

As we approach the club, I remember it's Friday, and even though it's getting into the evening, the gates are open with people bustling around going about their usual business. As soon as I slide the car into their

361

space, we have eyes all over us. I slam the door as I get out and Ash follows suit. I don't see Rebecca anywhere, but I spot Connor and his VP at the same time they spot me.

Connor tosses the cigarette between his lips to the ground, and then walks our way, "need something boys?"

"Calling in that favor." I bite out, and his eyes flick between the two of us and back to the car. I know he is looking for Elle and the lack of her presence fucking guts me all over again.

"I made that deal with your girl, not you."

"Yeah, well my girl is fucking indisposed right now." I snap out, and his eyes focus on mine.

"He has her?" He asks pointlessly, because I'm sure he can tell from the fury in my eyes that we lost her.

I just nod. He watches me in silence for almost a minute, before he nods and then whistles loudly in a pattern like a bird. It sets off a chain reaction as guys spill out from everywhere following his tune, whistling back as they appear.

He keeps his stare locked with mine when he addresses them loudly, "get ready for war boys, it's coming."

I nod and pull the burner from my pocket and toss it at him, "when I call you, you answer. Be ready." Is all I say before I climb back into the car. Asher doesn't move at first, until he pushes past Connor and heads straight for the guy, I know to be Killian and gets right in his face. I don't know what he says, but it has Killian smiling viciously and offering him a mock salute.

Asher stalks back towards the car and we drive out of there as quick as we came and head back down the road. My phone ringing breaks the silence and when I answer it, Zack's voice comes down the line with an echo, so I know we're on speaker. I answer it through the car's sound system.

"I got the MC on our side." I say, before he can say anything, "they're awaiting instruction."

Zack pauses and then blows out a breath, "that's good. Great thinking, Marcus. We need as many men as we can find." His tone already sounds defeated, and it has the hairs on my arms standing up.

"What is it?" I push, because I can tell from his tone that he called to tell us something that I know I'm not going to like.

"We got a security alert from the cameras at the main house." He replies slowly.

"You mean at your house?" I ask to confirm. We have been at the safe house for weeks now, so I don't know why something would set off the alarms there now. No one has been there so far.

"Yeah." His clipped response doesn't ease me at all.

"What was it?" I question, immediately on high alert.

He ignores me, "a few of the guys are on the way there, so if you two want to head that way and meet up with them that would be good." He is speaking to me without an ounce of familiarity, like this is just a business call.

"What set it off, Zack?" I push him, but he ignores me again.

"Wait for them to get there, the last thing we need is anyone else disappearing. I swear, when we get Elle back, I'm going to kill her myself." He huffs out and I can hear the despair in his tone, but I can't move past whatever he's not telling me.

"What set off the security alert, Zack?" I ask one final time and he sighs.

"Someone dumped something out of a van in front of the main steps."

I look at Asher and he looks ghostly white as he asks Zack, "dumped what?"

Zack takes one more breath before he delivers three words that gut me, "it's two bodies."

Chapter 42

ELLE

2 HOURS EARLIER.

There's a ringing in my ears, or maybe it's a buzzing, I'm not sure. Am I awake? I don't know. I try to move, but all I feel is pain. That must mean I'm awake, right? Alive. I attempt to lift up my head, but it's heavy. The pain sears into my brain and I cry out, but no sound comes from me, or at least I can't hear any. My vision is blurring in and out as I try to force my eyes to stay open, focusing on one spot until it clears. I'm cold, painfully so, and something bites into my wrists. As I finally manage to clear my eyes, I wish I hadn't. The room is strikingly familiar. *I've been here before.*

It's disgustingly the same. From the dirty mattress, metallic smell, and cracked tiles. It's dark, dingy, and the light is flashing on and off. I'm on the mattress, but I have been thrust up against the wall. I try to move but am immediately restricted. Of course, I'm tied up. I force a thick swallow down my dry throat, as my lips crack from the lack of water and screaming. I take a deep breath as I try to push past the pain and figure out how I got here.

I went for coffee with Jace and Mason. No. Wait. We lost Mason. We were being followed. I spoke to Marcus and then nothing but blackness. But I did speak to Marcus on the phone, right? He will come for me. Us? Fuck. *Jace.*

I whip my head around the room and the ache crashes into my entire body. I'm really fucking beat up. Flashes of blood and glass assault my mind, as memories of what happened flow through me. All of it pales in comparison though, when I spot Jace's lifeless, bloodied body on the floor. No. Please. No. His whole body is turned away from me, but I can see his arms are tied above his head, locked into a bolt on the floor and his legs are the same. If they tied him up, he must be alive.

"Jace." I croak out, but it's barely above a whisper, so I clear my throat and try again, "Jace." I can hear the panic in my voice as I breathe through the tears staining my cheeks.

An anguished grunt is followed by, "yeah, I'm here." His voice is low, and his words panted out through a struggling breath, but I hear them. The relief I feel is unreal, he's alive. He rolls onto his back with a hiss of pain, and I take in his injured form. Dried blood coats his face and arms and I can tell by the way his shirt clings to him that it's also soaked through. That's when I remember, the truck, it followed us, we thought we lost it, but then it came out of nowhere and crashed into us. His side of the car took the main part of the crash, and if I'm in pain, I know he must be. Fuck! How did a simple coffee run turn into this. It's only then I remember Mason and a fresh wave of pain hits me. If the truck was not only able to follow us, but get to us too, that only means one thing. Mason is dead.

I can't help the cry I let out, "Jace, I'm so sorry." My voice wobbles with the tears clogging my throat.

"Don't..." he starts, but I go on.

"I should have never brought you into this, this is all my fault." Mason is dead and we are here. I did this. Me.

"We're in this, together, right?" He grits through his pain, and I nod, even though I wish we weren't. Tears continue to pour down my face and I can't even wipe them away. This is it, how it started and how it's going to end.

I shake my head at the words he has spoken to me once before, closing my eyes tight, like I can just make this all disappear, "I'm sorry it's come to this, that we're here." He might not have been here before, but I have. I know exactly what kind of things happen in the Donovan's trafficking compound. This is the one thing we won't walk away from, not intact at least.

"Don't give up on me yet, Queenie." He pushes out, and the tender use of my nickname would make me smile, but not today. Today everything changes. Marcus promised he would stay with Cassie and it's a pinky promise I never want him to break. He isn't just going to lose me today though, but Jace too. Jace says don't give up on him, but I can hear the pain and fear in his voice. He knows how fucked we are. I take a deep breath and force a smile, as I respond.

"Never, pretty boy."

Loud footsteps approach, and for the first time, my eyes lock with Jace's and we both take a deep breath, "I'm glad I met you Elle King, you gave me a new purpose, even if only for a little while." He whispers, and my chest cracks open with the pain.

I shake my head, "no, don't you dare say goodbye to me, Jace Conrad." I push out through my tears.

"Not goodbye," he smiles softly, "just a see you soon."

I don't get to respond before the door slams open and the Devil himself walks through. Greg Donovan steps inside the same way I imagine he steps into every room, with a smile on his face and death in his eyes. He's wearing an immaculate gray suit, the kind you would hate to ruin, yet I bet he doesn't think twice about it getting covered in blood.

The grin he gives me makes my stomach turn, "Ah, there she is. My beautiful bride to be." He walks over to me and his hand strokes down the side of my face. I snap my head away in disgust, but all that does is make his smile wider.

Jace struggles against his own chains as he spits, "stay away from her." But Greg doesn't even spare him a glance. He just leans down, so his face is next to mine as he purrs, "you and I are going to have so much fun."

I know this is the fight to the death, so my sharp tongue isn't taking any prisoners, "unless it includes me stabbing you in the fucking throat, then we don't have the same idea of fun." I spit out at him.

He laughs wildly, not fazed by my words, "blood play is my favorite kind, princess." His arm comes out again to caress my cheek and this time I don't move away. I won't give him the satisfaction again. The gleam in his eye shines at my defiance. His hand drops to my neck and keeps going down to my waist until he pushes it between my thighs.

"That was my favorite part, you know. It wasn't the feel of that tight, virgin cunt." He cups me roughly, as he says it and I bite my tongue so hard I taste blood. "it was watching your blood spill down your stomach to cover my cock. Shall we spend our wedding night like that?"

Wedding night. This is all just a big fucking game to him. Getting off on something he thinks is his right. He claimed me that night, but I got away. Now, here I am again, but this time I'm ready to pay whatever price I need to, because he isn't getting a fucking wife.

"I'm not marrying you, you sick fuck." I pull forward on my chains until I can get in his space. Show no fear. Panic is what gets you killed. "Not unless you plan on dragging my decomposing corpse down the aisle. My daughter is safe and out of your reach and that's all that matters to me." My words are bold and brave, which is the opposite to how I'm feeling, but I refuse to go down without a fight. I have to get Jace out of here, even if it's the last thing I ever do.

He clicks his tongue at the mention of Cassie then moves over to Jace, "Oh, and what about your little friend here?" He brings his foot up and slams it into his ribs and Jace yells out in pain.

"Don't you fucking touch him!" I scream, and Greg laughs viciously as he smashes my defiant resolve.

"Don't worry, princess. I have other plans for him."
He bends down, brushing an escaped hair from Jace's
forehead. "He's going to make me a lot of money with a
face and body like his." He stands up, brushing off
invisible dust from his suit jacket and straightening his tie,
"but before all of that, I brought you a gift, one to make
you more..." He pauses, thinking about his phrasing,
"open to my plans, shall we say."

He has barely finished talking when two guards
drag someone in the room. It's a girl, she's wearing
nothing but a ripped shirt and her underwear, and when
the guard rips the bag off her head, I almost choke on my
sob in recognition.

"Taylor?" Jace's voice is barely a whisper as her
name slips past his lips. She tries to move her head in
the direction of his voice, but Greg slides behind her and
fists her hair to pull her back towards him. Her face is
covered in bruises and slightly swollen, but it's definitely
her.

"My boys have already had quite the afternoon
with her, haven't they Miss Kennedy?" She doesn't react
to Greg's words and I know from looking at her that she is
high on something and the bile burns my insides as I try
to cough it back.

"Taylor." I whimper, "Taylor, look at me, please."
Her glossy gaze collides with mine, and I see confusion
and fear dancing behind her eyes. Jace is still silently
staring at her in horror, as I speak to her, "I'm so sorry,
but it's going to be okay, I promise." She tries to nod, but
winces at Greg's grip on her hair and I watch the tear slip

down her cheek. She knows that I know how she feels. What we have now both been through.

"Not really in the position to be making those kinds of promises, are you wifey?" Greg laughs, and I take a deep breath through my nose, he knows he's got me exactly where he wants me. My tears feel bitter against my face, yet I can't keep them at bay. Jace didn't want her involved in any of this, yet here she stands, broken and bleeding and it's all my fault. Another innocent life caught up in my mess. Owen was on her, but I bet Max pulled everyone in when we were taken, leaving her with no one to have her back. Either that or he's dead too. How many more deaths will be on my conscience?

I'd risk my own life, but I won't risk Jace and Taylor's. I close my eyes, forcing my emotions to shut down into nothing, and when I open them, I reply. "You've got my attention, you sick, twisted, psychotic fuck."

He frowns down at the Elle King only my enemies see, "I don't think I do. Don't get me wrong, I enjoy your fiery side, my little bride to be, but make no mistake, you will submit to me."

"And if I don't," I ask pointlessly, and he grins that savage smile I hate so fucking much. I think about all the ways I want to hurt him. the way I'd mark his face with a different kind of smile, permanently. The way I'd carve his heart out of his chest and serve it to him. The way I'd douse him in gasoline and listen to his screams as I set him on fire. None of them provide enough pain and suffering for the kind of death he deserves.

"That's what the incentive is for," he replies, gesturing to Taylor and Jace. "Shall we begin?"

Before I can respond he stabs Taylor in the side.

"I'm going to fucking kill you," Jace fights against his chains, but Greg just laughs loudly, pulling the knife from her side and getting it ready to use again.

"Okay, okay! What do you want?" I yell at him, my eyes fixed on the blood pouring from Taylor's wound as she whimpers in distress.

"You know what I want, princess." He drags the knife down her arm, slicing it open.

"Okay, you win." I scream, and he pauses, bringing up his empty hand to smear blood across Taylors's face, as his arm comes around her.

"What was that? I can't hear you over all the screaming." He laughs again as Jace continues to yell threats at him.

"You win okay, I'll marry you, just stop. Let Taylor go and free Jace and I'll marry you." I rush my words out as panic attempts to assault me. She isn't bleeding that much, so he probably hasn't hit anything vital, she just needs to get to a hospital. If I can just get them both out of here, then everything will be okay. It has to be.

Greg preens with satisfaction, "You got yourself a deal, Miss King, or should I say, Mrs. Donovan?" He hollers out in celebration, bringing the knife up into the air.

"Except for one thing." The silver blade glints in the flashing light and then it happens so fast. His sadistic cheer, the grief-stricken scream, the vacant stare. I don't realize what he's done until he lets Taylor's body drop to the floor next to Jace.

"My wife needs to learn her place." He gleams, "do not defy me again."

I don't say anything, just stare at her lifeless body at his feet.

He slit her throat.

Chapter 43

MARCUS

Eleven minutes and forty five seconds. That's how long it takes us to get from the South Side up to the house. A house we haven't been to in weeks, not since the night we left to get Cassie. I never thought I would be scared to come here, but right now, as we pass the line of trees up the driveway, I'm fucking terrified. There's two bodies here, dumped onto the gravel like trash. Bodies that might just belong to my brother and my girl. A fact I try to prepare myself for, but how can I? What could ever prepare you for seeing something like that? Trust me, I know. My father's dead body has been imprinted onto my brain since the night I found him. I can't add to that.

The stones skid beneath the tires as I slam on the breaks and dive from the car, Asher right behind me. We didn't wait for Max's guys and I don't give a fuck about them right now. The only thing that matters to me is the identity of these bodies. I spot them lying side by side, one male and one female.

My knees give out and I stumble to the ground, as I stare at them. The hands and feet are bound and there is a bag on both of their heads. The girl is wearing nothing but her underwear and her blood. *Please don't be my Ells.* The bitterness of heartache bites at the back of my throat as I try to find any distinguishable markings, but there is just too much blood.

Asher passes me, slowly approaching them and crouching down. For the first time ever, I see him hesitate, like what could be under that bag is going to kill him as much as it would me. Grinding his jaw, he slowly reaches down to pull the bag off the girl's body, and I close my eyes, waiting in agony.

"Fuck." He mutters and my eyes snap back open as an anguished noise escapes me.

"It isn't her." He starts and I wish those three words could bring me some sort of comfort, but the next ones out of his mouth change everything. "It's Taylor Kennedy."

What? Oh God, no. I rush to my feet and move towards them just as my phone rings. I pull it out, answering it blindly as I stare down in disbelief at Taylor's corpse. What the fuck? How did they get to her?

"Marcus?" Linc's voice cuts into my sorrow. "We see you there, who is it?" His words are rushed and laced with panic, nothing like my quiet and reserved brother.

"It's Taylor." I choke out, bringing my fingers to my eyes, forcing them closed. So many memories assault my mind of her from when we were kids. She was the only true girlfriend Elle ever had, the only person from the North Side who didn't treat me like a fucking pariah after my dad was killed. She was getting close to us again, too close, and now look at her. Caught in the crossfire of a war we shouldn't even have to fucking fight. We should have done better, she deserved better. So why is it, the only thing I can think is, thank god it's not Elle. *It could still be Jace.*

I bend down, ripping the bag from the male's body and almost choke on relief when it isn't him. Instead, Mason's lifeless eyes stare up at me, his face battered and bruised. He put up a good fight before they killed him.

"Brother?" Lincoln whispers out and I know he's waiting for me to tell him who it is. Waiting for me to tell him our world isn't falling apart.

"It's not Jace." Is all I can manage. He might not be laying here dead, but all that does is remind me that he is alive somewhere and no doubt suffering. What's going to happen when he finds out about this? He didn't want Taylor involved at all. I know things were starting to change between them. Even if he wasn't ready to admit it, I saw it, we all did. And now she's dead. He probably already knows, it's probably the reason they were able to get to them in the first place. Fuck, how did we miss this?

"Fuck." Lincoln curses bitterly, and I can hear people in the background mirroring his sentiment. This changes things. Elle is strong, the strongest person I know. She would fight to the death if she had to. She's done it before, and she'd do it again. So many things could have broken her, but she never let it. She's always fought back bigger and harder and without remorse, because she knew she had her own back. Only now, it isn't just her own back she will be worried about.

"Marcus!" Asher snaps, and I open my eyes and lock in on him. He's holding a bloodied piece of paper in

376

his hand so tight that I'm surprised it doesn't rip to shreds. I don't need him to tell me who it's from. Only one person in this town would drop off a pair of dead bodies with a fucking note. He holds it out for me, and I snatch it from his outstretched fist to read it.

I've got the Kingdom. I've got the King.
We'll seal the deal with a diamond ring.

I want a wife. Those words plunge to the forefront of my mind. That's what Greg said on the phone the night he took Cassie. That he would hand her over in exchange for a wife. *The perfect wife*. He's going to make Elle marry him. Except I know Elle, my Ells would never agree to something like that. But then I look down at Taylor's cold dead body and I know she already has. This is why they were dumped here for us to find. The message isn't their bodies, it was just proof of Elle's submission. Mason would have been killed before Elle and Jace were taken in order for Greg to be able to get to them. But what about Taylor? Owen is supposed to be guarding her, he isn't with Max and he isn't here, so where the hell is he?

I look down at Taylor again and grimace. This would have pushed Elle over the edge. Taylor may be dead, but Jace must still be alive. She will do anything to protect him, even if that means she has to tie herself to a fucking psycho.

"Fuck!!!" This is bad, worse than I thought. We are well and truly fucked. Another car speeds down the driveway and before it even stops, Liam is jumping from it, followed by Oliver after he kills the engine.

I push towards them and halt them, I know these won't be the first bodies they've seen or dealt with, but their friend is here. "Wait a minute," I start, but Liam cuts me off.

"It's Mase, isn't it." He asks in a pained tone and all I can do is nod in confirmation. They both push past me so they can look for themselves.

"Fucking bastards." Oliver curses, as he looks down at his friend. "Spineless fucking bastards." He shakes his head in disgust as he looks back to me. "Owen?"

"Not sure." I answer solemnly and they both curse.

Liam sighs, "we need to get rid of her and…" He starts looking at Oliver, but before he can respond, I cut in.

"You can't fucking dispose of her like she's no one, she isn't one of them, she's one of us." I can't hold back the emotions in my voice.

"Marcus," Oliver starts, but then he's cut off too.

"I swear to fucking God, Oliver, don't." Asher starts, "what are you going to do with Mason's body?" He snaps, and I feel both Oliver and Liam flinch. "Are you going to dump him, like he was nothing?"

"Of course not." Liam replies. "We will sort it out, make sure she gets a proper send off. That they both do."

Asher nods, taking a deep inhale before snatching the phone from my hand where Lincoln is still on the line.

378

"Blackwell, I need a direct line to the board of Donovan Enterprises," he says coolly, "tell them we are conducting an emergency takeover. Do whatever you have to do to make sure they are ready to overthrow my father and brother." His tone is the one I'm most accustomed to: cold, serious, and completely deadly.

"And how am I supposed to guarantee that?" Lincoln responds, and I can hear the frown in his voice.

"I don't know help, impress me." Asher ends the call before Lincoln can answer him and then he looks between us. "I want her body to be handled with care and respect, ready for Elle and her family to pay their respects." Liam and Oliver both nod and then Asher focuses on me, "we're going to my house." He turns and stalks back to the car before I register what he just said, and I have to run after him.

I catch the driver's side door as he opens it, "what the fuck do you mean, your house?"

He rolls his eyes, "Marcus, do you really think my dad or Greg are going to be there when they finally have Elle back in their grasp? This is my one and only opportunity to get inside there."

"What about security?" I try to point out the obvious, because even if they aren't there, it will still be heavily guarded.

He pats the guns clipped to his sides, "anyone who gets in my way tonight won't survive." He pulls the door from my grip as he climbs behind the wheel and slams it shut. I round the front of the car, getting into the passenger seat and without exchanging another word, we head off into the night.

It doesn't take us long to get to the Donovan mansion and as we approach, Asher pulls out his phone and taps out a message, before sliding it back in his pocket. I don't bother asking who he sent a text to. One thing I know about Asher Donovan is that if he wants you to know something, you will. Clearly, he doesn't need me to know. By the time we pull up to the gates, the guardhouse there is dark, and I frown.

"What the hell?" I mutter out loud.

He looks my way as he says, "my father and brother aren't the only Donovan's that people are scared of." The gates open and we drive through without any trouble whatsoever.

His grip tightens on the wheel as we make our way down the elegant hedge lined driveway. "Greg is a psycho, has zero work ethic and my father is just lazy. They got cocky and overconfident. While they spent their days trafficking girls, I spent mine in the shadows digging. I have dirt on a lot of people on his payroll. He's just too busy abusing girls to notice."

"Why didn't we do this the night Cassie was taken?" Is my immediate thought.

He gives me a stare that would make a lesser man quiver, "do you not think I wanted to?" He snaps. "I was willing to walk right in here and grab her, damn the consequences, but you guys wouldn't let me. I didn't care that my father and Greg were here. I would have done it."

I can tell how serious he is and how hard it must have been for him to have held back. To put Elle before his daughter, and abide by her wishes of keeping himself safe.

"You did the right thing," I pat his shoulder, "we needed you." He doesn't respond, like I knew he wouldn't, but I still had to ensure he knows how important he is to our dynamic.

Slowly, we move down the driveway towards his house and the hairs on the back of my arms stand on end, it's been a long time since I was here. I don't know why Asher needs to come here, but I've got his back no matter what.

Asher continues, "I run multiple corporations and am the owner of several successful IPOs. With Zack's guidance, I now make more money than my father, but again, he is just too ignorant to realize it. He spends his time talking down to me, preparing me to live in Greg's shadow, when in reality, I have been working to take the company out from under them. I want Donovan Enterprises to be nothing but a vague memory in people's minds. Just like they will be."

He slams on the breaks and jumps from the car, just as two guards come out the front door. They have bullets in their head before I can even raise my gun. Asher shows no remorse and steps over their bodies like they're not even there, so I follow suit. Once inside, I follow after him and notice every maid and housekeeper pass him with a nod as they make their way out. It's like a chain reaction, as they come from everywhere. None of them batting an eyelash at us, as we pass. Asher kills three more guards and I kill two as we continue through the house. We make it to what I presume is his room and he taps a keypad outside the door. *Of course, his room has a lock.*

He stalks right over to his bed and then I watch in awe, as he taps a panel there and it pops open, revealing a small safe. He pulls out a lock box, some files, and a small black bag. He grabs another bag from his closet and shoves the contents from the safe inside along with some clothes, watches, and a few tech devices. Once satisfied, he zips up the bag and motions for us to leave the way we came. As we push back out into the hallway there is a woman down the hall from us.

"Gail." Ash shouts, and it halts her in her tracks as she turns towards us.

"Asher, my sweet boy." She gasps in relief, as she rushes over to him and grabs him by the shoulders. "You haven't been sleeping?" She scolds him and I can tell from her tender tone that she loves him. Like a mother should a son.

"Do I ever?" He smiles softly at her, "sorry for the late notice."

She shakes her head, "nonsense my boy, this has been a long time coming, I'm so proud of you."

He ignores her sentiments of course, "have you got everyone settled?"

"Yes," she nods, "they all know where they are going and appreciate the settlements you provided."

"It's the least I could do." He replies solemnly.

"I heard what happened with Cassie." she starts, and he stops her immediately.

"Hey, it's not your fault, you were busy with your own family."

"Look," she pauses, and I can tell whatever she is about to say, Asher isn't going to like, "I heard something, one of the maids, she's been bumping uglies with one of the guards. They're all being pulled to the compound tomorrow," she hesitates before adding, "for a wedding."

A wedding. Tomorrow. Fuck.

Asher nods at her before surprising us both and pulling her into a quick hug, "Thank you, Gail. For everything."

A tear escapes her eyes which she wipes quickly. "Anytime, my sweet child."

"Now get out of here and don't come back."

A smile spreads across her face, "not unless you do." She gives him a quick kiss before she disappears the way she was heading, and Asher leads me in the opposite direction. We head down a back set of stairs and into the kitchen. He turns on the gas on the cooker and then proceeds to smash numerous bottles of vodka on the floor.

He continues to pour liquor on the floor, as we head out of the house and when we finally reach the front door, he looks at me, nodding for me to go. Just as I turn, I see him pull a lighter from his pocket, he flicks open the flame and tosses it to the floor and we both run side by side and get into the car.

The house goes up in flames as we hit the drive and for the first time ever I hear Asher laugh. A full, throaty, loud laugh. "You have no idea how many times I have wanted to do that."

He slams his foot down on the pedal and we speed off into the night with the orange glow lighting up the sky behind us.

We've got a wedding to crash.

Chapter 44

ELLE

I should feel something, anything, but I'm numb. Void. Finally, completely broken. I don't know how long I've been in this bath, but the water is stone cold. I see the goosebumps covering my body and the wrinkles on the pads of my fingers and toes. I could have been in here for hours and I wouldn't notice. All I can do is replay what happened over and over again in my mind.

The knife slicing across her neck.

The sound of Jace's despair.

The look on Greg's face.

The vomit I choked out.

My submission.

All of it a never-ending stream in my head. The silent cries continue to wrack my whole body, but no tears come. I have none left. I have nothing left. My only salvation? That Cassie is safe. Marcus promised he would take care of her. She has him, Ash, and the rest of my family. So many people to look out for her and protect her. I want to hope that I'll make it back to her, but hope is for the weak. I'm done thinking I can win this war. Rebelling against them was a stupid idea. All it brought me was pain and death. No justice, no redemption, just pure fucking grief. I can't fight anymore, they won.

Jace is here with me, a constant reminder to why I can't win. I won't put him in any more danger. He's sitting in the corner of the room we're in. He hasn't spoken, not since Taylor's blood seeped under his body as he lay there, staring into her dead eyes. He's still wearing the same blood-soaked clothes and the same broken expression. His wrists are raw from the chains and handcuffs he has been kept in, and his injuries are still seeping blood every now and then. But he doesn't feel them, he doesn't feel anything. Just like me.

Under normal circumstances, I'd be worried about him seeing me naked, but he isn't even here anymore. The Jace Conrad I knew, the one I came to love quickly and easily, has gone. He may as well have died when Greg sliced Taylor's throat. I saw it, saw his own hope perish along with her life. We aren't surviving this, dead or alive, we are both just gone.

The door opens and three women rush inside, dropping an array of things on the table against the wall and pulling out a towel. I have no idea where we are, I can only presume we are still at the compound. After what Greg did, I didn't even bother to fight against the needle he slid into the side of my neck. Just kept my focus on Taylor's lifeless form as I let the darkness take me. By the time I woke up, Jace and I were in a slightly nicer room, I was laying on a bed with actual sheets on it and he was tied to a chair in the corner. I didn't move. I just lay and let the ache of my grief collapse inside of me.

I don't know why Jace is still here. I vaguely remember Greg saying we had a deal and maybe that's why. Did I save Jace's life only to offer up Taylor's? The old Elle would fight, kick, scream, do anything that wasn't just sitting here, but that was before. This is after.

Do not defy me. Submission is my only salvation now.

One of the women grabs me by the arms and stands me up, directing me out of the tub as the other wraps me in a towel. I am ushered over to a chair where I spend the next couple of hours being pricked, poked, and fucking polished into the perfect bride. Jace was led from the room, still in cuffs, halfway through my makeover and all I could do was watch him go. Broken and alone.

Once my hair is perfectly curled and my makeup pristinely finished, I am led into the bedroom and find myself stepping into a wedding gown. It takes two of the women a couple of minutes to get it on and fastened, and then they fit my head with a crowned veil. They give me one last check over, then gather up their supplies and take their exit. I wait until I am completely alone in the room before I turn to look in the dirty mirror in the corner.

A crisp white, silk dress molds to my curves. Hugging my breasts with a plunging neckline and straps going around my neck. The bottom isn't big, but layers of silk still fall all around me, giving the impression of a wide dress. It's covered in crystals and pearls that just scream 'obscenely wealthy'. If that didn't clue you in, then the real diamond crown would. It's nothing like I would pick for myself. The only thing that resembles me is the necklace from Marcus that still hangs around my neck.

Marcus. Just thinking of his name causes me pain. Yesterday morning we were tangled up in each other's arms. Now I'm about to marry another man. Everything we did, everything we planned, we were so close. Yet I still stand here, dressed as somebody else's bride.

The door handle pushes down, and I slowly turn as Elliot Donovan steps inside, followed by his son and a guard dragging in a now suited up Jace. When Elliot sees me, his smile could rival his son's. Dark, deadly, and disgustingly smug.

He blows out a slow breath, "you were always a looker Elle, just like your mother." He lets his gaze trail over me slowly from head to toe. Lingering on my barely concealed breasts. "But now you are truly breathtaking." He turns to Greg, "she'll make the perfect wife, son."

Greg leers at me as he stalks my way, his eyes roaming over every inch of my exposed skin. Once he's done, he picks up a piece of the skirt of my dress and grins, "this is going to look good stained in blood." He leans in grazing his lips against my cheek and I hold in my shudder, "I'm gonna enjoy making you bleed while I fuck you, raw princess. Just how I always planned." He hears the sharp intake of my breath as his sick words wash over me and laughs. Fuck. What I would give to have my knife strapped to my thigh, right now. See how much he could fucking laugh without an intact esophagus.

Elliot moves towards the both of us with a seemingly genuine smile this time, as he smacks Greg on the shoulder looking between the two of us with proud eyes. "A Donovan and a King. Just how it was always meant to be."

Unlike Greg's, his words do nothing to me. I've accepted my fate. Cassie is safe and I trust Marcus, Ash and my family to get her away from here. To run and never look back. To save her in a way I couldn't.

Elle King dies today, and Elle Donovan will be born.

We step out of the room, into a dark, barely lit hallway. I know immediately we are still at the compound as memories flash across my mind at the familiar surroundings. Guard's march both in front and behind us. I don't think about escaping, I just follow them to my fate. I ignore the weight of the ridiculous diamond on my hand, the feel of the silk gown against my body and the veil pinned in my hair. This isn't how my wedding was supposed to be. No, it's all wrong. I was supposed to be older, happier, marrying my best friend, my River. But the Devil found me first and now I must atone.

I wonder if Marcus and the rest of my guys are ripping the town of Hallows apart, looking for us. If I had any feelings left inside of me, I'd smile at that. But I can't. I don't want them to come for me. I want them to run, run and never look back. Escape this fucking pit and forget I ever existed. Take my daughter and give her the life she deserves, one without fear and pain. *One without me.* My life in exchange for hers. The best thing I have ever done.

We reach a door and when it swings open, we step outside, the sun blinding me after being held inside for so long. It pierces through the clouds, making my dress shine. The perfect weather for a wedding. Your wedding day is supposed to be the best day of your life. I should be happy. I should be free. I should be marrying the man I love. I am none of those things. I am empty, caged and about to make the ultimate deal with the Devil.

We head towards an outbuilding and I see an actual priest making his way towards it too. I almost laugh. Of course, they have a real priest. No doubt another sick twisted fuck who they have bent to their will with blackmail. My footsteps falter, but I am pushed onwards without a second passing as we descend towards our destination.

Greg pushes Jace to my side, "don't forget your best man, wifey. Be nice and I'll let him watch me fuck you later." He winks, before turning and heading into the building, no doubt to await my arrival like this isn't a fucking sham of a wedding.

I look to Jace and for the first time since yesterday he's staring back at me. I don't know what he sees on my face, but I watch the vein in his neck thump wildly and his chiseled jaw clench. He closes his eyes briefly, breaking our connection, before opening them again and I am greeted with a flash of my Jace. My reckless rebel and his tortured soul. We are in this together to the very end.

I take a deep breath as I cross the threshold into the building and mutter to myself, "Forgive me father, for all my sins."

Chapter 45

MARCUS

The signal pinged not even ten minutes ago and we are already out of the house and on the road. I haven't slept, I couldn't. Not when Elle and Jace are with those cunts, going through god knows what. I can't bear to think about it and from the way Asher has been raging around, I know he can't either. We all know exactly what kind of place the compound is. What crimes are committed there. Elle already bears the scars from one night spent there. What scars will she have after she survives another?

If she survives.

That thought constantly burns through me, turning my insides to ash. I already know what it's like to lose her and that's when I knew she was out there living somewhere. I hated it. I won't survive if I lose her for good. I don't know if any of us are going to make it out of this alive, all I know is that if I lose my brother, lose my girl. The grief will fucking cripple me. We're about to head into the biggest fight of our lives. We are going to be outgunned and outmanned, but none of that matters. I'll do whatever I need to do to get them back to us.

After setting fire to the Donovan Estate, we returned to the Royton house. We didn't see the point in going back to the safe house. When we got there, there was no trace of Taylor or Mason ever being there. The bodies were gone, and the blood cleaned. Like it never even happened. Max and the rest of his guys arrived a little later with Lincoln and Logan. Zack limped in behind them with a determined face while Max just grimaced at him. He is still recovering from Greg's ambush, but I know there was no way he was staying behind.

Max was barely through the door before Ash jumped down his throat, "Cassie?" He asked, with his jaw clenched so tight I thought it might break.

"Secured in the bunker with Arthur, Helen and Lils. I left Alex and Seb locked down in the house with them and I have another back up team incoming, just in case."

Asher didn't respond, just stared at him until he exhaled and stormed away. I can't imagine how he is feeling. I hate this. Hate the fact she's in danger and I've only known about her for two months. That's his little girl, his world. I saw what her kidnap did to him, what it did to Elle. If we make it out of this, that girl is going to be fiercely guarded for the rest of her life.

While we waited for everyone else to arrive, a bleeding Owen marched into the house. He looked like shit and angry as fuck. He told us how he was jumped outside of Hallows Prep when Greg's men turned up to get Taylor. He gave them the slip, trying to get to her, but he was too late. And when Greg's guys gave chase, he took a bullet to the arm and slipped into the woods to escape. All of his comms and stuff left behind in his car.

Zack was both furious and relieved, and I could see the regret on Owens's face when he learned of Taylor's fate. He was too injured to even think about joining us, but that didn't stop him. He showered, had Logan patch him up and then tossed back a few painkillers and strapped himself with fresh weapons. Whatever it takes.

It wasn't long before my boys from the South Side joined us, followed by the Crows. All of us packed across the den going over every bit of intel we had together. We discussed ideas for a number of situations and came up with as many backup plans as we could. Just anything we could think of that would prepare us for what we were about to do. It's war against the corrupted and it's time for the elite to meet their end.

The drive across town is ghostly silent. Asher is driving, with Lincoln in the front and me in the back. The only sound comes from Lincoln tapping away on his keyboard as Asher directs us towards the compound. It's another twenty minutes before we arrive, and he is pulling off the road. He continues a few hundred feet through the trees until he swings the car around so it's facing back in the direction of the road, and then kills the engine. We get out and I find myself looking around, thinking about the last time I was here. Remembering. Regretting. That day started with a double dog dare. This day is going to end with them dead at our feet.

I can't see the compound, but I know it's just through these trees. I can't tear my eyes away as car after car pulls in behind us. Max and all of his guys are the first to get out of theirs. He stops at each of them, checking them over, making sure they're sufficiently armed and protected. After what happened to Mason, I know he is taking extra precautions, he doesn't want to lose anyone else. Zack leans against the hood of the car he arrived in, with Logan by his side. Both of them staring through the trees just like I was, like they think if they stare hard enough, they will see her.

Jack, Kai, and the rest of my crew are here too, the only people not meeting here with us are the Crows. They are heading straight for the path that leads into the middle of the compound. The perfect distraction. We have no idea if Carter Fitzgerald will have told Elliot about Rebecca's rescue and his loss of leverage against the HCMC, but it doesn't matter. We are going in guns blazing, either way.

Asher and I move to hover around Lincoln's laptop as he shows us entry points, and we discuss our own strategy. Once we have a little instruction on what to do, we all make off through the trees towards the compound. We are going to come at it from different directions but need to get eyes on it first, so we know where to send more of our manpower. The only agreed instruction is whoever gets to Elle and Jace first, gets them out of there no matter what.

I push through the foliage with Asher and Lincoln by my side. All of us are in small teams of three and four, to ensure we all have backup. We are still dressed in our tactical gear and I have more weapons strapped to me than I could have ever imagined. I'm not going down without a fight. None of us are.

I look at Asher, who is silently brooding beside me as we walk, "I want to be the one to kill Elliot." Lincoln swings his head to look at me, but Ash doesn't respond, so I carry on. "He killed my father, took everything from me. I want to return the favor." I wait for his refusal, for him to fight me on it. Elliot might be a sick son of a bitch, but it's still his father. I don't know what plans he has for him, but I don't care.

He stares at me, like he is looking directly into my head until he just grunts, "Greg's mine."

The rest of the walk is silent and as we get towards the edge of the tree line that leads out into the grounds of the compound. We all slow down as Max, Elijah, and Oliver all step forward, binoculars in hand to assess what awaits us. I can see them whispering back and forth, trying to come up with the best way to approach with minimal sighting. They point things out to one another and when they seem satisfied, they gather us all around.

"Alright, we've got around twenty guards hanging around the front." He nods to Owen and Josh, "you two set up for sniper cover and take out as many as you can. More guards will be drawn there when the Crows get here, so Me, Oliver and Liam will cover the front too." He looks at Zack, "you stay by my side." He warns him, before turning to me.

"Split your guys up into two teams to hit from both sides. Harry and Landon will help cover them." The guy's nod as they listen to his instructions and start splitting up into two groups.

"You, Asher, Logan and Lincoln are going to enter through the back with Tyler." I nod at his final instruction and we all start pulling out our weapons, checking them, and getting ready.

We wait for the rumble of the bikes to come round the bend and as soon as they appear, Max gives the order. A smile spreads across my face as I raise my gun and run off into the trees. Hang tight baby, we're coming. I ignore the branches that whip into my face and the bite of the bitter cold. None of it will stop me from getting where I need to be.

Asher and Lincoln move silently beside me and I hear Logan and Tyler somewhere close behind us. All of us have a gun in our hand and look around, wildly searching for our first target. Once we see the edge of the back buildings, we slow our pace, as we creep closer. There are a few guards lingering around and none of them look like they expect much action back here. That's their second mistake. The first was helping to take my girl.

We stop in the cover of a few trees and all lock eyes with a nod before we step out and start shooting. The five guards are dead within a minute and we are pushing over the fence and opening the gate in the next. Ash approaches the back building first, followed by Lincoln and then me. Tyler leads Logan towards another, as we split up to cover more ground. We move between what look like two derelict buildings before we come to one that's manned by a lone guard. Lincoln fires a bullet in his head before Ash and I can even move. He cracks the door open and dips his head inside.

"Fucking hell." He mutters, as he swings the door open and reveals two semi-naked girls. "Motherfuckers."

395

He shakes his head and raises his weapon to show he isn't a threat as they bundle together in fear. "We aren't here to hurt you." He adds slowly.

"Two girls secured." Ash snaps down his comms. He secures his gun to his waist as he slowly approaches them. "We're here to get you out of here. We are here for our friend. She was taken too." They stare at him wide-eyed with fear, "she escaped once before, a few years ago. We just want her back and we can help you too if you want."

One of the girls slowly nods, before she whispers, "please help us."

"Alright. Come on then we need to be quick." He reaches out towards them and the one who didn't speak flinches.

"No." She cries and Asher freezes. "I'm not going. No. They'll find me."

"Come on, Kiera, this is our chance." Her friend pleads.

"I can't." She stares at the floor visibly shaking in fear.

Her friend looks up to us, "Her sister," she whispers, "her sister was here with us, she wouldn't stay quiet, so they shot her."

I grimace as soon as she says the words, but Asher doesn't falter, dropping to his knees before them. "I'm sorry about your sister, but she wouldn't want this for you. I promise it's going to be okay. We just need to get you out of here."

She looks at him, studying him, like she is trying to work out if he is genuine or not. She eyes all our weapons and just as she is about to speak, gunfire breaks out in the distance and she almost jumps out of her skin,

"No. I can't. They will shoot me."

"Here," Asher opens his hoodie and then rips off his tactical vest.

"Asher." I snap at him, he needs that fucking vest, but he ignores me.

"Put this on, no bullet is getting through that. It's about a hundred feet to the back fence, where we have opened a gate. You run that way and head to the right, you'll find all our cars. Hide there and wait for us."

She stares at the vest in his outstretched hand as her friend begs her, "please, Kiera. We can't stay here."

Kiera looks at her friend and back to the vest before reaching out and taking it with a shaky hand. Her friend helps her stand, and she puts it on. They are both filthy and weak as they stagger behind us to the door where Lincoln has remained the whole time. He looks around and when he sees it is clear, he quickly runs them to the fence allowing them to slip out. Fuck, how many more girls like that are we going to find, it makes me sick to even think about it.

Once Lincoln comes back, we carry on moving silently through the compound, the gunfire continuing ahead of us. I'm about to step round a corner when Linc slams my body into the side of a building, covering me as bullets start to whizz towards us. He leans around to fire back with Ash crouched beside him doing the same. Another guy comes up behind us and I fire at him, hitting his arm and forcing his own gun to the ground. He doesn't stop though, charging towards me as I fire another into his chest. He drops to the floor gurgling on his blood, and Ash reaches towards him and slams a knife into his throat, killing him instantly.

We continue to push forward and fight with every guard we come across. I'm bleeding and out of breath, as we move forward towards a building that the guards seem to be gravitating towards.

"That must be where they are keeping her." Lincoln pants out, eyeing the same spot I am.

"It's going to be fucking crawling with guards." Ash snaps and we both nod in agreement. He's right, it will be. But that's my girl in there, my brother. What would they do if they were us? That's when it hits me.

"Wanna smoke them out?" I ask and they both look at me as I pull the bag from my back. When Max told us to pack supplies, I thought about what extra stuff I would want on me. The only thing I could think about is how many girls have been hurt here, have died here. This place needs to go. I show them what's inside and when they don't say anything, I add, "it's what Jace would do. What Elle would do."

Linc is the first to react, his slight smirk tugging on the side of his mouth. "Let's burn this place to the fucking ground."

I look at Asher to see what he thinks and he's staring at the building up ahead of us. His fists clenched and shoulders tense, no doubt remembering all the terrible things he has seen happen here.

He turns to me slowly, before nodding in agreement, his stare burns into me as he tightens the grip on his gun once more. "This ends today. No matter what."

Chapter 46

ELLE

I have never thought much about the composition of the wedding march, but as I put one foot in front of the other and force myself to move, it's all I can think about. Who composed it? Why did it become such a staple piece of wedding music? Why do you even walk down an aisle at all? Stupid, pointless questions, but I'd think of anything right now that isn't about becoming Mrs. Greg Donovan. I think of my beautiful daughter and whether she will walk down the aisle to the same piece of music. I think of how it should be Zack walking by my side right now to give me away. I think about how it should be Marcus waiting for me and not the Devil.

I picture how this day would be if I had my freedom. My hair would be pinned up, my dress white lace, my ring a simple, platinum band. Marcus would wear gray to match the shades of us. Jace, Lincoln and Asher would stand by his side and Helen, Logan, and Lily by mine. Cassie would walk ahead of me in a dress to match mine, no doubt throwing rose petals everywhere. Arthur would officiate and we would all have a family party afterwards. Max and his guys would be there and so would the Rebels. It would be small, simple, and utterly perfect.

This is nothing like that. Inside is exactly how I expect it. Dingy, dirty, and completely Donovan. There is a makeshift altar up ahead with a large table covered in a white cloth. On top there is a bible, cream candles burning, and a large silver pointed crucifix. There are brown, run down pews lined up on either side that could have only been taken from a church. What did they do, fucking steal them? The thought seems ridiculous, but this is the Donovan's we are talking about. Nothing is beneath them. Unexpectedly there are flowers hanging off the pews and again I almost laugh. Just like a real wedding.

The priest is standing at the end of the 'aisle' with Greg off to one side, leaving a space on the other for me. I don't so much as walk towards them but get dragged.

Jace is forced ahead of me until he is placed to the left of the waiting priest, just behind Greg. He turns smiling wildly at him, patting his shoulder like they are buddies. Jace looks up at him with such animosity that I know he's probably imagining ripping off his arm and beating him to death with it. *If only.*

Guards have filtered in to line the walls, all armed and looking both bored and excited at the same time. I cast my eyes to the couple of guests standing at the front. I find Elliot Donovan's gaze blazing back at me, but what I don't expect when I move to the next person is my mother! Sarah King's void eyes stare back at mine and I can't hide my frown. What the hell is she doing here?

She looks at me with unshed tears ready to pour and I can't look away from her. I want to look her in the eye and let her see my broken expression. I don't turn away until I make it to the end of the aisle and the security guard releases me, pushing me towards Greg. He is already staring at me with the most genuine smile I've ever seen from him. Not sadistic or smug, just purely gleeful. He genuinely wants this and that scares me more than anything else.

The priest starts to speak, and I can't bear the crazy look in Greg's eyes any longer. I peer over his shoulder and find Jace glaring back at me with an unwavering intensity. It gives me the strength to take a breath, he's here with me, I can do this, I'm not alone. I want to smile at him, to thank him for the friendship he gave me without thought. For how he just accepted me, protected me, loved me.

When I made the decision to come back to Black Hallows, I never saw the South Side Rebels coming. Yeah, Marcus and I had our history, but it was tainted in lies and blood. He'd found himself a new family, and never did I think they would welcome me with open arms. They've had my back, killed for me, and even saved me. I will forever be in their debt. I hope the look on my face can convey my gratitude as I offer him the only smile, I can manage. The slight tip of his lips assures me he understands.

Greg gripping my hand, drags me from my moment with Jace and I hear the priest confirm that it's time for vows.

"Greg, if you will repeat after me."

"I, Greg Donovan, take you, Elle King, to be my wife..." Greg repeats his words in a tone that makes my skin crawl and I try to ignore them as he plays his role as dutiful husband to be. Forcing a diamond encrusted band onto my ring finger. "...till death do us part."

The priest turns to me and follows the same suit, asking me to repeat after him and when I open my mouth to speak, nothing comes out. I can feel the fear and despair clawing up the back of my throat as I try to force myself to submit to him. To say the words and become Mrs. Elle Donovan.

"Don't disappoint me, wifey." Greg grits out through his teeth, crunching my knuckles between his fist, where he still grips my fingers. When the words still don't come, he nods, and the click of the gun grabs my attention. A guard pushes it into Jace's temple, watching me, waiting. I close my eyes, breathing in deeply before I open my mouth.

"I, Elle..." My words mix with a rumbling sound in the distance and Greg's grip tightens once more. The sound gets louder, it's hard to decipher and the guards ready themselves, until Elliot speaks.

"Don't worry, it's probably just the Crows." His tone is patronizing, and I can tell just from his words, how much he looks down on them. He nods at the guards to check out the impending interruption and Greg's hand tightens even more on mine. I can feel my bones cracking within his fist and I fight against the grimace of pain.

"Vows." He spits at me and I can tell that smug resolve is starting to crack. If I continue my vows, it doesn't matter who is coming, I will still be married to him. I take in the gun at Jace's head once more and I see a savage sort of smile on his face. He honestly doesn't care, he is willing to risk it all to save me and so am I for him.

I look around for something, anything, that could be used against Greg, but I see nothing. How the fuck am I supposed to get us out of this. Just as I have that thought, gunfire breaks out in the distance, and I smile.

The cavalry has arrived.

Greg uses his grip on my hand to drag me towards him, spinning me so my back is against his front. A gun digs into my side, keeping me from moving. The guard still has a gun to Jace's head and the rest of them move towards the doors we came through. Gunfire continues to rain outside, getting closer and closer.

Greg nuzzles into my hair as he pushes his mouth to my ear. "When your little boyfriend gets here, I'm gonna make him watch as I fuck you. Then I'm gonna make you watch as I kill him." He bites the words out and I can feel him hardening in his slacks. I swallow down the bile in my throat, looking towards Jace again. He is staring back at me and then he nods ever so slightly. It's now or never. Just as I am about to try to escape his hold, a small explosion goes off behind us and we are all thrown to the floor.

Smoke pours into the room and I hear guards shouting and more gunfire approaching. Shattered glass from the windows above us, covers the ground and I roll over in pain, registering that I am now free from Greg's grip. The table we stood at before is on its side and I crawl behind it, trying to find some cover in the chaos as I get my bearings.

"Elle!" Jace's voice cuts through me, "Elle!" He screams again, but the smoke is coming in thick and fast, I can barely see anything.

"Over here," I choke out, "I'm here." I roll onto my front and peer around the side of the table. "Jace?" I call out to him, but before he can respond I hear him howl in pain. I look round wildly trying to locate him, but it's no use. Fuck. He's already injured, I need to get to him, help him.

The doors at the front slam open and I see figures stepping through the smoke, as the gunfire echoes throughout the room. Max, Zack, and Connor O'Sullivan step inside, none of them seeing the guards waiting behind the pews thanks to the smoke.

I scream, "Look out!" Bullets spray towards them and Max pushes Zack aside, slamming them into the wall, just as a bullet takes out the president of the Crows. He drops to the floor with a bullet to his head. Fuck. I can't watch another person be killed. I need a weapon and fast.

The smoke starts to clear out of the open door, and I notice Sarah staring wide-eyed at Zack, who stands just a few feet from her. Does she know who he is? I wonder if she thought he was dead. I wouldn't put it past Elliot to brag about what Greg did. I know they thought they'd murdered him.

Zack looks her way and then takes out a guard beside her. I can't see where Elliot went, but he is no longer with Sarah. As Zack kills the guard, another steps

405

towards him, raising their gun and firing. Sarah screams, diving in front of him and intercepting the bullet. It hits her in the chest, and she drops to the floor in the same instant that Zack shoots the guard in the head. He drops to his knees and uses his hands to try stop her bleeding, just like I did for him, not too long ago.

"I'm sorry." She chokes out and then her body goes limp in his arms. Neither of us have time to process it as more guards come into the room, having been pushed back by some of our guys as they continue to shoot at each other.

I try to crawl towards where Jace shouted from, broken glass cutting into me everywhere. A grip finds my foot, dragging me backwards. "Not so fast, wifey." Greg pulls me towards him, and my hands reach out blindly, looking for something, anything, that I can use against him. He flips me over and smiles sadistically, "till death do us part remember?" A piece of glass is plunged into my side and I cry out, the agony hitting me instantly.

He climbs over me, pulling my dress up around my stomach, "If I can't have you then neither can he." He grips the wound at my side, and I almost black out from the pain. My hand darts out again, desperately searching for any kind of weapon. My fingers land on something hard and sharp and I snatch it up tightly, using every bit of force I can muster to bring it up and slam it into his shoulder.

"Till death do us part, you sick fuck."

It pierces through his skin and his weight collapses on top of me and he groans out in agony. Blood pours from his wound, mixing with mine and soaking through my dress. I spot the silver crucifix sticking out between his neck and shoulder as he chokes out. "I'm going to fucking kill you, you little cunt. Not even death will separate us."

Before I can respond, his body is ripped off the top of me. I stare up and find Jace's wild eyes looking down at us. Hand fisted around Greg's own gun. He looks down at him in utter disgust.

"This is for them." He shoots him right between the eyes with zero hesitation and then drops to his knees as he succumbs to his own pain.

I scramble to my feet, ignoring my own pain and blood loss just as Logan and Tyler burst in from a side entrance. They move to help me, but I point to Jace, "Get him out of here." I order, as I stand up fully and lock in on Elliot Donovan. He is frozen to the spot where I am sure he was about to make his escape, staring down at his son's dead body. Marcus, Asher, and Lincoln appear from a back entrance as Elliot looks up and lets his gaze collide with mine.

Everything next, happens so fast.

Elliot raises his gun to me as Marcus raises his, both of them firing at the same time. Marcus hits Elliot right in the chest, killing him instantly as Elliot's bullet barrels towards me. I brace for the impact, but it never comes, and the last thing I see is Asher stepping in its path.

The bullet pierces him and he drops to the floor in front of me. My scream is unlike any I've ever heard as I throw myself to my knees beside him.

"No. No. No." I cry, "Ash?" I plead his name as I rip open his jacket and push up his shirt. Blood pulses from his body as he gasps out in agony.

"Elle." Marcus tries to pull me back, but I shove him away.

"Ash?" I choke out. I press my hands to his wound, "I'm so sorry, Ash." His blood feels warm in my hands as it glides out through my fingers.

"It's okay, baby girl," he pants out, eyes starting to close, and I grab his face, painting it with the crimson liquid.

"No. Don't you dare fucking die on me." Every word feels like a stab to my throat as I force it past my tears. "You can't leave me, you promised. I need you. Cassie needs you. Please just hold on." My silk dress begins to turn red as his blood clogs into it.

This can't be happening. He can't die. He saved me from this fucking place and now he's here bleeding out. I can't even process the satisfaction of both Elliot and Greg lying dead, just a few feet away. They don't matter. None of it matters. Because the only Donovan I have ever given a fuck about is about to die along with them.

I hear orders being shouted around me as Max and Zack make it over to us, but I ignore them all. "Ash, please." I croak out, leaning forward to drop my head to his shoulder. "I love you. I love you so much, okay?"

Marcus drops down beside me, "Ells." He pleas, but I continue to ignore him.

I feel Asher's staggered breath against my hair, "I can't do this without you. Please don't leave me, not here, not like this." I can barely breathe through the sobs choking out with my words.

My enemies are finally dead, my daughter is safe, but my best friend is going to die. What sort of sick justice is this?

His hand comes up to touch my cheek and it already feels cold. I lean into his touch as a thumb swipes away one of my tears. "I'll be with you, Hells Bells. Always."

I close my eyes and let my sobs break free. I can't lose him. "Yes, Ash, always. Which is why you can't leave me. Please." His arm drops from my face and my eyes snap open. His glossy eyes leave me and drift to Marcus. Just one look passes between them and it communicates everything. Marcus curls his arms around me, the pain in my side nothing compared to the hole in my chest, as he lifts me up to pull me away.

I fight against him and the pain, kicking and screaming. "No, please. Don't do this. No!" I battle with everything I have against his hold, but Marcus just tightens his arms. Smoke lingers all around us, burning my lungs. Blood spray coats the walls and bodies line the aisle. But all I can see is my best friend.

Marcus doesn't stop until we are next to Lincoln. He is standing frozen, looking down at Ash's dying form. "Get her out of here!" His voice grabs Linc's attention and he immediately wraps his arms around me, restraining me, as I continue to fight.

"No, River, don't do this. I'm not leaving him." I beg, but they both ignore me as Logan helps Jace to his feet and supports his weight against his own. My gaze roams wildly across them all as I see them getting ready to leave.

"We can't leave him," I scream, "somebody fucking help him." My throat is raw, but it's like they can't hear me.

"We've got to move, now!" Max snaps, looking between Asher and I with sorrow in his eyes. They are not fucking leaving him here to die.

"I've got him, brother." Lincoln starts, eyes still focused on Asher, but Marcus shakes his head.

"No." He snaps, "Logan's got Jace, and now you've got my girl. Get them out of here. I'll get Asher."

The tears soak my face as he grips my chin and brings my face to his. "I got this, baby, go."

I don't get to respond before Lincoln is hauling me out of there. Jace, Logan, Zack, and Tyler quick on our tails. I do nothing but cry as I try to break free from his hold on me. Lincoln doesn't stop, just strides out of the building and into the middle of a fucking battle. There are bodies everywhere and bullets fly past us, but Lincoln isn't fazed. He remains focused on where we are heading, and all I can do is watch as we leave it all behind. I see familiar faces everywhere battling against the Donovan fray and fire bursting out of several of the buildings.

There are girls screaming and crying everywhere and for the first time ever. I don't care about any of them. I know what they have been through, what they have suffered. But all I can think about right now is that we just left my best friend behind to die.

A thought passes through my mind that I never thought possible.

Too many Donovan's will die today.

The Crows are retreating to the front gates, continuing to kill the remaining guards as they go. Some of them drag girls along with them. It's fucking carnage. We pass Aiden and Killian who are covered in blood as they carry Connor O'Sullivan's dead body. I can't even let the guilt hurt me. It's too much.

We make it through the gates and towards the trees as more of our guys start to join us and I desperately search for signs of Marcus and Asher, but all I see is smoke and flames. I feel dizzy and lightheaded, and I know the blood loss is getting to me and my flailing around isn't helping. I collapse around Lincoln's body and feel him relax slightly as I calm myself.

"Superman." I whisper and he looks down at me, "I'm going to lose him." My voice cracks as the emotion and exhaustion starts to overtake me. I can feel myself starting to fall into a pit of nothing, but Lincoln's words pierce into it.

"It's gonna take more than a bullet to destroy Asher Donovan." His tone is strained, and I can tell he doesn't believe a word he just said. Asher Donovan may be a force of nature, an angel among demons, but he is still only human. He's saved me time and time again and his actions are finally catching up to him.

Elliot Donovan is dead.

Greg Donovan is dead.

Asher Donovan is dying.

Is this how it was meant to be? My punishment for so much chaos. I'm free and allowed to live, but my best friend has to die....

Crows continue to retreat out of the gates, running towards us and I see Max and his team coming in quick and fast too. Zack staggers beside us, with Logan holding up Jace. The only people missing are Marcus and Asher.

Is the payment for my sins that I have to lose them both?

The last thing I see before I fall into darkness is the Donovan compound perishing in flames like the true pit of hell it always was.

Always.

Epilogue

ELLE
Two months later…

The funeral was perfect, or as perfect as death can be. It didn't heal the hole in my heart, but it allowed me to say goodbye. *Goodbye.* I fucking hate that word. It's just so lacking for what it entails, but would any word ever be enough to let go of the people you love? To accept the fact that you are never going to see them again, talk to them. To hear them laugh or pull them in for a hug. They're just gone forever, and you're left behind to deal with the loss.

I stare down at the freshly tossed soil and think about how close I came to being in a box of my own. Not that I could ever forget. The scars and the dull pain in my side don't let me. The ache in my heart is a constant reminder as well. You'd think I'd be used to this feeling of regret considering this is the fourth funeral I've attended in the last two weeks.

First there was Mason's. Max pulled out all the stops to ensure he was given the sendoff he deserved. One worthy of his bravery, commitment, and sacrifice. His death will always remain on my conscience. His loss is felt by all of his friends, but they know we are lucky there weren't more. Owen escaped the same fate and it's the only salvation for Max and his team.

Connor O'Sullivan was thrown an all-out Crow affair as his chapter said goodbye to him. His daughter Rebecca right there by his graveside. All of them paying their respects to their late president. I guess he's the ex-president now. Aiden was voted in a few days after everything went down. I'm not sure how successful the transition was, I'm not exactly high on the list of the Crows' favorite people. If it weren't for me, Connor would still be alive.

Sarah King's funeral was the least emotional. Zack attended with me, but not for her, for me. Her last act doesn't change a lifetime of betrayal for him. It doesn't change it for me either, but I needed to go, needed to let go of everything she did and say goodbye.

There's that stupid fucking word again.

Today is the funeral I had been dreading the most. A death that will forever both stain my conscience and break my heart.

Marcus' fingers are entangled tightly with mine on the left as Lincoln takes up his spot on my right. Both of them silently offering me comfort as we listen to the priest talk about a life cut way too short. I don't listen to his words. Instead, I think of all the things I never got to say, the things we never got to do and the friendship I am going to miss out on. Like my own internal punishment for the part, I played in her death.

I stay long after the service is over and even after her parents leave. Just remaining there to bask in my grief. I stopped by their house this morning, like I do a lot these days and they were almost fully packed up. They are getting ready to say goodbye to this town and all that has happened here. I didn't lie to them about their daughter. They know exactly who wielded the weapon that killed her and know I'm the catalyst for it all. I didn't ask for their forgiveness. I don't deserve it, just like I didn't deserve a friend like Taylor Kennedy.

The FBI received a large number of anonymous files right after everything went down. It was a mix between what we got from Elizabeth Donovan, what we had gathered ourselves, and what the guys stole from the compound. All of it telling a damning and compelling tale about the men of the elite families of Black Hallows. The investigations are ongoing, and we've all been questioned multiple times. We spun our own web of lies to cover our backs and no one seems to be questioning it. I guess with the number of bodies found at the compound and the fact Carter Fitzgerald is still missing after clearing out his accounts, it's easy to not look our way. They are hunting what they deem to be bigger fish than the South Side Rebels.

Max and his team are still monitoring the situation in case anything changes. They aren't in Black Hallows anymore as they've moved onto their next job, but we still talk all the time. A lot more than we did before. I know I will always be able to count on them for anything.

Zack has finally returned to work full time and has even been commuting back and forth between his small office here, and his main office in New York. Logan and Lily have both gone back to college and Arthur and Helen have been extra manic about them checking in every day. They've chosen to stay in Black Hallows with us for the time being, they want to enjoy their retirement and be close to me and Cassie.

When I woke up in a hospital bed, Marcus was at my side, his face grief stricken. I waited for him to deliver the news that Asher was dead. That I had lost my best friend and my daughter had lost her father. What I didn't expect was for him to nod to my other side where Ash lay unconscious covered in tubes. The doctors described his survival as miraculous. That the bullet pierced into his chest cavity and lodged itself against his heart. It took a fourteen-hour surgery to ensure he survived.

He is still recovering, much to his distaste, but that hasn't stopped him. He still managed to successfully disband Donovan Enterprises. With Zack having zero interest in being the Donovan heir, everything went to Ash. Well, everything that wasn't seized by the cops. Asher was interviewed relentlessly about his father and brother's crimes until the police were satisfied, he wasn't involved.

We are both still struggling with what happened and decided the best way for us to grieve is to work through it. Neither of us aspires to go to college, wanting to ensure we can be around Cassie as much as possible. So instead, we have almost finished setting up a charitable organization that will help victims of sex crimes. The Kennedy Foundation will be a place girls and women can come and get the help they need.

Lincoln continues to work with Zack and will be helping run things at the office here in town whenever Zack is in New York. He has been intense since

416

everything that happened that day and I can see it haunting him. I know he's got a dark past of his own and I think everything he saw that day dredged some things back up for him. He's been more closed off than before and I know Marcus is worried about him.

Jace spent a couple of weeks in the hospital thanks to the injuries he sustained in the crash and from Greg's men. He's no longer my light and playful Rebel. Rachel's death tainted him, but Taylor's death ruined him completely. He's a shell of the Jace he was before, and I don't know if anything can save him now.

Marcus' arm curves around my waist as his hand finds the now healed wound in my side. Just another scar that speaks a thousand words. Every time I look at them, I won't think about Greg, that night or that day. No, instead I will think about my family, my future. A future I still get to have when so many others don't.

"Time to go, baby." Marcus leans down kissing my neck as he speaks the words directly in my ear.

I sigh, "I know, I was just saying goodbye." I feel his nod against my cheek.

I lean forward and place the white rose in my hand across the heaped ground. "See you soon."

Marcus guides me to the back of the black town car, and we head off. We are all going for a late lunch, choosing to skip the wake. We head to Big P's diner to catch up with everyone else. Asher left to go pick Cassie up and Lincoln disappeared too.

Marcus and I are the first to arrive so grab a booth as Pam starts to fuss over us. We have become regulars here lately, bringing Cassie at least twice a week. She loves it and Pam adores her, like I knew she would. The freedom I now have to be able to take my daughter anywhere I want and not have to look over my shoulder, it's indescribable. We can now live the life she deserves, the life I deserve.

"Usual?" Pam asks and I smile.

"Of course." She nods, shouting off our orders and making her way to the kitchen.

"Did you see Jace?" I ask, "he wasn't at the funeral."

Marcus sighs, "he was there, he sat in the back and left before the end. I saw him going to the graveside as we left. He just needs time, we all do."

The bell rings and the sight that greets me takes my breath away. Asher Donovan steps inside with our daughter in his arms. He knows he should still be taking it easy, but nothing stops him from carrying Cassie wherever she wants to go. The ache I feel whenever I look at them never goes away. I came close to losing both of them and I won't ever forget that feeling.

"Mommy!" She squeals when she spots us, and Asher puts her down so she can rush across the diner towards us. Marcus scoops her up before she gets to me, tickling her sides, "no, River. No tickles!" She cries with laughter, before he drops her next to me.

I pull her into my lap and snuggle her close and Ash slides into the round booth beside Marcus.

"How's my Hell's Bells?" He asks with that dark smile of his and I see Marcus smile with him.

"Better now you two are here." The anxiety that fills me when I'm not around them is something I struggle with every day, but they all help me with it.

He shrugs in such an unlike Asher move, and responds, "because I'm your favorite obviously."

"Always." I beam at him.

We order for the two of them and then just talk back and forth and let Cassie tell us all about the party she wants for her upcoming birthday.

Halfway through eating the bell dings again and Cassie yells out across the diner. "Superman!"

He stalks toward us and gives her a big smile, "princess." He beams at her and then nods hello to the guys before looking at me, "we need to talk."

No good ever comes from hearing those four words. I force the swallow of my burger down my throat and wipe my mouth with my napkin. Ash nods that he's got Cassie and I follow Lincoln to the corner of the diner. He hands me a file and when I open it there is a picture of a little girl. Her name is Sofia Decker and she's seven years old.

"Should I know who this is?" I ask, my stomach curdling in anticipation and terror, wondering where he is going with handing me a file of a beautiful little girl.

"That is the adopted daughter of Gerry and Ava Decker." He confirms. I frown in confusion and when I don't say anything, he adds, "turn to page seven."

I flip the pages and scan the words until I am a third of the way down and right where the birth parents are listed, I see a familiar name. *Trisha Conrad.*

"Jace's Mom?" I ask to pointlessly confirm, because he wouldn't be bringing it to me for any other reason. "Jace has a little sister." I whisper to myself in both despair and hope. Jace has a little sister. A sister he knows nothing about. A sister who looks well and cared for. This could change everything, change him. Bring him back from the path of destruction he's now on. This could be exactly what we need to save him.

I close the file and sigh, because as much as this could help him, I know he's not ready for it. At least, not right now. I look at Lincoln and I can tell he feels the same. He sees the way Jace is, barely sleeping, never eating, drinking, smoking, and taking God knows what. He's in a bad place and we need to handle this carefully.

"Get me everything on them..." I start, but he smiles, and I shake my head knowing he will have already done that, so I change course. "I want to meet with them, explain the situation and prepare them for what has to happen."

Lincoln's nodding before I even finish speaking, "I'll reach out to the dad, he works for a charity for foster children born to drug addicted parents." He explains and all it does is remind me of Jace's shitty past, and think how lucky his little sister is to have escaped it.

I feel eyes on us as he talks and when I look up, I find Asher staring at us. No. not at us, at Lincoln. Watching him like he is analyzing him. I flick my gaze back to Lincoln, but he must have followed my stare because now he's staring back at Asher.

Breaking into the tension I speak, "Keep me updated." I flick the file back open and stare down at the picture of the little girl again. Now I know who she is, I can see the resemblance. She's got his hazel eyes and her blonde hair is the same shade as his. I hope she can be reason enough to save him. I hand the file back to Linc and we walk back over to the table. We all finish our dinner listening to Cassie tell us about some ridiculous dinosaur game she played with Logan and we can't help but laugh.

Once we are finished eating, I have one more thing I want to do today, and I look at Cassie. "Baby, daddy is going to take you home okay. I've got to go somewhere."

She smiles easily, all that darkness from before Christmas forgotten. "Okay mommy." I lean down and give her a kiss and a cuddle before Ash scoops her up into his arms.

"Catch you at home, Hells Bells." He says to me, then nods to Marcus and then awkwardly lingers on Lincoln before just turning and walking away. *Weird.*

Lincoln watches them leave, then nods at us, taps the file in his hand, and goes on his way.

"And where may I ask, are we going?" Marcus flips me round and leans down to drop a kiss to my lips.

I smile into it before pulling back, "It's a surprise."

I slide in the back seat having already given my destination to the driver. Marcus slips in next to me and we go on our way. Marcus is silent until we make it to the road leading up North Hill.

"Ells, where are we going?"

"I told you, it's a surprise."

I don't say anything else until we pull into the gates of Marcus' old house. His grip on my hand tightens and we move down the driveway until we are stopping in front of the steps.

I turn to him and squeeze his hand back. "Just don't say anything yet, okay?"

He looks between the house and me before nodding. I take a deep breath and step out of the car and he follows close behind. I lead him up the steps and quickly type the code into the security pad that Max had one of his guys set up, and the doors beep open. We step inside and I lead him into the middle of the foyer, so we can see into the rooms that surround it.

I've spent the last three months having the whole place restored and renovated, and I did it for him. I turn so I can stand in front of him, but I can't decipher the look in his eyes, so I take another deep breath.

"I know you might not want to live here, after what happened to Michael, but that is just one memory. This place is filled with a million other good memories and someone deserves to make some more here." He looks over the entire place in silence, and I can feel the pangs of regret starting to circle inside of me. "This house was always more of a home to me and well, I just thought... I just wanted to give it the chance to create new memories. Even if they aren't ours."

He finally brings his eyes to mine and I see unshed tears dancing behind them. "Ells," he breathes out, "baby I don't know what to say. It looks beautiful. I never imagined... I never even thought." He shakes his head. "I love it. Thank you."

422

He cups my cheeks and uses his hands to tip my head so he can kiss me. The kiss is everything it always is. Passionate, heart fulfilling and completely and utterly soul destroying.

When he pulls back, he gives me that heartbreaking smile of his and my stomach rolls, like always, at the fact that he's mine. "That's not all." I manage to whisper out.

I take his hand and lead him through the house to the garage and once there I switch on the light. Standing in the center of the room is a black bike. An exact replica to the one he lost in the fire.

"No way!" He barrels past me like a kid at Christmas to inspect his gift. He walks round it smiling big, stopping to touch it and check out the things in it, before he steps back and looks at me, shaking his head.

I laugh a little and walk towards him and he pulls me in as soon as I get close.

"Just had to try and steal my thunder, didn't you, little King?" He whispers against my lips.

I laugh, as he pulls back and then he's dropping to his knee. I almost choke on my breath as he stares up at me.

"Ells, I knew the moment I first laid eyes on you that my life would never be the same." My eyes widen as he pulls out a small black box, opening it up to reveal a beautiful platinum band with six little diamonds in it. "I instantly felt this fierce protectiveness over you, I didn't know it then, at five years old, but I had met the girl I wanted to spend the rest of my life with. Now we have been through a lot," he huffs out a laugh, "more than most people, and I know we are only eighteen, but that doesn't matter. I know you're mine and I'm yours. So, marry me, baby, today, tomorrow, next fucking year, I don't care as long as we are together. I dare you."

The tears pour down my cheeks as I choke out my words "Yes, River, of course I'll marry you." I reach out my hand so he can slide the ring onto my finger, and it fits perfectly. "I've always been yours, Marcus, so what's forever?"

He smiles, curling my little finger with his. "pinky promise?"

"Pinky promise." I whisper back.

He kisses me breathless until my heart pounds against my chest, begging for this to never be over.

He pulls back, smiling at me mischievously and I can't help but ask. Now what?"

He licks his lip. "Now, little King, I'm going to fuck you on this bike."

THE END.

Thank you so much for reading Marcus and Elle's story, I hope you enjoyed it.

This is the end of their journey, but don't worry we will still see our favorite King and Queen in the future Rebel's books.

Reckless Rebel is going to be a wild ride just like our pretty boy, Jace.

Coming Soon!

Acknowledgements

Firstly, I would like to say thank you to my readers! To every single person who has joined me on this wild ride and fell in love with Marcus and Elle the way I did. You guys truly are the best! From every review, every edit, every tag. I am just blessed with the love you have shown my book babies! I LOVE YOU ALL!

Sammie, my ride or die. This has not been fun! Let's not play deadline roulette ever again!! God, with each book things just get crazier and crazier, and I am forever grateful for your friendship. It means the world to me and I love how you always push me to be better. I couldn't think of anyone better to have by my side and as my kid's future mother-in-law LOL! Just love you so much my insufferable little tater tot.

Andrea, Ders, my sexy little texy… you girl are the bomb! Thank you for every good morning stabby message, every song rec and for generally just listening to me when I fall into the pits of my anxiety. Love you girl!

Sam, my little bacon bitch. Thank you for putting up with my needy ass and allowing me to bug you every single day. For every vibe, every stunning edit, and every buddy book we read that I definitely didn't have time for. You are awesome. Love you queen.

To my betas Roxanna, Laura, and Dean. My level of gratitude for you guys knows no bounds. Thank you for taking the time to read and for not yelling at my severe lack of commas. You rock!

My street team queens!!! You guys... I can't even. Thank you for loving this story enough to want to be part of the team and hype me up. All your posts and stuff you tag me in mean the absolute world to me!! I will always be grateful!

Finally, to my husband (who doesn't read these books or acknowledgments but whatever). Thank you for putting up with all my BS and still loving me anyway.

Want to talk?

Come find me on Instagram @authorgnwright

Like me on Facebook G.N. Wright

Join my readers group to talk about the book and keep up with information on future books… --> G.N. Wright's Rebels.